The Project: Hero Saga Book 2

Alongside a Legend

Thomas Edward

Independently published through

Kindle Direct Publishing

Seattle, Washington

Cataloging-in-Publication Data has been applied for
and may be obtained from the Library of Congress.

ISBN: 9798862409260

Cover art by Jimbo Salgado
Cover colors by Anang Setyawan

This book is a work of fiction. Any reference to historical events, real people or real locales is used fictitiously. Other names, characters, places and incidents are the product of the author's imagination, and any resemblance to actual events or locales or persons, living or dead is entirely coincidental.

Published independently in 2023 by Kindle Direct Publishing.

This book is dedicated to my wife, Jean. Without her and her extensive time and effort, as well as believing in me, my novels would have never become a reality. I can't thank her enough for helping with everything that allowed me to get my first novel of The Project: Hero Saga to be published, Enter Alexavier. She has also gone out of her way to make sure this journey of superheroes continues with this new novel, Alongside a Legend. And for that, I love you and am forever grateful.

I would like to give a huge thank you to Roberto Corales. He has been a champion and supporter of me and these books, since the first day he heard about The Project: Hero series. It means the world to me, and I'll never forget it.

Also, I'd like to thank everyone who purchased Enter Alexavier through Amazon or came to one of the many book fairs and comic conventions and picked up your special edition copy and had it signed. I had the pleasure to meet so many of you and have you become a part of the Project: Hero universe. I appreciate all your support and hope the heroes and villains embedded in the pages of this novel continue to bring you more joy and excitement. Thanks again for your support!

Original artwork by Jimbo Salgado:

To see the art in color by Anang Setyawan in its entirety, go to:

http://www.instagram.com/p/CxoGEsAAyyD/?igshid=MzRIODBiNWFIZA==

Welcome to the universe of Project: Hero!

Provided at the back of this book is a glossary to help familiarize yourself with the characters in this universe or as you need a refresher as to who is who and what they can do. Listed are all the characters that appear in this story. First are the people involved with Project: Hero, listed in alphabetical order by first name followed with their hero names and abilities. That is followed by the names of the villains and their abilities, also listed alphabetically.

Thank you for purchasing my book. Hopefully, this story will bring you as much enjoyment and fun as it was for me to write.

Connect with me on social media:

Thomas Edward
Facebook: Thomas Edward
Twitter: @TEdwardWriter
Instagram: tedward_writer

"We have been given an opportunity to give back to the world. Being gifted with the abilities that normal citizens haven't been, we as heroes must use those gifts to help, to protect and to maintain the peace and tranquility for everyone around the world, no matter who they are or where they live.

To put limitations on those with such abilities will only hurt us who look to help and not harm. Anyone with thoughts of wrongdoing will not heed your wishes. If you put restrictions on us, the heroes who look to thwart those of evil will no longer be able to do so. What we saw happen to this city will only be the beginning of chaos. I beg of you to let us heroes, do what we do best and to never let that happen again."

Samuel Nelson, The Patriot Warrior

The United Nations hearing on superhumans.

New York City, June 6, 1983

CHAPTER 1

Alexavier Vankendreh'd was intensely focused on getting some reps in. Lying on the bench, he lifted the barbell that had more weights on it than he normally would attempt. His exercise was driven by what happened in New Jersey with the building collapse that nearly killed his close friend, Beth Breckenridge. That made him push harder through his workout, still hearing her words as she relived the nightmarish moments.

"I couldn't see into any of the windows, and every door was locked. I got more disappointed with every building I explored. I checked everywhere, but there was no sign of Bobbie. I'm guessing she was likely finding safety from The Tribe in one of those buildings.

So, I moved onto the tallest building situated in the middle of the industrial complex. Once I reached the first set of windows and looked inside, the darkness made it too hard to see anything. I was about to dismiss the building and move on, but I suddenly saw a shadow moving down a hallway. It was a dark figure, but I saw the shine of a gun, as they vanished through a doorway. I realized that I may have just seen The Infamous One! Thank goodness the door nearby happened to be unlocked. I slipped inside and hurried down the hallway to look around.

It was pretty dark inside, and I began to get anxious, knowing that The Infamous One was in his element, so I decided to call for reinforcements. I waited for the team to respond, but only heard static. I knew this might be the only chance to capture The Infamous One. With no one coming as back-up, I made the judgment call to go after him anyway.

I cautiously moved forward through the hallway, briefly stopping and listening to make sure the coast was clear. It is so dark that you could hardly see your hand right in front of your face! About a minute went by before I heard the sound of a swinging door, followed by footsteps. After hearing the door close and latch, I ran as fast as I could towards it, pressing my ear to the door. I could hear the sound of more footsteps which got softer and softer. I carefully opened the door of the stairwell and leaned over the railing. The footsteps stopped with the sound of the door closing behind me. It then became a waiting game. After another thirty seconds or so, I knew that he had to be pushed. So, I put my hand out over the middle of the stairs, and created a glow that got brighter and brighter, filling the entire stairwell with light. He knew he was in danger of being seen and made a mad dash down the last few flights of stairs. I hurried down as quickly as I could, hoping to not lose him. Unfortunately, my pace wasn't fast enough, and I heard the sound of a door being opened ring throughout the stairwell. I couldn't let him get away and I raced down as fast as possible.

Once I reached the bottom, I turned off the light from my hand and everything became dark again. I crouched down with my back against the wall next to the door and carefully slid over to peek through the window. The basement was pitch black. I dropped back down and gave one last attempt to contact anyone from the team, but The Com-Links still didn't work. I knew I was on my own, but still had to go after him. I don't think I've ever been so nervous in my entire life."

The image of Beth's face showing anxiety and fear lingered in Alexavier's mind as he remembered her telling more of the story.

"My worst fear was not being able to see, but I didn't want to give away my location to The Infamous One. I needed to counter his shadow powers the best way I could, so I waited a few seconds and then kicked the door open hard and shined the brightest, blinding light to fill the entire basement. I stepped forward and could see almost everywhere, except for a small portion of the basement towards the back. I then saw the masked, dark figure sprint from behind a cement post towards the back corner wall and vanish. Because there was a chance of getting shot while turning the corner, I intensified the energy around me, creating a shield of light and heat, so if a bullet came my way, I wouldn't get hurt."

Alexavier pushed harder with the weights as he could hear the fear in Beth's voice.

"*I knew I would have to go around the corner, but I wasn't sure if I was ready to come face-to-face with him. I approached the corner slowly, intensely shining the light on this whole new section of the basement. But instead of only seeing The Infamous One, Natural Disaster was there as well, protecting him.*

It was eerie with absolute silence and seeing him with an evil smirk on his face. He created a small energy field encompassing them both, which also touched the ceiling. This dome shaped field distorted my view, but I could see him, with hair flowing as if it was on fire.

Now my nerves were really on edge at this point. Having the two most wanted super villains in front of me was a once in a lifetime encounter that I never expected. I knew my powers were strong enough to defeat The Infamous One, but I was uncertain against the more powerful, Natural Disaster. As he has long been considered The Terror Tribe's strongest member, this would be my ultimate test going up against him. I decided to give the Com-Link one last try, but again only hearing static.

Then, Natural Disaster started taunting me. "Sorry, sounds like no one is coming to help you."

I tried not to show fear and replied, "If all I'm going to take on is you and Infamous, I won't need back up."

He issued a challenge. "You sound confident, little girl, but you've never tried."

"That can change." I said and lifted my arm and shot a mild blast of energy at them, which hit their shield and caused a slight disruption, but bounced off. The disturbance of his shield must have triggered something, as he increased the energy field intensity.

Seeing this, I thought maybe he could be vulnerable to my attacks, so I directed a larger, more intense blast at them. It hit the shield harder and forced Natural Disaster backup a step.

Even with his shield appearing to weaken, Natural Disaster seemed to be very confident. "You can't take me down, little girl. You're not strong enough, and you never will be."

"I'm not done yet." I yelled back, trying to not show my nervousness. I focused on generating enough energy in one beam of light to take him down. Willing a stronger blast, they were forced to brace harder, so I concentrated as much energy as possible to hit his shield, so I could end this. Even though I nearly broke down the shield, what I didn't realize was the rest of the blast had deflected away, doing lots of damage to the building.

Natural Disaster then dropped to one knee, pulling his shield in closer and yelled back to his partner hiding behind him, "Now!" The dark figure put out his arms, and that's when everything got heavy. It became hard to stand up."

Alexavier could picture the look of horror on Beth's face as she completed telling her terrifying story.

"That's when I noticed Natural Disaster's shield was also bracing the structure of the building as well. By lowering the shield with my light blasts bouncing off and hitting all parts of the basement, the building started to collapse. I couldn't get out of the way of the falling concrete fast enough. Several pieces hit my shield, knocking me to the floor. That weird gravitational pull had me pinned and unable to move. One by one, more pieces of the building fell down, slowly crushing me. I was barely able to keep one arm up to maintain my shield. The more debris kept piling on top of me, the harder it was to concentrate. The weight caused excruciating pain, but I wasn't able to scream in agony. As the final pieces of the building settled on top of me, I finally couldn't sustain my shield anymore. All I could do was to try to reach through the cement slabs for daylight. Unfortunately, I finally passed out from the lack of oxygen. I really thought that was the moment that I was going to die."

With her words lingering and the image of her scared face still circling around his head, the anger helped release more adrenaline, which allowed Alexavier to push the barbell even harder.

CHAPTER 2

Alexavier was so focused, that James Killus, the regular disruptor and resident psychopath of the recruits, and his crew were allowed to watch him uninterrupted. The band of thug heroes became more comfortable when Alexavier didn't acknowledge their presence. Hank Malberg, the big, lumber oaf, took up the whole doorway, forcing the weasel like Glen Euw to push his way through. His scrawny, little body made it easier to squeeze between Hank's massive legs and stand next to Killus. The swagger that Killus possessed made all of his cronies over-confident. As he walked around the weight room, Killus smiled with the fact that Alexavier paid them no attention.

Alexavier kept his focus, although that feeling of dread continued to grow. He felt it long before Killus got close to the weight room. He commented, not even turning around to face Killus. "We going to do this here?"

"Do what? You haven't done anything here for quite a while." Killus glared.

"He ain't gonna do anything now," Glen poked.

Alexavier put the weights on the rest, sat up and turned to face them. "Let's go."

"I told you," Killus chuckled. "He's not as lame as he looks. But not here, I've got the best place for you and your funeral, the hanger."

With all the stress and anxiety built up from reliving the horrific events that happened to Beth, not to mention being sick of dealing with Killus' crap every single day, Alexavier accepted the maniacal hero's invitation in hopes of shutting him up. Throwing his towel into the nearby hamper, Alexavier pushed his way through everyone, heading toward the hanger. April Dandridge looked away, wishing she was anywhere other than with the group. With Alexavier having a head start, Killus and his crew followed back far enough to make sure their journey and entry to the hanger wouldn't have any unnecessary spectators. Dwayne Cygnus stayed even further back, just like he had always done and barely entered the empty room.

"See," Killus said with a childlike excitement. "No helicopter at the moment. Best of all, no one to bother us, since everyone working in the hanger, it would seem, were called to a meeting."

"Too bad. I'm sure everyone would love to see you get this beating."

Hank stepped closer. "How about I give you a beating that-"

"Hold on my big and dopey friend." Killus pushed back his top goon. "This is my playtime, and my friend here is going to really enjoy the game I have in mind for him."

As only he could, Glen slithered over toward the entryway and pushed a button on the wall, laughing out loud as the doors leading to the complex slowly closed and locked. Hank backed away while circling the outside of the landing pad, all the while Alexavier and Killus stood near the center of the large, cavernous room in a face off reminiscent of a boxing match for a heavyweight championship.

The last several weeks had seen Alexavier behaving more different than he normally would. Having felt like he could have done more to prevent the building from collapsing on Beth and himself, he believed he now required a higher level of discipline. However, there was something different with this challenge, and Alexavier appeared ready to release some pent-up energy. If there was anyone who deserved to have some aggression taken out on him, it was Killus, the resident pain in everyone's butt.

Pulling his black hood over his head, Alexavier knew the standoff wouldn't last long. That feeling he had of sensing when something is wrong was screaming in his brain like a siren. Once the doors were locked, Killus, armed with his thirst for violence, instantly charged looking to get the payback he believed he was due. Alexavier sidestepped him easily, but Killus planted one foot and spun, throwing a spinning back fist that was blocked. With Killus' back to him, Alexavier landed a push kick that sent the maniacal hero stumbling forward.

With an acknowledging grin, Killus turned slowly, almost congratulating his opponent. It didn't last long, as Killus began walking aggressively in a circle, looking for his opportunity to engage again. He attempted a kick, which was blocked. Throwing a couple of lazy jabs, he tried to bait Alexavier into watching his hands. It didn't distract Alexavier as Killus' next kick was blocked again, this time causing Killus some pain to his shin.

Killus' only power was his love of hurting people. Unfortunately, that last one stung him. "Good one, brat. I see you're still as spunky as ever." Killus flexed his leg as he circled around. "We should have done this a long time ago."

"You're stalling."

Killus smiled and with a loud cry, he rushed in. His swinging punches were again blocked or went by harmlessly. Alexavier stayed on the defensive, letting Killus exhaust himself before punching Killus in the face, bloodying his nose. Killus wiped the blood away with an ever-increasing, malicious smile. Alexavier took a cautious step forward, enticing Killus to punch and kick even harder. The exchange was a clinic of offensive aggression and tactical counters, with each fighter getting their own attempts in. Whereas Killus used anger, Alexavier used skill and was able to kick the back of Killus' leg, buckling his knees, sending him down to the ground.

No longer able to contain himself, Hank lumbered over, wanting to get a piece of Alexavier. Although Hank had super strength abilities, he couldn't lift a building, but could use his powers when his anger pushed him to get violent. His cohort was scrawny and diminutive, which meant Glen hesitated, not being sure when to pick his shots. Dodging Hank was easy for Alexavier, but once his back was turned, focusing on Killus and Hank, Glen jumped in, although very haphazardly. A quick spin away and sticking his leg out tripped Glen having him faceplant, smashing his nose into the concrete, unable to use his power to produce sticky liquids. Groaning as he rolled over with his hands covering his face, Glen had blood pouring out between his fingers.

With Glen whimpering as he crawled away, Alexavier turned his focus onto the two people who were the most threating. Hank slowly made his way around to the left, but Killus stood his ground. Feeling the need to ramp up the intensity, Killus pulled out his favorite knife. Giving it a few twirls, he walked opposite Hank, looking to double their odds of taking down Alexavier.

Before they could double-team their prey, a deafening siren filled the hanger. It halted the fight causing everyone to look around in surprise. The overhead doors to the hanger cracked open, allowing rays of sunshine to rain down and wind to enter and swirl around. The wider the doors slid open, the stronger the wind became, until the doors came to rest, allowing the wind to whip around the hanger signaling the arrival of the jet helicopter. Everyone separated with Glen scrambling, trying not to get crushed. Killus quickly stashed his knife and backed away. The impressive aircraft gradually descended onto the helipad, achieving a nice, soft landing. Alexavier stood his ground, but Killus and his crew looked to find an exit. Before they could leave, the ramp lowered, presenting a figure they knew all too well, Samuel Nelson, the legendary Patriot Warrior.

CHAPTER 3

Sam walked down the ramp, hauling three full bags of necessities and setting them down at the bottom. He was no fool to what was happening when he arrived and wasn't too pleased. It took a few minutes for the wind to die down from the spinning helicopter blades. Almost everyone had that sinking feeling, knowing they were about to get a lecture. Killus was the exception to the rule, who kept smiling as he tried to catch his breath.

Being one of the greatest heroes of all time, Sam Nelson earned a level of respect that few others on the planet have gained. The sight of him was awe inspiring. Just his presence alone brought everything to a halt, but it shouldn't have required that. As so, it really upset him.

Sam started with Killus. "This is not what I expect to see when I get back from my commitments in Washington. Where are the technicians and mechanics?"

"I think it was an emergency meeting or something..." Killus' voice trailed off.

"Get that door open!" Sam commanded, motioning toward Glen. "We have daily operations that need to continue. What do you think you're doing?"

"Playing nice," Killus joked.

Sam walked over, standing right in his face. "Don't play me as stupid. I've known you long enough to see what's happening."

"I'm just getting a real workout in, one that really tests my skills."

"Your hand-to-hand combat skills are only marginally better than most of the other recruits. Unless you have a weapon in your hand, you're not going to take down most of The Terror Tribe. Rather than looking to cause physical harm, you should be learning from Alexavier, since his elite fighting skills may be what it takes to bring down The Infamous One."

Killus started to get infuriated, as there are only two things in this world that would make Killus mad. One is questioning his fighting abilities and the second is that he wouldn't be the hero bringing down the most dangerous man on the planet. That made him enraged, causing him to keep fidgeting with the knife that was behind his back.

Sam could see the maniacal hero's angered look, but was not intimidated. "You can get your goon squad and get out of here! Actions have consequences Killus. You'll be seeing me later!"

"Yes... sir." Killus' short and irritated reply was only matched by his nonchalant exit. He gathered his gang and meandered away, shooting one last look of death at Alexavier.

The young hero stood still, watching and waiting for his turn to be reprimanded. After Sam went back for his bags, he made his way to the apprehensive hero. Once face-to-face, Sam didn't hold back.

"Of everyone here, I would least expect this from you. What's going on that Killus, of all people, would get under your skin? Everybody here are supposed to be heroes. This stellar training and high-tech facility are avenues to a greater cause. Everyone is here, in this program, because they're the elite of all candidates that will one day carry on the traditions set long ago by men and women who gave their lives for the betterment of this world. This is unacceptable behavior from anyone, no matter who they are within Project: Hero. Go get cleaned up!"

"Yes, sir."

"We'll be having a discussion about this later," Sam stated, as he headed toward the complex.

With sweat running down his face, Alexavier dusted himself off while watching Sam vanish from sight. Feeling discouraged, he turned to walk through the hanger doors into the training complex thinking that he had once again let down the person he most respected.

#

Sam began his journey through the complex and noticed Major Constantine, the head of Project: Hero, heading directly towards him. Getting the casual greetings out of the way from the regular staff, Sam beat the Major to the punch. "Did you know Killus and Alexavier we're fighting in the hanger?"

"I just found out from one of the mechanics after they were told about a meeting that never happened."

Sam continued to walk briskly. "I'm sure that the source of this has to be with Killus and his crew. I thought you took care of that problem?"

The Major let Sam walk by. "I will address it, again." He sighed heavily, knowing that another serious conversation was going to happen very soon.

The rest of Sam's journey through the complex corridors was of multiple greetings. His arrival put everyone in a great mood, quickly changing the atmosphere throughout the facility. What people didn't see was Sam feeling a little on edge, not only from the possible chance of a nuclear threat, but also from what recently transpired in the hanger. Once inside his room, he quickly unloaded his gear onto the couch and took a moment for a few deep breaths. Before Sam could get too far tearing into the bags to unpack, a welcoming committee of retired hero, Jonathon Bender and program aide, Mike Mackinaw came strolling through his door.

"Good to see you, Sam," Jonathon reached out to shake hands.

Sam reached back. "Glad to be back."

"How are The United Outcasts doing?" Mike asked.

"Really good," Sam replied, continuing to put things away. "Downtown has quickly become the leader they need. Epic, DLX and Giggle Stick are really establishing themselves as hometown, New York heroes. Ordinary Joe is still... ordinary. No big surprise here, Getaway and Rosé are in a relationship."

Mike began helping Sam. "I knew there was something up with those girls, even before they left here. Can we even call them girls anymore? Both just turned eighteen this year, right?"

"Yes. Oh, there might be a couple of new members in the coming days," Sam mentioned.

"Who?" Jonathon wondered.

"D.T. didn't say, but I'm sure he will let us know as soon as anything becomes official." Sam finished putting away the last few things from one bag and turned around. "Did you know that Alexavier and Killus were down in the hanger when I landed? I'm sure my arrival broke up a fight."

"When? Today?" Mike asked.

"Just now."

Jonathon looked at Mike and stated, "That doesn't sound like Alex. Although, he hasn't quite been himself lately either, especially since the mission in New Jersey to rescue Beth."

Mike headed for the door. "Let me go check on him."

"Report back to me if there's something more going on."

"Will do." Mike left to go see if he could find Alexavier.

Sam gave another sigh. "I thought this thing with Killus was taken care of."

"When it comes to Killus, the Major has a soft spot for him," Jonathon stated.

"Just because someone has no problems killing people doesn't make it okay to let that person get away with these kinds of things. You know, I think the Major and I need to have a serious discussion about Killus' future here." Sam set everything down and headed toward the door. "I'll be back in a few."

Jonathon took a seat on the couch. He knew what was going happen in the Major's office and was happy just to relax and not be in that room.

#

Major Constantine left the door to his office wide open, knowing he was eventually going have a visit from Sam. He buried his head in the never-ending mountain of papers on his desk. There was a weird calm that came from having to review performance folders for his recruits. If his work was the calm, a storm arrived to bring dark-gray skies. That storm was Sam Nelson.

Sam entered the room with a purpose. He marched right up to the desk, not letting the Major have a chance to get comfortable. "What are you doing about Killus? I thought the last few weeks had been different?"

"So did I."

Sam paused, waiting for a better response. "And?"

"And what?"

"One of our heroes, notorious for violence against the staff, who you clearly favor, went out of his way to initiate a fight with another recruit and did so sneaking behind your back!"

The Major bit his lip. "I am well aware of what he did."

"And?"

"He will be disciplined accordingly!"

Sam became even more annoyed. "By now, I thought we would be done with him!"

"As I said, I will handle him," the Major barked.

"How is that? You cannot even handle what is going on with Alexavier's training. Yes, I heard about his last couple of training sessions."

The Major put down the papers that he was working on. "That's a different story. Alexavier has not shown any kind of motivation. He joins workouts only when forced to."

"Do you not think you should step in? Mike can only do so much."

"I can't hold his hand. Besides, I took him off his duties, and you wanted him back. Where does the blame fall if Mike can't handle even the slightest of issues with Alex?"

Sam gave a disgruntled sigh, "Mike has never been these recruits' therapist, as much as you might hope he could be. His efforts have always been to provide support. Sometimes that comes in the form of just being there for them, which happens to be the case with Alexavier."

"But that has not been enough. It's obvious there is something wrong, and nothing seems to make a difference."

"We obviously have not provided what he needs. Our goal should be to move recruits forward, not back."

The Major reiterated what they both knew, but he didn't like. "You're in charge. Ultimately, it is your decision that can make or break them as far as their chances to become heroes."

"Well, I am not making a decision to send Alexavier back."

"Maybe you should."

The comment really got to Sam, but didn't sway his decision. "I am not giving up on him yet. This facility was set up to bring out the best in people like him. We will get it figured out, even if you cannot."

As Sam turned to leave, all the Major could do was bite his lip. Once Sam had vanished from sight, the Major picked up a glass from his desk and threw it hard at the wall behind him. It took all his might to stop from tearing apart the rest of his office. Reaching for the bottle of whiskey on his desk, he let out a sigh realizing that the glass he needed was shattered on the floor.

CHAPTER 4

After the rough morning, Alexavier looked to get in an early lunch. It was less about being hungry, but more about not wanting to deal with anyone. The food was less than appetizing, just as it always was, but he figured he could stomach through it, even if the bread was harder to chew than a stick.

Several of the other recruits eventually found him and decided to provide company while he ate. He would have felt grateful having friends who cared, but for right now, he'd rather be alone to focus his attention on other things.

After gathering the various forms of nourishment, one of his best friends, Dave Headley, known as Dead Head, hurried over to grab a seat next to Alexavier. "Hey, buddy!"

"Hey." An awkward silence followed, as Dave for once didn't have something to say.

Taking the other seat next to Alexavier, was Beth Breckenridge, the Beacon of Light. "We heard what happened."

"Nothing really happened."

"Weren't you and Killus fighting in the hanger?" Beth asked.

"Sam arrived, so nothing really happened."

Manny Bautista, the young hero called the Human Battery, sat across from them. "Did you get in trouble?"

"Not yet."

Dave was shocked. "How do you get so lucky? I just breathe funny, and the Major throws the book at me."

"That's because you're a degenerate."

Dave sarcastically replied, "I love you too, Percy."

They were joined by Percy Shottenheimer, Wally Ryder, Bobbie Terpstra and Michael McKnight, the recruits known as Precision Shot, Wave Rider, Booby Trap and Mecha.

Beth looked over at Bobbie. "Are you ready to go on a recon?"

"Only a couple hours away," Bobbie responded. "I'm more than ready for tonight."

"Where's the Major sending you?" Manny inquired. "Some place cool, I hope."

"Sam said I'm going to New York City and making my way over to Brooklyn. There's some questionable activity being reported, so the Major wants the area checked off his list. That way he can narrow down the search for The Tribe."

Dave couldn't help but wonder, "So when am I going to be back out there doing recon?"

Bobbie blurted out, "Not any time this century!"

"Your workouts are terrible, man!" Manny stated.

Dave exclaimed, "Have you seen me? This body is not for working out. It's for working in, like staying in and watching a movie and eating popcorn."

Wally added, "Ain't that the truth. What you do isn't called a workout anyway. It's not like you actually win, so I think that's why you're not first to compete. At least you won't have to deal with Killus." Wally looked to Alexavier. "What's up with him in the hanger?"

"I know he was trying to get to Alex." Bobbie turned to Beth. "But I thought we put an end to it."

"At least I thought we did after Alex knocking him down a peg." Beth whispered loudly to Alexavier, "You didn't go after him, did you?"

Alexavier replied, "No. He came into the weight room, and I just got sick of listening to him."

Michael added, "They usually frown on that sort of thing."

"I'm surprised that you haven't already been to the Major's office," Percy exclaimed.

"I threatened to shove one of my Starburst missiles down Killus' throat. Then I got punished and couldn't go on missions for a week." Michael motioned to Percy. "I would have been happy with the punishment for actually doing it."

"I know that's right!" Percy reached over to fist bump Michael.

Slowly, the image of Jennifer began to appear next to Wally. "I can take him and drop him off of a skyscraper."

"I think you'd have to get in line," Manny joked.

Percy looked around the table. "I say we do it and ask for forgiveness later."

The table roared a collective agreement, but Bobbie pointed out, "I know it would make everyone feel better, but where would that put us for trying to become a hero?"

Dave appeared to be thinking hard, then replied, "Nope. I'd still push him off a building."

"She's right," Beth stated. "As much as it would probably solve a lot of issues, we're here to do good, not bad."

"Sometimes I wonder if doing good is good enough," Alexavier said with his head down, trying to eat.

A shocked Beth replied, "Sure it is. We're the good guys. There's a reason we're called heroes, because we do good."

"Not saying I disagree with you," Percy exclaimed. "But when was the last time we made a big dent in Terror Tribe activity? If you say Jersey, that's only because Alex didn't listen to orders."

"That's different," Beth argued.

"But how?" Alexavier wondered. "It took disobeying the Major and having him bite my head off. Even after having a building dropped on top of you, you almost died. Now they're somewhere safe in a new hideout, and the Major is upset with me. How is that right? I'm not sure if being good is better than them being bad." A silence swept over the table, as Alexavier put down his spork. "I have some homework to do. I think I'll be excused."

His early departure from the table quieted everyone. The only thing traded back and forth was awkward stares, until Percy exclaimed, "Man. Dude's taking it hard."

#

Sam returned to his room where Jonathon Bender, known as the iconic hero Time Bender, was laying back and dozing on and off. "At least one of us can feel relaxed."

Jonathon grinned, "It's easy when you're not the one who's having the uncomfortable conversation with Major pain in the butt. Speaking of discussion, maybe I can have a word with you about Alexavier?"

"I would welcome any intelligent conversation about him right now." Sam returned to unloading the next bag.

Jonathon sat up. "If you look at everything he's been through since he arrived, it's been a lot for a new recruit handle. He had no friends when he arrived. I don't know what Harvey's problem is with him and he has to worry about Killus being on him all the time. The first mission he went on Beth nearly died and to top it all off, she gets captured, and the both of them end up under a building. It's been weeks since he's been out on the hunt for any bad guys. I know I'd be getting a little itchy to see some action, if I was stuck here all the time too."

Sam realized, "It happened to you many years ago, didn't it?"

"Sure did." Jonathon stood up. "You know, we've had a lull. There's been so little going on as far as The Tribe is concerned, which is unusual."

"You think that might be why he took Killus up on his offer to battle it out? I can't imagine that would be enough to do something as having a brawl and possibly getting hurt."

"I don't know for sure, but it could be. I remember the boredom and having that itch just to do anything. I probably would have done something to get in trouble too, if it wasn't for you."

Sam gave a nod. "You and Alexavier are very much alike in needing something to focus on. Problem is, I thought he wouldn't get pulled into Killus' games. Getting into a brawl where many people could get hurt does not seem like something he would do. Maybe I'm reading him wrong."

"I think you're dead on. He never seemed that way to begin with. I think after the last two missions, reality may have hit hard about the consequences. Some of these recruits are still considered children, but they're dealing with life-or-death situations. Is he having a hard time handling it, and that's why he needed an outlet to let off some steam?"

"Not sure about the letting off steam though, but if comes to focusing his energy, I have an idea." Sam paused putting stuff away. "Can you get Bobbie?"

"Sure. Don't you think you should talk to the Major first?"

"I'll fill him in later. Not everything that goes on around here needs his approval."

"I'm cool with that. I'll be right back." Jonathon left, with Sam intently looking over his metal briefcase.

CHAPTER 5

In a partially empty office building located in downtown Pittsburgh, the man considered to be the most dangerous human on the planet stood facing out a full-length window, looking upon the early morning display of sparsely lit office buildings and streetlights. The Infamous One remained close enough to the pane of glass to see in nearly every direction. His arms were behind his back as he focused, concentrating on the ever-colorful scenery.

This building was one of many secret headquarters and safe houses that The Terror Tribe had spread out across the country. The financial gains from the many heists of various financial institutions and corporations over the years, as well as the Infamous One's knowledge of real estate investing, had allowed the group to acquire many properties, unbeknownst to the general public. The buildings were purchased under various companies and financial groups. So even when one of these buildings becomes compromised, they move their entire operation to another location and continue on without being discovered. It is a rarity that any of the secret locations get discovered, like what happened in New Jersey, so having to reestablish this new headquarters is uncommon.

Suddenly, the atmosphere of the room itself changed with a mist erupting from the floor. As it intensified into a thick cloud, the shape of a human figure slowly became visible. Once the mist disappeared, the hooded and caped Everlorne stood directly behind The Infamous One, his magical suit pulsing with the yellow, glowing sections of his outfit. "You were unable to neutralize the threat of Beacon of Light."

"While that may be the truth, there are still many pieces in play on the battlefield. It will not be difficult for us to capture them." Never looking back, The Infamous One spoke softer, "I fear the time is coming soon, my friend. This war is going to take its toll, and I don't want to pay it."

"Cryptic as ever. How long has it been? The time has yet to come for us to make your vision come true."

"Just because decades have passed, it doesn't mean that everything isn't finally cumulating, and building to an end with a final crescendo. Yet, I myself am surprised it has taken this long."

Everlorne pulled back his hood, displaying the glowing eyes of this magically powered villain. "Speaking of taking a long time, I see our new headquarters is only half complete. I assume you were not ready for an early exit from New Jersey."

"It's not the first time, although it had been a while since we were last outed. I have moved up the deadline. This building needs occupants to appear normal and inconspicuous. My decorating expertise is limited, but I am very good at sourcing those who can help. As soon as I can get this office set up, we will rent the other spaces. We can continue our operations here, as everything that we have planned may finally be coming to a head."

"What makes you believe it's about to happen?"

"A message, one that has been delivered to me by a messenger who has never failed me before." The Infamous One brought his hands in front to reveal a sliver of paper in the palm of one hand.

Everlorne looked confused. "What do you need of me?"

"Are you ready for a battle bigger than we've ever fought?" The Infamous One turned to face his disciple. "Will you stand behind me, even if it means fighting her?"

The glowing pieces of Everlorne's suit got brighter and pulsated faster. His face showed a high level of annoyance. "You don't have to question my loyalty. I will do what is needed of me."

Stepping closer, The Infamous One lowered his voice. "I know how you feel about Julie, and I appreciate you saying those words. I have put my trust in you from day one of your journey with us. You may have to do the deed that ultimately brings us victory, which may be facing her. I know you will not disappoint me."

Feeling that it was time to leave, Everlorne created another mist that slowly enveloped him, as he pulled his hood over his head. The black and gray portions of his suit blended and became one with the cloud with only the luminous pieces showing. Before the mist transported him away, Everlorne responded, "I will not, my leader."

The Infamous One watched his friend and fellow warrior disappear. He took the concern within his eyes and redirected it out the window towards the early dawn cityscape. He closed his hand, grasping the small, worn paper. There was some comfort in having it close by. However, would that provide enough comfort for what he knows will surely be difficult times ahead?

CHAPTER 6

Making a beeline for his room, Alexavier didn't want any interactions, so he kept his head down. The short trip was interrupted by an unseen presence. He kept walking, hoping the feeling would go away, but it didn't. "What do you want, Jennifer?"

"I want to see you smile." She gave her own.

"Not happening."

"But I like it when you smile."

Alexavier abruptly turned around. "You know when I'll smile? I'll smile when each member of The Terror Tribe is back here in a cell."

She let him turn and walk away. Confused and not sure what to do, Jennifer's body faded away until she disappeared from sight.

Arriving at his room, Alexavier was still thinking about The Terror Tribe. They have been on his mind ever since returning from New Jersey. After a few minutes of making his way through the populated halls of the complex, he finally made it to his room, his sanctuary. With all of the constant attention, at least he could block out the world outside the approximate three hundred square feet, that was truly his world.

He fired up his computer and began logging onto the World Net, hoping to do some research. His focus was exactly as it had been for some time now, combing the online world for any signs of the world's largest, villainous organization. He gathered the pads of paper and pencils for documenting any findings. Searching was tedious as always, with the usual sites providing no new information. Once through the social media and news outlets, he began the exhaustive process of focusing on the vague clues littered online. He was bound and determined to find that one little nugget that would lead him to The Infamous One or any of the other super villains associated with him.

As usual, with the limited Terror Tribe activity, nothing new could be found. Of course, that frustrated him even more. To try and settle his nerves, he stopped searching and just stared into space. He knew that somewhere in this virtual world was the tiniest tidbit of data that would put him on the path to bringing to justice those who caused him stress and anguish.

Before he could reset and give it another go, the familiar face of Mike Mackinaw showed up at the door. “What's going on, buddy? I tried catching you in the cafeteria, but they said you left.”

“I wasn't that hungry. Plus, I had some homework to do.”

“Are you sure you're alright? You want to talk about Killus?”

“Only if it's how I can punch him in the face.”

Mike walked over, standing next to the desk. “You shouldn't be thinking about beating the crap out of him. He does deserves getting his butt kicked, but not if it's going to get you in trouble.”

“Everyone says how Killus never gets in trouble. Then why should I be worried about getting in trouble?”

“He does get in trouble,” Mike leaned against the desk and folded his arms. “Especially from Sam, but he’s not the problem. Major Constantine always lets him off afterward.” Frustration took over Mike's tone. “I’ll tell you a story. Killus didn't like one of our doctors because he kept poking at him. Well, Killus decided to introduce him to that knife he loves to carry around, and the doctor had spent weeks recovering. Sam flipped out and threatened to kick him out, but the Major somehow stopped him from doing it. Look, Sam does try, but not even he can do anything, let alone the rest of us when the Major has his way."

"What is it with Killus? Why is he even here? I don't see him having any powers."

"We've asked that same question. That's what that doctor was looking into when he got stabbed. For some reason, Killus didn't want anyone poking around. That doctor quit shortly after being attacked."

"So, no one ever found out that he has powers?"

"The only thing we know is that something in his brain is switched off so he can kill without remorse. Also, he seems to go into situations where he should be dead, but somehow, he miraculously shows up alive. We don't think it's skill, as he doesn't have invulnerability. We're guessing it's a luck thing, because he should have been dead multiple times, but he's still here."

Mike walked over and took a seat next to Alexavier. "Look, I know things have been a little crazy since you arrived with a few unwelcomed encounters. I know Killus is one of them, and Harvey is another problem on its own. Don't let these guys get to you. Stay focused and be ready. You might have a workout tomorrow. The Terror Tribe might attack the White House. You never know."

"I just want a chance to take them down for what they did."

"You mean the mission to save Beth in Jersey?"

"Not just that, but I'm also talking about when Beth almost died from the building falling on her. I never felt so helpless. It's something I never want to feel again."

"The problem is how it's making you feel now and how that's affecting you. You don't need to continue down this path. You've made so much progress, but now it seems like you're taking a step backward."

"I just wish-"

“Knock, knock.” They had a surprise visitor, as Bobbie stood just outside the door. “I am I interrupting?”

“Kind of,” Mike replied. “But it’s fine. Come on in.”

Bobbie entered the room. “I just wanted to come by and tell Alex the good news.”

“Really?” Alexavier perked up. “I could use some.”

"You, my grumpy friend, are going to be getting your first taste of going on recon... with me!"

Alexavier's eyes lit up. "Wow! When is it?"

"Oh… just maybe… it could be…”

Alexavier couldn’t take the suspense. “Come one. Tell me!”

“We take off in a couple hours.”

“A couple hours?” Alexavier exclaimed. “How did that happen?”

“Bobbie sat on the edge of the desk. “I just came from talking to Sam and Jonathon. I was going to be heading out to do some recon on my own in New York, but they had a change of plans. They think it's about time to get you in the field and for me to show you the ropes when it comes to doing reconnaissance.”

“Hey! That's awesome!” Mike patted Alexavier on the back. “Weird that they didn’t include me on making that decision.”

“I'm going to be guiding you through the steps of the mission and give you any pointers if you need them,” Bobbie explained. “Should be a pretty straight forward recon.”

“I should probably start getting my stuff-”

“Hold on.” Mike held Alexavier’s arm as he was going to stand up. “Just so you know, this is kind of like a homework assignment. Bobbie will be reporting back on how well you do. Sam and the Major will be grading your performance.”

"I didn't know that. I figured it would just be training."

"Even when you're training is done, and you're going on regular missions, you're still being evaluated on your performance." Mike turned to face the excited hero. "You know that folder the Major has with your name on it? What's inside can make you or break you. Every workout you do, every recon that you go on and every mission you participate in gets documented. Every negative mark hurts you. Take Dave, for example. He can come back to life from being dead, which makes him a great candidate to be put in dangerous situations. Yet, his numbers aren't that great, and it's holding him back from being deployed more. That folder goes directly to Sam and he sees everything. If you really want to impress Sam, make that folder something he's pleased to look at."

"The last I'd seen, your folder was leaving with Sam," Bobbie stated.

"There you go. He's probably already opened it up and reviewed it. He'll probably notice a few things that have been documented lately that aren't that great. But that can change, starting with this recon mission. So, grab a few tools that you think you might need. I'd start with any lock picks and a flashlight. But leave the weapons behind."

"Why is that?"

"If you guys want to present yourselves as normal people," Mike explained. "Carrying around a three-foot sword will make you stick out, like... well, a three-foot sword."

Bobbie added, "Plus, if we were ever questioned, we wouldn't look as a threat of any kind. Police officers really frown upon finding hidden weapons."

"Makes sense." Alexavier set down the throwing knives.

"Not to mention, you're really good without weapons. I'm sure you could improvise."

"I think you'll do great." Mike looked over to Bobbie. "What do you think? You think your new student will give you any problems?"

"We'll be just fine. I have faith in him." Bobbie gave Alexavier a playful punch to the shoulder as she got up to leave. "I should be ready within the hour."

Mike nodded as she left to pack. Once she had made it out of the room, Mike continued, "Here's your chance. No matter what went down before, this could be what puts you in Sam's good graces, especially if good things end up in that folder. Go out and eliminate anything that doesn't provide any clues. Gather the necessary data and when you return, this recon mission will add to the great things that make that folder something special. Alright?"

"Yes," Alexavier smiled.

Mike stood up. "Time to get ready. Bobbie is probably already close to being packed. Show these guys what you can do."

Alexavier gave an enthusiastic nod, assuring Mike that he was as good as gold. After a quick pat on the shoulder, Mike left him alone to get started. Alexavier jumped up, hurrying to grab his backpack. He put together a bag of things that would accompany him on what would hopefully be the first of many recon missions.

CHAPTER 7

Technicians were buzzing all over the hanger, finalizing the preparation for lift-off. They had a spectator in Alexavier, who had arrived early and was eager to go. He had his backpack leaning against his leg, just watching the crew work. It gave him the opportunity to focus and get mentally ready for the time away from the complex and what might lie ahead.

The first recruits to join him were Beth, Dave and Wally, with the slight image of Jennifer floating behind them. All were excited for the prospect of Alexavier going on his first recon mission. Beth, who had brought Morkie, ran over with her usual bubbling enthusiasm. “I can’t wait! Are you ready?”

“Yeah. I actually started gathering my stuff the second I found out.”

Beth put her hand on his arm. “You’re in such good hands.”

Dave agreed, “Bobbie’s the best.”

“She helped train me,” Beth stated.

“Just have fun, dude,” Wally added with Jennifer hovering over his shoulder. “We rarely find anything, so just enjoy the time away from here.”

Jennifer floated over. “Can I go with them?”

“No,” Wally said, trying to wave her back. ”You have to keep me company.”

“You get to bring any weapons?” Dave wondered.

“No. They said not to pack any.”

Beth added, “The Major usually doesn’t care, but Sam frowns upon it.”

Finally, Sam escorted Bobbie and her entourage of Mike, Percy, Manny, Michael and Harvey Stringer for her departure. Missing was Killus and his gang, which meant whole team were happy not have to deal with them. Bobbie planted her bag next to Alexavier. The others gathered near them, providing their support. Harvey stayed back, keeping his distance with the frown on his face as he stared down Alexavier.

Percy gave Alexavier a high five, as Mike instructed, "Stay safe. Use those skills."

Alexavier gave a nod. "I will."

"Bring me back a few tacos. I know this place on the west side that makes-"

"Not this time, Manny." Sam disappointed the recruit of Mexican descent. "If anything, I think it's Percy's turn for comfort food."

Percy smiled, "Just send me with them, and I'll get my own."

"Then we're all going for a ride." Michael's comment brought a collective agreement, although Harvey could care less about the proceedings.

"Can I tag along? They literally won't know I'm there."

"Sorry, Jen," Sam replied. "You're going to have to stay here."

"Oh. Darn it!"

Wally came up behind her. "You still got me!" She smiled with cuteness only matched by being shy.

Sam let everyone mingle before takeoff, but motioned for Alexavier to join him away from the others. Once they were far enough from being heard, Sam addressed the young hero, "I just want you to know that I'm giving you this opportunity so you can prove to me the truth or falsehoods of exactly what I have read in your folder. I really wanted to address how disappointed I was in your actions in the hanger. Actions like that could have you grounded from missions or even have you sent back down to Philadelphia, until such time as you can prove how to behave, let alone a hero. Killus has disobeyed us so many times, which is no surprise, but you're different. You are supposed to be the next big recruit, and you should be held to a higher expectation. Getting into fights warrants disciplinary actions. But as much as I want to deal with that situation, as our rules dictate, I got some advice from someone who thinks really highly of you."

"Was it Mike?"

Sam nodded, "Yes. He made some compelling arguments. He also brought up the fact that you've been through so much, but haven't really had an opportunity to go through the normal processes of training and field work. He thought that might be one reason you lashed out and fought Killus. I am not one for second chances, because there is not a bad guy alive that will give you a second chance. You need to be right. You need to do right. Most importantly, no mistakes. However, I will make an exception for you, because I think you've had a lot in your past, and perhaps this is what you need, a second chance."

Alexavier sighed, "Thank you, sir."

"Don't screw this up."

"No, sir."

Sam moved closer. "How are you feeling?"

Alexavier looked his idol in the eye to respond. "Been waiting for this. I've trained for recon for years. I really want to show that I can get out there and gather the information we need to go after The Tribe."

"Be careful out there. Even though we never expect to find any info, you never know what the situation might come your way."

"I will, sir."

"You can call me Sam."

"Yes, sir." Sam smiled, patting the young hero on the back.

The Major entered the hanger, visibly upset. "Nice to be informed last minute of the changes to this recon mission." He gave the hand signal to the pilot, and the blades of the helicopter began its spin, slowly getting faster, which signaled that the wait was over. He returned to give them instructions, also giving Sam a dirty look. "Do a bit of recon before setting up camp. The hotel reservations indicate you arriving around sundown. Take the time before turning in to plan your reconnaissance for the next day. Keep in contact, but remain as silent as possible in the field. Once on the ground, use your hero names, not real ones. Both of you ready?"

Bobbie nodded, and Alexavier gave an approving glance. After a quick goodbye to Beth and Morkie, Alexavier grabbed his gear and followed Bobbie up the ramp. He slowed before entering so he could look back one last time. The approving nod from Sam felt good, but seeing Beth smile brought back triggered a feeling he hadn't had in a while. He bashfully smiled back before turning away and vanishing into the belly of the helicopter. Everyone had smiles on their faces with Beth having the biggest one. Dave stood by, keeping her company, as the rest of the team watched the aircraft prepare for takeoff.

After a couple minutes of continued spinning, the rotors on the helicopter reached their proper speed to allow it to lift off and rise through the roof. It always felt special when a recruit went on their first recon mission, even though they had previously proven themselves just to be there. The one person not excited about the helicopter vanishing from sight was Harvey, who watched from far down the hallway, with a scowl on his face. He pounded the wall with his fist before turning back.

#

Sam joined the recruits walking back to the center of the complex. Unfortunately for him, being at the back allowed the Major to pull him away so he could vent some frustration. "I don't appreciate not being kept in the loop."

"Why do you have to be informed every time I make a decision?"

"I've been put in charge of this program, which means I oversee all aspects of this complex."

Several of the recruits noticed Sam falling behind, but Sam motioned for the group of heroes to go on without him. "I am just as capable as you are. In fact, I've made many decisions that never went through you."

"Still, I would have been able to review their plans and make any necessary corrections to their mission."

Sam turned to continue walking. "We have a long list of targets that need to be investigated. It has been quite some time since we've sent anyone to investigate these. Now we can start crossing some locations off the list."

"I wouldn't have used our valuable resources for ghost hunting." The Major's agitation was evident in his waving arms. "I reviewed the itinerary you have for them and we have much better leads that could have been prioritized. If I was included in choosing a target, we could have sent them to a possible area with guaranteed Terror Tribe activity. What sense is there in checking out places that have no chance of bringing in information or even a villain?"

"I would rather send Alexavier into situations to learn about doing recons than submerge him into unnecessary combat. He's still green on exactly what we do, especially when it comes to our expectations for reconnaissance."

The Major became even more annoyed. "He's more than capable of handling himself, or haven't you noticed?"

"I have, but Alexavier has never been out data collecting. One of the deficiencies of our training program is the little details of our business. Getting information could mean a break that brings us a major villain."

"I'm all for bringing in bad guys, particularly if we have a chance to do that right now."

Sam looked perplexed. "Weren't you the one who didn't want to send Alexavier out into the field?"

"Sure," the Major agreed. "And I still feel that way. But if he's going anyway, why not go after real criminals, rather than wasting our resources on what is unlikely going to provide us with any valuable information?"

"There are still too many potential targets that may contain even the slightest clues, evidence or otherwise. We won't know if there's any information to be had unless we check out these places."

The Major appeared to want a way out of this discussion. "If you want, we can meet after they return from their mission to discuss things further."

"That works. I'll find you in your office." Sam headed off, leaving the Major to his anger once again.

CHAPTER 8

The wind was swirling around the rooftop helipad, as the helicopter landed on a government building in Lower Manhattan. With the cargo door lowered, Bobbie led Alexavier off and toward the stairwell, all while feeding him tips for his training. Their descent to the street took some time with the lengthy elevator ride. Coupled with a slow cab ride through New York City traffic, Alexavier was adding a plethora of information to his knowledge base.

Their trip ended in an industrial district in Brooklyn, which happened to be their first scouting location. Once they had been dropped off and the cab vanished in the distance, Bobbie took in their surroundings. “We need a safe place to change where there’s no prying eyes.”

They began walking toward an alley that had little in the way of windows from the abandoned buildings on either side. An entrance to the largest building had an enclosed overhang that was perfect for changing into their hero outfits.

Bobbie pulled the padded skintight shirt over her head “We have more than a dozen buildings in this area to cover. Arriving late in the afternoon like we did, most of the businesses that are still open will be closing soon, so civilian interference is unlikely, but be cautious. Gauge whether there’s a possibility of each building you’re scouting to be a good candidate for Tribe activity. If you feel like you should check one out, don’t break in, especially if there’s a business occupying the space.”

“What if the business looks questionable?”

After getting her dark blue and gray super suit on, Bobbie placed her full-face mask on her head. “We don’t want to do anything illegal. But if one really feels like it needs you to investigate it, be very careful how you enter the building. You do have your lock picks, right?”

“Yup.” Alexavier all but finished changing into his all-black outfit, putting on his black, hooded sweatshirt.

“Perfect. Look, I know the Major really wants me to show you the ropes, but I think that’s overkill. You’re probably better trained for recon than most of the others. I say we split up to cover more ground.”

“Okay,” Alexavier answered with a bit of surprise in his voice.

“I figure we can cut our time in half and get back so we can settle in for the evening before the big day of scouting tomorrow.”

“I’m good with that.”

Bobbie looked at her watch. “Let’s meet back here in two hours. That should be sufficient time. We’ll have to think about getting some food too.”

“How often should we keep in touch?”

“Actually, we should keep it to a minimum. Last month, I was ambushed when a couple of bad guys somehow intercepted our signals and overheard my conversation with the Major back at the complex. That’s not to say don’t ever call, but only if you really need to.”

“Got it.” Alexavier looked around. “Where do you want me to start?”

They exited the enclosed entrance, as Bobbie pulled out a pocket map. “We’re to the south. I figure if we take one half of the area, you to the East and me to the West, then we can meet at this middle building.”

“Sounds good to me.” Alexavier put on his mask.

“Before you go, I just wanted to see how are you feeling? The Major has been worried about your performance lately. I just want to make sure you’re ready.”

Alexavier sort of brushed off the question, still surveying the landscape. "I'm good." Bobbie still looked skeptical. "Really, I am."

She wanted to believe him, but time was wasting. "Okay. If you have any issues, you're to contact me immediately."

"Will do."

Alexavier started a brisk jog toward the first building. Bobbie was reluctant that maybe her partner wasn't ready. But her intuition said he was, so she let him venture out on his own. She placed the rest of her civilian gear in her compact backpack and threw it over her shoulder. As she began her search, one last look saw her trainee looking into a window. She started to feel comfortable that he would do just fine.

#

After an hour of scouring empty buildings, Bobbie hadn't had much luck. Having searched some of the outlying buildings so far, Bobbie entered a smaller one in the main warehouse area. She opened the door very quietly and scanned the partially illuminated area. Not a sound could be heard. After several seconds of staying absolutely still to ensure no one was near, she felt comfortable to enter.

Taking one careful step after another, Bobbie made her way toward the back entrance area, where the boilers were located. She slowly moved into the center of an open area continually listening for sounds. It was so quiet that she could hear her own heart beating. The layers of dust gave the building a creepy, abandoned feeling. Mezzanines hung above with several incinerators placed upon them. She eyed certain platforms, seeing which ones were large enough to have some kind of extraordinary usage.

Feeling no significant threat from the main area, she made her way up the stairs, keeping her eyes and ears open. With each step, the floor of the next level came closer to eye level. She could see various pieces of equipment scattered around the mezzanine, covered in dust. That along with the undisturbed dust on the floor indicated a good sign that no one had been there in a while.

Bobbie scanned the areas above, with her eyes set on the next work area on the upper floor, which housed the primary incinerator. Again, she cautiously climbed each step, creeping ever so slowly. The mechanical feel of this area was more complex than the rest. Most of the actual labor probably took place here. There were a several chutes and conveyors leading to this large incinerator, as well as an emergency exit just behind it. The massive size overshadowed every other piece of equipment. The incinerator door itself was large enough for people to move in and out of. Having no backup, apprehension was her new friend. Everything around her felt like it could be a hideout for The Terror Tribe.

Before she could fully investigate the incinerator, a sound caught her attention. She immediately stopped moving and held her breath. Listening intently, she could make out more than one noise, and it were getting closer. To her surprise, it was the sound of voices. Quickly, she slid as close to the incinerator as possible, leaving very little of her body to be seen.

Down below, the voices grew louder as guests entered the doorway of the building. “It’s not my job to care, ya know?” said a male voice.

Bobbie turned her head to look and immediately recognized them. Topher was the man with the abundant attitude and Jersey accent. He was joined by Faducia, a woman of African descent with whom Bobbie had a personal interest in. They were also scouting the nearby buildings.

As Topher walked through the door, a black cat suddenly jumped out, scaring him. “Damn cat!”

“Told ya,” Faducia looked around, “Stupid thing just chasin’ the birds. You know you gonna have a heart attack one of these days.” She took a step in the building to look around. “With your brats and beers, you be dead by Wednesday.”

“Don’t give me no crap about my eatin’. Not like you really care anyhow.” Topher took a deep breath. “There’s got to be someone here.”

“You right, I don’t care,” Faducia stated. “But since you covering my ass, y’all no use to me if you dead.”

Topher straightened himself up and adjusted his shirt. “How touching. Makes me all gushy inside.”

Faducia stepped out of the building. “Yeah, you a big softy, like a Pitbull with a fat, pink bow.”

Topher became defensive. “You callin’ me fat?”

“However you take it, my pudgy friend.”

“Okay, because… Wait. Now I’m not sure if you makin’ fun of me,” Topher pondered.

Faducia started to walk away. “Yes. I’m completely making fun of you.”

Topher's voice mellowed. “Why you got to be like that? You know my ego bruises like a grape. You hungry?”

Ever so quietly, Boobie found her way to the closest window and poked her head up slowly to look through the broken glass. Topher and Faducia were leaving, having walked halfway across the dirt covered, parking lot. Even from a distance, Bobbie could still hear their conversation.

“Coney dogs are da best,” Topher stated with pride.

“I don’t care. If it don’t have real meat, I don’t eat it.” Faducia's face showed her disgust.

“What, ya a wimp or vegetarian?” Topher's voice slowly disappeared once the duo got close to the next building. “Let’s see if someone’s over here. I’m tellin’ you, there is.”

Bobbie quickly made her way down the stairs. Being careful not to make too much noise, she raced to reach the outer doorway. Taking a peek outside, she saw the villains turn the corner of the opposing building. Bobbie made a mad dash over toward that corner. Once at the wall, she slid along, walking briskly. Reaching the corner, she carefully looked around to get an idea of where the villains were. She could see them casually walking along, headed toward the main street and storefronts. She waited until they were far enough in the distance before attempting to contact the complex.

Even though these two were lowly henchmen, it was still as if a birthday gift was dropped in her lap, and she could wait to reach for the button on her Com-Link earpiece. A quick press and she heard a connection. She peeked around the corner again to make sure that she had the time to talk.

A voice on the other responded, “Go ahead.”

“This is Booby Trap.” Bobbie settled back behind the building for cover. “I just got done watching Topher and Faducia. They are moving on from my location, but still within intercept range. Should I pursue?”

“This is Major Constantine. That’s a negative on the intercept. Keep looking for any signs of The Tribe.”

“Aren't they part of The Terror Tribe? I could still-”

The Major replied, “No confrontations are authorized, unless unavoidable. Keep on the lookout for identified Tribe members while looking for signs of recent activity.”

“But I could-”

“Negative! Your personal vendetta can wait. I need you to investigate if there’s any Tribe activity in that area. Am I being clear?”

Bobbie sighed, "Affirmative. Booby Trap out."

She ended the transmission and was not happy to let them go, particularly Faducia. Bobbie refocused her energy into examining the remaining buildings. Unfortunately, there were no exciting prospects among them, so she headed toward the nearest one, still having the desire to go after Faducia. The road ahead was dusty and abandoned, but the walk was short. A partially rusty door looked promising. With a quiet turn of the knob, she slowly opened it enough to take a peek. Seeing no signs of life, she quickly slipped inside, vanishing like a magic trick done right.

#

Alexavier's afternoon was about as eventful as it was for Bobbie. The difference being that he had yet to nearly get spotted, but he was making good time. He only had a handful of places left to check out. The next location was different than the others. From across the dirt and weed covered lot, it appeared to have a number of doors and windows, with all of them in really good condition. He thought to himself, if you're wanting to hide somewhere and keep your anonymity, this would have been the place. Alexavier was excited to investigate and tried looking into the windows. Unfortunately, the cloudy day didn't allow for enough light to illuminate the inside. He grabbed his flashlight, hoping to get a better look. There was still only so much that he could light up, so he decided to venture inside.

The first goal was to find an unlocked door. After glancing around to ensure he wasn't being watched, he walked briskly over and turned the handles, but the double-door was locked. With picks in hand, it took him a couple of turns of his wrist, and it was no longer locked. He opened the door quickly, getting inside before anyone might notice and shutting it behind him. Before he could get underway, he heard a voice.

"See, I told ya!" It was Topher, who was excited to find a masked figure. "We get ta kick some ass and drink beers!"

Faducia ran over to join her partner. "Wait 'til the ass kicking is done before you open the first one."

"I didn't mean to invade your space," Alexavier expressed, hoping to not get into an unnecessary confrontation. "I'm just looking for Terror Tribe hideouts."

"It looks like we've got a real life, government hero here. He could be our ticket to join the big guys." Faducia responded, beginning to circle around as Topher tried going the other way.

Alexavier could tell that the limited space in the building would make it difficult taking on more than one bad guy, so he backed out the door into the open area outside to assess the situation. Seeing the young woman with various weapons on her person, she was obviously well skilled in combat, but the slightly out of shape, middle-aged man posed a question. Faducia stopped, taking a combative stance, pulling out a Katana sword.

Topher exuded excitement. "Whoa, pullin' out da good blade. Must be a frickin' moron, 'cause he's ain't runnin' already."

Wanting to test the young hero, Faducia advanced forward. Alexavier matched her pace backing up, still eyeing the unknown man waiting behind her. Faducia stopped and began to swing her sword vigorously, as Topher cheered from a safe distance, "She's gonna get ya good, boy!"

Alexavier was curious. "What's your name?"

"Call me Faducia. I'm going to be the one to slice you good." Her blade stopped, pointing directly at him.

Feeling left out, Topher barked, "And I'm Topher, who's gonna stomp your freakin' head in when she's done!"

"We don't have to fight. Because if we do, this will only end poorly for both of you," Alexavier exclaimed.

"You jokin', right?" Topher said, laughing as he spoke.

Faducia stepped forward slowly. "You think this should end peaceful? Why wouldn't I slice you into pieces?"

"Fine," Alexavier conceded to her violent request. "Let's make this quick."

Faducia lunged forward and swung hard. Alexavier stepped quickly to his right, and kicked. His foot landed on the inner part of her forearm, throwing her arm back. She used the momentum and spun for another swing that sliced through the air, waist high. Alexavier hopped back and planted his right foot. Once the blade had cleared his proximity, he kicked the thigh of her lead leg, causing her to buckle slightly, unable to try another attack. Alexavier took advantage and grabbed her wrist, twisting it so hard that her hand snapped, dropping the sword. Pushing her away, he stepped over to the sword, giving it a strong kick and sending it far out of reach.

Alexavier once again offered a truce. "Like I said, I'm only interested in The Tribe. You can just walk away."

"You wantin' us to run? No way, punk! We got more for ya!" Topher exclaimed.

"We as good as Tribe members." Faducia regained her footing. She reached back and pulled out another Katana. Her small amount of frustration gave way to the satisfaction of feeling the sword in her hand. She slowly moved closer, ready to strike again. As Alexavier advanced, she lunged at him with a stabbing motion. Alexavier contorted his body sideways, allowing the blade to pass by. He reached out and grabbed her wrist, stepping closer using this momentum for a Judo throw. Faducia's body flew through the air, causing her to land hard on her back, dropping the sword. Quickly rolling to her stomach, she scrambled to reach for her sword. Once it was in her grasp, she slowly rose to a crouching position and swung at Alexavier's feet. He easily jumped over the attack, although Faducia began to swing much more aggressively for his ankles. Jumping prematurely, as her sword swept back, he stomped down with his right foot, pinning the blade to the ground as it swung by. Using his free leg, he kicked her hand, sending the sword harmlessly away.

Although he was standing over her and in control, Alexavier felt a sensation again indicating something was wrong. He ducked, and a flat, disk-shaped rock flew dangerously close to his head. Alexavier moved away from Faducia to a safe distance to watch them closely. Topher had become much less amused by the events and decided to help his partner. Muttering to himself, he reached down and picked up another rock and began to stretch and mold it like putty. Within seconds, the baseball-sized stone transformed into a throwing star made of rock. Topher quickly threw it at Alexavier, but the trajectory was quite poor, whizzing by and to the ground.

"Damn it!" Topher's attitude quickly changed when he saw Alexavier staring him down. As he slowly backed up, he stumbled over more rocks, looking quite clumsy. "Hey kid, you ain't gonna want none of me. I'm like the caged lion, waiting to strike."

Alexavier cautiously proceeded forward, but did not get too far when Faducia reached into her pant leg, pulled out a pair of knives and quickly jumped towards him. She took a wild swing, catching Alexavier off guard. He stepped back, losing his balance. She lunged at him, forcing him to spin away and distancing himself from her partner. Soon, her failed attempts to cut the young hero gave way to desperation, forcing unwarranted movements. Alexavier used her carelessness and side stepped one of her attacks and executed a backhand strike to her wrist, causing one knife fall to the dirt.

Looking up in surprise and becoming even angrier, Faducia turned around with a more aggressive swing. Alexavier blocked her attack with his forearm and reached for her wrist. With a slight twist and chop, she dropped the other knife. Desperate, Faducia landed several lazy punches to Alexavier's chest forcing him to break away.

Topher stood in shock. He grumbled and muttered inaudible swear words while picking up a slightly larger rock. He began to pull and stretch it like an artist fashioning his piece of clay. It got longer with each crafted pull. The rock soon became as long as his arms and as thin as a stick. Once satisfied, he threw it to Faducia. "Here! Smack the punk with this!"

Once the heavy, fashioned stone touched her hand, Faducia used her powers of transformation to turn it into a real wooden fighting staff. Faducia slowly turned around and stared down her opponent. "You fight good for a newbie. The government's dollars are being spent well." She twirled the staff around, taking a battle-ready stance. "Now you get to taste a little bit of payback."

Topher laughed, "I like it when ya sport wood."

Faducia twirled the staff in a spectacular display. She brought it back to her side and pointed it at Alexavier. The stare down was short lived, as Alexavier took the role of the aggressor. Faducia was caught off guard, so she tried a thrusting jab, but Alexavier contorted his body and spun away. She brought the staff back, aiming at his head. He dropped down, ducking the attack. One overly aggressive swing was followed by another. Eventually, her attention gravitated toward his feet, hoping to have a better outcome. The result was the same as the others, he moved away without any harm. A quick chopping swing causing him to stumble a bit and roll to his back. Looking to deliver a sweeping attack along the ground, Faducia swung even harder. Alexavier sensed the attack and did a kip up, lifting his legs over his head, thrusting them out and under, raising his body to allow the staff to pass underneath. He landed on his feet in a crouched position. Faducia aimed low to the ground, but Alexavier performed a no-handed cartwheel to avoid the attack. Faducia's aggravation forced her to swing with more power. The length of the staff kept Alexavier at a distance, although with each attempt she got closer. Finally, one hard swing had his left arm in its sights. A quick adjustment allowed the staff glance off his upper arm and careen over his head. The sting from the blow was evident on his face as he winced

"Ha! Rat bastard got caught!" Topher shouted, becoming the cheerleader. "Shove it down his throat!"

Alexavier stepped back, hoping to resolve the confrontation another way. "You don't need this."

Faducia crept forward. "What, you getting your head busted open?"

Alexavier held his ground. "Nope, me taking you down. It's going to end badly."

"Only for you." Faducia swung again, forcing Alexavier to back his mid-section away. She changed the swings to jabs and back again, slowly building her confidence. Alexavier waited for a wild swing and stepped forward. He attempted a straight front kick, but missed, as she tried to get within striking distance. As quickly as possible, she brought the staff around for one last attack. It arrived suddenly catching Alexavier off guard. He lifted his left arm and braced for contact with his ribs, while moving with the staff, lessening the blow. The impact still hurt nonetheless. Wincing from the pain, he dropped his arm and grabbed the staff. Tugging back and forth and trying to get her to lose her grip, Alexavier found his strength and pulled hard, causing Faducia to jolt forward. Stepping forward too, he twisted around and faced the other direction while watching Faducia end up within a few feet of him. Taking this opportunity, he used a mule kick, landing his foot in the center of her stomach. Faducia bent over gasping for air, losing her grip on the staff. With a quick stomp on one end, it caused the staff to come up, and the other end to smack her on the chin. A quick reach had Alexavier grab the staff. He spun around quickly, delivering a swift swing that hit her legs, knocking her down. With a couple of twirls of the staff, Alexavier stood up, looking down at his opponent. He tossed the staff in a show of confidence that had Faducia second-guessing her chances. She scrambled back to her feet, breathing heavy as Topher once again began grumbling and mumbling, searching for more rocks to shape.

“One last chance, it's your choice.” Alexavier issued a challenge that made his adversary irate.

Faducia rushed forward, throwing wild punches. Alexavier countered with a leg kick to her left outer thigh. She stepped in and threw a couple of jabs, both of which were blocked. Alexavier executed another strong kick to her inner leg with the force knocking her leg out, nearly sending her to the ground. She regained her balance and cautiously progressed closer.

Faducia was not ready for his kicks and became even more aggressive to counter them. She charged at him, hoping to land precise punches, but Alexavier instinctively backed away, not allowing her to get close enough to do any damage. With a hard stop, he ducked under, shooting in and grabbing a hold of both legs. He pulled her to the ground where she was clearly at a disadvantage. Fortunately, she had a one knife left and grabbed it from her belt. Sensing a dangerous situation getting worse, he rolled off before she could use it. Alexavier reached for her hand, as they struggled for control. He twisted her hand sideways and thrust it back, stabbing a broken wooden signpost. Alexavier slipped away, allowing her a moment to try to pull the knife free. An unsuccessful attempt to extract the weapon just infuriated her, so she charged him again, unloaded another barrage of punches that pushed Alexavier back. He sidestepped her attack, but she attempted a backhand swing. He leaned away and kicked at her lead leg, which buckled. Alexavier placed another kick to her inner knee, dropping her completely to the ground.

Topher screamed from the sidelines, “He ain’t nothin’! Punch him in da groin!”

The now angry villain was desperate and jumped up, putting every ounce of fury into her next attack. Unfortunately, the sloppiness that went along with it enabled Alexavier to capitalize the situation. He caught her wrist from a punch, but she swung with her other arm. He was able to duck it and quickly move in, putting his right arm under hers and over her opposite shoulder, with a stranglehold on her head and neck. Clasping his hands, he squeezed tight, applying a maneuver called a head in arm triangle. The pressure placed on her neck cut off the blood supply to her brain making Faducia dizzy. She struggled, but had very little leverage to counter this move. In less than ten seconds, her eyes rolled back, and she passed out. Alexavier continued with the pressure until her body went limp. Only then did Alexavier released his hold as her body slumped to the ground.

Topher, who was gathering rocks to shape into more weapons, stared at his fallen partner with a blank expression. He dropped all of the rocks, but one. In a feeble attempt, he threw the last remaining rock towards Alexavier’s direction but missed him by a several feet as he duck out of the way. By the time Alexavier turned back, Topher was already running in the other direction.

Alexavier let the stumbling villain escape, as his power to shape rocks made him very much non-threatening. The most important thing was to secure Faducia. Alexavier pulled out the zip ties and within moments she was bound and awaiting extraction.

#

Running for what seemed like the first time in years, Topher tried hard to catch his breath and staying on his feet. Even when he thought he was in the clear, everything changed when he turned the last corner. His luck ran out when he came face to face with Booby Trap. She disobeyed the Major's order to not engage the two villains by staying on their trail and was gifted Topher who came running at her. He nearly face-planted trying to stop. "Get out of my way, sweetheart."

Bobbie had an offended look on her face. "I'm not your sweetheart."

"What ya are is dead meat if ya don't get out of my way." Topher knuckled up, trying to look as imposing as possible.

Bobbie stood her ground, knowing exactly how this was going to go. "Why don't you try and go through me?"

Attempting to psyche himself up, Topher kept grunting and waving his arms in a less than masculine manner. Once he had achieved the point of overconfidence, he crept forward until he was a couple feet away. He let out a war cry and rushed her. With the greatest of ease, Bobbie gave him a front kick to the stomach, which dropped him instantly from having the wind knocked out of him. Topher gasped for air, making some awful, but almost funny wheezing sounds. Knowing the out of shape villain was in no condition to put up a fight, Bobbie brought out the zip ties and secured him. As he continued to desperately bring oxygen back into his lungs, she started running off to find Faducia. But as she turned the corner, Alexavier was off in the distance and running towards her. She yelled out, "Have you seen Faducia?"

"She's tied up about three buildings over. What about the big guy?"

"He's kind of in pain and out of breath… and on the ground… and really out of breath." Bobbie let out a relaxing sigh and gave him a high five. " Great job! I've been wanting to get her for a long time."

"Why? What's the deal with her?"

“It’s a story for another day. Let’s get them ready.” Bobbie tapped her earpiece. “I’ll radio it in. The helicopter will be on its way.”

Alexavier could tell something had happened, but didn’t want to push if she wasn’t ready to divulge the history between them. He walked with her to help bring Topher for extraction, but was still curious. He hoped that in time she would eventually tell their story.

CHAPTER 9

As the blades of the helicopter began their long, slow deceleration, the cargo door gradually opened to a large crowd of spectators. Even Killus and his crew joined in the festivities. Everyone was thrilled about the results of the reconnaissance mission, except Major Constantine, who was less than ecstatic. Once the door had come to rest on the ground, the Major instructed Dirk Henderson of the Elitesmen Guard and his armored Guard members to handle the prisoners. A path was made to allow them to be escorted toward the holding cells. As usual, Killus, Hank and Glen poked and prodded them as they walked by.

After getting a chance to disembark, Bobbie led the way to a plethora of high fives and congratulations. It continued for Alexavier, until they were surrounded by the other recruits. For the first time in a long time, you could see a smile on Alexavier's face.

Dave couldn't stop patting him on the back. “First recon out! That's so awesome! Was it easy? How quick before you had her tied up?”

“Give him some room.” Beth pushed her way between them. “I'm sure he's tired after a fight like Faducia can give.”

“I'm fine. Really, I am.”

“How quick did you beat her?” Dave was bouncing like a five-year old with a sugar high. “Did you have to take her to the ground?”

Percy interjected, “Give him a break, man!”

Beth leaned over to Bobbie. “How did he do?”

"Amazing." Bobbie looked over to the Major who was still in a foul mood. "There's no reason why he shouldn't be thrilled."

"I'm glad I'm not you," Beth admitted. "You're debriefing is going to suck."

"Yeah. I know."

Mike finally arrived. "What are you ladies talking about?"

Beth smiled, "How well Alex did."

"I heard." Mike turned to Bobbie. "Congratulations to you too! I hear you now have the fastest capture, beating Harvey's time."

"Thanks," Bobbie put down her backpack. "But Alex did all the hard work. He made it easy for me. I only had to put one boot to Topher."

Percy smiled, "And what a pretty boot it is."

"Thanks," Bobbie grinned, as Percy came and stood next to her. "Hey, Alex!" She gave a big thumbs up, as he smiled and nodded.

Alexavier wondered, "Is that it? Are we done?"

"I have to meet for an initial debrief," Bobbie responded, not sounded enthused. "Go see the doctor, as it's required if you engage in any type of combat during a recon. We can meet after, in case they want you to do some debriefing too."

"Got it." Alexavier strolled over to Beth. "You want to come with me to the doctor's office?"

Finally seeing a break in the homecoming celebration, Sam walked over, pulling Bobbie away from the group. He led her away from the hanger, following the Major. There was minimal conversation along the way, since the real discussion would begin shortly in the Major's office. Once they were all inside, the Major closed the door and lowered the shades.

Sam was first ask, "Give me your thoughts on Alexavier's performance."

"Alex did well. He listened to my instructions and did what he needed to do."

The Major impatiently interrupted her, “What about Faducia? Why weren't you there?”

“I decided to split up to cover more ground. After they left the building I was in, they must have wandered over to where Alex was.”

“But you're supposed to be training him.”

“Yes, I was. I gave him every piece of advice I thought he may need for this recon. I read up on him when he first arrived and did a follow-up on his file before this recon. He's been doing this kind of stuff for a while and is better at recon than almost everyone here. He could probably show the other guys a thing or two.”

“That might be true, but I gave specific orders to-”

Sam interrupted, “I don't think her call was too far out of line.”

“He needs to understand our processes and exactly how we do specific things, which means being present and with her for every part of the recon. Plus, if Bobbie experienced any issues, he wouldn't have been there to help.”

“She didn’t need help,” Sam countered. “She is one of the best recruits we've ever had. I know, because I've been working with her since day one. She has experienced some difficult situations and has always dealt with them appropriately and come out on top. I’m not worried about whether she can handle herself.”

The Major heaved a big sigh, “Again, that might be true, but what if the next time she's cornered by the whole Tribe, and can't call us? We know that's a possibility. We've lost communications on several occasions now.”

“I understand your concern, but we are training these recruits to think on their feet, even go with their gut instinct. Hell, Alexavier's success is based off of his ability to feel... or whatever you want to call it.”

“But what if that feeling proves to be wrong?”

"He hasn't been wrong yet." Sam looked over to Bobbie. "Can you give us a minute?" Once she was outside, Sam continued, "You have been telling me for more over a year that this recruit was something special, our shining star. If that is true, then let him go out there and do what he is trained to do."

"His performance within these walls has been disappointing thus far. He has not been the stellar hero that we need him to be. We are basically rewarding him for his unacceptable performance."

"Recruit performance is important and a criteria for going on recon and missions. But you have to look at the big picture, we haven't had someone that is physically capable of handling themselves like Alexavier, since we worked on getting Bobbie to that level. That was two years ago."

The Major started to become agitated. "It's going to be another two years if his performance doesn't improve. How will I explain Alexavier participating in these missions when the documentation shows he underperforming?"

"But he executes well in the field."

"Yet, he doesn't here in this complex." The Major handed Sam a folder. "We set up this revised evaluation system to insure the recruits are ready for action. We have data to back it up, and the hard numbers say Alexavier is not ready. His workout with you should have proven that. If we're going to make judgment calls, when are we going to bring up a random kid from our Portland complex without being ready and throw him straight on a helicopter."

Sam could see the point and backed down. "I agree with you. We should be tracking and evaluating their training, but Alex is different."

"So is Manny. So is April. So is Harvey."

"I see your point." Sam didn't want to get too frustrated with the Major's one-sided argument. "Let's just table this discussion until we can sit down and evaluate this in more detail." Sam attempted to hand back the folder. "Maybe we should bring Senator Steinberg in on this as well."

"Fine. Hold onto the folder and look it over, until our next meeting. Still, I don't feel that we can really afford for him to go out and make a mistake. We will keep him here and have Mike and Jonathon work out some of his issues."

Sam nodded and exited the Major's office. Outside the door, he quickly pulled Bobbie's arm to have her walk with him and didn't speak until they were well outside of hearing distance from the Major's office. Sam gives one final look and made sure they turned the corner before speaking. "I want your honest opinion. Don't hold anything back. After being out there with him, how would you feel if Alexavier was on your team or in the field? Do you feel confident that he would have your back?"

"Definitely."

"You'd have no qualms about working together? If he went with you on another recon, would you do it again?"

"In a heartbeat," Bobbie answered without hesitation.

Sam was quick to counter, "Even with his lack of performance here at the complex?"

"That's not my call, but his performance in the field is what counts."

"I appreciate your honesty." Sam let her leave. It has always been Sam's job to evaluate each recruit and their progress, keeping in mind what was right for the individual trainee. Sometimes it took looking at the numbers. Other times it meant using his intuition. In this moment, he had no more words. All he had was the information in a folder.

CHAPTER 10

With the doctor's office located next to the hanger, Alexavier and Beth didn't have far to walk. Setting up her standard set of instruments used for a post-reconnaissance mission check-up, Dr. Jean Dennis waited for the recruits. Any combat experienced during a mission resulted in a visit with the medical team, to ensure there were no unforeseen or sustained injuries.

"How are you feeling?" The doctor waved Alexavier over. "Any major sore spots?"

"My upper arm and ribs."

"Let's take a look." The doctor helped him pull off his shirt, exposing the bruises.

After a quick observation, she placed her hands over the injured areas. Instantly, a soothing sensation washed over him like a warm waterfall raining down. The doctor's healing powers began repairing his injured ribs, as the hypnotic effects kept his mind from focusing on the pain. Beth watched in anticipation, waiting for him to open his eyes.

Dr. Dennis removed her hands and stood back. Alexavier slowly opened his eyes. He looked around, eventually focusing on the doctor. With a slight smile he said, "Thanks. I feel a lot better."

The doctor continued her evaluation, "Any other aches or pains?"

"Nope." Alexavier settled in comfortably for the examination.

"I need to find a way to relax like that," Beth smiled.

"Good. Relaxation is definitely important." The doctor pushed on his elbows. "Any joint pain or anything that is limiting your range of motion?"

"No, nothing."

"Any blows to the head, hard hits or landings?"

"No."

"Let me check your pupils." The doctor examined his eyes, eventually shining a light into each one. Satisfied, she put the pen light down. "Perfect. Now the fun part. I'm going to take some blood to again run some genetic tests. We want to further explore the previous results and see what else we find."

It took a minute for the doctor to prep the needle and syringe. Alexavier looked over to Beth, who waited patiently. She smiled, which made him feel warm all over.

A swipe of an alcohol swab prepped the area. "Okay. It's the same poke you've had before. Just relax and..." Remembering her previous experience, Dr. Dennis knew the difficulties of obtaining blood from Alexavier. Using additional force to puncture the skin didn't work again, so she pressed harder, pushing the tip of the needle against the skin and finally piercing the epidermis. With the blood flowing through the thin tube and into the syringe, the doctor inspected his blood a bit more closely than usual. The process of collection was efficient and took very little time.

Having completed the blood collection, Dr. Dennis pulled the needle from Alexavier's arm and placed a bandage over the sight. She began labeling his blood, as Alexavier hopped off the chair.

"We'll analyze these samples," the doctor acknowledged. "The results should be back in a few days. We should also have another result for your DNA and genetic makeup."

"Are my genes still showing up weird?"

"Strangely, every time we test your blood, the results are slightly different. It's puzzling, especially to the experts. The geneticists are curious as to why it is happening. One test indicates you're a Non-Meta. The next test doesn't show the mutation at all. We've even seen one test a few years ago that showed the Meta human mutation. I'm hoping that this sample today will provide enough blood to analyze and obtain a definitive result. Alright, let me finish up so I can send these out."

Alexavier hopped down and started to leave, but the doctor stopped him by adding, "Oh, I've requested some information from a couple of doctors out of southern California about memory recovery. Their research is quite interesting and has proven to help some of their patients bring suppressed memories back from their subconscious."

"Awesome news! I can't wait."

"I won't receive the information for a few days, so we'll plan another visit and appropriate time to attempt another recovery of memory. You guys enjoy the rest of your evening."

"Thank you, doctor."

"Thanks, Dr. Jean!" Beth's enthusiasm was infectious, making the doctor smile, followed by Alexavier.

Once they were out in the hallway, Alexavier looked around, seeing that the welcome party in the hanger had moved back into the complex. He took a second to gather himself and then turned to Beth. "Hey. I just want to say that I'm sorry that I've been in such a mood lately. Things have been frustrating for me. I've realized, that for a while, I've really been shutting everyone out, including you."

"That's okay. There are times when we all need to hunker down and work a little harder."

"But I could have handled it better. Things haven't gone the way I'd hoped. My workout with Sam was such a big disappointment. We barely made it out alive in New Jersey, then to have the Major get mad at me. I wanted to be careful about what I do and don't lose focus. I started to concentrate on what I need to do in the field rather than here. Not to mention, Killus is always looking for a reason to fight and Harvey won't stop being such a douche."

"What if you extend an olive branch to Harvey?"

"Really? I'm not sure what I did wrong for him to hate me so much."

"You might find out if you try to make peace with him."

Alexavier sighed, "I guess you're right."

"I'm always right," Beth smiled.

Alexavier chuckled, "I won't argue that. My biggest fear is if I do something wrong out in the field, I may get sent back."

"Just think positive. You're here, and you're saving lives. That's the role of a hero."

"I can say, after going on that recon, I do feel better."

"Good! You should. You did great." Beth wrapped her arm around his and pulled him down the hallway. "I'm in the mood for a snack. How about we get some ice cream?"

Walking back through the complex, Alexavier's mood quickly changed. He was starting to really look forward to a spoon full of ice cream, as much as sharing it with Beth.

CHAPTER 11

The day of spending time with friends morphed into a night of continued searching on the World Net. Spending so much time scouring, Alexavier didn't realize it was getting late. This current round of searches didn't bring him any closer for his quest to figure out where The Terror Tribe might be, but he felt confident enough to rule out the general warehouse area near the New Jersey docks. If there were any legal evidence, it wasn't present online.

With an overall mood change that had him feeling better, Alexavier put away his gear from the recon and readied himself for bed. Recent events had him worked up, but the doctor's visit made him feel at ease. Exhausted, he threw back the covers, plopped into bed and reached over to turn off the lights. He took a moment to clear his mind, hoping to relax and have a great night's sleep, so he could be reenergized in the morning.

Laying back, settling in and letting out a big exhale, Alexavier closed his eyes. The darkness eventually overtook his consciousness and deep sleep ensued. Hours of sleep brought many dreams, but in the middle of the night, one dream in particular became extremely vivid and real.

Entering into what appeared to be in a long and endless tunnel, Alexavier started walking through the darkness. Everything about it felt creepy, causing a bit of uneasiness to sweep over him. Finally, off in the distance, a point of light began to shine. Just like how people have described a near death experience, the light was warm and inviting.

Suddenly the tunnel began to take a different shape. He stopped, unsure of what was happening. Dark portions of the walls moved toward the center, eventually taking the shape of a man and a woman. The bright light behind them hid their faces, but something felt familiar. It was as if he knew these people.

Before he could interact with them, they began moving towards the light. He reached out desperately wanting them to stay, but his feet wouldn't move. His cries to have them wait made no noise. It seemed to take a lifetime before they slowly melted into the brightness, becoming one with it. With his hand still desperately trying to grab a hold, a stranger's hand reached back, touching his. Instantly, a new sensation took over his body. The comfort of her touch eased his anguish and the only sound he heard was her voice.

"Never stop looking. Only then will you discover the truth."

Suddenly, Alexavier's body jolted, as he woke up. Feeling drenched from sweat, he sat up looking around to determine where he was, only to feel safe with the sight of his room in the middle of the night. Not wanting to lose any of the memories of what he just experienced, he got out of bed and grabbed his journal.

For anyone flipping through this journal, they would see just an ordinary every day journal containing memories from his time within Project: Hero. Over the years he would record events from his daily life, people he would meet and at times, detailing choice conversations with friends. He started to log these memories for fear he would forget something important, especially after the expected and mostly reversible, short-term memory loss experienced after each scheduled Session. He began to see others lose not only their short-term memory, but at times, their long-term memory. For fear of losing any critical memories, especially during his childhood, he began to document his life.

Turning to the back of the journal where he kept his dream experiences, Alexavier began detailing the strange woman's hand, voice and words. Not knowing what any of this may mean, Alexavier continued to keep details of these complex pieces until the puzzle is complete.

CHAPTER 12

Even though he had slept well, the vision from last night had his mind racing early in the morning. Rather than lay in bed, Alexavier decided to be productive, so he got out of bed. His usual agenda would include some kind of physical activity to start with, but today was different. Today he was hungry. Knowing that everyone else would be asleep at 5am, it would be the best time to grab a bite to eat without any drama.

The cafeteria smells that were wafting down the hallway were surprisingly inviting. Usually, the smells would make you ask yourself if you should run the other way. Walking through the doorway, Alexavier could see that the room was almost empty, except for one table. Oddly, Harvey was the lone occupant of a large table, even though he hardly ever got up early enough to be the first in line. Alexavier had the pick of the room and looked to stay away from Harvey. But he stopped, remembering what Beth had mentioned the day before. Alexavier decided to set up shop right across from Harvey at the same table. Harvey's recent actions towards him had bothered and confused him, so he took this opportunity in an attempt to figure things out and possibly resolve any issues.

"I get up this early to eat alone and not be bothered, if you can take a hint." Harvey didn't look up from his food.

The response to his presence was not unexpected, but Alexavier was going to try being tactful. "Look, I don't know if we got off on the wrong foot somewhere-"

"There's no we in this conversation. I'd actually prefer to not have a conversation with you."

The words caused Alexavier to pause. "We're teammates in this. We need to be working together."

"I'm working on bringing down The Infamous One. I don't care what you do."

"You can't do that if you're always being left here all the time."

The comment angered Harvey, and he slid his tray forward and got up, leaving the rest of his uneaten food. As Alexavier watched the disgruntled hero exit the cafeteria, he could only wonder how things have gotten to where they are, having absolutely no idea why.

#

Sam felt a little guilty for some of the comments he made the last time he was in presence of the Major. Wanting to make sure there wasn't any heat between them, he found his way through the complex and straight to the doorway of the Major's office. The Major was stationed behind his desk with his hand rubbing his forehead, looking particularly annoyed. Feeling that an interruption to whatever was causing the stress might be welcomed, Sam knocked on the frame of the door. "Are you busy?"

"I'm always busy." Major Constantine closed the folder in front of him. "What do you need?"

Sam slowly entered the room. "I just wanted to clear the air about my last visit. I wasn't judging your ability when it comes to the recruits. I think I was on edge from catching Alex and Killus in the hanger. Something like that is unacceptable and should never happened in the first place."

"I understand. But you have to understand everything I have to deal with."

The Major slowly rose to his feet taking a confrontational stance. "That includes trying to go after the worst bad guys on the planet. Sometimes that decision includes having a recruit that tends to have psychopathic tendencies. I agree that Killus' actions aren't proper for what we expect of our regular recruits, and he probably could be locked up if the circumstances were different. You and I both know that we need to have that one person who isn't afraid to get violent when the opportunity arises. We teach everyone to try and deescalate dicey situations, but you know that rarely happens. The worst thing is when someone defies everything you ask, and then try to kill you. You then have to be merciful to them. Our compassion has gotten recruits killed because we wouldn't do what was needed. Killus provides what we need in those special times. I know he isn't the model recruit, but I'm not going to let another hero die because we can't pull the trigger. I will handle him. It's not right what he's doing, but rest assured it will be handled."

"I appreciate it," Sam said, feeling some relief. "There is a lot we have to handle, and it gets more complicated with each new kid that walks though those front doors."

"April is such a complicated girl. I'm still trying to figure out Michael's limits, which almost don't exist."

Sam nodded, "Then we add Alexavier and all of his unknowns. I really think our level of compassion needs to be higher than ever. This is where Mike is priceless. He works so well with our younger heroes to get accustomed to life here."

The Major's phone rang, but he ignored it. "I get it, but Mike needs to follow my expectations as well."

The phone rang again, finally making Sam pause. The Major glanced at the phone, but left it alone, however Sam couldn't ignore it any longer. "You should answer that."

The Major quickly reached for the receiver. "Hello?"

Sam could see the look on the Major's face change. "What's going on?"

"Okay. Send out a Code Green. We'll be there." The Major hung up the phone and frantically searched his desk. "There's a bank robbery in progress in D.C. right now. Eyewitnesses say it's a couple of Tribe members."

Sam slowly retreated to the door. "I'll take point on this. We can be there in less than ten minutes with the new helicopter. Have any available recruits with gear in hand meet me in the hanger, except Killus!"

With a nod that sent Sam on his way, the Major compiled enough papers to take with him to central command before reaching for the phone.

#

As the minutes went by, more and more of the hungry heroes began to fill the cafeteria for morning nourishment. With Killus and crew finally arriving, all recruits other than Harvey, who had left earlier, were gathered to eat.

For the most part, everyone was enjoying their meal, with the only exception being Alexavier and his glum demeanor. Everyone at the table were well aware, but not sure why, so the conversation was kept light. Even with a recent reprimand, Killus and crew were tickled to see Alexavier bummed, even laughing and joking about it.

"I don't need another workout," Dave exclaimed.

Wally rolled his eyes as Bobbie added, "You need a successful one."

"Ha, ha." Dave sat back and stared at his food.

Jennifer was floating by and noticed Dave becoming grumpy. "You're not smiling."

Percy piped up, "He got served the truth with his breakfast."

"I thought the point of us being here was for training?" Dave wondered. "I don't think becoming superheroes is a competition. Who'd even want to keep score anyway?"

Wally smirked, "It's not hard to keep score when you never win."

Dave threw his hands up. "I can see I'm never going to win this argument."

"Just like with your workouts!" Beth's response had everyone nearly on the floor in laughter. Even Alexavier had a little grin.

Suddenly, an announcement from the Major erupted over the PA system, interrupting their verbal barrage on Dave. "Attention all recruits, Code Green! Attention all recruits, Code Green! Collect your gear and meet in the hanger! Repeat, Code Green! James Killus, please see me in my office."

"Code Green?" Alexavier asked. "Is that-"

Beth jumped up. "It's a bank robbery in progress. We never get the call while it's happening. It's got to be The Tribe!"

"Let's go!" Wally grabbed a handful of food before weaving through the tables.

Jennifer vanished in her own way, as most of the young heroes sprinted to their rooms. Seeing Alexavier rush off, Killus stayed seated, eyeing the new recruit as he quickly exited the cafeteria. With a disgruntled sigh, Killus finally got up and headed to find the Major.

#

Back at his room, Alexavier needed very little time for a quick turnaround, since he was a master of gathering his gear. He whipped off his clothing with little regard to where they fell on the floor. The realization that he might finally see some action was motivation enough to hurry and grab his black hooded sweatshirt while putting on the last glove, before heading towards the door.

Cutting through the sea of people in the hallway wasn't easy, especially with everyone having their own roll in preparing for this mission. Careful enough, Alexavier moved through the congestion within the center of the complex. When he got an opening with fewer people, he sprinted to the hanger. To his surprise, the only thing he saw was the helicopter, spinning its blades faster and faster. Within seconds of each other, Sam, Beth and Hank arrived. Not far behind was Bobbie.

The only thing bothering Sam was Hank and what he had brought with him. "Leave the weapons here, Hank. We're going to be coming in as heroes and protectors, and we don't need to give anyone the wrong impression. Plus, the world doesn't know you yet, which can also work to our advantage."

With the sound of the spiked mace and massive hook dropping to the floor, Sam looked over the assembled group. He had hoped more recruits were present and really couldn't wait any longer if they were to catch The Tribe members. He got his wish when Dave, Wally and Jennifer came running and flying in. "Let's get on board!"

Everyone hurried up the ramp, finding their usual seats to begin the pre-flight procedure. As they began finalizing their preparations for takeoff and inserting their Com-Links, Sam moved toward the front to address the team while the flight crew and ground crew were nearing procedural completion. Only when the helicopter lifted into the air did Sam start to provide details about this crucial mission.

"Reports have come in that there is a bank robbery currently in progress in downtown Washington, D.C. Early information reports a number of possible Terror Tribe members present at the scene."

"Do we know who?" Beth questioned.

"Negative. I'm waiting to hear back from the Major. I was in his office when the call was received. He briefed me with the current status, while I was getting my suit. The bank they are robbing is an older bank. In fact, I believe they have robbed it before, although it has been quite some time since they did. They entered through the front door with no regards about being seen, so we may encounter some heavy hitters. Be on guard."

"Did they break through the front doors?" Alexavier asked.

"They walked in."

Alexavier thought for a second. "Then we're not looking at the top members of The Tribe. With them, it's always shock and awe to confuse."

"Makes sense," Beth added.

Sam continued, "Which probably means they are lower ranking Tribe members, possibly from the area. Still, I need you to be on alert in case something else is happening. It could be a trap. We don't know. I question how we were made aware of this so easily."

Bobbie raised her hand. "Are we fighting them or hunting them?"

"As long as civilians are safe, our first priority is to capture one or all of them. I will assess the situation on arrival. If the opportunity presents itself to follow one leading us to the rest of the Tribe, I wouldn't rule that out."

"What do you want me to do?" Jennifer wondered.

Sam replied, "I need you to stay up high and keep a watch out in case they run, and we need to track them down."

"Got it, boss!" Jennifer saluted him.

"What is the area like we're heading to?" Alexavier inquired.

"The bank is located downtown in an older business district with tall buildings, lots of people and traffic. There will be civilians present, but most should already have fled for safety. There are always thrill seekers in the midst of the action, so watch for those people. I may need to be the distraction for them and able to get their attention, so be ready to head out on your own. The great thing about you guys is that you're anonymous heroes to the public right now. Therefore, it can be to your advantage in capturing these villains. Alright! Finish suiting up!"

It only took a few seconds before everyone was ready, allowing Sam to speak the words they all wanted to hear. Words that have been said for so many years, "Alright Beacon, Dread, Hack, Dead Head, Booby Trap, Syphon and Wave Rider. Let's do this!"

Alexavier watched as Sam put on his super suit. Seeing the red, white and blue, with various stars gave him goose bumps. He had seen the outfit, but only on TV, in comics and movies. Now he was getting to see it in person. When Sam finished putting on his last glove and stood up, the sight was inspiring. This was the greatest moment in Alexavier's life, and a moment he will never forget, going to be on a mission with The Patriot Warrior.

CHAPTER 13

With the training complex located not far from D.C., the flight time was extremely short. The helicopter came in hot, circling over a several block area, surveying the layout of the city streets. The location of the targeted bank was in an area where landing a jet helicopter was not impossible. Several buildings nearby were only a few stories tall, which allowed the helicopter to hover low enough to drop the heroes with the help of Wally. Sensing the jet was at a constant altitude, Sam lowered the rear ramp and began directing traffic.

"Everyone make sure your Com-Links are activated. From now on, we are using code names only. Stay tight and stay close. I will assess the situation and begin issuing commands. Wave Rider, bring me and Hack 'n Maul down first, then come back for Booby Trap, Dead Head, Beacon and Dread. Syphon, head out to scout from above. Pilot, achieve a safe altitude and flight pattern until we need a lift out!"

"Roger."

"Let's go, Wave Rider!"

Wally nodded and grabbed the two heroes, floating away and out of sight. Using the air currents from the helicopter's spinning blades, he made his way down, swooping in and slowing for a soft landing. Upon Sam getting his secure footing, he turned to see numerous onlookers with stares of disbelief with his arrival.

Sam quickly instructed, "Hack, keep alert for any surprises. I'm sure that my presence will bring a lot of attention."

Hank grunted and felt naked without his deadly toys wrapped around his wrists. He rotated meticulously to gage their surroundings, moving his head frequently to maintain Sam's location.

Wally arrived back and dropped off Alexavier and Beth a safe distance from Sam, so not be noticed. Wally flew back up for one last transport, as Alexavier began assessing the situation. Something didn't feel right. "This is such a small bank."

Beth looked over the building. "Yeah, and an old one too."

"But why go through the hassle of almost getting caught in broad daylight for such a small payout?" He pointed across the street to one of the biggest banks in D.C. "That one should have so much more."

As Wally brought down the final heroes to street level, Sam started delivering orders. "I need eyes in the sky."

"On it." Wally lifted into the air, high above the crowded streets with numerous people chanting Sam's name.

"Can we see anyone trying to flee?"

"Negatory, boss!" Jennifer exclaimed.

Being the world's most famous hero can have its advantages. Right now, Sam was being overwhelmed with the attention, and it was hindering their mission. To lessen the distraction that the enthusiastic fans might have, Sam headed for the growing mob. He greeted as many fans as he could, using himself as a diversion. "Hack, you and Dead Head examine the bank over for any clues."

"On our way," Dave said, joining Hank as they weaved through the crowd towards the front door.

Suddenly, Jennifer shouted over the Com-Link, "I see a two figures being carried off through the air! They're only a few blocks away!"

"Wally! Pick up Booby Trap and Dread. See if you can catch them."

"Yes, sir!" Wally dove back quickly, reaching his arms out to grab ahold and take his teammates over the crowds.

If having The Patriot Warrior in front of them wasn't enough, the sight of flying heroes made many awestruck. The growing crowds created concern that Sam and the team hoped not to get. The unneeded attention could result in massive causalities, so Sam begin to head away from the bank in question.

The race to catch up to the villains was easier than expected. The wind was significant enough for Wally to move quickly and the villains could see it. They immediately flew down to street level, with the two villains transferring the loot bags to Bootlegger who took off, trying to escape. Wally glided in for an easy landing, allowing Bobbie and Alexavier to chase after The Tribe members. Like a rocket, Wally took off after Bootlegger. "Patriot Warrior, come in! I'm on Bootlegger's tail right now! Dread is in pursuit of Landfill, and Booby Trap is after Empty!"

Concern continued to grow, and you could see it on Sam's face. "Roger. Be advised, we're bringing too much attention to ourselves. I'm moving away from the combat zone. Remember your training. Dead Head, Hack, what is your status in the bank?"

"I think we're about done. There's not much evidence left behind."

"Evacuate the building and head toward the others in case they need back up."

"Got it." Dave led the way, skirting the crowd that gathered around Sam. It was hard for Hank to remain inconspicuous, but they were able to do so enough to eventually race away to aid their comrades.

#

Landfill wasn't a particularly fast bad guy, so the race to catch him was easy. But the hard part for Alexavier was the powers this villain possessed. Landfill's manipulation of the ground made for a tricky confrontation. Even before Alexavier could get close enough to him, a large section of the pavement opened up, allowing a huge mound of dirt to shoot up. It did little to block Alexavier, as he easily changed course and continued to gain ground.

Seeing his first attempt fail, Landfill threw up a stretched-out wall right in front of Alexavier. The persistent hero kept his momentum and dug in with one foot, hopping up to the top of the earth structure and staring down at his target.

Slowly stepping back, the plan for escape now included a confrontation that Landfill wasn't happy about. "Stay out of my way, or I'll bury you alive."

Remembering how triggers had an effect, Alexavier decided to use a trick that had worked during a previous altercation. "That's not happening, Terracon."

"The name's Landfill!" he roared. "And you're stupid if think you can take me in a fight!"

"You have one chance to surrender."

The answer was a shower of dirt filled with rocks that sprayed all over the crouched hero, but his body felt a sensation to move. The wall beneath him began to crumble, and the sides came flying in to crush him. Alexavier jumped forward, but was met with a mass of dirt shooting up, propelling him into the air. Leaping off a large clump of dirt, his hands reached out to the bar of a streetlight where he was able to steady himself.

"Ha! Sitting duck!" The sight of Alexavier hanging unharmed made Landfill anxious. He erected several more mounds of dirt, scattered around in front of him, hoping they would protect him. Noticing a hesitation in

Alexavier, Landfill tried to take him down, thinking he was an easy target. With a raise of his hand, a stream of dirt erupted from the cracks in the street and shot in the prone hero's direction. With an urgency to move, Alexavier swung back quickly to gain momentum and leaped to dodge the projectiles hurled his way. He landed atop an awning of a nearby building and pushed forward, hopping from one to another. The massive field of dirt piles reminded him of the posts from the W.A.R. Room, so he jumped over to use them, racing toward his opponent.

In a move of desperation, the once confident villain sent all the debris he could muster in Alexavier's direction, hoping to stop the rush. The weak attack had Alexavier adjust his route, dropping down and using the various piles of dirt to mask his movements from side to side. Once within reach, he rushed forward too quick for Landfill to react and delivered a strong flying kick that sent him skidding on the ground. In another desperate attempt to put space between them, Landfill pulled up multiple columns of dirt, sending several cars into the air and on their sides. Alexavier scampered away to avoid being crushed, but quickly felt a strong uneasiness. Suddenly, two large deposits of earth broke through the street on either side. They swelled up like tsunami waves, crashing down with a thunderous boom, sending a cloud of dust in the air reminiscent of a nuclear bomb. Landfill felt some satisfaction that he could no longer see his opponent, until he looked up and was stunned to see the hero emerge through the dusty cloud. Alexavier had leaped with a forward momentum that allowed him to land, thrusting both hands out and making contact with Landfill's chest. The attack caused Landfill to stumble over some loose rock and gravel. Grasping for stability, he was able to place his hand against the nearest car to keep from falling. Alexavier hid behind one of the mounds, not allowing Landfill to get a bead on him. As if being shot out of a cannon, Alexavier jumped up, using the top of the closest mound to propel him forward in a surprising move that had Landfill unprepared. Alexavier landed in front, but Landfill could only attempt a weak thrust of dirt that was easily sidestepped. Once he was clear of the earth born projectile, Alexavier planted one foot and swung his other leg forward. It landed hard on the villain's face, driving him back into the car, causing another collision. One that saw the master of dirt mounds knocked out cold.

With a deep breath, Alexavier reached for his zip ties to secure the unconscious villain. But before he could do so, a familiar sensation came over him. Gravity pulled on every inch of his body. His muscles didn't have the strength to hold him up and the pull continued to get stronger. He desperately grabbed for the hood of an overturned car, but his hands kept sliding down, as he could no longer keep himself upright. The only thing to grab a hold of was the old car's antenna, but that did little to help. Once he was flat on his back, he turned his head in time to catch a view of a completely, dark figure.

The pull on his body wouldn't allow Alexavier to do anything, as the mysterious person attempted to lift Landfill. For some unknown reason, this person was unaffected by the overwhelming gravity. Alexavier's struggle to make any kind of movement to halt this escape had him grunting and groaning, even struggling to open his lungs for oxygen.

"Booby Trap and Dread, report in."

Alexavier couldn't respond, but he realized the dark figure pretty much ignored him and didn't notice his hand grasping the antenna. Using all his strength, Alexavier yanked hard, ripping off the antenna. In one motion, took a swipe at the unknown person's leg. The firm contact and whipping effect hurt so bad that the dark character screamed in pain, making the first noise since arriving and lessening the gravity slightly. With much difficulty in standing up, he hobbled away leaving Landfill lying face down. Once the injured villain disappeared completely, gravity started to ease even more, eventually becoming restored and Alexavier slowly pushed to get to his hands and knees. Now being able to survey the area, he could see the copious mounds of dirt and no one else, leaving Alexavier alone with his captive.

"They were fighting, but now they're running away!" Bobbie answered.

"Keep after them if you can." Sam called out, "Dread, report in!"

"I'm securing Landfill right now," Alexavier huffed and puffed. "I also had a run in with a dark figure. What was weird is that I experienced the same gravity effect that took down the building that nearly killed Beacon. I think I hurt him enough that they ran off."

"We'll be right there," Sam replied. "Wave Rider, what's your status with Bootlegger?

"She got away!"

"Okay. Come back and grab Hack. Give Dread support."

"Be there in a second. I'll grab Dead Head too."

"Dread, was that person The Infamous One?" Sam asked.

"He was dressed in all black, but somehow wasn't affected by that insane gravity." Alexavier finished cinching the last zip tie. "Landfill is now secured."

"Infamous couldn't cause that, at least not that I know." Sam paused, still fending off the adoring public. "What's your status, Booby Trap?"

"I'm good. I had to get away. The fight wasn't going my way and had to abort. I kept falling through portals. I set enough traps that deterred any pursuit."

Alexavier climbed to the top of the closet mound of less than stable earth. Seeing a flying hero in the distance, he waived his hands high. Wally dropped down with Dave and Hank to marvel at the sight of Landfill being neatly tied up. Wally and Dave high fived Alexavier as Hank began carrying the bonded villain. They met up with Bobbie and Beth, who were also excited about the capture. As much as the rest of the young heroes were thrilled about the results, Alexavier remained hesitant.

Walking away to distract some close-by fans and spectators, Sam called for the helicopter to drop down for extraction. "Team, it's time to leave. The helicopter will be over your location momentarily. Have Wave Rider pull up everyone to a safe building top and come back for me so I can sedate Landfill for transport. Keep out of sight as much as possible, but be aware that I have a flip phone pointed on me. You may have someone recording you as well."

Beth acknowledged, "Will do, sir."

One by one, the heroes readied for Wally to take them away, with Hank holding onto the restrained villain. The helicopter made a landing on a mid-sized building with an open roof. With his team finally up top, Wally flew back for their leader to finalize the extraction and head home.

CHAPTER 14

The wind whipped around the hanger, as the jet helicopter landed, delivering its heroes safely to the Project: Hero complex. The blades began to slow down, signaling the closing of the roof doors. The pilot shut down all the systems and prepared everyone for exit. The sound of the alarm for the roof was met with the beeping of the ramp lowering. The group's enthusiasm could be felt pouring out long before they did.

Bobbie joked with Wally and Dave, excited to give details of her encounter with Empty. "He was scrambling just to stay on his feet! I'd never seen a bad guy that afraid. He was making holes everywhere. The more I missed, the more he freaked out!"

"But you weren't able to get your hands on him," Wally pointed out.

Bobbie elaborated, "He was so terrified, that anywhere he could make a portal, he created one. When he got lucky, and I fell through one and came out the side of a building a fair distance away and became disoriented. Empty finally decided to come after me."

Dave wondered, "Did you set any traps?"

"A few, including one that affected his portals. Weirdly, one of his portals fell on him, sending him across the street." Bobbie motioned with her hands and laughed. "You should have seen the look on his face. He was so confused when he landed on his head that he wasn't able to follow me after that."

Running into the hanger, Manny came to greet them. "I heard it went alright."

“Alex got Landfill, but they got away with the money,” Bobbie responded.

“I hope it wasn’t too much,” Manny cautiously wondered.

Percy arrived. “Why didn’t you guys wait?”

“Sam said we had to go. I barely made it to the hanger,” Beth replied.

Hank had Landfill over his should, with Alexavier closely watching their prisoner. But unlike the others, there was no chatter. Alexavier was calm, almost too relaxed for having just fought a super powered member of The Terror Tribe. Jennifer floated out of the cargo hold with Sam being last, sorting through some papers.

Mike strolled over to Alexavier. “You got Landfill!”

“I almost didn't. As I was securing him, the same heaviness came over me that I felt when that building was dropped on Beth. It had to be somebody causing it, but I couldn't lift my head to see who it was. Luckily, I was able to hurt him enough to get him to leave. I'm sure his leg will be sore for a few days.”

“Do you think he was the one making things heavy?” Percy asked.

“It had to be. I could hardly move, yet he wasn't affected.”

Mike pointed out, “You said he.”

“I could tell it was the figure of a man, dressed in all black.” Alexavier used his hands to help describe the person. “He wasn’t that tall, so I would assume he wasn't a grown person. He yelled out when I whipped him with a car antenna, and I could tell it was a younger voice. I couldn't see any features, but I'm positive that he wasn't The Infamous One, even with the dark outfit.”

Mike began scratchy his scruffy beard. “There was this kid that the Major was trying to recruit and never could. He was able to amplify gravity, but that was a while ago that the Major tried getting him.”

“Do you know what happened to him?” Beth wondered.

"I couldn't tell you." Mike could hear the footsteps from behind. "Although, I know who can."

Major Constantine arrived, bypassing the talking heroes and focusing on the captured villain. He walked through the first trio to look over Landfill and instructing Dirk and the Elitesmen Guard, "Put him in a cell and keep an eye on him until Dr. Dennis can properly sedate him to nullify his powers so he can be interrogated."

Hank dropping the sedated villain and walking away, allowing the armored security to transport Landfill. Sam stopped next to the Major and shouted, "Great work, everybody!" He looked over to Alexavier and gave a thumbs up, which made Alexavier smile and nod. "Everyone must get checked out by Dr. Dennis before getting debriefed!"

"I'll follow up with the Major later." Mike led the group as they started walking toward the center of the complex, following the Elitesmen Guard and discussing the mission. Dirk and his convoy veered off toward the containment cells. It wasn't long before they encountered Harvey, who didn't even acknowledge them.

Wally had to yell to get his attention. "Hey, Harvey!" Harvey stopped, but didn't go over to them, acting more annoyed than usual.

Beth jogged over with excitement. "Did you want to join us? Alex caught a Tribe member."

"You're so happy he caught just one. I've done that many times. You can come talk to me when he gets to a dozen."

"But you're not catching anyone right now." Percy stated forcefully.

Dave pointed out, "At least he brought down Landfill."

"I'm trying to catch the bad guys, just like you. We can take down more of them if we work as a team." Harvey just stared at Alexavier's out stretched hand. Alexavier's peace offering felt like an insult in some odd way.

Mike tried to offer an olive branch. “Just come with us to the cafeteria and get some dessert to celebrate, like a team.”

“You might be happy only tackling insignificant Tribe members, but I'm not. I have more important things to do, like taking down The Infamous One.”

“You can't do that if you're not going on missions,” Wally pointed out.

“As you guys go after the minnows, I'm going to land the whale. Just don't get eaten by the shark in the meantime.” Harvey eyed Alexavier, as he walked away.

“C'mon, Harvey!”

“Let him go, Dave. He doesn't need to ruin this for us.” Mike placed his hand on Dave’s shoulder and steered them away, hoping to keep whatever happiness was left by getting them to the cafeteria. Alexavier did look back, knowing that things aren't finished between them.

#

Back at the hanger, Sam’s optimism about the mission was met with the Major’s skepticism, as he hunted down Sam. Sam had heard all these negative reports about their newest recruit, but the mission was anything but negative in regard to Alexavier's performance. “I know what your concerns are, but Alexavier was impressive on this mission. He is as close to being a ready to go hero as we’ve got. The way he performed, I would include him with Bobbie, Beth and Percy of those with the skills of a candidate to graduate.”

“He’s only been here a short time,” the Major stated with negativity in his voice. “I’d hardly say he’s ready.”

They embarked for the Major’s office as Sam countered, “How does being here years prove readiness. He’s been here shorter than anyone else before they caught a bad guy, and he’s caught multiples.”

“Will that mean he’s ready for The United?”

“That is quite possible. We’ve graduated many others who didn’t perform at his level.”

Hating being involved in another conversation he wished he wasn’t a part of, the Major agreed, “I guess so.”

Once they arrived at the Major’s office, Sam set his gear on an empty chair and proceeded to reach for some water, as the discussion about the mission quickly changed to a much darker topic. “Downtown and The Outcasts haven’t heard any chatter. There is absolutely nothing circulating the New York area about a possible nuclear threat. Have you contacted The United?”

Strolling toward his desk, the Major wasn’t keen on where the conversation was going, which could be heard in his tone. “No. They have been trying to address a few Tribe leads on the West coast and Colorado. We have good intel that either location may hold a safe house for Tribe members. I will inform Dynamic when they return, however I don't think we are looking at any plausible leads. The possibility of a nuclear attack seems remote. We are too aware and vigilant after what happened the first time, so I don't believe there will be a second.”

Sam disagreed, “What’s confusing is that if The Tribe wanted to destroy a city, they have more than enough firepower to do so with their superpowers. The fact that they haven’t done so makes finding medical equipment with low level radioactive material very disturbing. At any moment, they could set things in motion that could prove deadly. We just need to be prepared.”

Desperately needing a change of topic, the Major asked, “What about the bank robbery?”

“There wasn’t much evidence at the scene. Dave and Hank scoured everything. It didn’t matter since we found the villains responsible as they were trying to escape.”

"I would say it was The Terror Tribe, especially since Landfill was involved. Empty and Bootlegger must be new. Up until now, they weren't affiliated with anyone that I knew."

"But why that specific bank?" Sam asked. "Alexavier had a very good point. It is small and didn't hold much money."

"I don't know. Maybe they were thinking people wouldn't expect a smaller bank?" the Major guessed.

Sam wasn't convinced. "The larger commercial bank across the street makes more sense. It had millions, at least ten times the cash. Even their better security wouldn't matter. I'm sure Landfill is more than powerful enough to have taken out their security."

"Sometimes it's about not getting captured."

"Speaking of captured, we had a guy with his flip phone recording us. He had more of me than the others. The only good thing is how grainy it will be."

"We can always explain the recruits away. Civilian technology hasn't caught up to what we can get from the military."

"I think we should be worried," Sam responded with concern. "Enough grainy footage will bring more questions than you have answers for."

"Why me?" The Major appeared more annoyed.

"You want to keep this secret. We should have gone public years ago."

"Anonymity is our best ally. The less The Tribe knows about us, the easier it will be to pursue them. Plus, the public mentality is to hate superheroes right now."

Sam was getting more annoyed. "Hate us? I was swarmed by fans. I couldn't even get to the bank to investigate because they were excited to see me."

"But there's a huge segment of the population that views heroes as the problem. Even if you save everyone in a burning building, you're still the villain. I don't have to remind you of this, do I?"

"No." The comment appeared to hit very close to home with Sam because of a recent incident. He swallowed more water before continuing. "It doesn't matter right now. We need to focus on the fact that The Tribe escaped with the money. It may not be a lot, but they still have the money. Bootlegger lost the extra weight by dropping off the others in exchange for the cash, which helped increase her speed. Wally can't go any faster than the wind can carry him, and the wind began dying down as soon as we set foot on the ground."

"We need to increase his flight powers. Most villains who can fly can achieve triple digit speeds. Wally is severely limited to whether or not it's a windy day."

"There's not much we can do. Only Riva had the power to affect the elements." Sam leaned against one of the tables, trying to rest. "Unless we have another recruit who can manipulate the weather to aid Wally, we're at a big disadvantage."

"Not really," the Major responded, pulling out a folder. "We always have the Session for Wally."

"No, we don't." Sam left him hanging, not taking the folder.

"We just completed a successful Session with Alexavier not too long ago, and he received an extra strong treatment. We can do the same for Wally."

Sam sighed, "I disagree. Alex is a special recruit, able to handle the intense regimen that the others likely cannot."

"We don't know that the others can't. We haven't tried."

"Those Sessions wreak havoc on them. These recruits get bombarded with lights, noise, drugs and radiation that causes some damage to both short-term and long-term memory. It also puts them in a near comatose state. The suffer through these Sessions as it is. Now you want to intensify them and worsen the experience?"

The discussion was about to get a lot more interesting, as Jonathon, Mike and Senator Frank Steinberg arrived. They could hear the last part of the conversation from down the hall.

"I thought we put that to bed, administering Sessions, being bad and all," the Senator stated.

The Major countered, "Just for Alex. How's Washington been treating you?"

"Still the same bipartisan B.S. that hurts everyone in this country. Glad to be away. So, where are we at giving everyone new Sessions?"

"We haven't tried and we won't know until we do." Jonathon said, taking a spot near Sam. "But do we risk causing permanent trauma to one of these recruits in hopes it will work?"

The Major pulled out a few results from the folder. "We had no idea about Alexavier until we did it. We're in the same situation, just with a different person."

"Yes, but Wally is not Alexavier." Sam continued to sip the water. "There's something about him that's different. We shouldn't be treating the others the same way and exposing them to permanent injury."

Jonathon made a surprising offer. "I'll do it."

"You can't," the Major stated.

"You keep saying that, but I don't get it."

"You're not a candidate for Sessions." The Major flipped through a few stacks of papers looking for something specific. "You've been tested. We know your brain generates an extreme amount of energy that you are able to channel throughout your body." He pulled out several pages stapled together. "Every doctor has said you can never get in that chair."

"Then they're wrong."

Sam tried to deescalate the growing tension, taking the papers. "We can take a better look into Jonathon's eligibility. Having an increase in your powers would bring a better tool to fight these powerful Tribe members."

"Thank you, Sam"

"And speaking of using powers," Sam faced the Major. "Alex followed my orders precisely. There was no hesitation in taking down Landfill."

The Major began thumbing through the folders again. "That doesn't make any difference to how he's been doing here, and how lackluster he's been over the last several weeks. The great performance he showed when he first arrived hasn't been there since he and Beth came back from New Jersey." Finding Alexavier's file, he hands it to Sam.

Sam flipped through the pages, as Mike interjected, "Honestly, his recent performance before this mission hasn't been bad, just subdued."

"It like he's in power save mode or something," Jonathon added.

"What about sending him for another Session?" the Senator asked.

Sam looked up, even more perturbed. "It's not about Sessions. He did great out there."

"But not in here," the Major countered. "His time in the W.A.R. Room has been pretty much forgettable lately."

"How do we change that?" the Senator wondered.

Sam closed the folder. "By having a sparring match with me." A hush fell over the room. "We will schedule a workout with everyone, and we will do it all over again."

"I think that's a great idea," Mike said while Jonathon nodded.

"I'm not sure what you're trying to get out of this. We haven't been able to make any headway with him, and I'm not sure if this is going to make any difference." The Major pointed to Alexavier's folder. "There's nothing to track, since he has literally stood on the sidelines the whole time."

"Maybe the problem isn't him." Sam moved to the side to address everyone. "I have been giving this a lot of thought lately. Perhaps I should be spending more time with these recruits. We are supposed to be crafting the next generation of great heroes and honing their abilities. What better way than if I am more present?"

Everyone gave collective nod, except the Major. "You don't really need to. Things are going fine. Not to mention, you have all those meetings and goodwill appearances scheduled on a constant basis."

"Personally, I'm sick of all the publicity. I am a hero, trained as one and will always be one. I need to give back what I have learned. I can be more involved with the day-to-day operations here. Along the way, we can decipher what is happening with Alexavier."

"It would be nice having you around," Jonathon smiled.

Mike agreed, "Absolutely!"

"Alright then." Sam placed the papers on the desk. "Let me get settled away. We also need to discuss the possible nuclear threat with The Terror Tribe." Sam picked up his stuff and was escorted out by Mike and Jonathon.

The Senator turned with a smile. "It will be nice having Sam around." He noticed something was bothering the Major. "Are you okay?"

"No. I know what's going to happen." The Major threw down all of the folders onto his desk. "Everything I've been working on will be ruined. We'll be starting from square one."

"That won't happen."

With a big sigh, the Major sat in his chair. "You don't know him like I do."

"I'm sure Sam will be an asset. Just give it a chance." With a reassuring smile, the Senator went to join Sam and the others, while the Major was left to stew over what the next few weeks might hold. It wasn't making him very happy, but that been par for the course lately.

CHAPTER 15

The lights were dimmed in the office of the most dangerous man on the planet. The Infamous One was hovering over his desk, studying the multiple papers strewn about, as the city brightly illuminated by the sun shined in through the window. As always, his mind was at work, plotting and planning. The various pictures and random sheets of paper appear to have no consistency, yet they all made sense to him. His eyes darting back and forth between one sheet of paper and another, then to the picture close by. There was a story being told, even if he was the only one who knew the plot.

Game Over came barging in, which usually was frowned upon. Today was a different day. “I’m home! What’s the deal, oh mighty leader?”

“We are nearing that time.”

“Thank goodness! You’re finally going to wear colorful spandex or tights? I said the black was a little too blah. I’m glad you’re coming to your senses.”

“I say we put a bullet in him.” Getting up from a chair situated on the side of the room was Cavalio, the Infamous One’s girlfriend. She walked by the mouthy villain, saying as she exited the room, “I think that’s what it’s time for, if you ask me.”

Once she had left the room, Game Over walked closer. “Did I ever mention that she scares me?”

“She must like you, since you’re still breathing.”

“Does that mean I’m still getting a Christmas card this year?”

The Infamous One walked from behind the desk. "Alright, joking is done. It's all going to happen and happen starting now."

"Yes! How long have you talked about this?"

"Too long. But with recent events, including specific incidents and the introduction of this new hero, Dread, the timeframe has been moved up significantly. It cannot be a coincidence that they have this well-trained hero who literally disrupted the operations of one of our main safe houses."

"That may be true, but we need to stabilize things." The humongous villain Natural Disaster made a slightly dramatic entrance, carry a couple of duffel bags. "Our financial score a few weeks ago was more than sufficient. But if we're going to become heavily involved with this, the last thing we should worry about is money when we're worried about fighting heroes."

The Infamous One pondered, while Game Over stated, "I'm always about the green. Unfortunately, that job really put everyone on high alert. We're on everyone's radar now, like an F5 tornado."

"We don't need to how worry about how to fund things or if we run low while all this is going on," Natural Disaster explained.

"Speaking of funds, how did the operation go?"

Game Over threw his arms in the air. "Like I said, they weren't even out the door, and they were on our guys like they'd been waiting for us, like they were in our planning meeting."

"Please elaborate."

"The crew got in and out fast, but as they were making their getaway, several heroes arrived chasing after our group." Natural Disaster drops the duffel bags next to Infamous. "They were able to hold onto the money, but Landfill was captured."

"Highly unfortunate."

"And once again, it was that Dread guy!" Game Over exclaimed.

"Most curious."

Game Over's face lit up with surprise. "That's it? Really? What's curious about a dude who's making our lives miserable? The only thing I'm curious about is how we're going to take care of this problem!"

The Infamous One placed his hand on Game Over's should. "Patience and planning are what we would best do now. There's too much at stake to make rash decisions."

"But this Dread could be our downfall. We need to act with him in mind," Natural Disaster stated.

"You're right." The Infamous One walked back to his desk, putting his palms on the edge. "Oddly enough, I believe the wheels are already in motion for how we can eliminate this threat. He's good. I believe he's smart. Both of these things will help us, but we cannot take him lightly, even with as little as we know of him."

"All I want to know is when and where. Then I'm going to drop a building on that miserable, little superhero," Game Over said defiantly.

The Infamous One smiled at his two most trusted colleagues. "In due time. But for now, let's get to work. It is time to make our plans a reality."

CHAPTER 16

After everyone had finished with their post-mission medical exams, a small group of recruits congregated in Alexavier's room. The talk was light and upbeat between Bobbie and Alexavier, as they began to relax after a semi-successful mission. He caught one of The Terror Tribe, but they were unable to recover the money. Still, he was in decent spirits as he removed his black, hooded sweatshirt for his favorite gray one. With having a guest, he would wait to take off the rest of his outfit, but soon had more company when Beth and Dave arrived, both very excited.

"It was cool seeing Landfill all tied up!" Dave was incredibly excited. "We really needed a capture."

"I'm so happy for you!" Beth exclaimed.

Bobbie added, "I think we all are."

"Thanks."

It brought a bit more enthusiasm out of Dave. "I can't wait to get my first capture. They're going to erect a statue of me."

"That'll be because it took you so long to get your first one," Bobbie joked.

"It is kind of hard if you're always going in first and getting shot at."

Alexavier's statement made Dave stop and think. "You know what? It is. I really need a new job. Can I be the head of Tribe capturing?"

Bobbie quipped, "That's not really a job."

“Who’s to say we don’t need one?” Dave pointed at Bobbie. “You’re great at sneaking around. Alex is great at fighting. Beth is great at being a ray of sunshine in this dreary place. I can be the head guy in charge of zip ties.”

Beth walked over to Alexavier’s belt, pulled out the zip ties and handed them to Dave. “Now you’re in charge of the zip ties.”

Bobbie followed suit, pulling out every one she had and placing them on top of the others. “Here, you can manage mine too.”

Dave looked down at the pile in his hands. “That’s not what I had in mind.”

As much as that brought a smile and a chuckle to everyone, including Alexavier, he remained a bit more serious, and Beth noticed. “Hey, smile. You just captured an important bad guy.”

“I’d have a smile so big that I couldn’t walk through the door,” Mike said, entering the room. “This is the biggest capture we’d had in a year! There’s no telling what information we could get out of him.”

Percy followed behind. “I can’t wait to start working him over. As soon as we can get the location of a hideout, I’ll be ready to go in locked and loaded.”

“It’ll be a tough battle, taking on the full Tribe at one of their headquarters.” Mike sat on the corner of the desk. “We’re going to need to be heavily armed, both with weapons and our best recruits.”

“Don’t you think The United would be sent in instead of us?” Alexavier wondered.

Mike fiddled with the mouse to Alexavier’s computer. “Most of the time, any intel we collect is given to The United. They’re considered the professionals and known to the public. We’re still like a black book operation. Plus, if you’re talking about the most dangerous of villains, The United are usually the ones being sent in. Unfortunately, they can't be around all the time, so we're here, and they currently are not. That's why we need to be ready at all times.”

"If we're going to be the ones going in, I'm going to need access to some heavy-duty weaponry," Alexavier stated.

"I think I can accommodate you." Mike ventured over to Alexavier's closet. Finally reaching the door in the back, he punched in a code, unlocking it. "I just set up the code here so that only you and I know it." Mike handed Alexavier a piece of paper, which he quickly shoved in his pocket.

As the door swung open, the amazing contents inside immediately became visible. A plethora of bladed weapons were on display on opposing walls. The high quality of these is well beyond the ones Alexavier had been training with.

Mike pointed out, "These are all handmade Japanese swords, some being hundreds of years old. They're so sharp and forged so well, they can even resist nicks and dings if you happen to unintentionally hit other objects."

"They're amazing." Alexavier's eyes scanned the sharp edges, over the hilt and wandered through the beautifully wrapped handle. His fingers carefully caressed the blade, completely in awe that such majestic weapons were brought in just for him to use. Pulling down one of the Katanas, he could instantly feel how balanced it was. As he slowly tilted and waved the sword, a smile grew on his face. However, something else grabbed his attention. Hung up on display was a superhero suit. It appeared that those in charge had an idea about what Alexavier would look like as a superhero and had created his outfit. The suit was half white and half dark red. The gloves and boots were opposite color of what was on that side. The chest had a dark red 'D' that came out as a part of the red side onto the white. It had a small mask which covered a large area around the eyes, and wrapping around the head, but nothing more.

"Is this mine? Am I supposed to be wearing it now?"

"Currently? No." Mike stretched out the suit to see more. "There's usually a grace period of being here before recruits get approval for hero uniforms. Some don't get to wear them, while others refuse to. You can also look to do some modifications, if there's something that doesn't suit you."

Alexavier looked over the chest, fixated on the dark red half circle that was protruding on to the white area. Mike could tell that the young hero was contemplating something. "What ya thinking?"

"I understand the big D, but still come back to the name Dread. Heroes shouldn't be scary or put fear in people. I know the whole putting fear into villains thing, but I don't want regular people to dread me as well."

"That's where you establish yourself in the public eye by the actions you take. You could be known as The Axe Murderer. But if everything you do is helping save lives and fight the bad guys, they'll know the true hero in you."

"I guess that makes sense." Alexavier continued fiddling with the outfit.

Mike placed his hand on Alexavier's shoulder. "Once you make it out of here, all that can change. You can change your name. You can change your super suit. Heck, you can even change sides, as it's so often happened."

Alexavier smiled, appreciating Mike's attempt to lighten the mood. "I don't think I'd go that far."

"Maybe I can change my outfit?" Dave thought out loud. "It's pretty plain for a hero."

After spending enough time watching, the others decided to join Mike and Alexavier to see what all the fuss was about. Dave was the first to enter the long closet. "What are you guys doing in here? Whoa! Look at all the swords and knives! Why can't I get any swords? Oww!"

"I think we see why.'" Mike took the sword from Dave's hands, so he was no longer a danger to himself.

Percy picked up a Bowie knife. "I like this."

"You have one already," Mike reminded him.

"Yeah, but not as nice as this."

Alexavier noticed Percy admiring the knife. “You can have it if you want it.”

“Seriously?”

“Sure. I really don't like using knives that much, particularly for combat. Give me a sword any day. It’s easier as a long-range weapon and also keeps bad guys at a distance. I mean, if you think it will help you, it’s yours.”

“Man, I owe you one.” Percy twirled the blade and smiled. “I just might have to save your butt one of these days.”

Even with everything in the closet that could cut you, Bobbie ogled over a six-inch metal bar. Confused, Alexavier went over to check it out. “What is that?”

“Stand back.” With the press of a button, both ends shot out, becoming a five-foot long hardened metal staff. She stood it on end, presenting it to Alexavier.

“Wow! I always used wooden ones in training. I didn’t know there were metal ones that can become compact. I can even put it in my belt!”

Beth was amazed at all of the neat stuff, but headed for the super suit. “See? Now you know you made it when they give you a superhero uniform.”

“I don't know that I've made it yet. At least I hope I’ll make it.”

Beth gave Alexavier a light shove. “Hope you'll make it? You better start believing in yourself, the way the rest of us do. Isn't that right, guys?”

A collective approval came from the group, except for Percy, who kept fiddling with the knife. Beth leaned over and nudged him. “Isn't that right, Percy?”

“Well, he did give me the knife so maybe-”

“Percy!”

"Fine! I can say it if you want, but I don't need to. I know he'll be there for us any time we need him. He let The Tribe drop a building on himself just to save you. I'm sure he'll do it again for any of us."

"You'd let them drop a building on you just for me?" Dave grinned at Alexavier.

"No," Percy interjected. "We'd drop the building on you instead."

Dave sighed, "Geez. I never get any love around here."

"You know you'd survive it," Wally stated.

Beth added, "Yeah! You'd survive anything!"

"I hope so."

Not yet done, Percy wondered, "Can we try some of them out, just to be sure? I'd really like to drop a car on Dave."

"You know what, Percy?" Dave folded his arms. "You're not invited to the next sleepover."

"How about a bus? Can we try a bus?"

"You too, Alex?"

Everyone was having a good laugh, when Alexavier noticed some interesting items. "Are those throwing needles?"

"Yes, they are," Mike acknowledged. "They're perfectly balanced, properly weighted and sharpened to a surgical quality, needle point. They're a great non-lethal weapon if you know what you're doing."

"They'll also fit nicely in my belt."

Percy pulled down some throwing stars. "These will take up more room, but they do more damage."

"Where did you get them?" Alexavier asked.

Mike picked up a needle. "I made all of this stuff."

"Really?" Alexavier exclaimed

“Yup. The needles were an idea I had to make a non-lethal, but highly damaging weapon that makes no noise. Its range and accuracy are as good as the person wielding them.”

Beth took a needle from Alexavier’s hand. “It doesn’t look like any needle I’ve seen before.”

“It’s not a needle to crochet with, but you can knot together a few bad guys.” The moans and groans echoed loudly throughout the room at Dave. “Okay. Okay. Bad pun, I know. Why don't we head over to see what's happening with the interrogation? The Major should be starting the questioning any minute now. We can fondle the rest of Alexavier’s toys later.”

Everyone finished placing the all of the shiny trinkets back where they belonged. Once the last person exited, Alexavier looked back before closing and locking the door. He was thrilled to finally have an arsenal of weapons to use, hoping it will level the playing field for when he takes on a villain with Meta human abilities.

CHAPTER 17

The streets of Pittsburgh were heavy with traffic. Pedestrians were going about their everyday lives. Some were meandering down sidewalks, while others made a mad dash for the other side of the road. Two people who were mixed in with the unknowing, general population were Bootlegger and Empty. These villains didn't talk much, trying to stay inconspicuous. Their path through the city led downtown to an inner-city building housing several restaurants and bars, where they set-up shop at one of the diners and blended in with the locals.

A waitress arrived, taking their drink order. Soon, she brought over a basket of tortilla chips and salsa that they eagerly dove into. With the drinks delivered to their table in a timely manner, the waiting game began.

Within the establishment was a figure, taking up space at the bar. With a drink in hand, he left got up from his stool and weaved through the occupied tables, eventually finding his way to the two bad guys. Pulling out the chair and taking a seat, the man joining happened to be the monstrous and dangerous villain, Natural Disaster. "I see you made it from D.C. Must have been a tense flight."

"Yeah. Our nerves our almost shot." Empty put down the chip in his hand, wiping his mouth. "But we're ready."

"Even without Landfill?"

"It's not like we haven't worked without him before." Bootlegger leaned in so she could speak quietly. "We can steal a wallet or take a life. What do you want?"

Natural Disaster waffled a bit, mulling over what to do. "You're both not regular members of The Terror Tribe. Landfill was. You must understand why we have to be careful."

"Our record speaks for itself, if you haven't noticed."

Empty placed his hand on Bootlegger's arm. "What my colleague is trying to say is that we've proven ourselves before. That's why Landfill chose to work with us."

"He did, but he also got caught."

"It's not our fault he couldn't beat a trainee in diapers." Bootlegger grabbed a handful of chips to stuff in her face, wanting to exit the conversation entirely.

"I know you're trying to ensure the safety of the rest of The Tribe, but why did you contact us after we gave you the money from the heist?" Empty looked around, not wanting to be discovered.

"You have a point, and I have a job for you, if you're interested."

Bootlegger dropped the tortillas and leaned forward. "Is it a babysitting job, or are we doing something special?"

"This will be a big-time job." Natural Disaster smiled, "And you'll be working with me."

Bootlegger's eyes lit up. "I mean, I'm all for causing terror and mayhem, but not at our expense. We've gotten hosed before and taken the blame. I'm not interested in being the fall girl again."

Empty once again held back his cohort. "I think what my associate is trying to say is, we need some assurances, particularly ones that come with being a part of a team."

Natural Disaster sat back and made a proposition. “If you help me, I’ll help you.”

CHAPTER 18

No one had ever said James Killus was normal, and he preferred it that way. When someone like him spends much of his waking hours within the prisoner confinement section staring down the captives, all while twirling his knife, you become something more than unusual. Over the years, Killus had moved well beyond creepy to downright terrifying. All the captives were uneasy. Having such a crazed lunatic stare at you all day could make you just as crazy. Attempts to remove Killus to ease the torturous stares to the prisoners only lasted so long. Within minutes, he would sneak back and continue with his quest to terrify anyone behind the unbreakable glass-like cells.

But this time, Killus was not alone. Hank and Glen enjoyed the games of psychological torture just as much. In fact, this was when Glen was most aggressive. Being one of the shortest and skinniest recruits, having protective holding cells to keep the danger away meant he could be as obnoxious as he wanted.

Their campaign of psychological assault on the prisoners finally ended with the arrival of the Major, Dr. Dennis and Harvey, followed closely by a number of recruits. The others tried to hide their actions, but Killus kept pacing back and forth with side glances at all of the prisoners. Bobbie became fixated on Faducia and wouldn't stop staring at her. The Major looked them away, but Killus only moved back and kept watching from a distance.

The bad guys that they were interested in interrogating were not of the super villain status. Landfill was, but they had no interest in him at the moment. They wanted to cross-examine Faducia and Topher. Topher had his hands bound together in a clasping position, to limit his ability to mold objects, including the restraints and the cell itself. Although Topher was an ideal candidate for cross-examination, the Major's focus was on Faducia, the principal lead of their small two-person team.

The Major pressed the intercom button and took a step back. He waited, giving a dramatic pause before talking. "My name is Major John Constantine. You are currently being held as prisoners for having committed crimes with the use of your superhuman powers. I am here today to give you the opportunity to provide us with information. Your assistance will not be leaked outside these walls. Thus, you will have nothing to fear as far as retribution. This cooperation will show that you are remorseful. In exchange for your cooperation, you may receive a lighter sentence. If you do not, we will be forced to extract whatever information we can, and you will be prosecuted to the fullest extent of the law."

With a lack of response from either, Harvey focused his stare on Faducia, using his power to control the iron in her blood, called the Brain Drain. It was named that since he could pull the blood from someone's brain, forcing it elsewhere within the body, it would cause the person to pass out. The first thing Faducia noticed was the lightheadedness. But as the sensation became stronger, a woozy feeling hit her, causing some imbalance. Through the fogginess, she looked up with anger at her captors. Harvey created a much harder assault, his Brain Drain sucking the blood from her head. She slumped over, struggling to hold herself up. Finally, the lack of oxygen led to a lack of coordination, as she rolled over onto the floor.

Hoping that she was in a state to talk, the Major wasted no time questioning her. "Where is The Terror Tribe?" She gave no response, only getting up to her knees and bracing herself. He asked again, "Where is the location of The

Terror Tribe headquarters?"

"I don't think she's going be a very willing prisoner. Should I turn it up?" Harvey inquired.

Annoyed, the Major instructed Harvey, "Please proceed."

Over the past few weeks, Harvey had very little to be happy about. But the one thing that did make him feel normal was an interrogation, where he was able to use his powers freely. With a faint smile on his face, he began to unleash a dangerous level of attack on the helpless victim in the prisoner cell. Mike arrived, leading the group that included the heroes who were checking out Alexavier's new toys. They lined up against the back cells to observe. The Major eyed them with a stern look to maintain their silence. Harvey kept his focus on Faducia who was close to the point of passing out. Her delirious state brought about confusion, but not enough to get her to crack. The more that Harvey focused, the less coordinated Faducia became.

Having had felt the effects of Harvey's Brain Drain, watching Faducia starting to stagger had Alexavier concerned. "What is Harvey doing?"

The Major overheard and answered, "It's called an interrogation."

The answer didn't sit well with Alexavier. "So, depriving her brain of oxygen is the answer? You could kill her!"

"Don't be naïve. It's confusing her," the Major responded. "It's making her more likely to talk."

"But if they lose too much oxygen for too long, it could cause brain damage."

Harvey couldn't take the defiance anymore, "The only damage that needs to happen, is to you."

Alexavier stepped forward. "I'm waiting."

The Major shouted, "Alright, you two! That's enough! Harvey, continue the interrogation!"

Harvey looked away with a smirk and focused his attack on Faducia once more. Mike pulled Alexavier back, but it wasn't easy with Alexavier wanting to get in Harvey's face. Having another go at her, Harvey focused harder, causing the blood in Faducia's brain to stop flowing, causing her to drop to her knees again. Harvey eased up, allowing enough blood to circulate for her to be questioned in a dazed state.

"Are you willing to talk now?" The Major's question was met with defiance in the form of spit against the glass where the Major's face would have been.

Bobbie balled up her fists in anger, as she knew she could get Faducia to talk.

The Major noticed Bobbie step forward and placed his arm out to restrain her. "Cool it! I know your hate for her for what she tried with Percy, but now's not the time." The words, coupled with his glare made her back away and leave the cells.

The Major refocused his attention. The unsuccessful attempt to extract information from Faducia wasn't met with frustration, as the Major knew she would be the tougher one to give up anything usable. They intentionally used this display of Harvey's skills to put fear into Topher, which was successful. Topher was shaking. He could hear everything that was going on and became terrified at what was coming. Harvey stepped over and began to stare at the pudgy villain.

"Wha… what are ya doin'?"

Topher's visible shaking made Harvey even more aggressive with his mental attack. "Making you squeal like the fat pig you are."

The cries from Topher went unanswered, as everyone watched intently. Some, like Alexavier, looked with concern. Even Faducia pressed up against the unbreakable glass in hopes of hearing what's going on with her partner. For as much as Topher felt like passing out, he kept his self-control in defiance of his onlookers.

The Major asked again, “Where is The Terror Tribe?”

“I ain't tellin' ya nothin'!”

“We can do this all day,” The Major decided to counter him with an offer. “Or we can make your stay a bit more comfortable, if you tell us the locations of hideouts.”

“Screw you!”

Mike stepped up. “We know you're not real Tribe members. You don't owe them anything. Help us. We can work with the both of you to lessen anything that you might have coming. You're already going to have charges brought upon you for previous discretions. Just cooperate with us.”

“I can't trust ya. Ah! You ain't never done us no good before!”

Alexavier leaned in close to Dr. Dennis. “Harvey’s going to hurt him bad.”

“I won’t let anything happen,” she assured him.

“He’s enjoying it too much to care about stopping in time.”

Dr. Dennis placed her hand on his shoulder. “Just give him a minute.”

“Maybe this will change your mind.” Harvey unleashed a targeted Brain Drain that dropped Topher to the ground, barely able to hold himself up.

Alexavier rushed over and pulled on Harvey's arm, standing face to face with him. “You're going to cause permanent damage!”

“So what?” Harvey responded, “It’s not like he hasn’t hurt people himself.”

“Alexavier! Stand down!” The Major tried getting in between them.

Harvey got nose-to-nose and softly stated, “Maybe the person I should hurt is you instead.”

Before Alexavier could respond, an announcement came over the PA system, “All recruits, report to the W.A.R. Room in five minutes. All recruits to the W.A.R. Room in five minutes.”

"To the W.A.R. Room, now!" The Major motioned to Harvey. "Stay and continue with the interrogation."

The stare down continued until the Major pointed. "Go!"

Alexavier backed off, as reluctantly as Bobbie did. Knowing the importance of being on time for any kind of meeting, any beef he had with Harvey could wait. Alexavier and the others made their way from the prisoner cells, with Bobbie looking back when she got to the end of the hallway. Once everyone had vanished, Harvey gave one last smile, then returned to attack Topher's mental stability.

CHAPTER 19

One by one, the heroes in training began to congregate in the W.A.R. Room. The first to arrive in a hurry were Alexavier, Dave, Manny, Beth and Wally. Once in the room, everyone looked around, slightly confused as to what would be of such importance.

"Any idea what's going on?" Dave wondered, standing next to Alexavier, who was still visibly concerned about the prisoners.

"I'm as clueless as you are." Beth responded.

Manny added, "It didn't sound like an emergency."

Alexavier noticed the anger in Bobbie and asked, "Are you alright?"

"I'll be fine once I can get my hands around Faducia's throat."

"What happened, if I can ask?"

Bobbie responded softly, "Maybe another time."

Feeling hesitant to further the questioning, Alexavier was cut off when Mike led a caravan of recruits, including Percy and Michael through the complex, eventually ending up in the W.A.R. Room. Surprise meetings happen, and usually Mike is informed, but not today. Mike scratched his scruffy chin. "Hmm."

"They didn't tell you?" Wally wondered.

Mike threw his hands up. "Not a clue. I guess we're all going to find out together."

Soon after, Killus arrived, flanked by his misfit entourage. This time, April was with him, but as it usually goes with these meetings, Dwayne wasn't. The group took spots on the steps, but Killus decided to encroach on other's conversation. He stood as close to Alexavier as possible, giving him that weird feeling. A look from Alexavier in his direction did nothing to get Killus to move away. Mike moved toward the front of the room, waiting for more orders, but kept his eye on the potentially problematic interaction.

"I'm playing nice," Killus said, noticing Mike's stare. "Isn't that what you wanted?"

"I don't ever see you playing." Percy stated.

Killus smirked, "Oh, we will."

Alexavier turned around. "Whenever you want to do this-"

Killus backed away with his hands held up. "Whoa! You see who's the one not playing nice?"

Before having a chance to go after him, Beth grabbed ahold of Alexavier's arm. "He's just trying to get under your skin."

"Hey! He's not worth it," Bobbie added.

"Who cares what you have to say?" Killus taunted.

Beth pushed back both of her friends. "You know, one of these days you're going to be in trouble and need our help. We might not help you."

"I've never needed your help, and I never will." Killus joined his crew. "I have a team that will watch my back." As he glanced back, April shied away, trying not to make eye contact. Alexavier saw her reaction, which only angered him more.

Mike on the other hand, was trying to keep the team camaraderie. "We're all a team, whether you like it or not. Having your little cliques here might be fun, but not out there. It's not something you'll want Sam to see if he were evaluating you guys."

Everyone paused and looked, as Sam entered the W.A.R. Room, being accompanied by a man all too familiar to everyone, the hero Downtown. Their entrance signaled for the recruits to take their places.

Satisfied with the mostly compliant team, Sam began the introduction. "Sorry about the last second notice, but I'd like to introduce you to a former Project: Hero recruit, Downtown."

A round cheers and applause erupted from most of the audience, with Dave rooting the loudest. As usual, Killus was less than enthusiastic.

"Robert Baun is of Filipino descent and has been made the head of a new group of heroes called The United Outcasts. This team has been in the planning stages for a while now. He will be working closely to build a team that has been desperately needed for some time. Project: Hero has trained multiple heroes over the years and not everyone has the opportunity to join The United. However, this new team will be an option for those who want to continue their career as a superhero. With how busy The United has been lately, traveling to cities throughout the country, they are limited in handling every situation that comes up. The United Outcasts provides us with a secondary team to intercept the various villains. They will help to manage many dangerous situations to keep civilians safe."

"Why are you called Outcasts?" Beth wondered. "It doesn't seem like a very positive name?"

Robert replied, "Everyone on this team was either overlooked or denied becoming a member of The United for one reason or another. None of those reasons sat well with us. I spoke with the members about not using the name, but the entire team was in agreement. They wanted to use this name that would provide motivation to show that we can be the heroes this world needs."

"Who decides who joins?" Dave asked.

"Both of us," Sam responded with a nod to Robert.

Wally asked, "Are there going to be team members around the country like The United has random members?"

"For the moment, they are only based out of New York City," Sam stated. "Once there is a large enough team, there could be some branching out, but how long that will proceed is unknown."

Robert added, "We are actively recruiting members for the team as we speak."

"So, this is another option for us once we graduate?" Alexavier asked.

"Yes," Robert replied. "We hope to be a favorable choice rather than just an afterthought."

"There is a formal, public introduction planned very soon. We are expecting to finalize things within the next few weeks, even though they have been active with pursuing The Terror Tribe." Sam explained. "I am hoping things will go smoothly with Robert in charge. I need to spend as more time here, but I will be lending my expertise to his team every chance I have. So, everyone can welcome the leader of our newest hero team and maybe the best yet. Please welcome, Downtown! Alright! Meeting is over!"

With the dismissal and through some cheers, Alexavier was quick to head over and get an introduction. Beth hurried to tag along, dragging Wally and Dave with her. Sam had entered into a conversation before Alexavier could get to them so he waited until Sam noticed them.

"Robert Baun, I would like you to meet the newest, shining stars of our current crop of recruits. From left to right, we have Dave Headley, Bobbie Terpstra, Wally Ryder, Beth Breckinridge and Alexavier Vankendreh'd. Over there is April Dandridge." Sam pointed to where the Killus crew was loitering. He then began looking around the room. "I'm not sure where Jennifer is."

"It's a pleasure. Sam has been keeping me in updated with as many of you new faces as I can."

Beth gushed, "We're so excited to meet you. I arrived here just after you left and missed the opportunity to meet you."

"Thank you. I wouldn't be too worried. From what Sam has been telling me, I'm sure I'll be seeing you out there with me pretty soon."

Dave pushed to the front of the group to speak to his idol. "Do you take recruits who haven't graduated yet? I mean, I'm as good as graduated."

"You'll never graduate," Beth joked, which made everyone chuckle.

"Unfortunately, you need to graduate first and receive the recommendation from Sam and the Major."

Dave wondered, "How does that work with heroes outside Project: Hero? Does Sam have to approve of them?"

"No. If they've moved on from here, but later want to transition back to the life of a superhero, I can make that call. I'm negotiating with a couple heroes right now, some really big additions."

Bobbie asked, "Anyone we know?"

"I can't give anything out yet. There are still some negotiations happening. Let's just say, the team I'm putting together will rival any other, whether past, present or future."

Dave joked, "It's actually me, but they don't want to spoil the surprise."

"The only thing spoiled here is you, Dave," Percy stated, while pinching his nose.

"I was wondering what the smell was around here," Manny chuckled.

Everyone had a good laugh, but Sam settled everyone down. "Does anyone else have a question for our guest before I let him go?"

"What is it like being the first gay superhero?" Dave wondered.

Robert paused. "You know, it wasn't easy. Not that I wouldn't do it again, but it was difficult coming out while being in the public eye. I really had no idea what would happen and figured there would be some rough roads ahead, being labeled as much as everyone wants to label things. The only label I wanted was that of a superhero, not even a gay superhero. I just wanted people to look at me as someone who saves lives. Good deeds are universal, so why do we have to distinguish it by who they are, and why they're different? It's fighting crime and saving lives that's important. It makes us heroes, and that should be the focus. Those heroes who might not have fit in with The United need a team, one that can let them be the hero they always wanted to be, without judgement. That team is The United Outcasts."

The feeling in the front of the room was electric with goose bumps everywhere.

"Any chance you can stay?" Beth asked. "I think we'd all like hearing some stories about crime fighting in New York."

"I really need to get back. Things are getting crazy, and I need to address some issues with The Outcasts. Big things are coming. If you can convince Sam to bring you to the Big Apple, I'll have you meet the team, and we can tell you stories all night long."

Sam gave a sarcastic look. "Me?"

"Yes." Robert patted Sam on the back. "I've now designated you the chaperone for their upcoming visit."

"Apparently, there's now a field trip in your future." Several cheers went up. Sam waved his hands to settle down the group. "Okay! Okay! Let me do some work to get the Major on board. Anyone know where he is?"

Percy exclaimed, "Getting his kicks kicking around prisoners!"

Sam nodded, "That would explain things. Maybe we'll have to-"

A sergeant rushed into the W.A.R. Room. "Sam! We have a situation!"

CHAPTER 20

The whole complex was buzzing from the news of another bank robbery, and how The Terror Tribe was responsible. Sam came running into Major Constantine's office, having raced across half the complex and weaving through the mass chaos the news had caused. "Did you hear the news? I went to the prisoner cells, but they said you left."

"Just got done talking with local authorities in Pittsburg." The Major picked up his coffee that he had brewed earlier in the morning, but hadn't had a chance to drink down. The Major took a sip and let out a big sigh, putting down the mug of cold coffee. "They went in by force, meaning one of their heavy hitters had to be there. From their description of the damage, I'm betting it was Natural Disaster."

Sam started to contemplate, "So, they're branching out. I wonder if they are trying to distract us by diverting our attention to various target areas throughout the country."

"I don't think so. From the blast-"

Jonathon ran into the office. "I just heard."

Followed by Mike. "Me too."

"It appears to be a Terror Tribe heist. The Major was just filling me in on the details."

Mike shook his head. "Two high profile heists in the same day? That's ballsy, even for The Tribe."

The Major continued, "I have the authorities collecting information and will report back soon, but here's what we do know. A large blast took out the back of the building while several civilians were inside. By the time the police reached the vault, The Terror Tribe had vanished. From intelligence reports, their getaway seemed to be by a portal that began disappearing as they arrived. There was no one inside in the vault, so they went back outside and discovered that there was another dark circle that was vanishing as well."

"I'd say it was Empty and his portals," Sam responded.

"Yeah, definitely Empty," Jonathon agreed. "It would appear that the Washington robbery wasn't the only withdrawal they were looking to make."

"But they didn't have Natural Disaster with them in D.C.," Mike noted.

The Major grabbed a few papers. "That's where things start to get confusing."

"Maybe they just met up along the way?" Jonathon asked.

"Could be," the Major answered. "We were fortunate to snag Landfill, so they were down a man."

"With losing one team member, it would make sense to add another member, but then why was Natural Disaster in Pittsburg?" Jonathon asked.

"We're not sure if he was there originally or met them there. That's quite a distance to travel from the coast. It would seem easier if he was already there."

"You said them?" Sam wondered.

"Eyewitnesses in the area, at about the same time of the theft, claim to have seen someone flying through the air, carrying a couple of people."

Jonathon agreed, "Sounds like Bootlegger."

"So..." Sam paused. "Empty and Bootlegger are continuing a crime spree in Pittsburg. They lose a man, but pick up another who happens to be a significant Tribe member in Natural Disaster."

"We know Landfill is a part of the Tribe," Jonathon stated.

"I bet you there's a connection," Mike said emphatically.

"But what?" Jonathon reached for the papers on the Major's desk. "They're moving away from the coast. Are they looking to raid the Midwest, hoping to stay away from us? That doesn't feel right."

"Yes," Sam agreed. "They've tried to stay out of our crosshairs, but have not been afraid of potential confrontation if a big financial windfall is possible."

Jonathon handed the papers to Sam. "Sometimes it felt like they welcomed a fight."

"There's a grander scheme, and we just don't know what it is," the Major stated.

Sam paused. "Maybe... maybe they're heading away from the East coast because they know our response time would be slower. Even if we left the pad at the same time they hit the bank, our helicopter still would take 60 minutes to get to Pittsburg. They would be long gone by then."

"Makes sense," Jonathon admitted. "I take it that means we're not heading to the scene."

"No," the Major stated. "Authorities there are handling the best they can. I hope to have an update within the hour, including photos for evaluation. They hit where and when The United couldn't handle this."

"Do we need to branch out from this complex? We're not meant to go face-to-face with them, although that's happened more lately than in years past," Mike wondered. "We can't solely count on The United. They're just one team travelling the country after Tribe members. Once far enough away investigating possible Tribe activity, such as in Colorado, they're ineffective if needed on the east coast."

The Major disagreed, "Setting up another high-level facility like this would take too much time and money. The logistics of it does not make any sense."

"We can start with more local teams like The United Outcasts," Sam said enthusiastically.

"How would we control them?" the Major asked.

"Why would we want to control them?" Sam challenging the Major started to get on his nerves.

"If we don't have control, how are we supposed to ensure they will do what we say?"

"We don't command them. We work with them," Sam pointed out.

The Major countered, "How does that work? If they don't agree with us, they'll just refuse, and we are back at square one."

"Why wouldn't they agree to help?" Sam argued.

"You mean to tell me that a group of powerful human beings, under no obligation to us is going to do our bidding every time we tell them? How likely are they to agree with everything we need them to do? Hell, everyone in this room is committed to this program, and we still don't agree on things."

Jonathon agreed, "Good point."

"Then what do you suggest?" Sam wondered. "We have limited options."

The Major paused, giving a sigh, "Let me talk to Senator Steinberg. He's about as important to what we do here, as we are. Maybe he can help us in some way we don't know."

"Where is he?" Sam asked.

"He should be in the command center. He had a conference call. When he gets done, I'll go talk to him."

"Good," Sam gave a sigh of relief. "In the meantime, send me any information you have on Pittsburg when it comes in."

"Will do," the Major responded.

"Jonathon and I will go over the reports. Mike, can I see you outside?"

"Sure can." Mike followed Sam into the hallway. "What's up?"

"Where are we with using the Deerdron Scanner to locate new superhumans?"

"Uh, we're not. With the latest generation of people developing powers, it's rare that we can detect their power signatures, so we've stopped."

"Wonderful," Sam groaned. "We need to circle back to using it or improve its detection capabilities. I was thinking it could help us find someone who might be able to fly. Can you go through all of the current Project: Hero rosters around the country and get me files on those who can fly or teleport?"

"What about Wally, Michael and April?"

"Wally is well trained, but limited to using the wind or telephone lines. Even during the windiest day, his top speed is only that of highway speeds. Michael is very inexperienced. His flying is good for regular exercises, but hasn't been pushed to where we need him to be. His stamina also plays a factor and working to increase it should be a priority. April is a whole other question mark. The mysterious body parts she pulls out of nowhere is a mystery as to what or where they came from. We understand little about her abilities, which is hampered by the fact that she doesn't open up to anyone. Plus, she hasn't worked on flying too much. I wouldn't want to put her in harm's way."

"Okay. But wouldn't the Major be able to access-"

Sam put his hand on Mike's shoulder. "I need you to do it. He tends to pick and choose certain recruits based on his wants and needs. Right now, we need a recruit that can get somewhere fast. A teleporter would be ideal. Check anyone with the ability to fly and where they are in developing their powers. Maybe if we can bring them here and focus on improving those abilities, we can fill that slot."

"I'll get on it."

"Please stop by my office later. I want to review the status of Wally, Michael and April and what plan we can come up with to increase their abilities. Until we can get another flyer in here, we need to improve them quickly."

"Looks like I've got some homework for once."

Mike smiled as he walked away. Sam grinned, but that changed when seeing the look on Jonathon's face as he exited the Major's office. They began walking together when Sam asked, "I imagine he's mad?"

"Saying he's mad is not quite the word to describe him right now."

"I don't expect him to be happy, but what can we do? We have no way of effectively going after The Tribe right now. Most times we're playing catch up. If you've got some time, I'd like to have you and Mike go over a few items regarding Wally, Michael and April."

"Sure. What's going on?" Sam and Jonathon continued down the hall, unaware of the Major watching from behind the shades in his office. Most times, Major Constantine isn't regarded as a very happy individual. Right now, he's furious.

CHAPTER 21

The best thing about committing a crime in the town you're based in is how quickly you get back to your hideout. It also helps when that hideout happens to be a legitimate office building with multi-million-dollar corporations as tenants. For Natural Disaster, it meant getting to cover and getting out of the public eye much faster, in case any do-gooding heroes happen to be close by.

The elevator arrived at floor that would be the eventual home of The Infamous One and The Terror Tribe. The look of the floor was much of a surprise to Empty and Bootlegger, being unoccupied and still under construction. They cautiously followed Natural Disaster through the skeleton of rooms with only frames of doors and walls present. They eventually came to the doorway of an office with the lights on. As they entered the room, they were provided incredible views of the city and allowing the visitors to finally see who the occupant was.

The Infamous One turned around with a curious look on his face. "How did everything go, my powerful friend?"

Natural Disaster brought over two large bags, filled to the point of not being able to be zipped closed. "We were in and out faster than ever before."

"My portals make getting in and out of tough places a breeze," Empty stated.

"I appreciate your help." The Infamous One slowly wandered over to the bags.

Bootlegger responded, "I'm glad you do, since the deal was that we become members of The Terror Tribe."

"Deal? Young lady, I was not aware of any deal."

"Look! We had a deal! We've gone out of our way to help you. We lost our partner the first time." Bootlegger pointed. "Then we get your vice president of destruction over here into a secured vault and out without hardly being noticed. We showed how easy it can be to pull off a job with our help. We're a valuable asset to any team. You're stupid to not have us."

"I am?" The Infamous One strolled over to them, standing directly in their faces.

"No… that's not what we're saying."

The Infamous One sported a devious smile. "Perhaps I should take what you said into consideration. Perhaps my gut instincts are wrong. I've been able to keep everyone safe and had this team survive for decades with just my decisions."

"We're not telling what you should do, but if you're worried about getting caught, you can't do any better than us," Empty stated.

"He's right." Bootlegger took a step forward. "Once he gets you out of wherever you are, I'll get you home."

"How, pray tell, do you plan on doing that?"

Empty added, "I'll set up an escape path with a portal. No matter where we go in, we're coming out safe… and rich."

"Really?" The Infamous One smirked and looked over to Natural Disaster. "I guess I should defer to you since you have experience with them."

"I can say, it was much cleaner than it would have been if I had to blast through the building twice." Natural Disaster walked over to stand by his leader. "We got in and out in record time. Empty's portals allowed for easy exits and jumping away from tricky situations. Bootlegger has some of the best flight abilities, which is something we continue to lose. They had my back, even with the possible threat of an armed security guard."

"Natural Disaster trusted us to get the job done," Bootlegger stated. "I'm not sure if there's anything else we can do to prove ourselves."

"No, you can't. I do believe you have both proven yourself more than capable, more than worthy. If your wish is to be a member of our team, I grant you that wish." The Infamous One slowly walked up to them, standing face to face. "Now that we have finished with the formalities at hand, there is Tribe business that we need to attend to."

CHAPTER 22

The next morning arrived, and everyone was informed of an incoming surprise. Getting to experience that new car smell, that's if the car were a multi-million-dollar, super-secret, jet helicopter. Project: Hero had a few helicopters in the past, with the current one being as good as anything else flying in the blue skies of Virginia. But times are changing and so is their air fleet, thanks to Senator Steinberg. They were adding a second, even better aircraft to enhance the crime fighting capabilities of the team.

The entire complex personnel were pumped, especially Alexavier, who was up early to be ready. The arrival of the helicopter was a big deal, particularly since only few outside of the military have ever seen this level of experimental aircraft. He needed to finalize his thoughts in his journal, but was now on his way. The landing was just mere moments away, and if he waited any longer, he might miss the dramatic aerial unveiling.

Getting to the main hallway, he weaved around those not heading toward the hanger. He could hear a voice in distance, coming from behind. There's only one person who could be later than he was. Dave came running, accidentally knocking into people. A few excuse mes and a couple sorrys later, he finally caught up. Alexavier pointed out, "You're more dangerous to us than The Terror Tribe."

Dave desperately tried to catch his breath. "I wouldn't have to run... so much... if you weren't... always on time."

"I think I'm late too. The helicopter should be arriving any second. We need to hurry."

Rushing into the hanger they could tell they were the last to arrive with the Major, Sam and the Senator addressing the gathering of heroes. The Major was in the middle of his presentation, with everyone listening intently. Alexavier and Dave circled to the backside of the hanger to get a better view of the Major.

"Our current helicopter is one of the fastest in the world with a top speed of just over 250 mph. This new one has a revolutionary design that sets a new benchmark. It can achieve speeds of over 400 mph, thanks in part to help from Mike and his mechanical expertise." A collective awe emanated from the group, while a couple of the team patted Mike on the back.

"Response time has been limited of late, especially with the recent string of well-organized thefts. This aircraft is almost twice as fast, so for battling The Terror Tribe, it will be a game changer. No longer will we be delayed when The Tribe makes their move. Our current helicopter takes about ten minutes to get into the heart of Washington, which is about 20 miles away. This new aircraft will get us there in under five. New York currently takes about forty-five minutes. Now we can be there in twenty. This will truly be revolutionary in the way we fight crime, and we are truly fortunate to be able to acquire such a fantastic piece of technology. This is a project from one of the government's black sites. Even less people know about this aircraft than about our training complex."

"Wait. So, if this an expensive, super-secret, experimental helicopter, how are we lucky enough to get it?" Jonathon wondered.

"That would be me." Senator Steinberg stepped forward. "Ask for help, and you shall receive."

Jonathon was suspicious. “Are you involved with other highly secretive operations that we don't know about? Am I allowed to even ask?”

“I'll tell you this. My family’s wealth definitely helps get me into places, especially when it’s somewhere people aren't supposed to go. If for some reason I'm not able to get what I need, a hefty donation to a fellow politician's re-election campaign can get my foot in the door. Most of the funding for this came from my backing, but I also promised some help for research and development, coming from a particular friend of ours.” The Senator placed his hand on Mike's shoulder.

“I don't mind. I can get my own foot in the door for new technology too. I can get upgrades for outfits, weapons and gadgets.”

Suddenly, a loud alarm began to ring through the hanger. The roof doors slowly slid open. Everyone quickly backed away to the perimeter, away from the helipad. The wind started gusting, even worse than before, but no one could hear any noise. An image soon appeared through the sun, lowering down and eventually landing in an eerily quiet manner. The rotors slowed as the engines shut off. Before them was a sleek, futuristic helicopter with sleek lines and sharp angles.

The Senator took center stage for the introduction. “Let me introduce you to the new VTR120 AV-1 Air Viper. Originally designed to be a quick strike, attack and deploy helicopter, this aircraft slowly mutated into a long range, high speed intercept transport. Gone are the weapons, which saved several thousand pounds, which allowed for increased acceleration and top speeds. Although, we will not be using it for any combat purposes, but it can easily be converted back within a moment’s notice. The design of the fuselage was intended to enhance speed, but also provide maximum stealth. The body panels, like everything else, are made from a synthetic material with which helps dissipate heat and is coated with a non-reflective, noise dampening outer shell. With the help from Mike, the aircraft has an onboard silencer that emits a strong volume of negative soundwaves, making it almost completely silent when the device is activated. Having no heat, synthetic materials and no noise, this helicopter is completely invisible to all but the naked eye. We should be able to approach situations with surprise on our side."

"If this can help us bring down The Tribe, maybe more people will be persuaded to back heroes like us," Mike commented.

The Senator continued, "The war on terror is funded through the government, as well as the war on crime. For as much as there's people out there with super human abilities committing crimes, there's little push to throw money into fighting them. The main backing for The United comes from some very inventive ways to make the government funds available to them. Certain legislators are trying to disband the team. The fact that The United Outcasts even formed is a miracle. We need more teams like this, since the number of villains continues to be more than the heroes fighting them."

"When do we get to go for some New York style pizza or Coneys?" Dave joked.

The Major shut him down. "It's not here for going to get take out."

Dave mocked the Major for being such a buzz killer. "Our goal is to have this helicopter ready and prepped by this afternoon and in service. This will be our primary mode of transportation from now on. The old one will be as a back-up, since we're likely to have the need for more than one at a time. Everyone can have a quick look before the techs and mechanics need their space."

Everyone broke off into the usual groups. Mike escorted Alexavier and friends toward the back, lowering down the cargo doors. The area for personnel was a major advancement compared to their old helicopter, but also had some shortcomings. Beth noticed the smaller interior. “How many people does the cargo bay hold?”

“The old one holds up to twenty people sitting comfortably, not including prisoners. This new one can only handle twelve. We rarely needed that much seating, so why not trim the fuselage. The less width means better aerodynamics, while less weight also equals more speed.”

Killus joked, “Hey! They planned ahead with less seats. I guess that confirms it. Mike's too chicken to go on missions.”

Killus' laughter was met with Beth's annoyance. “That's funny coming from someone who can't go on any missions.”

As much as Killus wanted to engage in a battle, whether verbal or physical, he glanced over seeing the Major staring him down. He waved to his gang to follow him. Once close to Beth, he whispered, “One day, you'll be seeing this face, but you'll be feeling my knife.”

“Any day you want to try.”

Alexavier saw the face-to-face confrontation and attempted to get between them, but Killus began to leave. Alexavier stood next to Beth, waiting to make sure the band of thugs had left before saying, “I really want to punch him again.”

“You're going have to get in line.” Beth gave a slight grin and pulled his arm, bringing him back to look at the new aircraft.

Everyone was enjoying the personal tour Mike was providing. Having spent countless hours going over every inch of the design, it gave him intimate knowledge of the details which made things very insightful.

“It is slightly smaller, so we going to have less people on board. However, having two helicopters means we can split the team up and do more. Storage is better. With this new helicopter, you can now keep certain gear in small lockers under the seats. You'll have less turnaround time when you don't have to grab all of your stuff. That will lead to better and faster departures, also enhancing our ability to reach destinations quicker. We've provided duplicate gear that's already being stored on the new one, and we're working on it for the old helicopter. We have expanded the number of monitors around the cargo area. They have been enhanced to display a more intuitive and interactive computer system that has a virtual link to the training complex and World Net. Comfort has been drastically improved with the seats being contoured and conforming to individual body shapes. They should provide better comfort for the increased G-force and speed. The belts are on tensioners that sense every movement of the helicopter, providing constant adjustments during takeoff, flight and landing."

"How does it get there so much faster?" Wally asked while marveling at the new monitors.

Mike led them outside and down the cargo ramp. "There's a really cool new idea that I was able to implement. The top rotor tilts much farther forward than standard helicopters, allowing the aircraft to angle up and begin accelerating almost instantly upon take off. This tweak in the design cuts the time of liftoff by at least half. All of the modifications have boosted speeds, even though it's not really twice as fast as the old one. My goal was to determine how to decease flight time, since that's our Achilles heel."

Percy was tracing his hand around the jet engine's inlet. "What kind of engines does it use?"

"This one is a highly modified, jet turbine engine. There are two of them that each produce about 3500 pounds of thrust. With that much more power, everything had to be redesigned to withstand the greater pressure being put on them. Even the rotors had to be assessed for the increased forces put on them. We tested every design tweak to ensure that the added stress wouldn't cause a catastrophic failure at any point. There's a stealth mode that negates the sound, so we can enter into a hot zone without making any noise. The body is of a hardened composite material that is light, but can withstand extreme conditions of its increased flight capabilities. The matte black finish is from the Navy's stealth fighters. I found a lab outside of Los Angeles that has a dull coating that not only negates radar signals, but also reduces heat while increasing rigidity. Every part of this helicopter can withstand most forms of small artillery."

"If it can't be shot down with bullets, what about lasers or a blast from Natural Disaster?" Alexavier wondered, rubbing the hull of the aircraft.

"The tiles are impact resistant, but a highly concentrated blast will still cause damage. Then again, Natural Disaster is who he is. I doubt the helicopter will survive too many direct hits. Let's hope we never find out."

"Alright, everyone needs to clear the hanger!" The Major's voice echoed louder than the conversations, bringing a halt to the guided tour. "We have a scheduled test flight, and there's prep work involved!"

Sam had a great idea. "The heist that just went down shows us that we need a better way to intercept The Terror Tribe, especially when criminal activity is happening at that moment, and we need to get there quickly. What if we use the inaugural flight as a trial to see how it works in the field?"

"That's perfect!" Mike motioned to the recruits. "Grab your gear and hurry back."

The Major opened a folder, pulling out a paper to review. "Incoming intel says that there's a couple of low-level villains currently located around the north D.C. area. They have been on our radar, but never with enough interest for concern."

Jonathon took the paper. "I'd say it's a good test without putting everyone in too much danger."

"We could also drop off Robert back in New York when we're done." Sam began heading toward the center of the complex, following the recruits. "I'll take the lead. Have the information loaded to the onboard computer for our departure. How long should it take before it's ready?"

"We'll just need to look everything over and do a quick refuel." The Major looked at his watch. "I'd say 15 minutes or so."

"I'll meet you back here for liftoff." Sam vanished down the hallway, followed by Jonathon.

The Major looked over to Mike who was loitering, still marveling at the amazing piece of aerial hardware. He walked closer, standing right next to him. "Are you going to grab your stuff for this flight?"

"There's a few things I still need to handle back at my workshop."

Mike slowly turned and walked away. Before he could leave the hanger, the Major yelled out, "You need to deal with this. You can't run forever!"

"I'm not running!" The Major could only watch, as Mike continued to walk down the hallway. As much as this was supposed to be a historic event that could be remembered fondly, unfortunately for the man coordinating it, it ended on a sour note that has been lingering for a while now.

CHAPTER 23

With the whole gang arriving at the hanger around at the same time, the inaugural flight of the new helicopter could get underway with Sam and Major Constantine completing their preparations for the launch. The roof was already opened in anticipation of takeoff.

Before anyone could get aboard, the Major addressed the group. “We will be underway in just a minute. Sam will be giving you a briefing once aboard. First is picking the team. I want Dave, Wally, Michael, Hank, Killus, Bobbie, Beth and Manny to get on for the mission. Hurry up. Take off is in minutes.”

“Is that it?” Beth questioned.

“That’s it,” the Major responded.

Confused, Beth responded, “Why not Alex? He’s one of our best heroes.”

“He’ll be staying here for this mission.”

“But that’s not-”

The Major hated the back talk. “If you question me, you can stay with Alex.” He stared her down. “Get on the aircraft now.”

Everything inside her wanted to stay and fight for her friend, but Alexavier gave her a nod that it was okay to go. Reluctantly, Beth walked over and entered the helicopter, looking back one last time to see Alexavier give a smile and a nod.

Without any acknowledgement to his presence, the Major dissed Alexavier and walked passed him and got on board. Although he wasn’t going either, Harvey watched from the entryway with a smirk on his face. The cargo door closed, as the blades spun faster. It wasn't long before the aircraft lifted into the air and through the roof. Alexavier watched his teammates vanish into the sky. Mike arrived to see the disappointed hero. He stopped next to Alexavier, but didn't say a word. Alexavier had questions. "Why am I not going?"

"You know what? Sometimes it's about different people going on missions. I wouldn't think too much into it if I were you. Besides, it's not a mission. How about you keep me company?"

Alexavier nodded, still bummed about not going, but at least he got to hang out with Mike.

#

The space age helicopter quickly achieved top speed, racing toward their destination. The recruits raced to get prepared for action while listening to an update from Sam. "Having this new helicopter is a blessing, since we can take more risks to go after criminals who we might not have considered in arresting. So, for today, we're attempting to tackle a small crew based around Washington, D.C. that have been consistently causing trouble for local businesses and entrepreneurs for a few months now. These three are basic criminals who do not have any affiliation to The Terror Tribe, so there shouldn't be much resistance from any big and powerful Metas."

Bobbie asked, "Any intel on who these guys are?"

"The head of the group is Dodgeball. She doesn't really have a power, but throws various objects that have different effects, like exploding or electrocuting. She's more a long-distance fighter with really good aim, so stay close when fighting her. Air Raid is their getaway driver with the power to fly. His flying is different than most others as he can support an incredible amount of weight or cargo when flying, without having any real super strength. Tether is a Meta that is able to grab a hold of objects with a psionic grip. Essentially, he can lift massive objects with his mind. You can understand why these three have banded together to commit a bunch of robberies."

"It's weird to me that with their abilities that The Tribe wouldn't want them," Wally said.

Sam responded, "Rumors circled that they were contacted, but needed to proves themselves, which seems to be how The Terror Tribe operates when recruiting. These recent heists could be just that."

Manny pulled the mask over his head. "How are we going to find them?"

"Yeah. Are they like, committing a crime right now?" Dave asked.

Sam pushed a button on the remote in his hand, pulling up a map onto the large monitor. "Their crime spree has been all over the surrounding area outside the main D.C. cityscape. Activity picked up this morning, particularly on the northside. A tip came in that they were sighted less than an hour ago. We're heading to where they might be if we calculate their progress. Once we get into the general vicinity, we'll attempt to locate and engage them. Have all of your suits and gear on before we arrive. This flight is only a few minutes. Let's be prepared."

Over the next few minutes, everyone finished assembling their uniforms and weapons, ready for the encounter. It wasn't long before they could see the monuments of D.C. and watch them vanish in the distance as they passed over the city. When the helicopter arrived in the targeted area, it slowed and circled to find an appropriate place to land. The Major was in contact with local authorities and found the approximate location of their targets. The visual search began for any out of the ordinary activities. But before they could narrow down the area for landing, Wally inquired about the environmental conditions for how he would use his powers. "What are the winds like on the ground?"

The Major scrolled through several pages before pulling up the weather report on the big screen. "We have clear skies and calm winds up to five mile per hour."

"I can't use the wind. Once I'm away from the helicopter, I've only got the power lines to use."

"I'll inform the pilot to drop you off as close as possible to some."

As he stepped up to the cockpit give instructions, the Major received a status update from the pilot of possible movement just a few blocks away. "Major, central command has received word of the current location of the possible Tribe members not far from here. Should we change course to intercept them?"

"Affirmative. Take an intercept course, and give this chopper a good speed test using stealth mode. Let's get there so fast the bad guys won't have a chance to react."

After relaying the information to the pilot, the Major returned and addressed the group, "We have confirmed sightings of Terror Tribe members not far from where we are. Have your gear on and be ready for deployment. We are coming in hot and hoping to catch them off guard, so be ready and hero names only."

Everyone raced to finish having their gear on, Killus and Hank were giddy with the thought of combat. Sam noticed the need for someone to head up the mission, so he walked over to Wally. "Take point and direct the others. Do what you can to catch up to them once the others are giving chase."

"Yes, sir." Wally pulled the mask over his face and headed toward the door to wait.

The aircraft arrived almost instantly and began a calculated pattern to determine the best spots for deployment. As the cargo door opened, Wally searched the terrain for the closest wire. The helicopter slowly hovered toward a set of taller power lines, eventually being in close proximity for Wally to jump out and use the swirling winds of the helicopter to propel him towards the lines. Once he made contact with the energy, he surfed to the top of a pole for the best vantage point.

Finding a suitable open area that was a parking lot, the pilot lowered the helicopter down for soft landing. The remaining heroes jumped out, allowing the pilot to take off. Sam stayed with the aircraft and began scanning the surrounding landscape, hoping to spot their targets. Before Sam had a chance to locate them, Wally spotted the team of three sneaking along the small businesses lining the closest major road. "Sam, I've found them!"

"Team, follow Wave Rider's direction to intercept!"

But before any of the heroes could begin the chase, Air Raid noticed Wally hovering about the telephone pole and shouted, "We've been spotted!"

The fleeing bad guys quickly found an opening into an adjacent lot where Air Raid could grab his partners and fly into the air. Tether and Dodgeball held onto several large sacks, as Air Raid soared high into the sky, gaining more and more speed.

The first one out of the helicopter was Michael, who attempted to follow with rockets emerging from his calves. Trying to balance and take off after these criminals, Michael struggled to stabilize because of his inexperience at flying and could not catch up to them.

Killus and Hank followed with Bobbie, who tried to pushed her way past them. Dave, Beth and Manny were last and tried to keep pace with the others. Sam decided to help, but was no more able to get to the villains than any of the recruits.

Knowing he was the only one who might have a chance to bring them down, Wally set off atop the wires, using their electrical impulses to drive him forward. But with each post that he passed, he lost ground to the increasing speed of the villains. The only thing he could do was continue along at a mild pace, hoping they would make a mistake and slow down. They didn't and continued soaring higher and farther away. Once the three vanished from sight, Wally slowed down and gave up the chase. With a sigh of frustration, he headed back toward his team. "Sorry! I couldn't catch up to them! They're gone!"

CHAPTER 24

The helicopter hovered over the slowly opening roof casting a shadow over most of the hanger. Those who remained at the complex gathered to welcome back their comrades. Ready for the physical and mental evaluations required after each mission where any kind of action has taken place, Dr. Dennis was primed and ready. She was joined by Mike, Percy, Alexavier, April and Glen, who were all ready to welcome back their teammates. April and Glen kept their distance, while Alexavier was visibly anxious to see their arrival. He ignored the small talk, focusing on the landing aircraft. Harvey stayed back down the hallway, almost out of sight. Once the helicopter touched down, the cargo door lowered for the heroes to return home.

Of everyone exiting the helicopter, Wally was less than enthusiastic. That didn't stop Beth from trying to cheer him up, but her words of praise didn't have an effect. "I heard your transitions from pole to pole were some of your best! You're making progress!"

"Hey, what's got old blondie in the dumps?" Percy asked, as he and Mike came over to greet them.

"They got away, and Wally's taking it hard," Bobbie replied, setting down her gear.

Wally added, "I can't chase people when there's no wind. Even using electrical wires doesn't help. I'm actually slower than if there's a nice gust of wind."

Dave mentioned, "We were on the ground and couldn't board the helicopter fast enough to give chase."

"We'll get them next time. We now know where they're operating," Mike assured them.

Beth was the first to greet Alexavier and apologized, "Sorry you couldn't go on the mission. I tried."

"That's okay. What happened?"

Beth answered, being mildly disappointed. "They flew off and we couldn't follow. Wally gave it his best shot."

Wally sighed, "I just can't fly without wind. I don't even know why the Major selected me with the obvious weather conditions. It would have been better for Alex to go instead of me." With his head down, Wally took the gentle breeze that flowed through the complex and lifted into the air, gliding over everyone and heading to his room.

"Sucks when it's all up to you, and you blow it." Harvey commented from a distance.

Alexavier gave him a dirty look. "I thought you and Wally were friends?"

"I am. That's why I can be honest about failures and success." Harvey turned and walked away. "And that I'm not the one responsible for letting the bad guys to get away."

"It's really nice that you want to bring people down instead of help!" Beth's voice carried, but Harvey could care less if he heard it. He kept the smirk on his face as he vanished from sight.

"It wasn't anyone's fault." Sam passed by, saying with a little disappointment in his voice. "Unforeseen circumstances can happen, and you have to be prepared. Today, we weren't."

Alexavier rubbed his chin. "Would it have made difference to go back to the helicopter to chase them?"

"By the time we all got picked up, they were probably ten or twenty miles away," Bobbie pointed out. "And we had no idea what direction."

They watched Sam continue toward the pilot, who was giving the new helicopter the once over.

"I feel like I could have helped." Alexavier kept watching Sam. "Maybe I should go ask to be on more missions."

"It might not be the best time to do that," Bobbie stated.

"Yeah," Mike agreed. "Especially since the mission didn't go as well as anticipated."

After finalized many of the little details while consulting with the pilot, Sam headed toward the complex entrance and was met by the Major. His demeanor was of disappointment. He stood there clutching multiple folders, sifting through them to find the one he needed. He opened it and began commenting to Sam as they made their way into the complex.

"The fact is, we can't count on Wally to catch anyone with the slightest amount of speed. If all he has is power lines with no wind present, he's practically useless. Do we only conduct exercises when there's certain weather conditions from now on? We knew going into this test flight what Wally is capable of, especially if we encountered anyone, which you did. That's not going to change unless we look to boost his powers or modify them entirely."

They arrived at the elevator, where Sam hit the button. "I know where you are going with this, and I disagree."

"Wally isn't going anywhere with his powers in the state they are."

"I don't know. Just sending these kids into that chair every time things don't go right isn't accomplishing anything."

"We weren't seeing results with everybody, as almost everyone is plateauing with their treatment." The Major hands Sam a folder. "But

Alexavier's Session opens the door to a whole new level of treatments. We could see gains in abilities again, maybe even levels we've rarely ever seen."

"There are so many unknowns with this. Wally's powers may never develop any further with these Sessions. Then we are left without having any competent flyers."

"But we have a couple of recruits who can fly."

"We have Michael, who is one of the most amazing Metas we've seen," Sam stated. "But his control over flight is nowhere near where it should be. Just hovering, landing and taking off isn't acceptable if he is to be a major asset to the team. Until we know he has achieved this, the only thing he should be working toward is being the best flying hero we have ever put out."

The Major pulled out a form to fill out. "I'll submit orders for non-stop training in aerial control and maneuvers."

"But we also have an issue with April. Since she's been here, there has been minimal focus on her development."

"I can put that in for her as well." The Major grabbed another paper off his desk. "Our biggest problem is that outside of Wally, there's no one here who can fly or teach them."

"Our lack of capable flyers puts us at a major disadvantage. Where are we with locating recruits throughout the various Project: Hero sites?"

"There has to be a number of candidates throughout the system. We need time to evaluate each person to know who is ready to bring up to the complex."

"This needs to happen quickly. We can't continue to ask these same question several months from now. I have Jonathon looking into it, but haven't heard back yet."

Sam's comment felt like being undermined with someone else doing the Major's job. Before he could make a snarky comment, a voice interrupted them, coming from the doorway. "I know two recruits who could really help us."

Sam turned around to see Alexavier standing at the entrance to the Major's office. "Who do you have in mind?"

"Brad Stryper has trained with me for quite a while," Alexavier stated, cautiously entering the room. "He's one of the few who was willing to take me on in combat exercises. Not many of the other recruits wanted to. His fighting skills are really good and his powers are cool. He becomes light that can travel long distances and come back together. It's sort of like teleporting, but without vanishing."

The Major sorted through, finding a folder. "His name is Broadstripe. He's a Meta who can dematerialize by breaking down into strips of light that move from location to location, coming back together in human form."

"Can he transport others with him?" Sam asked.

"Not at this time," the Major responded. "But his powers haven't been as extensively developed as many of the others. With a few more Sessions, he could very well take others with him. Currently, we have been working to improve the distance he can travel. I don't feel he's ready, unless he's had a few more Sessions to judge his abilities."

"I don't know about the Sessions. We need to develop his powers and not just hope to increase them. You said you know of someone else?"

"Yes, sir," Alexavier answered hesitantly. "Her name is Valery Grayson. She goes by the name Gray, and she teleports."

Sam looked over to the Major. "How well can she use her powers?"

"Actually, what she seems to do is jump through portals from one place to another. So far, she's been able to do a couple dozen miles and carry a limited number of items." The Major quickly found the file, handing it to Sam. "She's a Meta and has barely been through any Sessions, so her powers should have a lot of potential for growth."

Sam browsed the data, quickly skimming through to the most interesting part. "Creates portals, huh? We should bring her up as soon as possible."

"But the only way to get her any closer to taking anyone with her is with Sessions."

Sam began rubbing his head. "Have you tried to have her teleport with anyone?"

The Major sighed, "Yes. The cat died."

"Crap," Sam sighed, tapping on a table.

"Sir?" Alexavier cautiously spoke up. "The cat dying appeared to be more from shock, at least that's what she said. I'm sure I could survive the trip."

Sam stated, "I say we bring her here and give her a try, but I don't want to go through Sessions immediately. Let's do a few test jumps to establish benchmarks for evaluation purposes."

The Major countered, "Really, if there is anyone who needs a Session, it's Wally."

"It's not necessarily just about getting Sessions."

"With no other way to improve his powers, how else do we go about it?"

"I'm up for anything that doesn't require these kids sitting in that chair every ten minutes. Until you can tell me that we have no other option, I'll hold off ordering one."

Looking over and seeing Alexavier, the Major gave an attitude. "Actually, why are you here?"

"After not making this last flight, I wanted to ask if I could be on every one from now on."

"The decision to keep you here at the complex was-"

Sam interrupts the Major. "It was a mutual decision after lots of consideration to give other recruits a chance to go. You will definitely be going on more missions." The Major wanted to correct Sam, but was cut off. "Major Constantine and I will follow up you about the possibility when the next mission comes available."

Feeling better, the young hero nodded. But before he departed, he made one last point. "Can I put in a good word for Brad? I really believe he's worthy of being here."

"There's nothing in his file that constitutes him moving forward to-"

"Hold on," Sam interrupted the Major. "Give me your honest thoughts."

Alexavier looked a bit nervous. "Well, I know he's really inexperienced. His powers may not do everything we need, but he can travel distances pretty quickly. Back in Philadelphia, he was able to make it from one end of the complex to the other in only a few seconds."

"That's nearly a mile." Sam started doing the math.

The Major wasn't impressed. "Yeah, but that won't help if we need others to go with him."

"That can be worked on, just like we're doing with Alex here." After a few seconds of silence, Sam turned to Alexavier. "We'll work on it."

Alexavier gave a grin and a nod before exiting the room, leaving Sam with a furious Major. "How can you undermine my decision like that?"

Sam put his hands up. "How was that undermining you?"

"I give my thoughts and concerns, and you disregard them."

"I'm just trying to add someone to this group that is desperately needed, recruits that can fly or travel distances quickly. They seem to be two of the only candidates we have right now. Nowhere in the system do we even have someone who can run fast. We're running out of options and need to work with what we have."

The Major opened a folder and attempted to hand it to Sam. "Here's what we should be basing our decisions on."

"I don't have to look at numbers to know we're in trouble with the lack of skills and powers we need to fight The Terror Tribe."

"So, we're supposed to take the word of a recruit that has struggled while here to prove they should be going on missions about who they believe would be appropriate to train for use on missions?"

Sam took a more confrontational stance. "But when it counts, that recruit has shown more than so many others have about how to be a hero. And as far as Alexavier goes, I personally think he should go with us on every mission from now on."

"And how does that help? We're just taking steps backwards in his training."

"Again, we haven't had any problems with him when he is sent out into the field. The recon with Bobbie and mission to D.C. with me proved that." Sam held up his hands. "Look, you're beating a dead horse here."

"I'll keep beating that dead horse until we see results or changes that matter, like what should happen with Mike."

"What about Mike?" Sam asked, becoming highly agitated. "He's not a recruit."

"But he does have roles and responsibilities, including leading our missions, which I've had to start doing."

"Do you want to tell him what he went through doesn't matter? Are you that insensitive?"

The Major pulled out a different folder, handing to Sam. "It's not being insensitive. It's being realistic about what you should be doing."

Sam refused to take the folder. "I'm not going there."

"Well, somebody should."

Frustrated, Sam grabbed his stuff. “No. We’re not.”

“We still have a Session planned. Wally needs the boost more than anyone else.” The Major threw a file on the desk in front of Sam. “If you have a better idea, now’s the time.”

Sam sighed, “Fine. But if this doesn’t work, we’re reevaluating all Sessions, even so far as to eliminate them entirely.”

As the Major watched Sam walk away, something inside of him was very pleased to know he upset his colleague. The Major picked up his phone. “Let Dr. Dennis know to come see me so we can prepare for a Session tomorrow.”

CHAPTER 25

It seemed that the only consistent thing happening around the complex was mealtime. Be it breakfast, lunch, dinner or just a snack, getting a bite to eat was the only guarantee. The need for nourishment was just as strong as the need to discuss the most recent crime-fighting endeavor. As the group made their way through the cafeteria-style line, everyone played follow the leader as Beth selected the table that would be their final destination.

Although everyone's mood was pretty upbeat, there was a slight air of disappointment from the very first flight of the new high-speed helicopter. The jet helicopter performed flawlessly, demonstrating amazing speed and capabilities beyond what the heroes previously had at their disposal. It added another tool to capture the villains of the world, but the real work would need to come from the heroes. Limitations have now been exposed, bringing a sense of uncertainty among the recruits, with some more than others.

"I don't think I've ever been so happy to indulge in this mostly tasteless food," Wally admitted.

"It just sucks," Beth sighed. "We were so close to those bad guys who have been bothering the locals, but couldn't catch them."

Wally apologized again. "I'm sorry. I'm so sorry, guys. I could only travel so fast."

"You can only do what you can," Michael reassured his friend. "I'm still learning how to fly. So, it was up to you, and I thought you did your best."

Alexavier sat down. "They have to know your limits. How can they expect you to do something they know you can't do?"

"But they expect me to fly, since that's my powers. Unfortunately, I'm limited to what energy sources I use. I've always been jealous of heroes who can fly without help."

"Yo. You gave it your best shot." Percy joined them. "I've never seen you do anything otherwise."

"We're all proud of you," Bobbie added.

Beth rubbed Wally's back. "We'll never think anything of you other than a hero."

"Thanks everyone." Wally gave a slight smile. "I really appreciate it."

Jennifer materialized from above and floated over Wally's head. "You are my hero."

Wally attempted to reach up and touch her. Jennifer let her hand materialize enough to provide a bit of comfort to her favorite solid life form. Everyone could see the deteriorating condition of Wally and tried to boost his spirits.

Bobbie stated, "You're the best guy we have at pursuing flying bad guys. No disrespect to Michael."

"Hey, none taken," Michael replied. "I'm still so green with flying around. I almost crashed just a week ago right outside here."

"Do you need any help?" Wally wondered.

"Yes," Michael nodded. "Thanks, man."

"Maybe we can go on the next recon," Wally added. "No better way to help than being out in the field."

"And speaking of being out in the field, why weren't you on that flight?" Manny motioned to Alexavier.

"I don't know. The Major has been against me doing anything and everything lately."

Manny smiled, "Yeah, he didn't like me smart mouthing off to him one time and kept me off missions for a month."

"But that's not always the truth." Dave motioned to Harvey, who decided to eat elsewhere. "He's been a pain in everyone's rear and even to the Major as well. Yet, he's still finds his way onto the helicopter."

"The Major still considers Harvey the best to bring down The Infamous One," Bobbie said. "Being able to make anyone pass out at any time makes you valuable. Harvey gets away with all that stuff because the Major sees him as the solution to capturing The Tribe."

"I just want to punch that dude," Percy admitted.

"You and me both," Manny agreed.

Bobbie gave them a fist bump. "I'll hold him down for ya."

"What we need is to become heroes to take all of them down. That way, he won't favor Harvey." Everyone agreed with Beth. "Especially after the way he acted with Alex."

"I still don't get what his problem is," Dave responded.

"The problem is he's a jerk!" Beth exclaimed

Everyone agreed with her blunt assessment, but the group's conversation quickly halted when Major Constantine entered the room. His path toward their table never meant anything good, and they were all on edge. It was obvious to one of them what was happening, as only Wally kept his head down.

The Major bypassed everyone, stopping right in front of Wally. "We have a Session for you tomorrow morning. Be ready at 0845. We will get you at 0900."

"Yes, sir."

The Major paused before informing Wally, "Also, we will be using the information gathered from Alexavier's Session to deliver stronger treatments from now on. Your Session will be the first."

Everyone remained silent, letting the Major turn and walk away. Once the messenger of bad news had left, Percy was the first to speak up, seeing Wally not as upset and would be expected. “What’s going on, man? You don’t seem mad.”

“I’m not sure,” Wally admitted. “I don’t remember what happened the last time I did a Session. I’ve seen it with you guys. I guess I’m not sure how to feel.”

The person most upset was Alexavier. “I’m really sorry. Can I help in any way?”

“No. I’m fine.”

Mike finally arrived, confused about who passed him at the entrance to the cafeteria. “Was that the Major?”

“Yup,” Dave answered.

Mike took a seat at the end of the table. “He never comes down here unless…” The realization hit him with Wally’s head down.

Percy sat his spork on the tray. “These Sessions are going too far, Mike. Now he wants to use that enhanced Session crap they used on Alex, even without knowing how it’ll affect Wally.”

“I wasn’t informed of this plan. He never included me on this decision. Excuse me.” Mike stood up and exited the cafeteria, leaving his tray of food behind.

“That’s one pissed dude,” Percy said.

Alexavier reassured, “It doesn’t matter what happens, Wally. We’re all with you.”

Jennifer gave Wally a tighter hug. He closed his eyes, reaching up and holding her hand. The others continued to reassure their friend, as he slowly started to understand what the next day had in store for him.

#

There's not much that makes Mike mad more than not being included in recruit decisions, especially when it comes to Sessions. He really didn't need another confrontation with the Major, but he was determined for a face-to-face meeting. Barging into the office, Mike marched right up to the desk. "When was I going to be consulted?"

"The decision was made."

"So?" Mike put his hands on the desk. "I've been quiet about the last couple of meetings that you haven't included me, but this is too important not have my input."

The Major carefully set down his paperwork on the desk. "Fine. Wally couldn't catch another Meta-Human trying to fly away because there was no wind. He needs a boost, which hopefully will enhance his powers."

"But you're using a regimen that worked with Alex, and we know he's a different hero."

"Sam is aware and agreed with this plan."

"I don't! I wouldn't have just agreed to it without some serious discussion about the physical and mental impact on Wally."

The Major sat back in his chair, becoming highly annoyed. "I've asked Dr. Dennis to review this plan. Since she is the doctor, I trust what she has to say."

"But it's my job to take care of these recruits. You assigned me this job years ago, because you felt I would be the best person to look out for them."

"I may have been wrong about that."

Those words threw Mike off, rendering him speechless for a few seconds. "We'll see about that. I'm not letting anything happen to the recruits if it's going to hurt them." Mike stormed out the door to the Major's amusement of getting under his skin.

It was as if Sam heard Mike stomping through the halls, since he came walking directly to him.

"I thought I was to be included in these recruit discussions."

Sam placed his hand on Mike's shoulder. "I know. I even brought up your name."

"The jerk even told me he regrets assigning me to help the recruits."

"That's not true."

"He just told me!"

Feeling bad, Sam directed Mike down the hallway. "From now on, I'll do what I can to bring you in."

"But that doesn't do me any good if he doesn't respect me and my opinions."

They stopped in front of Mike's room with Sam giving one last reassurance. "I care what you think, more than you know. Son, if there is one thing I know it's that you will always do what's right by the recruits. I'm happy knowing you are looking out for them, especially if I'm not around. I wouldn't have it any other way."

Mike relaxed a bit. "Thanks. Still not sure if I really feel better."

"Why don't you get some rest or food. You're going to need to be up early for Wally. I really don't want to be away while Wally is getting his Session, but there's an appointment I really need to keep. Watch things for me. Don't hesitate to call me anytime, okay?"

"Yup. You got it." Mike entered his room, feeling in a slightly better mood after the discussion, although not hungry anymore. But it was Sam who wasn't feeling so hot. His expression was one of confusion. He paused to recover before rubbing the sweat off his forehead. Trying to clear his mind, he headed off to have a much-needed discussion.

#

After leaving his office, Major Constantine headed towards the command center. As he was walking along the hallway, he replayed the heated conversation with Mike in his head, smirking with how frustrated Mike became. Being distracted with this memory, the multiple file folders slipped out of his hands creating a paper mess on the ground. Heaving a big sigh, the Major began picking up the individual papers and folders. Although, it would have been easier to carry a tablet housing the same information digitally, his distrust of technology overshadowed its convenience. Straightening himself, he turned to continue his path to the command center, only to see Sam standing within inches of his face.

"What gives you the right to be that way toward Mike?"

"Me? He obviously didn't tell you how he stormed into my office without an invitation or being invited."

Sam lowered his voice. "The only thing I care about when it comes to Mike is that he does what he's good at, and that is helping the young heroes."

"He's being defiant! It doesn't matter if he wasn't in on the conversation. He has no right to come at me like that!"

"Maybe he'd feel different if you hadn't taken him off his duties!"

"He continues to question my authority! Senator Steinberg brought me in to run this program. You were brought in because of your expertise in the field. Your role is to be here for evaluations and graduations. You can do all the crafting and honing you want, but if you have constructive input on any of the recruit's development, you can address it with me. As the head of this complex, I have that ability to make a final decision. If you are so intent on having a say, then you can make the decision on your own." The Major tried to hand Sam the same folder as before. "Wally's numbers haven't improved in almost two years and that includes receiving two Sessions. The regular treatments have done nothing for him. The only thing left to try is the new, stronger regimen, unless you want to remove him from Project: Hero."

Sam's face was mixed with the frustration of knowing there was nothing he could say or do to change the facts, but also the possible change to Wally's status. "We can't lose somebody that we have invested so much time and effort into. I truly believe he hasn't yet reached his full potential and have agreed to this one Session. If it goes well, I'll consider further treatments down the road. However, before we even think about that, I will be checking with the doctor to see if Wally has been harmed in any way from the Session. I have to prepare for my flight."

The Major gave a lackadaisical nod, which was all Sam needed. He took his bags and briskly walked away. With so many frustrating moments happening lately, this one small victory felt huge to the Major. A rare smile occupied his usually frowning face.

CHAPTER 26

You might think the person having to endure the horrors associated with a Session would be least likely to sleep; that honor went to Alexavier. He was unfortunate enough to remember them. In fact, he remembered nearly all of them. That kind of mental trauma kept him up most nights before and after each Session. The fact that Wally would be going through one, kept him up last night.

Sometimes, if he couldn't sleep, Alexavier would pull out his journal and start jotting down various bits of the day's events. Having to recount even the smallest of details of the day would usually distract him enough to ease his mind. But anytime he looked at the journal, he felt no motivation to even pick it up. Feeling that he needed to do something, he decided to get up, get dressed and check on Wally.

Peeking in the doorway, Wally was getting dressed, being accompanied by Jennifer, who was hovering in the air above him. The conversation between them was light, yet somewhat playful. It wasn't what he expected from somebody who is about to be locked into a chair that Alexavier equated to a torture rack. After a moment of hesitation, he knocked on the outside of the door.

"Hey! Didn't think you'd be up so early." Wally was chipper.

"Sessions keep me up."

Wally gave a funny glare. "But you're not getting it."

"Yeah, but knowing you're going through kept me up. I don't like it when anyone has one."

"That's so sweet," Jen smiled.

Wally grabbed his shoes. "You can have this one if you want?"

Alexavier declined, "No thanks. Not that I'm wishing the Session on you."

"I know. It's cool. I should be done and back fighting bad guys real soon."

"You're so upbeat. I don't think I could be like that."

Wally looked up "Being down's not going to help, so I might as well smile."

"And I like it when he smiles." Jen began to smile herself.

Alexavier saw Wally begin messing with the radio. "What station are you trying to listen to?"

"I don't really listen to that much music. What I like most is the white noise, which reminds me of the wind when I'm flying. I find it soothing, and it helps me to sleep at night."

Jen stated, "He used to toss and turn a lot."

Puzzled, Alexavier wondered, "Really? How did you know?"

"I used to watch him sleep at night."

"Isn't that kind of creepy?"

"He let me," Jen replied. "Plus, he's just so cute when he sleeps."

"Yup. Creepy."

Second to arrive after waking up early, Mike looked concerned and couldn't help but show it. "How are you feeling? If you're not up to it, we can call it off."

"I'm actually not that nervous. Jen has been keeping me company, so I really haven't been thinking about it too much."

"I wish I could be that relaxed," Mike stated.

Beth walked in with Morkie. “Who can be so relaxed? Why didn’t you get me?”

“I didn’t want to worry you,” Alexavier admitted. “Especially if you were still asleep.”

“I woke up early, thinking about today.”

Wally patted Beth on her knee and rubbed Morkie. “I really appreciate you being here. When is the next movie night?”

Beth looked surprised. “How can you think about a movie at a time like this?”

“Why not? I’ll be done with this in a couple hours, and then it’s onto eating popcorn.”

“Who said popcorn?” Percy led a motley crew of Bobbie, Mike and Dave. Harvey tagged along, but stopped at the doorway once he saw Alexavier. Manny and Michael pushed passed when he wouldn’t enter the room. Bobbie gave Harvey a glare to get him to join them, but he didn’t budge.

Beth asked, “So, you want a movie night?”

Wally perked up. “I’m all for it.”

“I say Wally gets to choose what to watch,” Dave added.

“Really, I’m cool with anything, as long as it’s not one of those goofy westerns again.”

“They’re called spaghetti westerns,” Beth clarified, while straightening up a table. “They’re fun!”

“Not my thing,” Manny admitted.

Percy agreed, “I’m with you there, boss. It’s all car chases and shootouts for me.”

Alexavier wondered, “Do you guys ever watch the movies about The Patriot Warrior and The United?”

“We can’t,” Manny replied.

"Yeah," Michael agreed. "The Major doesn't like us watching those."

"I'm sure the Major would let us watch them if he was the star."

"I say we watch one anyway," Dave suggested.

Mike began to clarify, "The movies with Sam and The United are only based on real events. I know Sam sees them as entertaining, but not the Major. That's why he forbids them."

Alexavier wondered, "Even the cartoons?"

"Yes," Mike stated. "But I'm sure we don't have to tell those in charge."

"Okay. So is there one that you really would like to see?" Alexavier inquired, not caring if it was frowned upon.

Wally thought deep, not sure what to pick. "You know, anything with Sam kicking Major Disaster's butt would work."

Beth set Morkie down and picked up some papers from the floor. "I think they did three movies like that."

"I don't think the actors really did that good of a job," Bobbie proclaimed. "Sam sounded like a whining sixteen-year old."

"And the camera work sucked," Percy added. "Why would anyone let a camera guy record like he's shaking from too much caffeine?"

Beth gathered some of Wally's papers. "It just looks so amateurish."

Wally noticed Beth taking care of more of his stuff. "It's okay. You don't have to do everything for me."

"You're going to need to rest afterward. How are you going to do all this?"

Bobbie and Michael pulled the stuff out of her hands. Beth tried to be as brave as she could. "I'm just scared."

Wally went to give her a hug. She wrapped her arms around her dear friend, holding tight. Silence enveloped the room. But it soon became too uncomfortable for Dave. "I swear if you guys make me cry," he said, fighting back tears.

Everyone began to get a little emotional. Even Wally, who had been so strong, finally showed the first signs of worry. Knowing the mood in the room needed a change, Dave jumped up to grab something to drink and tripped over Mike's foot, landing on the floor. Laughter broke out, which first annoyed Dave. Seeing that the dread of the upcoming Session was being washed away by his face plant, he began chuckling, joining in on the lightened mood.

#

Enough time had passed, and Major Constantine's arrival signaled that the start of the Session was close at hand. The grumpy, military man had been accompanied by several doctors, including Dr. Dennis, who immediately checked on the patient. Finishing her brief examination, she wondered, "Do you want a sedative? I have several medications that might give you a bit of relief from worrying and help you to relax."

"I'm good, but thanks."

"I also have some Propofol, if you want to be knocked out during this one."

"I appreciate it, doctor. But I think I'll do this as usual, just like Alex did."

Mike interjected, "Maybe we should see what Alex thinks, especially since he went through it."

"I'm not completely sure what happened when I got my Session, but I didn't have the drugs." Alexavier turned to Dr. Dennis. "Was it an option for me?"

"Actually, no it wasn't. Since that specific treatment had not been tried in quite some time, it had been determined that there was a need for data collecting. What makes you unique is your resiliency and recovery. If we could see how well you handled this new regimen, that information could be used for everyone else here. You did well, but what would be helpful is how you feel about it."

Alexavier sighed, "To be honest, it was the worst thing I've ever been through."

"There is one difference though. Alex remembers them while the others don't," Mike added. "How much of a difference will the drugs make if you don't remember?"

"It's truly up to you how you feel." Dr. Dennis waited for Wally.

Wally deferred to Alexavier. "Would you take them?"

Alexavier paused. "If you won't remember it, I would say it wouldn't matter. But what if you do? If I could have been put under, I'd do so every time."

Wally thought about it, but still had a question for the doctor. "Will having the drugs make a difference in the treatment?"

"No. Nothing would be affected."

"Then I'll take the sedation."

"Alright. Are you prepared?" The Major kept eyeing all of the others.

"I don't think there's anything else I need to do." Wally stood up.

Jennifer lowered down, wrapping her arms around him. "You better stay safe, okay?"

Wally nodded, "You going to come with me?"

"I'd take that treatment with you if they'd let me." Wally placed his hand on her arm. She solidified enough that he could squeeze and hold onto her. They began to walk away. The doctors followed closely, with the Major not too far behind. Everyone else accompanied them, as they usually did with every Session. The distance to the room was pretty far from Wally's room, so it gave him time to enjoy having Jennifer being near.

Tensions were high and grew even higher the closer they approached the Session room. The once calm Wally slowly began to show the increasing anxiety on his face of what was about to happen. With the look easily visible to all of those around him, the rest of the spectators became even more nervous, some even taking up the bad habit of biting their fingernails.

As Wally was escorted through the doorway into the Session room, Alexavier moved to still get a view of him. With the preparations continuing around him, Wally waited, seeming unfazed. With nervousness enveloping him, Alexavier became fidgety, and Beth could see it. She moved to closer, putting her arm around his.

"I'm sure he'll be alright." Beth's voice gave little reassurance.

"Yeah. He'll be fine." Neither sounded too sure.

"We've got to keep our heads up." Mike offered some positive energy. "The doctors are going to take good care of him. Dr. Dennis would never let anything happen."

"I trust her, not him," Percy stated, looking at the entrance to the Session room.

Exiting quickly, the Major passed everyone on his way to oversee the procedure from above. He gave no one a look, but Percy stared him down from the moment he came into view until he vanished up the stairs. Beth grabbed a hold of his arm too, hoping to refocus his energy into thinking about their friend.

Michael looked around. "Has anyone seen Jen?"

"I think she's still hanging around Wally."

"Can she stay in there?" Dave asked. "I mean, her Sessions never really seemed to affect her."

"She'll get out of there before it starts," Mike assured them.

Beth said, clinching tighter, "At least she's able to keep him company."

Slowly, Jen's form started to appear outside the room. Bobbie and Beth went over, attempting to put their arms around her. She gradually solidified her body, welcoming the hugs with Morkie jumping up to give his assurances as well.

The only thing the Major was concerned with was getting underway. He stared down every worker, becoming increasingly impatient. Even as efficient as they were, it wasn't enough, and he let them know. "Why aren't we ready?"

Many nervous faces were everywhere, except for Dr. Dennis. She didn't miss a beat, getting everything in place. "We are proceeding with all the routine steps for preparation and also adding a dose of Propofol to his medications."

"Isn't that used for sedation?"

"Correct," she continued her work, never looking up. "With the new treatment, and after talking to Alexavier, we decided on sedation, just as a precaution."

"We've never done it before. Is it really necessary?"

Dr. Dennis finally looked up. "For the extra hard treatment, yes."

"Is there a problem that you're not telling me?"

The Major's lack of trust really got under her skin. "I'll tell you this, the normal treatment was always difficult on anyone enduring the procedure. Every once in a while, one of them has some lingering effects or slight memories of the Session. The use of Propofol will help lessen any chance of those with proper sedation. If I can do anything to alleviate the negative effects, I will, unless you have a concern with this."

The Major didn't like the slight attitude given to him and reluctantly backed off. "If you're close to being done, I'll leave you to it."

Dr. Dennis turned away, doing her best to forget the interaction and complete the preparations. A few adjustments had to be made to the radiation panels before returning to Wally. She gave him one last nod, then placed the helmet on his head. With a squeeze of his hand being reciprocated back, she placed the tray of I.V. needles next to his arm and began the placement of the I.V lines. She opened the valve to allow the drugs to take effect. Within moments, Wally was unconscious. The final preparations were completed with all personnel leaving the room. Dr. Dennis gave one last check on her patient before leaving. She closed each door, securing them for everyone's safety outside.

With the preparation for the Session finalized, everyone outside held their breath. The chatting amongst various groups quickly dissipated with each second. The anticipation began growing, as the wait was immensely longer than normal. Time seemed to stand still.

A flicker in the overhead lights signaled the start of the Session. The sounds grew louder the more the sonic waves increased. Equipment roared to life, as the radiation panels started to emit pulses of energy. Those standing outside the room began hearing more and louder mechanical sounds emerging from inside the Session room. Beth closed her eyes tightly, clutching Alexavier harder than she ever had before. Mike, who had never showed too much emotion, quickly started sweating and running his hands through his hair. Sessions usually last a couple of minutes, but this one had a few extra added on. The intensity of the energy used caused a complex-wide drain, but as the power levels fluctuated, energy was rerouted, and a rush of electricity sent everything back up to normal levels, allowing the Session to run its course.

As soon as the Session ended and the equipment shut down and the warning signs turned off. The medical and technical personnel rushed back into the room and quickly shut the doors behind them. Everyone waited patiently. No noise was coming from the Session room, causing some to become even more concerned. Usually, it would be only a few minutes for the recruit to be prepared for transport back to their room or to the nearby medical area, if something had gone wrong. After ten minutes, Mike became highly agitated, even walking by the stairs leading to the Major's observation room.

Percy noticed. "You're going to need medical treatment yourself if you keep this up."

"I'm tempted to run right up there." Mike stopped by the steps. "They closed the doors, so he's the only one who can see what's going on."

"If you do, you'll be in even more trouble than the last time." Percy patted his longtime friend on the back. "If they don't bring him out soon or the Major doesn't come out, I'll go up there for you."

They didn't have to wait much longer, as the heavy doors to the Session room opened. The Elitesmen Guard led the way, followed by Wally on a gurney, surrounded by the entire medical staff. They turned a corner, but did not head back toward the center of the complex where Wally's room was located. Instead, they guided him toward the infirmary. All who were waiting outside the Session room quickly followed with concern on their faces.

Upon arriving at the medical ward, the medical staff quickly prepped a bed with several IV pumps, medications and syringes. The flurry of activity saw the necessary equipment corralled near the bed in the corner of the room. The gurney was positioned as close as possible, as several Elitesmen Guard moved in to help transfer the unconscious hero with a nurse moving his medications to the nearest pole first. Once the covers had been pulled back, the guards picked up and carefully placed him in a resting position on the infirmary bed. Dr. Dennis covered him up and adjusted his I.V. to begin administering fluids.

Watching the medical staff quickly care for Wally, the Major motioned for everyone standing near the door to leave. Almost everyone complied, except for Alexavier. He stood his ground, continuing to watch his recovering friend. Beth pulled on his arm, hoping to drag Alexavier from the room. He refused, still hovering, with his eyes glued to Wally's body resting in the bed. Before Dr. Dennis could finish, the Major returned and attempted to remove Alexavier.

Knowing Alexavier's history of better than expected recoveries, the doctor walked over and held off the Major. "I'd like to keep Alex here if you don't mind?"

"This is not the place for him."

"He won't be in the way, and I can use his strength if I'm in need of it."

"You have the other doctors and nurses here to help you. He's not a qualified medical personnel."

"I also would like to find out about what he does after each Session. There may be more Alex can offer us to aid Wally with his recovery if this Session is to be a success." She stared at the Major.

He reluctantly backed away, knowing that he had no chance to argue her logic and having the need for this new regimen to be the norm. She motioned for Alexavier to take a seat on the far side of the room. He obliged, and waited quietly and patiently. Once the medical professionals finished and could take a moment to catch their breath, Dr. Dennis turned to the waiting hero. "So, tell me, what's next when he wakes up?"

#

With the collective group hovered around the door, the Major and Dr. Dennis were the last to exit the room, leaving Alexavier to wait inside. Both were bombarded by questions concerning Wally's status. The Major put his hands up, shushing everyone. "Settle down! If you want an update, we are not going to talk over each other!"

Once the questions had died down to a minimum, Dr. Dennis addressed the gathering of recruits. "Wally is doing just fine. He's in recovery right now, and all his vital signs are normal. Everyone will get a chance to go see him, but we want to limit the numbers until he is awake and responding. For now, Alexavier will be the only one allowed inside. I'll make room for more of you to visit and let everyone know within the hour how each of you can do so. We want to make sure there are no unforeseen complications before we open up the room so many visitors."

"So, we don't know if he's really okay or not," Percy interjected.

"Wally is fine, and he is recovering," the Major said bluntly.

Dr. Dennis added, "What the Major is saying is that Wally handled the treatment without any immediate issues we can see, especially with the new sedation protocol. He has also been given a few other medications in case of any side effects, but we won't know more until he wakes up."

Hoping to end what he deemed an unnecessary gathering, the Major ordered, "You can all go back to your rooms and wait for-"

"And why can't we wait here?" Manny wondered.

Dave added, "Hey, we're just worried and want to make sure that he's gonna be okay."

Dr. Dennis responded before the Major could, "Waiting outside is not a problem so long as you are quiet. With time, we will cautiously allow everyone inside."

"Your worrying isn't going to make a difference in his recovery. The Major became highly annoyed. "I don't want him to be put in any danger if there is any interference-"

Percy shouted, "Damn, man! Don't you think we'd know how to be careful by now?"

“Apparently, we didn’t do a good enough job in our training to know how to be careful,” Dave added. “Maybe we should just pull the plug now.”

Bobbie stared at the Major. “Or do you think we’ll kill him another way?”

Mike saw the need to step in and defuse the brewing frustrations. “Alright, everybody! Let’s just take a deep breath! Remember, this is about Wally, and we need to focus on what’s best for him. If you guys want to head out and take a break.” Coming from Mike, the once frenzied mob settled down. “I’ll speak with Dr. Dennis and get constant updates. I’m sure they’re just wanting to take every precaution possible with this new treatment. So, go chill! Get a semi-edible meat-like burger and shake. I’ll join you guys in a second.”

The doctor leaned in to whisper, “Thank you.”

Catching her words, Percy needed to get in one last shot. “Yeah. Thanks, Mike. At least one person around here seems to care about us and how we feel that our friend is in there.”

Rather than continue to get berated, the Major walked away and headed to his office so he wouldn’t have to deal with any more crap. Once he had taken the elevator and arrived at the second floor, he was met by the presence of Jonathon Bender, who knew where to corner him. The Major’s day was a mild success, just with the Session, but it was about to implode with the impending conversation.

“So, we’re moving forward with stronger Sessions, yet I can’t even do a regular one.”

“We’ve been over this.” The Major pushed Jonathon aside to get to his office, leaving the perplexed hero behind in hopes of cutting the interaction short. “Plus, I’m not in the mood right now.” Once the door shut, the Major locked it, ensuring that he would receive a reprieve from any further harassment.

CHAPTER 27

It had been several hours since Wally had been transferred back to his room from the infirmary. Alexavier had stayed the whole time, only stepping out for a bathroom break. Enough time passed allowing the medical staff to approve visitors. Many of the others would take their turn to stay with him, keeping them both company. Jennifer could be seen every so often at Wally's bedside with her hand over his.

Beth arrived with Morkie, taking her turn to sit with them. She brought a caffeinated beverage for Alexavier. He began taking larger sips, trying to get enough caffeine into his system to keep away the sleepiness.

"Thanks."

"Has anyone else stopped by?"

Alexavier took another drink. "Everyone, but Harvey, the Major and Killus' gang. They've all been stopping back and checking in. Since I'm here, I don't imagine Harvey will."

"I wish I could tell what's wrong with him. He's always been kind of a jerk, but it's gotten worse lately."

Alexavier hesitated, thinking about the vision he had when Dr. Dennis put him under sedation. "Did I tell you about the appointment I had with the doctor not too long ago?"

"I remember you saying you had some visions or something."

"One of the visions was of Harvey and I as kids, and he was picking on me. It was as if both of us got our powers at the same time. What made it weirder was the fact that his name was Harry."

"That is odd," Beth stated. "It's unfortunate that what you saw could be a real memory, but because of Sessions, they get stripped away. I hate it every time I get one, because I know I'm going to lose my memories."

"When was the last time you had a Session?"

Beth poured herself a drink. "Oh, I'd say about a year or so."

"Is it normally that way? Back in Philadelphia, it was pretty regular. You usually wouldn't go six months without a Session."

"You never know here. It depends on what they want from you. Michael has had two Sessions within the last nine months. They're really hoping the treatments can push his powers into the superhuman territory. Only Michael and I are close to being there. The Major doesn't consider Manny, Wally, Dave, Harvey and Jennifer to be close to being classified that yet. But since they really need someone who can fly really well, the focus has been Michael first, then Wally."

Alexavier sat back in the recliner. "I wonder if they're hoping this Session will help Wally. I heard the Major doesn't like how limited his speed is."

"When we're out on missions, I never think about him doing more than his powers will allow. For the Major to expect him to do something he can't, is wrong."

"That's our beloved Major." Mike arrived, jumping in the middle of their conversation. "If you don't meet his expectations, he'll try and push you as hard, as he can to get you there or get rid of you. If you overachieve, he thinks you should do even better. Then if you're like Percy, who never misses a shot, you're expected to shoot and kill on command."

"What does Sam think?"

"It's a struggle. Sam keeps pushing back, but the Major was hired by Senator Steinberg. Sam literally has no power to change his orders. The only thing he tries to do is steer things in the direction he thinks it should go. But when you're trying to go against the greatest hero of all time, you'll have to back down, and the Major has done that a lot. How long will that go on for? It's anybody's guess."

Alexavier looked over at Wally. "I hope this isn't the beginning of lots of Sessions for Wally. Who knows what this stronger treatment may do."

"You didn't hear this from me." Mike leaned in to talk quieter. "But I think they're desperate to find a way to make Sessions productive. Most recruits don't see much improvement once they get close to the age of twenty. Most of you arrive here around eighteen years, so that leaves little room to use that machine to make improvements to your powers. The fact that you were able to handle the new treatment gave them hope they could extend these Sessions beyond where they previously thought."

"But I thought I was the exception to the rule," Alexavier said.

"Many think you are the exception," Mike stated. "But they won't know unless they attempt it on others. Wally just happened to be next in line."

"How does getting a treatment work? I mean, how does it specifically enhance our powers?" Beth wondered.

Mike rubbed his head. "You're asking the wrong person. That medical stuff is way out of my area of expertise. You have mechanical questions, I'm your guy. Even Dr. Dennis doesn't fully understand how the Sessions work. The treatment for every Session comes from experts that the complex has on staff. I'm not even sure where these experts are located, but they're the ones making the recommendations that Dr. Dennis follows. Since she doesn't fully understand it, she's been trying to look deeper into it to comprehend the details."

"I would question whether or not it's really safe for us to go through, but they've been doing these Sessions for a decade or more," Beth mentioned.

"The real question is how the Sessions affect you long-term. There is already data and even cases of recruits getting treatment and experiencing extreme side effects."

"Wasn't that what happened to the original Beacon?" Alexavier asked. "I heard she flipped out or something."

Mike slowly shook his head. "That's what the Major wants everybody to think. Personally, I think she just got to see things more clearly and didn't want to deal with all of the issues that happen around here."

"We also had a recruit who died," Beth revealed.

"Yeah. The Session didn't cause his death, but reactions to the treatment from some underlying conditions."

"How do we know that won't happen to any of us?" Alexavier motioned to Wally. "It could happen to him, and would we be able to do anything about it?"

"Let's just pray that-"

Everyone stopped, hearing a groan coming from Wally. They all jumped up to check on him. His eyes opened wide enough to look around, but he kept squinting because of the ceiling lights were so bright. Eventually, he was able to see those in the room. "What's... going on?"

"How are you feeling, Wally?" Beth inquired. "Dr. Dennis!"

"Who's Wally?"

"That's your name," Beth replied with an anxious tone while looking for the doctor.

"Oh." Wally glanced around the room. "What happened?"

Mike knelt down. "You just had a Session."

"I don't… understand."

Beth bent over. "It's okay. We're here to help. You just have to rest."

“But why do I need to rest?”

Alexavier leaned in. “Can you blink for me?”

Still with a confused look, he blinked a couple times. “Yeah.”

“Great. Now do that another fifteen to twenty times.”

Wally began to blink repeatedly, as Dr. Dennis rushed in, beginning her evaluation of him. Beth wanted to help, but Mike stopped her from interrupting them. Mike remembered glancing at Alexavier’s journal when he had his Session and that the journal had things Alexavier used to help with the after affects. They stood back, as Alexavier continued to direct the groggy hero through more exercises.

CHAPTER 28

Another morning had arrived. Mike slept well, but had to quickly complete some projects that Major Constantine had demanded. So being up early was the plan and sucking down a jug coffee was a necessity. On the agenda was an improved Com-Link, one that operates like existing mobile phone, but could jump to satellite signals for improved connections when cell towers weren't efficient or the signal to them interrupted. The disruptions of late have rendered them practically useless. Mike had an idea about what was causing the problem, and his hope was to give the Com-Links a better connection. First was to modify two devices with the same exact technology. Part of the problem was that the needed technology was in the hands of the military, but having the Major around proved beneficial with pulling strings to get access to the technology.

The worst part of inventing anything new is figuring out how the individual parts work, especially if you didn't design it. The overly confusing manual was laid out across the back of the bench. He struggled with the descriptions and notes for each individual part. After getting through less than half the parts, he could not deal with the manual anymore. He wadded it up and tossed it towards the corner of the room, landing three feet from the trashcan. "Missed again. I'm definitely not Percy."

A knock at the open door was a welcome surprise, but was even bigger when it happened to be Harvey. The disgruntled recruit strolled in, but with slight reluctance, since Mike had been such a big supporter of Alexavier.

Mike smiled, “Hey! Long time no see.”

“I want to know what’s going on.”

“Well, first of all, I’m happy that the oatmeal is keeping me regular. I found a great shampoo that-“

Harvey became quite annoyed. “You know what I mean.”

“No. I don’t. What’s your problem?”

“I have a problem with you not giving me as much help as Alexavier.”

“Correction. Your problem is you. Alexavier’s been the one to come to me consistently since he arrived here.”

“He’s been a problem since he got here.” Harvey got into Mike’s face.

Mike sat down the parts still left in his hands. “Let me state this again. The only problem since he’s been here, is you. You’ve had these issues that everyone tries to help, but we get nowhere. Then, when someone comes along who might be the next great hero, you become even more problematic. So, I should be asking you… what’s going on?”

“I am the go-to hero when it comes to catching bad guys.” Harvey became highly sarcastic. “That hasn’t changed, and it never will. I’ll be the one to bring down The Terror Tribe.”

“Killus says the same exact thing, but you don’t have a problem with him like you do with Alex.”

“You don’t give him any help.”

“He never asks for help,” Mike explained, being a bit perturbed. “Not sure I’d help him anyway, but that’s another thing.”

“So, who’s the one with the problem, if you can’t stand Killus?”

Now Mike became really annoyed. “My thinking that Killus is a jerk has nothing to do with you being a jerk.”

“Now you’re being a jerk to me.”

“I’m being honest. It’s part of my job when I’m helping any of you.”

"But you haven't been helping me, which means you're not doing your job." Harvey put his finger in Mike's face. "Now, I'm being honest."

Harvey left in a hurry, not letting Mike respond. He tilted his head back and sighed. Needing something to divert his thoughts, he reached for the coffee and took a big drink. "I think I might need more oatmeal after all this."

#

After a quick visit to the nation's capital, Sam returned early that morning, eager to get some things crossed of his list. First was the results from yesterday's Session, which meant a long journey through the complex so he could stop by Doctor Jean Dennis' office. It was unfortunate that he had to miss the Session yesterday due to an important matter in Washington, D.C., but he hurried back to check on Wally.

Doctor Dennis was at her computer, working hard at logging in various recruit information. A quick knock on the door announced Sam's arrival. She motioned for him to enter. He was eager to discuss the events he had missed. However, the doctor was first to engage in conversation. "How did things go in D.C.?"

"About as well as can be expected considering you're dealing with politicians. I'm stepping down as the head of the TFSA, the Task Force on Superhuman Affairs. It's been a rough battle over the years to have the committee members understand the importance of what we do and to not restrict those gifted with abilities, who want to fight for and help society. We do not need to be regulated by unnecessary laws. I feel the TFSA is in a good place now, and hope to have everything wrapped up in the next few weeks. That way, I can devote all of my time here. Things need to be reigned back in, even if that means taking control away from the Major."

"He's not going to like that."

"I don't care if he likes it or not." Sam carefully cradled his backpack. "The current state of things around here is not what I had ever envisioned when Project: Hero initially started. I threw the idea to the Senator who wants to talk more. How is Wally?"

"He's recovering really well. Alexavier has been quite helpful in his recovery. We may have Wally back up on duty in a few days rather than weeks."

"Impressive. We need to document all that Alex has done. It will be useful for all upcoming Sessions." Sam was reluctant, but asked, "What were the test results for Alex? I heard your message and hurried back as soon as I could."

"We received some significant results from a couple DNA testing centers, which adds to the existing data we have on Alex from when he first started in the program. This may answer some lingering questions and determine how we proceed."

"Sounds like we should continue this conversation in the Major's office."

They left immediately, still discussing more of Wally's recovery. Soon, they arrived at the Major's office, still reviewing many of the details from the Session. This brought about a close as they aimed to focus on the importance of Alexavier's test results.

Working on his own computer, the Major quickly turned off the monitor, as if he was trying to hide something. "Were you filled in on Wally's Session?

"Yes," Sam answered with an inquisitive tone. "I didn't get specifics, but I did hear it went better than planned."

The Major tossed a folder onto the front of his desk. "I've got the details so far from Dr. Dennis for your review, unless she already did. Nothing surprising, but everything is good."

Sam set his backpack against the far wall for safety. “No, she didn’t, but that’s perfect.”

The Major nodded. “How did things go with the TSFA?”

“Really well. Everything is progressing with the Task Force, but they still need to be reined in about restricting people’s use of powers. That could have a massive impact on what we can do here. I will be meeting with them again in the next few weeks to discuss some important things. Were you able to get any information from Faducia and Topher during their interrogations?”

“No.” The Major pulled out another folder. “But being low level criminals who have no connections to The Tribe, I wasn’t expecting much either. Seeing that you brought the doctor with you, I take it there’s more to this visit than just having you briefed.”

“Yes. I stopped by to see Jean, and she mentioned that the genetic test results came back for Alex. I figured you would want to hear the results.”

“Yes, I would. Please proceed.”

Dr. Dennis handed a file to the Major. “We know the genetic markers determining hero status as a Meta or Non-Meta human has been sketchy, even appearing to change from time to time, which has been confusing. I repeated Alex’s initial tests, which returned with similar results showing no Meta mutations. However, it also doesn’t show the very slight Non-Meta one either.”

“Okay.” The Major had a confused look. “Still makes no sense with his intuition and the reaction thing he does.”

Sam inquired, “What about his extensive combat skills and being able to absorb information with all that fighting knowledge?”

“That may be his brain and how he is able to process, store, recall and use the information.” The doctor reached over and turned a few pages. “It’s like how a pro-athlete learns how to handle and shoot a hockey puck or shoot baskets consistently.”

"So, I'm right about Percy and his ability to never miss a target."

"Very likely. We also have to account for muscle control, since some of Percy's weapons are extremely high powered, and he can hit each shot, even with a strong recoil."

"Would that also be muscle control from the brain?" Sam asked.

"I believe so. It is another level of hand-eye coordination skill beyond even the highest-level, pro athlete."

"So, Sessions are a definite no for Percy," the Major pondered.

"We know what Alex can do, and it's coming from the brain," Dr. Dennis reiterated. "We've been giving him regular Sessions and has not produced negative effects. In fact, he's got the strongest improvements in skills percentage from any recruit."

Sam added, "Plus, his memory retention is beyond anyone to ever sit in that chair."

"That may be true, but there could be more to the story." Dr. Dennis pulled out another folder, flipping through the pages.

"And how so?" Sam inquired.

"I took extra blood samples from Alex and sent them to several genetics experts throughout the country. Depending on the tests and how they processed the samples, they came back with different results."

"Interesting." Sam asked.

"Even with similar results, each geneticist had a slightly different interpretation. Most of them were able to duplicate my results with slight variations. None of the responses were of significance, however three reported something different."

The Major perked up. "That sounds promising."

"Two of the results showed a gene having a slight mutation. In fact, it has never been documented before."

The Major got excited. "Okay. And?"

"It's not a Meta mutation, but it's also not a Non-Meta mutation. It's something different."

Sam cautiously stated, "So he is something special."

"He very could be, especially with the results of the last tests."

"Continue," the Major instructed."

"Well, I sent two samples to one scientist at Caltech. His tests not only break down the structure, just like the others, but also the make-up of the DNA itself. You see, all DNA is made of chemical building blocks called nucleotides. These are made of three parts: a phosphate group, a sugar group and one of four types of nitrogen bases. When forming strands of DNA, nucleotides are linked into chains, with alternating the phosphate and sugar groups."

The Major sighed, "I knew you were going to lose me, but go on."

"What you need to understand is the basics of DNA first. What's stored in DNA is a code, made up of four chemical bases: adenine, guanine, cytosine, and thymine. Human DNA consists of about 3 billion bases. What's important is that more than 99 percent of these bases are the same in all of us. The order of these determines the information for what we are and how we function as an organism. It's like how letters in a certain order will form words."

Sam looked puzzled. "How do those differences matter to what's going on with Alexavier?"

"We know slight differences are common among everyone. When we notice the mutation that is the Meta and Non-Meta gene, it's very significant. The Meta mutation and Non-Meta mutation both occur at the same location, it's never in another spot. However, with Alexavier's last two test results, we saw something never documented before. One result appeared to be a different mutation than the ones we attribute to Meta or Non-Meta."

The Major became ecstatic. “So, we finally have the proof that Alexavier is what we believed all along.”

“That’s not quite as defining as you’d think.” She handed Sam the folder. “If you look at the final results that just came back, it shows that Alexavier has consistencies with the Meta gene.”

“I thought the other tests had him as a whole new super human.” The Major was highly confused and disappointed. “Then this is just a regular Meta human result.”

Sam countered, “If he’s a Meta, that would be amazing, since that means we could focus our training knowing he’s got powerful abilities.”

“Not really,” the Major argued. “Look at Ordinary Joe. He’s supposed to be one of the most powerful Meta humans according to our tests, but he has never shown any powers.”

“Maybe I can shine some light on this.” Dr. Dennis pulled out one specific print. “The images in this picture are several genes that are mutated from normal into Non-Meta and Meta human. The first is a normal gene. The second is Hank’s Non-Meta human mutation of that same gene. Next is Dave’s, Michael’s and yours, Sam. As you can see, the genes that identify a person as Meta human look exactly alike. When you look at the final picture of Alexavier’s gene and compare it to the others, you would think it was the same. Now the last two are images are a side by side of his and yours, using a high-powered electron microscope. Yours is what would be the normal Meta gene. For Alexavier’s, you can see the slight line running directly in the middle. That’s a slight split and rebuild of the crack. Meaning, the gene was changing itself into another type of gene. More importantly, it’s a new kind of Meta gene.”

Sam was speechless, but not the Major. “You’re telling us that Alex is some kind of Super Meta?”

"I can't say he's a Super Meta, but a different kind of Meta would be more accurate, at least until we can really analyze the gene itself."

"It's pretty amazing that we can find such a small anomaly in a single gene where there are so many genes in the human body," Sam pondered.

"About 20,000 of them," she clarified. "For there to be a mutation of a mutation nonetheless is unprecedented for Meta and Non-Meta. This explains why there was so much confusion when it came to his results. He is the only one to have this complicated result, making him probably the only recruit to exhibit this gene."

Sam tilted his head further and stared at the pictures. "When can we conduct more research to find an answer? I'd like to know more about his powers and any potential powers we haven't discovered yet. Outside of the uneasy feeling that he gets, I don't see any real Meta human power being utilized."

"I can't be sure how to classify it, since that feeling causes a reaction," she explained. "I've studied the workout videos and can't conclusively say it's a Meta power. If I had to say right now, his sense or feeling is a Mutate or Non-Meta kind of power."

"Will more testing clarify it?" the Major wondered, getting the pictures in his hands.

"I don't know if another test can clear that up, but it may give us a more definitive answer to his possible Meta status. Right now, we're still looking at a possible mutation, but unsure what it truly means. Again, we still have more questions than answers, when it comes to Alex."

Sam inquired, "What do we need to do next?"

"I am already in contact with the geneticists, who want more samples for testing. I'll have to get Alex back to my office again before I can proceed."

The Major instructed, "Have him report to your office as soon as possible. Thank you very much, Doctor. If I could have the room with Sam."

"Certainly." Dr. Dennis took the folders from them.

As she walked by him, Sam said, "Thanks for everything, Jean."

"You're very welcome." Once making it into the hallway, she closed the door securely.

Seeing the room was clear to talk real business, the Major asked, "Are you excited yet?"

Sam pulled out the metal briefcase and sat it on the table. "It really puts things into perspective when you look back at what everyone has been seeing with him."

"But he still has to perform. It's inexcusable to not participate in daily sparring and training."

"There's more to Alexavier than just sparring, and now Jean has confirmed it."

"Then, by what means do we determine if they are ready for action? We need a way for them to prove they can perform in the field. He hasn't been doing that."

"Not everyone is the same. We should be assessing them on a case-by-case basis, with systematic reviews and individualized action plans. Look, we're supposed to be helping these recruits. They have special powers and don't understand why. So, we promise to help them, give them purpose and set them on their own path, but I don't feel that has been happening lately."

"We're doing all we can. What more do they expect?"

Sam walked closer. "Less than ten percent of the kids who enter into this program end up succeeding. It's hard enough for the kids at the entry level of Project: Hero to graduate and come here. Of the ones who actually make it to this complex, even less than will end up making it to The United. We're not providing them with a light at the end of the tunnel. We need more teams like

The United Outcasts and what Beta Star is putting together. Because right now, they feel like they don't have anywhere to go. We are not doing our job, and things need to change."

"What about starting with the Sessions? If we are to help them, the old regimens only go so far. We are failing them by not bringing them to their full potential. This new regimen will jumpstart their development. When was the last time we produced a Meta with a high enough level of power that could go one-on-one with any of the top Tribe members?"

After opening the briefcase and extracting a large syringe filled with a strange blue liquid, he injected it into his arm. "We have a couple now."

"But where can we go with Michael or Dave or even April if we can't get them to a level worthy of their powers? How else will we do that?"

"I've watched everyone get tortured in that chair." Sam started to get emotional with anger slowing creeping up. "How far are we willing to go to accomplish our goal? The after effects are too much for some recruits. If we increase the intensity and cause more damage, how are they going to recover from it?"

"Wally has recovered much better than we anticipated. The fact that he received the stronger treatment and is almost back to his routine speaks volumes."

"I understand what we are striving for when recruits receive a Session. However, my concern is the long-term damage, either physically or mentally. We know the memory loss is unavoidable, but we're lucky that the short-term memory comes back fairly quickly. I will agree to the possibility of stronger Sessions, as long as I review Wally's charts and results first. I'll assess him to review his progress before signing off on this Program-wide dosage increase."

“I think I should inform you that Alex was present when Wally woke up. He sat with him and worked with him to help gain his memories back quicker than usual. If his techniques helped Wally recover faster, do we consider another Session for Alex?”

Sam protested, “Putting him through another Session won’t accomplish anything we’re trying to do.”

“Why wouldn’t it? Maybe it will get him out of this mood that he’s been in around here.”

Sam closed the briefcase and set it on the floor. “We don’t need to change anything with Alex or increase any powers he possesses. He’s already a top-level hero. The lingering problem is his productivity here. So, let’s have him prove that he’s worth his status at this complex.”

“And how do we do that?”

“Alexavier and I go at it one more time.”

“You mean a workout?”

“Exactly.”

The Major paused. “But why not have him go against Bobbie first? The last time you tried, it didn’t work out so well.”

“We didn’t really get a full workout because of Harvey. This one will be different. Alexavier’s diet has been modified enough that Harvey’s Brain Drain will have a no effect. I’m not taking chances this time, as Harvey will not be present for this one. That way, we can spar like any other recruit.”

“I really don’t think that is necessary. Harvey was just-”

“He was just interfering. I didn’t ask for his help, nor did I need it.” Sam picked up his backpack. “I am just being proactive, and he can sit this one out.”

“Fine.”

Sam looked back as he left the office. “I will let everyone involved know and to be ready." Although this was not one of the worst experiences with the legendary hero, the Major felt so much better to see him walk away.

After a brief stroll, Sam walked past Alexavier’s room and saw that the lights weren’t on. Knowing that he was helping with Wally’s recovery, he made Wally’s room his next destination. Once within viewing distance, Sam could see the whole group was there, except for Harvey, who stood down the hallway, mostly out of sight and quite unhappy. Sam approached, with Harvey not acknowledging his presence.

“I’m planning a workout for tomorrow morning, but you don’t need to attend.”

“Whatever.” Harvey walked away, even more disgruntled.

Letting him go to brood on his own, Sam turned his attention to the whole crew that was keeping Wally company, including Morkie, who was licking his face. Slowly making his way to the door, he smiled seeing how much love was there for a friend in need.

Bobbie was the first to see the newest visitor. “Hey, Sam!”

“Hi everyone. How are you feeling?”

Wally smiled, “Great! I can’t say I remember too much before the Session. Besides that, I feel like I could go on a mission.”

“Let’s wait and get you evaluated first,” Mike responded.

“I agree.” Sam entered the room. “The most important thing for you is to recover completely. Then we need to see how your powers have been affected, or if they’ve even been affected at all. I hear Alex has been doing a great job of helping you with your recovery.”

Wally gave Alexavier a nod and a smile. “He’s helped a lot. I would have never recovered this quickly without him.”

"We need to bottle that stuff you used on him for the rest of us," Manny requested.

Sam grinned, "I'm not sure if the doctors can do that. Any adverse side effects?"

"None that I know of," Wally replied.

"Dr. Dennis has been checking on him several times a day," Mike stated. "Anything odd has been documented in his chart. But so far, no issues. Even the nausea never happened."

Sam started nodding. "This is fantastic. I worry about you guys and those Sessions. I feel better now that you've made such progress. I really do miss being able to just stop by any time."

Wally replied, "I really appreciate your visit."

"I wanted to be here for the treatment, but had a prior obligation and a promise I needed to keep, kept me away. I'm actually here for two reasons. First was to check up on you and see how you're doing. But secondly is to let Alex know that there will be a workout in the morning, and we will be having another sparring match."

The announcement brought about an awkward moment of silence in the room. Feeling the need to break the silence, Dave spoke up. "Well, I for one can't wait. We haven't had a proper workout with any good sparring matches in a long time."

Sam acknowledged, "I'm going to change that very soon. We need to make a goal of improving, all of us. There is no better way than going against one another. Let's just say that it's going to occur more frequently. Everyone will have to participate, even Harvey and Killus' gang. Just be ready for a fight."

Alexavier replied, "Yeah. I'll be ready."

"Perfect." Sam placed his hand on Alexavier's shoulder in acknowledgment. "See you all in the morning. Make sure you get some rest."

“I will,” Wally replied.

“And if you need anything, just let me know anytime, day or night.”

“Thanks, Sam.”

They all said a goodbye, but a quiet soon followed until Sam was far enough away for them to feel comfortable enough to speak up.

Dave was itching to ask, “Dude, how are you feeling? We all know what happened the last time you two went at it.”

“Hey! You don’t have to be insensitive!” Beth exclaimed.

“I’m fine,” Alexavier assured everyone. “I guess it was gonna happen sooner or later.”

“You don’t seem too excited.” Mike noticed.

“I guess I’m just nervous because of what happened last time.”

Beth pointed out. “But that was last time. I know you’ll do awesome this time!”

“Yeah. You have another opportunity to whoop some butt,” Percy said enthusiastically. “But then again, you’re taking on the man.”

“Sam doesn’t lose,” Mike added. “He’s spent so many decades sharpening his skills. You really need to be on your game.”

Morkie barked at Mike, making Beth comment, “He doesn’t like you being so pessimistic.”

Alexavier smiled, “I’ll take that as he thinks I’ll do good.”

“We’re all behind you,” Bobbie proclaimed.

Michael added, “If there’s anyone who can bring it to him, it’s going to be you.”

“And if you don’t, I’ll have to get out of this bed and kick your tail.”

Wally’s threat brought a small grin to Alexavier’s face. Even with all the compliments and praise, it was also very evident how uncertain he was. Everyone else may be enthusiastic, but he knew that his failure wasn’t something normal. For a hero who always performed to the highest level, such a bad performance was very unusual. It was something that worried him more than anyone could see.

CHAPTER 29

At a secret location somewhere in Pittsburgh, Nib made his way through a less than hospitable neighborhood. The abandoned homes only housed squatters and some very questionable individuals. You wouldn't venture to this part of the town unless you're one of the deadliest people in the world.

Adjacent to this neighborhood was a once thriving office building. Now empty, an example of the hard, financial times from decades of poor political and economic decisions, it became the perfect location to meet and discuss less than legal activities without being watched by anyone who may question your intentions.

Finding his way to the third floor, Nib located the only room that appeared to have any inhabitants. He entered into the sight of the top members of The Terror Tribe, all gathered together. Even Cavalio and Everlorne were present, meaning something big was going to be discussed. His presence signaled the start to the meeting.

The Infamous One took a couple steps forward, putting himself in the center of the group. "It has been some time, and things are now progressing to where everyone's attention needs to be focused on the plan. Our success hinges on its execution"

“Losing Landfill hit us hard,” Natural Disaster stated. “We can't afford to keep losing our best members if we hope to succeed.”

“There are many cogs in the machine that need to work precisely for our plan to be successful. Losing Landfill wasn't expected, but it doesn't slow us down,” The Infamous One responded.

“Hopefully there are no squeaky wheels that need to be oiled,” Nib replied, eyeing the two new members. “I don't need any problems that have to be taken care of.”

The Infamous walked over to the two new partners. “Empty and Bootlegger are both to be trusted. They helped us during Landfill's mission and Natural Disaster's as well.”

“But you're forgetting the most important thing,” Nib reminded them. “Landfill got caught.”

“You may not like that fact, but it may be a blessing in disguise,” The Infamous One said.

Game Over gave a puzzled look. “How do you think that is?”

“His capture gives them hope.” The Infamous One pointed out, walking towards him. “Since they haven’t captured any of us for so long, this could give them the false sense of security that would be advantageous for us.”

“They might actually believe they can stop us,” Cavalio agreed.

“Correct,” The Infamous One agreed. “And that is where their overconfidence will work perfectly for our plan.”

Nib kept an eye on the new villains. “How does our plan involve these guys?”

Natural Disaster stated, “Empty is a unique Meta. In fact, he provides escape routes we previous didn't have.”

“Everlorne could give us coverage,” Cavalio responded.

“I can't give you that kind of escape route. I can manipulate objects, but only so much. My vanishing is only good for covering my escapes.”

“Bootlegger can fly. We all know how hard it's been to keep someone on the team who can fly.”

“The real question is, can we trust them enough to have them work this close to us. We've never brought in anyone from the outside to be this involved with our plans. They're standing here listening to us and could turn around and snitch. I've gutted people for getting too close,” Nib brought out the crimson energy blade from his hand, almost as a threat.

“Wait a second. I thought we were cool!” Empty exclaimed.

“You are,” The Infamous One assured. “The rest of the team needs to be informed of your cooperation.”

“They have my approval,” Natural Disaster stated. “They had my back. Now I have theirs.”

Game Over stood next to Natural Disaster. “If this big, ugly mountain of a Meta says they're okay, then I'll let them into the clubhouse.”

Natural Disaster gave his cohort a dirty look, as Nib continued to stare at the new associates and wave his energy blade. “I'm not so easy to win over. You only get stabbed in the back for so many times before you do it to them first. If you all are good with it, I'll agree for the moment, but they better play nice, because if they screw us over, I won't hesitate to gut them.”

Cavalio added, "We can always have the fun of separating their limbs before they lose their heads."

“Let's give them a chance first,” Everlorne responded. “We were all in their shoes once.”

"You're no fun anymore. When did the big bad magician get soft?" Cavalio queried.

“I'm not. I'm present in this world and living by these rules. Here, I can only do what is best for the team and myself.”

“What do you mean here? You're not including that magical place you float away to when you're not with us?” Game Over poked.

“What I do when I'm away from here is none of your concern.”

The Infamous One put his hand on Everlorne's shoulder, hoping to calm him down. “We all decided a long time ago to not let our time as a member of The Terror Tribe affect our personal lives, if at all possible.”

Game Over apologized, “Sorry, man. I didn't know it bugged you that much.”

“It doesn't,” Everlorne mumbled softly, not to be heard.

“Well then, are we in agreement, that Empty and Bootlegger are a part of our team?” The Infamous One looked around to a general consensus. All but one. Nib was still unsure. “How about this, my friend. I give you my guarantee that they will be loyal to each and every person in our extensive network of Tribe members, or I will personally hold them so you can carve them open.”

The thought brought a smile to Nib's face. “Agreed.”

“Perfect,” The Infamous One grinned. “Our plan has been set in motion, and we are almost at the finish line. Let us execute the final phase.”

CHAPTER 30

The morning of the workout arrived. For Sam, these were usually a passing thought if it ever came to mind, but this one was special. It actually meant something. A recruit that had been deemed the golden child to some, was provided a chance to redeem himself. In many ways, the success of Project: Hero hinged on this physical encounter. Everything they were trying to accomplish in training young recruits to become heroes, including the progress they have made since the inception of this program, could have a major setback if another failure were to occur. For the first time in a long time, he was anxious.

He wouldn't have to go it alone. A buzz at his door signaled a visitor. Unlocking the door, he was pleased to see Mike outside.

"Wondering if you need some company this morning?" Mike queried.

Sam headed back to finish gathering his gear. "You're always welcome to join me, anytime you feel like it."

"You have a plan in mind for this morning?"

"Not really. What I normally hope is that we both engage in some kind of physicality and see how it goes. Last time was pretty rough. No contact, and he backed away. I can't judge someone on their skills if I don't see any."

Mike walked closer. "All I can say is, when he needs to be at his best, he is. I know these workouts with you show how they've progressed. But for Alex, it's not everything. There's more to him. We just need to focus on the part where he overachieves."

"That doesn't happen during the workouts." Sam zipped up the bag and threw it over his shoulder.

"Yeah, but it does happen in the real world, when lives are on the line. Maybe that's what we should be focusing on."

"Let's go meet the Major." The wheel in Sam's head began to turn, as they left the room, and the lights dimmed. Maybe this evaluation would provide better insight into a recruit he's hoping would become the next great superhero.

#

For Alexavier, his morning was an early one as well. He had no problem getting to sleep last night, but got up early when his mind kept racing about the upcoming workout. Workouts never really made Alexavier nervous, but this one did, especially after what happened with his last encounter with Sam. Since then, Alexavier had been focusing all of his energy on finding The Terror Tribe. Now he needed to focus harder than ever on using his combat skills.

Putting together his workout gear, it was the standard routine of throwing gloves in his bag. Pile in the clothes, and one by one, the boots. But after setting the second one inside, the first was no longer there. A moment of confusion was cleared up when the boot appeared on the desk behind him. Upon grabbing it and turning back to place it next to the other, that one had vanished as well. "I have to get ready."

Jennifer couldn't stop giggling, her body still very see-through. "I'm helping."

"How's unpacking my bag helping?"

She tried grabbing the other. "I'm keeping you busy."

"Still not sure that's helping."

"Are you thinking about the workout?"

"Actually, I wish I was already there."

"Then let's go!" Jennifer flew off threw the wall, never looking back, leaving him to finish gathering his gear.

Before too long there came a knock on the door. Standing in the doorway were Beth, Dave, Bobbie and Manny. "Come in, guys. You're all up pretty early."

"I wouldn't miss the big rematch for the world!" Manny stated exuberantly.

"You're going to take down Sam!" Dave exclaimed.

"I hope so. Where's Michael?"

Beth ventured over to see if he was ready. "He went to get Wally, as long as he's cleared to move around."

"We don't know what Dr. Dennis said?"

"I think Percy was supposed to find out if he can go, but you know how he sometimes forgets to ask on purpose and just does what he wants, meaning going to the range to shoot."

Bobbie smiled, "For a guy with such a hard, outer shell, Percy can be a softy."

"You're blushing," Beth poked.

"Hey! What can I say? I like my guys with a rough outside and a soft inside."

Alexavier brought his bag over and sat it on the floor to join them. "Are you guys dating?"

"I don't know what we are. I guess you could call it that. I don't think we've actually been on a real date."

"I thought we weren't allowed to date while we're in here," Alexavier queried.

"It doesn't matter," Beth stated. "The Major's so clueless, he wouldn't even know if you guys had gotten engaged and were planning a wedding."

Manny added, "He cares about planning, but only when it comes to the next mission."

"Speaking of the Major, should we get going?" Alexavier moved closer to the door. "I know how the Major frowns on people being late."

Dave joked, "Personally, I think he likes to frown, and anyone being late gives him an excuse to do it."

The gang began exit, but Beth slowed up near Alexavier. "You're going to do great. I know you will." He grinned, with her enthusiasm being infectious and followed her out the door.

Upon arriving at the W.A.R. Room, Percy and Michael were already there, having pushed Wally in his wheelchair. They were resting comfortably after finding a place to occupy on the steps by Wally, who was dressed in more comfortable clothing. Anytime a workout was scheduled, all heroes in training needed to have their gear on or in hand. Having a recent Session provided Wally with a little bit of a reprieve that he found most welcome.

Beth went to sit next to Wally. "They let you come!"

"That's what I hear, at least what Percy said."

Percy clarified, "Actually, he wouldn't stop yapping at us to bring him until we were pushing him down the hallway. I got sick of his whining."

"I got you to bring me here."

Percy rolled his eyes. "And I'm starting to regret it."

Entering shortly after was Killus and his crew, minus Dwayne, which was starting to become the norm. Their usual disregard for everyone else could be felt with glares and laughs at anyone and anything they could mock. The others did their best to restrain themselves, but you could see Percy ready to put his fist through Killus' face.

The mood changed once Sam and the Major finally emerged through the doors, both with a very business-like demeanor. Jonathon lagged behind, taking care of some business with Dirk of The Elitesmen Guard before joining everyone inside. Major Constantine went to the table located near the front and began displacing folders and paperwork. Sam placed his bag and briefcase in front of the table, giving a quick glance back to the attendees who had arrived. “I don’t see Dwayne.”

The Major sighed from having to hear the same thing every workout or meeting. “Let me get someone to bring him here.”

“I can go,” Jonathon offered.

Sam halted him. “We don’t have time to deal with Dwayne’s issues. That should have happened a long time ago.” Sam’s look at the Major made for an awkward moment.

Jonathon broke the tension by adding, “Let’s get him in to meet with us. Maybe we need to find out why he doesn’t feel like participating.”

“It doesn’t matter why,” the Major retorted. “If he’s a part of this team, he’s going to be participating.”

Mike came over, overhearing the conversation. “Obviously not. If he doesn’t want to be here, why are we putting the effort into training him. I’m sure there’s a dozen young kids wanting to be here and getting the chance to fulfill a life-long dream of training to be the next Patriot Warrior or Time Bender. We just need to determine if he’s even interested anymore.”

“Hard to change a mind if you’re not willing,” Jonathon stated.

“Maybe he’s having doubts about something. He came here pretty motivated, but not so much lately,” Mike recalled.

“If we can’t change that, we should really consider what his future will be with us.” Sam left the comment simmer in the Major’s head and turned to officially start the workout. “Good morning. I’d like to start with various updates. But first, it is a very welcome sight to see Wally up and around. I know we had you go through a much tougher Session, so your attendance today is fantastic." Wally smiled and received a plethora of support from those who cared. Killus and his gang, on the other hand, couldn't care less, making comments as April shied away.

"I hear that you've recovered pretty much all your memories without any losses, which is a huge barrier to overcome. Dr. Dennis informed me that you are improving physically, but still showing some signs of pain and fatigue. Her written recommendation is continued rest with a follow up visit with her in a few days.

"I'm fine. Really."

Sam shut down any hopes of getting back to doing hero stuff. "Sorry, but I do not want to take the risk that this attempt to gain an increase in your power will put yourself or someone else at risk. That being said, Wally's Session was a huge success, as his recovery has been ahead of schedule. I would like to thank Alexavier for sharing some of the techniques that have helped him in the past, to recover sooner than expected with his own Sessions. I believe Dr. Dennis will be documenting and implementing these for all future Sessions." She nodded in agreement.

"I'm sure you have all heard about the recent Tribe robberies. Well, we have a few details to share. It's not much, but here's what we know. First, regarding the heist in Washington. Lucky for us it was nearby. We were able to engage and bring down Landfill thanks to Alexavier. Landfill has been going through standard interrogations, and has not provided any information yet. Empty and Bootlegger were the accomplices, but escaped with a sizable amount of money. They have stolen larger amounts before, but only focused on a smaller and much older financial institution."

Bobbie wondered, “Were they targeting the bank because of it being old? Maybe a small and safer heist was what they wanted.”

“We cannot confirm that,” the Major added.

“But it does sound logical,” Sam admitted. “It makes sense with the second bank that was targeted in Pittsburgh. Reports we have received from authorities indicate the bank had similar security measures for its size and age. Bootlegger and Empty struck this bank as well, but with a new partner, Natural Disaster.”

Wally commented, “From one Tribe member to another.”

“Yeah, but they ain’t Tribe,” Percy pointed out.

“Maybe not then. But if this was some kind of initiation, they could be now.” Mike’s thought had Sam contemplating.

The Major countered, “Or they could be used as pawns. Now that they are not needed, we may be finding a couple of Meta bodies discarded in a ditch.”

“I’ve never known the Tribe to kill their own people,” Sam stated.

“Have you ever found a body?” the Major asked very aggressively.

“No.”

“They’re just good at hiding their handy work.”

Jonathon interjected, “I think that’s a stretch.”

With another dose of attitude, the Major reiterated, “Again, have you ever found a body? Dynamic and The United got a message a few years ago about several of their ranks wanting to defect. Cataract contacted us directly. He was willing to disclose the location of several hideouts, until communications stopped. No one has seen him since.”

“He could have gone underground,” Sam argued. “You couldn’t guarantee his safety. If The Infamous One found out, he’d have to hide, or who knows what might happen.”

“He’s a big boy. If you can handle doing The Tribe business, don’t decide to double-cross them.”

Annoyed with the Major, and looking to get the updates back on track, Sam sifted through some paperwork. "Okay. Let's get down to business. Due to Wally's impressive recovery, we will be discussing the future of these Sessions. You are all aware of the limited progress recently, specifically after receiving enough of Sessions and reaching your late teens. After we review the data surrounding Wally's recovery and potential increase in his abilities, considerations will be given to determine if future Sessions will follow this new regimen."

Jonathon asked, "Has there been any thought about comparing Wally's and Alex's recent results with the ones from their past?"

Dr. Dennis moved to the front. "Absolutely. That will happen, although it may take a bit of time. There will be a lot of data to review from both cases. We didn't really know what the numbers meant years ago. Now that we have the results from the last two Sessions, we are hoping to discover new information to make better informed decisions moving forward."

"Thank you, doctor." Sam took center stage again. "A number of you should be getting assignments shortly for a recon mission. A source has come forward providing intel on what appears to be Terror Tribe business dealings. Operating at such a high level of criminal activity and continue to be so elusive, we know there is a network of supporters across various areas of corporate and legal America. Candidates to go on this recon will depend on the needs of the mission. Sharpen your skills and stay ready."

"I will be compiling the schedules and teams and will be informing those involved with your assignments very shortly," the Major added.

Sam nodded. "I have one other update. The aim of our enhanced Session with Wally was to refine his powers and evolve them for faster speeds. One of our deficiencies has been having a fast intercept and engagement for those heroes who can fly. We have Michael and April, but both of you are new and inexperienced with your flight capabilities. While we work to make you into top-level flyers, we are also considering transferring in a couple other recruits that may suit our needs to fill this void."

"We are looking into candidates as we speak," the Major stated. "We will let you know if there are new additions to the complex shortly."

Looking through his papers one last time, "I don't think there is anything else. Well, I think it is time for the workout to begin." Sam placed everything on the table and pulled off his jacket. The heroes scrambled to the steps to grab a good viewing seat. Alexavier paused to allow everyone to get settled. Suddenly, that funny, awkward feeling overwhelmed him, screaming in his head. He spun around, using a backhand swing to knock away the arm reaching for him and pushed Sam off to a safe distance. Sam turned around and charged, hoping to keep Alexavier off balance. During the previous workout, Sam conducted the exercise like a real fight and attacking aggressively. Since Alexavier was able to keep his distance, the plan for this encounter was to keep him close, so he would have to engage physically.

Alexavier kept thinking to himself to be aggressive and take the initiative. Over and over again, he ran it through his mind. But when it came to taking the fight to Sam, Sam was the one who pushed forward, even able to get his hands on Alexavier's shoulders, grabbing a handful of his hooded sweatshirt. They jockeyed for position, with Sam doing the bulk of the forceful tugging. Alexavier continued to keep his balance, not to be forced down or into a compromising situation. Unfortunately for him, Sam's strength was so much greater, that he was able to gradually push him towards the wall. Wanting to avoid being confined, Alexavier quickly jerked Sam around, switching their positions. But the savvy veteran used this momentum to twirl his opponent back again, placing him tight against the wall. Instinctively, Alexavier kicked up his legs, planting his feet and shooting forward. The force sent Sam tumbling back to the ground, pulling Alexavier with him. But before he could get caught on the ground, Alexavier flipped over Sam, throwing his body away and clear from Sam's control.

Sam rolled to his hands and knees, eyeing his prey, but he stood his ground. With a slight grin, Sam kicked his feet to get up quickly and shot forward, reaching to get his hands on any part of Alexavier, but was only fortunate to grab one of Alexavier's pant legs. To avoid being contained, Alexavier shifted his arm under Sam's free arm, lifting up and twisting Sam away to land him on his back. Still within range to try another attack from the ground. Sam pulled his legs to wrap around one of Alexavier's. Having enough leverage, Sam squeezed as hard as he could to hold tight, hoping to haul his opponent down with him. Unfortunately, Alexavier's balance and counter fighting skills had him defending the grappling hold, twisting his body and sliding his leg to safety.

Sam rolled quickly to his stomach and leaped at the legs, which were his closest target. Alexavier kicked his legs back, dropping down onto Sam's upper body with his chest and negating any chance of Sam gaining control. But having a limb within reach, Sam grabbed onto Alexavier's arm and reached around with his other, going for the head to pull him closer. Alexavier did the same, locking them together to wrestle for position. Sam's power was greater than Alexavier could counter, allowing Sam to pull the young hero towards him and lifted into the air. With Alexavier's legs dangling, he pulled one up, planting his foot on Sam's stomach to push up. Dropping back down, he rolled back, taking Sam with him. Once Alexavier hit the ground, he kicked as hard as he could, throwing Sam off and onto his back.

The action brought excitement to the spectators, who were on edge especially knowing how the previous encounter turned out. Sam could sense the change in the room and scrambled back to his feet. He felt rejuvenated as this positive interaction reinforced that this fight with this program's next superstar was exactly what was needed.

Alexavier waited, forcing his heels back to brace for the next, inevitable collision. Sam didn't disappoint, charging towards him, using his incredible power and strength. Alexavier took the collision solidly to his chest, extending a foot back to slow them both. Just as their speed slowed, Sam adjusted his feet to generate some leverage and thrust Alexavier around and towards the floor. After landing on top, Sam placed his body squarely on Alexavier's upper torso, to not give any room for separation. Before Sam could restrict him, Alexavier swung his legs upward and placed them around Sam's head. Sensing the possibility of getting caught in a hold of some kind, Sam attempted to pull back, but Alexavier rolled the other direction. Sam was pulled with him, rolling over Alexavier and on his back. Being at a disadvantage on the ground, Sam reached for Alexavier's body hoping to gain physical control and maintain close proximity. Rather than being pulled back into a secured grasp, Alexavier popped up to alleviate the pressure and stay clear of any submission holds.

This positive engagement and interaction gave Sam hope for a real test of Alexavier's skills. His expression began showing a stronger look of determination to keep his counterpart close. Sam circled with an emphasis to have his arm within reach, forcing Alexavier to use his hands to keep from getting corralled. Sam's strength, along with a quick grab and death grip on Alexavier's arm had the recruit spin off. Sam kept with him, able to wrap both arms around his upper body and haul him up into the air. Upon being lifted, Alexavier hooked his foot outside and around Sam's leg, causing Sam to stumble. As he failed to maintain his vertical base, Sam dropped down, working hard to keep control. Once they landed on the floor, Alexavier used the impact to distribute his weight squarely onto Sam. The pressure loosened the grip, allowing Alexavier to slide an arm through, breaking the locked arms and giving a chance to squeeze free. But Sam under hooked the closest arm, following Alexavier backing up. Feeling a bit of leverage, Alexavier used the outstretched reach, grabbing to twist his body quickly, throwing Sam off.

Sam hopped up from one knee, anticipating a follow up, but his opponent stood in a defensive posture. He reached for Alexavier once again, looking to pull him into a closer physical confrontation. Alexavier moved to the side, sweeping his legs around to find a more advantageous position. Not wanting to give him a second to evade, Sam rolled with him, but Alexavier pulled away, backing up to gauge the threat of the next charge. Sam's persistence to stay on his opponent put Alexavier back on his heels. Just stopping for a split second gave Sam the opportunity to stand up and rush forward, locking into a test of upper body strength. Alexavier was no match for Sam's huge power, with Sam driving them away from their viewers and onto the open floor. Any attempt to wiggle free was thwarted by the hero's legendary strength, making Alexavier adjust his position ever so slightly to insert his arms inside Sam's. With slight control, Alexavier's arms were now putting pressure to move his bigger opponent. Sam realized he was losing his upper hand and tried to readjust. The split-second release of his grip gave Alexavier the chance to pull down on Sam, freeing himself from the strong clench. A fast reach to not lose distance had Alexavier evade again, pushing Sam to the side. Sam turned quickly, thrusting a hand out, but having no success to keep close to his opponent. His frustration deepened as he took a last desperate leap to grab any part of his elusive target, but Alexavier quickly dodged, sending Sam face first into the ground.

Slowly, Sam got up to his hands and knees. He pushed forward, waving his arm to grab a leg. Alexavier easily dodged the attempt, adding more to Sam's frustration. Using that as a motivation, Sam's next leap was more aggressive, backing Alexavier further, but still forcing Sam to reach desperately. Every wave of the arm came with a jump and stretch, but Alexavier's superior swiftness allowed him to continually evade each swipe. Having no chance to get his fingers on his opponent, Sam rushed toward him with as much force his muscles could drive his legs. Alexavier backed away, doing the same with each subsequent attempt, putting them at a stalemate.

After enough attempts at some kind of physical confrontation and getting almost nowhere, Sam finally stopped. Alexavier crouched down, ready for more and waited, but nothing happened. The Major could see the disappointment on Sam's face and raced over to Alexavier. "Why aren't you fighting back?"

"I'm sorry. I…I-"

"Sorry isn't good enough!"

The outcome of the sparring match was disappointing to almost everyone, creating a very tense environment. It was made worse with the Major berating Alexavier publicly with no consideration of how it looked. Seeing a need to divert the attention away from the Major's unnecessary outburst, Mike shouted, "Everyone is excused!"

Killus and crew bolted, never looking back. Although April slowed down to glance back with concern for Alexavier. With guilty look, her eyes focused back to the exit and caught Killus giving her a death stare. She hurried to leave, bowing her head and squeezing around Killus as he tried to block her path through the doorway. Everyone else waited, even Harvey. As much Harvey couldn't care about his complex adversary, something had him glued to the verbal beat down. His expression was one of slight indifference, which was unusual for his feelings towards Alexavier.

Wanting to take a moment to process and assess the workout, Sam hurried to gather his gear. But before he could leave, Mike pulled him aside. "I know this didn't work out quite the way you wanted-"

"At this point, I am not sure what to think. I just want him to give me a challenge. I thought the first couple of tries might prove differently. But by the end, he was still waiting for me to make the first move. Granted, he didn't run away this time, but there's still no initiative. I thought shifting away from throwing punches to grappling would change things. I don't know what he's waiting for and why he's just reacting to my moves. He just needs to initiate more."

Mike kept an eye on the Major. "Like I said before, he might not show what he can do here, but he has performed when it counts."

Sam sighed, "I get it, but should we take into account his lack of performance?"

Mike walked with Sam. "How does he perform when he's faced with a bad guy threatening him... or threatening Beth?" Mike motioned toward the Major. "You should stop him."

Sam paused, noticing Alexavier getting an earful. There was no need for the degrading language being thrown at Alexavier, so Sam brushed himself off and marched over to provide a reprieve. "Okay. I'm sure Alexavier feels bad enough already. Yelling at him is not going to be helpful."

"Well, I don't know how else to get through to him!" the Major exclaimed.

Sam motioned with his hand. "Why don't you head on out, and we will talk to you later, okay?"

With a defeated look on his face, Alexavier nodded and grabbed his bag to leave, not waiting for anyone to join him.

Both the Major and Sam had frustrated looks on their faces, but it was the Major who was really boiling over. "I'm not sure if he can get it through that head of his what it means to do well in here! The only thing he seems to be aiming for is failure!"

"Yes," Sam agreed. "There's an issue that we need to figure out."

"How hard is it to figure out? If he can't prove he should be here, then he shouldn't!" The Major's voice echoed throughout the W.A.R. Room for everyone to hear.

"You should keep your voice down." Sam stared at the Major, but it had little effect on his tone and volume.

"Maybe if he hears how upset we are, he'll realize how much of a mistake he's making! How else are going to get through to him?"

Sam folded his arms. "I don't know, but discouraging him is not the answer."

"Maybe you're asking the wrong question."

The Major's continued lack of compassion, as well as lack of respect offended Sam. He grabbed his bag and stormed out, which really gave the Major no satisfaction. The rest of the recruits left, pushing Wally out the door.

CHAPTER 31

Trying to take your mind off something can be difficult, especially when you can't change your environment. Alexavier roamed the halls, hoping to find something that could distract him. As much as he enjoyed the company of Beth, Dave or even Mike, he didn't feel like talking, so he tried to avoid everyone. Even the few acquaintances he did see, he steered away from them. After one full lap of the complex, he finally settled on April's usual hiding spot. It seemed to provide her with some kind of solitude, so he thought he'd give it a try.

Ducking down the corridor, he made sure no one saw him enter. April had found sanctuary in the shadows of this corridor where the light couldn't reach. Having a couple access doors that were recessed into the wall provided room to lean back and not be seen. He let out a big sigh, feeling down over the results of the workout. He bowed his head, letting the silence drown out his thoughts.

After what seemed like an eternity, April ducked into the corridor, only to stop once she saw him in her place. April hesitated, not sure what to do. That's her spot. No one is ever in her spot. But Alexavier didn't flinch, even when he heard her inching toward him. She paused, waiting to see if he heard her enter. Alexavier did. "You shouldn't be here."

"But this is my spot."

"No. I mean Killus won't like you being around me."

"But this is where I like to be."

Alexavier didn't want to find another place to drown in his negativity. Really, he would have preferred to be alone, but maybe having another person who is trying to separate themselves from the real world might be what he needed right now. “Can I stay?”

April hesitated, never having had someone sitting in her spot. He noticed her staying back, so he moved over. April quickly planted herself next to him on the floor, taking back the property she truly cherished. After settling in, an awkward silence ensued. The only sounds came from the random person who happened to need access to the outside hallway. April had these puppy dog eyes and kept looking over at him and then turning back. After several glances, she finally broke the ice. “Thank you for sitting with me.”

Something in her words broke through the rock-hard shell he had put up. “I just wanted somewhere to get away, and you always liked it here. I really needed some space to think. After doing so well and capturing a couple of Tribe members, I couldn't even take on Sam in a friendly workout.”

“But you do so much better than I do. I can never beat anyone in a workout.”

April's words brought Alexavier back to reality. He's had so much success in such a short time. Even the failures he had weren't anywhere near what she's endured. Realizing that no matter how bad things were for him, there was always someone else who had it worse. Clearly April was dealing with much more than he was.

He stood up, feeling bad. “I can help you train. I know Killus won’t like it, but I'll do whatever I can to help you.”

April hesitated, afraid of what might happen if Killus found out, but she really wanted to have a real connection to someone who wasn’t going to threaten her if she did something they didn’t like. However, it was that fright that held her back. “I… I don’t know. I have a lot of homework. They gave me homework to do, but I really don’t feel like doing it.”

“I hate homework too.” Alexavier looked to open up with her. “What do you have to do?”

“Something about laws. The Major said I should know them for when I’m fighting The Tribe.”

“It’s not very fun, but we should know them.” Alexavier paused, thinking that he had his own homework to do, but it might mean more to help someone in need. “I’m not the best at homework, but if you need any help, just ask.”

Alexavier slowly walked to the hallway, stopping to allow a cart being pushed pass by. Before he could leave, a petite voice from behind said, “Thank you.” He turned back and gave a nod and a smile before vanishing from sight. She might be alone, but at least for now, she started to feel like she was welcomed. For the first time in a long time, she started to smile.

Focusing on homework might get him to get back into the swing of things, so Alexavier stopped by his room and grabbed a few notebooks before heading to the library, including research he was doing on the mysterious Death Blossom. Being that Project: Hero is essentially a school, but with physical training and development for those with special abilities, there was still the need for learning. Most of the recruits didn’t spend much time researching, so the library was usually deserted. That was the case for today, with the exception of the librarian. He scanned the room, trying to motivate himself to dive into his homework, but his mind continued to wander. Focusing his attention on studying was going to be an issue. Unless he could concentrate, sitting in a room with thousands of books of words and information wasn’t going to do him any good. What he needed was something different, so he decided to leave.

Traversing the complex, nowhere in particular seemed to be calling to him. Even seeing Killus and his crew walking by, making rude comments didn't faze him from continuing on his path. Keeping a cool head, he made them disappear behind him down the long hallway. It wasn't until he walked past the W.A.R. Room and looked inside that he felt like it was a place that he needed to be.

The W.A.R. Room was a place of accomplishment and a place of torment that provided a plethora of emotions. The lights were on, which is normal during standard, operating hours, but nobody was inside. It was usually hit or miss if somebody was going to be working on their training. Alexavier walked inside, looking over the cavernous, empty room. Just located inside the entryway were the raised stairs used for bleachers and a couple of tables set up for when Major Constantine needed somewhere for his paperwork. The only way you could tell that the W.A.R. Room had more to it than just walls was by the outline of the various doors and plates that adorned the walls, ceilings and floors. It was what was behind and underneath that interested Alexander the most.

Having been given permission to use the obstacle course whenever he wanted, a tap of the touchscreen pulled up the menu where he selected the obstacle course. A collection of mechanical noises, as well as some typical clanging and banging, brought up the extended wooden posts that populated most of the room.

His books and homework instantly became insignificant with the sight of the challenge before him, so he set them on the table. With a sigh and shake of his arms, he hopped onto the first post. Staring across the field of posts, the world around him began to disappear. The last row of posts against the far wall became his primary focus.

With a heavily determined look on his face, Alexavier leaped forward, pushing off as hard as possible to hop on one foot as the challenge has always required. Each post had him gain more momentum to where he could push harder and jump farther, bypassing posts in the process. The end came quickly, with a heavy plant of his foot. A quick twist of his body and a kick off the wall jettisoned Alexavier back toward the finish line. Suddenly, the ceiling opened wide releasing the massive metal hammers that swung at different intervals. As he had done before, the direct route was preferred plan of action. Racing at full speed, he gained enough distance to bypass the first hammer with a slight lean, but his trajectory forced him towards a collision course with the second one. To avoid contact, Alexavier flipped sideways in the opposite direction the hammer was traveling. A stretch of his arm secured a point of grip to allow a forward arch back to his feet, still carrying plenty of momentum. The last hammer was timed so that it interfered with Alexavier's path. But rather than to try and avoid it like the previous hammer, he vaulted high, pushing off the top of the hammer and contorting his body for a sharp, quick landing. Once he dropped down to the last post, a steady posture left him just inches from the passing hammer that blew the hair in front of his face.

Unknown to him was a familiar face, staying out of sight, but viewing the event. Jonathon took in the spectacular display, but quickly scurried down the hall when Beth turned the corner, heading his way.

Having completed the course, he let the feeling of satisfaction and accomplishment settle in. Even blazing through the dangers and landing with the confidence that made him believe he could do whatever he put his mind to, there was still the nagging feeling making him doubt himself from the less than stellar performance earlier. Having no answer to explain the inconsistency, Alexavier heaved a big sigh and stepped off to the floor and grabbed his stuff.

As he stood facing the posts with his books and folders in hand, Beth happened to walk by the W.A.R. Room entrance with Morkie in hand. Seeing her close friend just standing and staring made her pause. Curious as to why he hadn't moved, she placed Morkie on the floor, who ran up and jumped on Alexavier's legs.

Beth strolled up to look out on the sea of posts with him. "Hi."

"Hi."

"Are you thinking about taking a run at the course?"

"I just did."

"How did you do?"

"I don't know the time, but it felt good doing it."

Beth leaned in, nudging his arm as Morkie started hopping up, wanting some attention. Alexavier leaned over picking up the young pup. After a couple licks on the check, he started to smile.

"I've done so well when I've been in this room, only to fall short when I'm against Sam."

Beth rubbed his back. "It's okay. Everybody has challenges when they first get here. You've only been here for a month or so. It takes time. Everyone has struggled and had to overcome different obstacles, like this course. Maybe just like you completed this obstacle course, you need to show everyone why you deserve to be here. I know the workout wasn't the result you were hoping for, but we all believe in you."

"Except for Harvey, the Major and maybe even Sam."

"Screw Harvey! If he doesn't want to be a team player, he doesn't have to be on our team. If it comes down to picking who's to be on my team, I pick you. The Major can just kiss my butt! And as far as Sam goes, I'm sure he's on your side, just like the rest of us."

Knowing Beth was in his corner brought a certain level of satisfaction that was reinforced by a few more licks on the cheek from Beth's cute, little ball of fur. Alexavier smiled, which only enticed the puppy to lick some more, and Beth to giggle. Seeing his mildly improved disposition, she inquired, "Are you doing okay?"

"Yeah. I'm good. Thank you."

A grin occupied Beth's face. "Did you want to go get a snack? Something sweet would be great right now."

"I could go for that. Will we get something for Morkie?"

Beth nodded. "Oh, Morkie always gets something, even if he has to beg, which is so cute. He lays his head on his paws and gives me those big, sad eyes. How can you refuse those sad eyes?"

"I guess treats for everyone?"

"Treats for everyone!" Beth's excitement had Morkie wagging his tail hard enough to hit Alexavier in the nose. The desire to wash away the negative atmosphere with treats came with a little bit of puppy love and some smiles.

CHAPTER 32

Taking a break for a change was nice, but wasn't enough to squash his feeling of failure. He still couldn't shake it, and didn't know how to. For once, Alexavier wasn't the dominant opponent. Back in Philadelphia, at the lower level of Project: Hero, he was undefeated at 131-0 in combat exercises. With both workouts against Sam not having a final outcome, he felt like he was 0-2. After taking some time to let things settle and contemplate what might be next, he decided to visit someone who might have a different perspective to the recent events.

The lights were on in Mike's room, meaning he was hard at work on something important. Alexavier pressed the buzzer and waited to be let in. After getting no response, he knocked on the door, which got Mike's attention to let him in. "Sorry. I had my headphones on. What brings you to this part of the dungeon?"

Alexavier followed Mike into his room. "I don't know. I guess I'm just trying to figure things out after I failed again with Sam."

"At least it's not the worst performance you've had."

Mike's attempt at a joke fell flat. "Not by much. I don't get it. I really tried to push myself. But every time I attempted some kind of move, it felt like I was standing in quicksand."

"You mean like you couldn't move?"

"No. It's hard to explain." Alexavier started to fiddle with some of Mike's tools. "I guess, it's like I wanted to, but I couldn't."

"Was there something holding you back?"

"Maybe. I don't know. I really tried to stay in there with him and not back away. I did that the first time and really wanted to change that. Something kept pushing at me, as we fought, to not get caught rather than to catch him."

"Interesting." Mike could see Alexavier struggling. "What did you feel when Sam jumped you from behind?"

"I had that feeling I usually get, so I reacted. Then when we were face-to-face, everything felt, I don't know, normal."

"Did you want to engage Sam or go after him?"

"Kind of. I mean I wanted to, but for some reason I just couldn't move my feet."

"Like they were stuck to the floor?"

"No. More like they wouldn't listen to me."

Mike sat down the tools in his hands and leaned against his workbench. "That's weird. I've never known you to be sick, so I don't think you have something affecting your brain. I don't think there's an infection or anything. The only thing I can think of would be something psychological or some kind of outside stimuli that's affecting you."

"I was pretty nervous both times."

"Were you ever that nervous before?"

"The first couple of times I had combat exercises, I was kind of nervous, since I had never done it before."

"Did you freeze up then as well?"

"No. I mean I was more cautious to begin with, but more so nervous."

Mike scratched his scruffy beard. "Hmm… and there's been no other times that you were frozen?"

Alexavier paused and thought really hard. “There’s the one time with Dave, but it wasn’t like I froze up. It was more like hesitation. Once Dave punched me in the shoulder, I ended up taking him down and beating him pretty good.”

“Speaking of beat downs, I remember when you were back in Philadelphia, and you took on the New York complex recruits. You tore through everyone! It didn’t matter who they were, including Hank. At the time, Hank was considered one of the top recruits coming out of that campus. You sure did give him a whooping that day!”

“Yeah. He was mad.”

“I think you were the first person to beat him.”

“I did it twice. We fought again a year later, just before he came up here.”

“That was your second win against him?”

Alexavier smiled, “Beat him worse than the first time.”

“That might explain why he was so ornery when he got here. I wonder if that’s why he hangs out with Killus. There’s always so much hate around Killus. Killus probably used that hate to lure him into his little gang.”

“I can see why they would get along, if he was always that angry.”

“Actually, he wasn’t. When he was down in New York, he was cocky, but not like now. With his ego and how you beat him the way you did, I can see how he ended up this way. He really thought he was unbeatable, especially if no one could use their powers in the combat exercises. The best about you is that your fighting expertise is not part of your powers. It’s just your skills. That’s why you excel when it comes to any kind of hand-to-hand combat.”

“But why can’t I perform like that now with Sam?”

“That’s the million-dollar question.” Mike patted the young hero on the shoulder. “Look, I’ve made it known that when it really counts, you’re there for everyone. You’ll get the job done. You’ve proven it time and time again. I don’t know how much that does to change things, but we’ll see. All I can say is that you need to go and relax, chill out somewhere and hang with your friends."

"I guess I can do that," Alexavier agreed with a little reluctance.

"I tell you what. Over the next few weeks, I'll come and work with you personally. We'll see if we can figure this thing out, okay?"

Feeling about as good as he could over the situation, Alexavier agreed, "Sure. I heard Michael talking about doing some board games. You interested?"

"Oh yeah. Count me in. Just give me a little bit to work on this slide and barrel for Percy's semi-auto pistol."

Alexavier nodded and turned to leave. Before he could vanish through the doorway, Mike shouted, "We'll figure this out! Trust me!"

"I do!"

#

Sam needed time to digest the workout and the results of it. Out of the blue, an idea hit him, unlike Alexavier during the workout. Never feeling more certain about anything than now, Sam needed to discuss an important matter with Major Constantine. The Major had no plans for the next several hours, so Sam knew he wouldn't be interrupting anything. Sam had spent his time since the workout to contemplate where the young recruit in question is headed within Project: Hero. For several decades, this 'Secret Garden' had produced some of the greatest superheroes the world had ever seen. They entered into this program being young, inexperienced and were molded into heroes. Through extensive training and with Sessions, dozens of heroes have progressed and moved on to fight crime and protect the world. To graduate, everyone had to go through the system and be considered field ready by the

Major and Sam, which was by no means easy. That process had been in place since day one. Compliance to certain criteria was always important, especially if these new heroes were to engage with the public and be held to a to a higher standard as superheroes. The walk to the Major's room gave Sam more than enough time to put things into perspective. Now it was time to discuss his opinion with the Major.

The Major was diligently working away with his paperwork, having no clue Sam was standing at his office door. With enough time wasted, Sam knocked on the open door. The Major refused to look up, frantically scribing from one page to another.

Wanting the Major's attention, Sam asked, "Do you have a minute to talk?"

"I've been meaning to talk to you too. I think we need to deal with the issue of Alexavier."

"I completely agree." Sam entered the room and pulled up a chair, sitting in front of the desk.

"His continued failure needs to be dealt with now." The Major quickly began gathering the paperwork. "I say, if he has to be judged just like everyone else, his failures during both of your workouts requires some kind of action."

"Agreed."

"Good. I've taken the time to write up his development plan."

"I think his development can only move forward if he goes out into the field with me."

The words rendered the Major speechless. "Uh... okay?"

"Let me stop you."

"Stop me? I've already filled out the orders to send him back to Philadelphia."

Sam leaned forward. "Why would we send him back?"

"The workouts he's had with you have been extremely disappointing. His overall performance for training sessions has suffered, especially since coming back from New Jersey."

"I know he's got issues that's not up to what we aim for in his development, yet his overall performance when he's in the field is exceptional, maybe the best any recruit has done yet. What he did in Washington was everything we hope these recruits are trained to do. I am impressed that he has only been here a few weeks and is demonstrating such advanced abilities and skills."

"But that is not how we determine these kids progress or whether or not they get to go out on missions." The Major waved a folder. "It's through the workouts!"

"Stop saying kids! They're all adults. As a matter of fact, Percy is over 30 years old! Why he hasn't graduated by now, I don't know."

As it had always been when it comes to these topics, especially Percy's graduation, the Major clams up, providing no real answer to why he was still there.

Sensing the mood in the room change, Sam eased off, returning to his original agenda. "I'm taking Alexavier to New York to run through a few leads on a case and give him some pointers. I know you had scheduled Bobbie and Beth for a bit of recon. We'll be going on that same flight."

Reluctantly, the Major gave in. "I'll get things ready, and have Alexavier notified."

As Sam was leaving, he took a look at the folder and the paperwork the Major had been completing. He was unsure if he should have taken it with him, not knowing if the Major would submit it anyway.

Before the Major could even consider if he should move forward with demoting his newest recruit, a furious Harvey entered the room, marching right up to the desk. "Why am I not going on recon with Sam, but Alex is?"

"Were you listening in when you shouldn't have been?"

Harvey put his hands on the desk, leaning forward. "Does it matter? How is it that I'm not going? I'm the top recruit here. I've been so since the day I arrived, and you haven't been giving me my shot lately."

"Do you really think you should be going after how you've been acting?"

"What are you talking about? I've done nothing but bring down bad guys since I've been here."

"You have also been disruptive to everyone, including Alexavier."

"He's not the one who's going to take down The Terror Tribe. I'm the one who's going to bring you The Infamous One!"

"You're the one who's not going to be doing anything, especially with this attitude. Why should I send you on any missions? You've put yourself in hot water with your shenanigans. You want to know why you're not going with Sam? Don't make the person who makes the decisions on field assignments mad."

"The only reason why I'm not going with Sam is because of you not pushing for me to go."

"The reason why Alexavier's going is because Sam feels the need to give him some extra time for training. You're much further along than Alexavier."

"If I'm so much further along, then why haven't you sent me on any missions after The Infamous One?" Harvey started shoving the folders off the desk.

"We haven't had any tangible leads to where he may be. If we did, it wouldn't be just sending you in. We would have the whole team go."

"You wouldn't need the whole team when you only need me."

"I wouldn't send you to take on the worst killers they have, all by yourself."

Harvey flipped a folder on the desk. "Why wouldn't you? I can stop anyone before they see me."

"You're not going to if you're stuck here."

"Then don't keep me here!"

The Major leaned on his desk, getting close to Harvey's face. "Then do something for me to not keep you here! And get off my desk!"

The hard stare coupled with his words sent Harvey walking out of the office. Needing a reprieve, the Major pressed a button, closing and locking the office door. He took a deep breath and hung his head, enjoying the silence, which he wished could last forever.

CHAPTER 33

After a long relaxing evening with Beth and taking his mind off of the recent events, it was time to get settled in for what would hopefully be a restful night. With his usual routine, Alexavier sat down to document the important events from the day. While in Philadelphia, he documented many important things. Since arriving at the main complex, there has been a substantial increase in the amount of information recorded in his journal. After many years of jotting down events, he realized there were a dozen or so pages left. While giving the journal one last look before closing it up, a visitor arrives in the form of a knock on the door and Jonathon Bender.

"Come in!"

Jonathon used his access key to open the door. "I hope I didn't catch you too late."

"No. No. I was just finishing up some stuff."

"Perfect. May I?"

With a nod from Alexavier, Jonathon proceeded over and sat next to him. "I know things have been a little complicated lately, but I have some news that I think you might like."

"Okay."

"I just came from a meeting with the Major, and it's been decided that you're going to be heading out tomorrow for a reconnaissance mission with Sam."

Alexavier's eyes opened wide in surprise. "Really?"

"You'll be flying out on the same flight as Bobbie and Beth."

"Wow! I wonder if they know about it."

"Actually, I just came from speaking with both of them, and they are aware of the change in plans, although they won't be affected that much."

"I would've never thought I'd be going out to do recon with Sam, after what just happened."

"Can I say something and give you a little bit of advice?"

"Sure!" Alexavier was excited to receive words of wisdom from such a legendary hero like the Time Bender.

"First, I noticed you running the course again. It's impressive that you care so much to keep pushing yourself. It can be hard when things don't go your way." Jonathon leaned forward, making the conversation more personal. "So, with Sam, he's always focused on having everyone being at the top of their game. Any little bit of information that can help you in any way, he will provide it, even if it's in the middle of throwing punches. Always listen and take in everything as being valuable knowledge, because it is."

Alexavier nodded as Jonathon continued, "I thought when I made it to being a part of The United Superheroes of America that I knew it all and was going to bring down every bad guy who looked at me funny. I learned a quick and valuable lesson about overconfidence, but Sam really helped guide me. Rather than ruin my chance to make a difference, he helped mold me into who I am now, a cartoon character."

The comment got a laugh out of Alexavier, especially with Jonathon, as well as most of the legendary heroes from over the years being turned into various forms of media for entertainment, like the very popular cartoons on television.

"But seriously, I would have never become the hero I am now, if it wasn't for everything Sam did for me. He can do that for you too."

"I understand, sir."

Jonathon smirked, "You know, you don't have to call me sir."

"Yes, sir... Jonathon."

"That's better. Now, onto the mission at hand. Since this is a reconnaissance mission, in and around New York City, you're going to be dressed in civilian clothes. You'll be bringing along your outfit and gear, preferably in a backpack. Leave your weapons behind, so there will be no issues if you happen to come into contact with any kind of authority. Even though you're going to be with Sam, you have to abide by whatever laws and regulations of the jurisdiction you are operating in. Definitely bring along your tool belt. You never know when you might need a good, old fashion, lock pick set. We'll provide a few little things like money and such, but you shouldn't have to need much since Sam will have most of the necessities. This could be for a few days, so a change or two of clothes is recommended, but you don't want a suitcase full of sweaters to weigh you down. Just make sure to have your black outfit packed."

"Got it."

Jonathon stood up. "You'll be taking off at 0800. Get some rest and be in the hanger thirty minutes before liftoff. I won't be there for your departure, but I think Mike should be there for any last-minute needs or updates."

"Awesome. Thank you."

Before Jonathon walked out the door, he turned back. "Remember, this is a mission and it's important, but enjoy your time and learn. Not many people get the opportunity to go out into the field with The Patriot Warrior."

Alexavier nodded and smiled.

Once Jonathon had left, Alexavier jumped up and grabbed the backpack from the chair across the room. Venturing into his vault of goodies, he pulled out the standard black hooded sweatshirt that has become his signature outfit.

Before stuffing it into the bag, he glanced over to see the red and white superhero suit in the storage area that was made specifically for him. Venturing on over, he pulled on the sleeve to getting a better view. He wondered at what point would this colorful outfit replace his current dark and drab duds. Contemplating that a wardrobe change would have to wait, he picked up the belt and a few implements that might prove useful. Before exiting back to the room, he stopped and pulled out a drawer that housed the throwing needles. He was instructed not to bring weapons, but these were small enough to be concealed and might provide some help, especially for something at a distance. For up close interactions, the compact staff would be more appropriate, as it resembled a small metal rod. It wouldn't look suspicious if noticed. He stored them into a compartment on the belt, and went back to packing, placing his boots, gloves, mask and pants into the backpack, feeling satisfied that everything was in order.

With the excitement of going a mission with Sam still fresh on his mind, Alexavier was not ready to go to sleep, but knew he had to try. If he wasn't rested, he might not perform well and could cause a bad guy to get away. He needed to excel, now more than ever. After putting his journal away and shutting everything down, he eased into his bed, trying to get comfortable. But he just couldn't stop fidgeting. No matter how hard he tried to shut off his brain, he couldn't stop thinking about the next morning. He had already gone out on a mission with Sam, but that included the others, as this was to be just the two of them. All the crappy workouts could be wiped away with this visit to New York. All he needed to do was use the skills he had been perfecting for combat.

As weird as it might seem, thinking about the next day's events made him tired. Maybe his mind working overtime made him sleepy, and he began to yawn. Feeling the need to turn over, he pulled the blanket over his shoulder and closed his eyes. Slowly, the thoughts of going to New York brought the darkness of deep sleep.

His rested state finally allowed his dreams to take over. Before long, the vivid images of Beth and his friends morphed into the disturbing sight of The Infamous One and his evil team. He became restless the more they continued to stay in his unconscious mind. Their faces moved in and out, playing with his anger and emotions. He twitched and moved about in the bed. As much as he wanted to get his hands on any one of them, the limitations of his dreams only tormented him more.

Then, a piercing light in the distance shooed the villains away. A moment of serenity enveloped his dream and provided a comforting feeling until two blurry images appeared. They stayed back, never coming closer, but felt so familiar and comforting. Alexavier tried reaching out toward them, without success. None of his attempts to make contact had any affect. The two figures disappeared into the light, pulled back by a hand. Once he was alone with the light, the hand reappeared, slowly reaching out toward him. He hesitated, unsure if he should welcome the outstretched hand, but the warmth proved inviting. He couldn't resist the urge to reach out. The closer the hand came towards him, the more it felt right.

The inevitable touch was interrupted by the sound of her heavenly voice and outline of a face. "When you see the light, know that there's always more than what you see."

Waking up and opening his eyes, he blinked a few times. Once again, he had been visited by the mysterious woman in the light. Looking around the room, he was able to see that he was back to reality. Something about the last few moments felt significant, but figuring it out would have to wait until the morning. The need for sleep was much stronger, especially with the eerie comfort that the vision provided. He rolled over, closed his eyes. The thoughts of the recent dream had him fidget again. It took a bit of time, but he used some meditation techniques to settle himself down and drifted off, falling asleep once again.

CHAPTER 34

Looking into the mirror, Sam brushed his hand down his newly shaven face. No longer did his signature beard occupy the image across from him. Sam was one of those rare heroes whose real identity was known to the public, which can have negative consequences, but good ones as well. For the upcoming mission with Alexavier, being as inconspicuous as possible would attract as little attention, thus allowing him to provide as much insight and training without much interruption.

With a grin, he placed his electric shaver on the counter and threw on some aftershave. After a quick dusting of the random shavings, the iconic hero headed back to the front room. To complete the inconspicuous look, he sorted through several hats before settling on a baseball cap with an American flag on it. He went to the couch and grabbed the casual jacket lying over the arm before picking his backpack and slinging it over his shoulder. That grin came back again as he exited the room, excited for the opportunity to work with one of the most promising recruits Project: Hero has ever seen.

#

The morning had also arrived for Alexavier, who slept incredibly well, even with the dream interrupting his shut eye. He felt an anxiousness, but this was one he welcomed, so he jumped up to prepare for the big day ahead. It didn't take long before he had finished gathering all his gear and grabbed his favorite gray sweatshirt. Pausing for a moment to realize what was ahead of him, he made his way from his room to what he hoped would be an amazing adventure with his idol.

Alexavier arrived at the hanger extra early, but not beating Sam, who had been working with the pilot and mechanics to prepare the new helicopter for the flight. Mike was also present, watching Sam's gear and directing traffic. Alexavier dropped his bag toward the wall closest to the entrance and began zipping up his favorite sweatshirt. Appearing calm, he successfully hid his nervousness. Mike finally noticed the young recruit's arrival. He ventured over to Alexavier, smiling in anticipation of their departure. "You ready for an adventure of a lifetime?"

"It's still unreal." Alexavier scooted over closer to talk more quietly. "The greatest superhero of all time is taking me with him."

"Don't be surprised." Mike placed his hand on the young hero's shoulder. "He's gone out with a few others too. He'll do it from time to time and you know it's something special when he shaves. That means he's taking the training serious and not wanting to be noticed. Rather than be interrupted by every fan, he can quietly work with you on various aspect of becoming that next level hero."

Alexavier kept looking up while having his head down. "I just don't know how I'm getting to go. I don't feel like I proved myself entirely."

"If there's one thing I can tell you about him, he's fair and knows how to treat people. Even when you do your worst, he knows there's always better to come from you, and he'll pull it out." Mike nudged his shoulder. "Enjoy this. Come on. Smile."

The smile slowly appeared, only interrupted by a giddy squeal that came from down the hallway. Beth ran ahead of Bobbie, planting herself right next to Alexavier. "Good morning! We heard last night, but didn't want to keep you from getting rest! Isn't it awesome?"

"I'm ready for this," Alexavier stated, showing a bit of excitement.

"You're getting to go with Sam!" Beth exclaimed. "I almost couldn't sleep I was so happy for you. I wanted to come see how you were doing, but I knew you needed the sleep."

Bobbie agreed, "This is huge, dude. You can really feel like you're making progress by going with him."

"She's right," Mike added. "Sam doesn't just go out for recon. If it's that important, you can be sure he needs someone who can provide the right support."

Alexavier looked around. "Where's Morkie?"

"Dr. Jean's going to watch him. He looked sad, but he really likes spending time with her. I thinks she spoils him," Beth responded, still bouncy with excitement. "This is going to be epic!"

"You ladies have all your stuff and instructions?" Mike glanced over the recruits and their items.

Bobbie sighed, "It took suffering through a lecture from the Major, but yeah."

"We even got an allowance increase. So tonight, it's all about room service." Beth's comment had Bobbie nodding with a smile.

Alexavier asked, "Are you staying in a nice hotel?"

Bobbie stated, "It's one that tends to a contract with most businesses for out of town guests, new clients or possible employee shenanigans. It's pretty sweet."

"I heard going to bed is like sleeping on clouds." Beth nodded as well.

Percy joined them, with Dave pushing Wally's wheelchair. "I really don't need to be in this thing."

“Stop being a baby,” Dave said, struggling to push against Wally’s fidgeting.

Dr. Dennis, Manny and Michael entered as well, excited just like the others. They pulled up to their departing teammates, but Beth looked behind them. “Wait, no Harvey?”

“He’s in one of his moods again,” Manny sighed.

“What do you mean again?” Percy questioned sarcastically.

Dave rolled his eyes. “He’s been in a mood ever since I got here. I think his whole life is one, big, crappy mood.”

“Speaking of moods,” Percy patted Wally on the back. “Our cheery, little pal here has been singing like a songbird. That Session tried to whoop him. Didn’t happen.”

“I can honestly say I feel really good, besides a bit of weird fog. From what the doctor says, it’s normal memory loss.”

Dr. Dennis nodded. “That should clear up. You’re progressing well with your recovery, so your mental clarity should improve soon. Then we can move on to assess any advancements with your powers.”

Michael started to grin. “It will be great to have somebody to fly through the skies and help my control.”

“That’s a bit of a stretch since I need the wind to fly.” Wally stated. “It would be nice to be able to do that someday. I dream of the day to fly whenever I want to.”

“You’ll get there,” Mike assured. “If your recovery is any indication of success, you’ll be flying to the moon by next week.”

Dave gave Mike a funny look. “Fly to the moon? I want to kick him there. Stop wiggling!”

“This thing is so uncomfortable. I need some padding!”

“I’ll give you some padding!”

Dave wrestled with the wheelchair as Sam joined the gathering of recruits, providing a break from Dave and Wally's verbal battle. "Okay. Everything has been checked out after the initial flight. The preflight checks have been completed, and we are ready to get underway. Wally, how are you feeling?"

"Good enough to not be in a wheelchair," Wally commented in protest.

Dr. Dennis responded. "It is standard protocol that we follow after every Session, Wally"

"Maybe we can revisit that down the road?" Mike inquired. "Alex didn't spend much time in the wheelchair after his Session."

Sam placed his backpack between his legs. "This is only because of being a special circumstance for us to trial a much harder treatment. Since Alex was able to handle Sessions differently, we wanted to see how well he would do with the new one. So, we relaxed our standards and recovery protocols for him. Until we can determine that the recovery for others will be as positive, we will keep to the same standards as before."

"Sorry, buddy. I tried," Mike said with a playful pout.

"Man, I'm going to be stuck in this thing forever."

Bobbie wondered, "Can you feel any difference? Do you feel like you want to take off and fly?"

"Really, I don't feel anything at all, but I haven't tried."

Sam straightened the street clothes he was wearing. "I'm sure the doctor will be running some of evaluations over the next couple of days, and we'll see you how things turn out."

Dr. Dennis stated, "He's scheduled for a blood draw later this morning and a physical as well. If everything checks out, we will start standard tests to measure the progress in his powers shortly after."

"I'll make sure to follow up with Dr. Dennis and keep you and the Major informed," Mike said.

"Perfect." Sam looked back, seeing the sleek, Black helicopter start to spin its rotors. "Time to board, people."

Those going on the mission grabbed their bags and headed off. Everyone gave one last look back and wave, with Beth nudging Alexavier. Sam put his backpack over his shoulder and handled a couple of final details with Mike before heading up the ramp. Reaching the top, he palmed the touch screen to activate the menu and closed the door. Once it had shut and securely locked, Sam found his way next to the three waiting recruits, who were already buckled in. Alexavier continued to wear an apprehensive look on his face, wondering when the subject of the workouts would be brought up.

Vibrations became stronger with the increasing speed of the turning blades. Noise levels increased as well, prompting Sam to signal for the pilot to implement the noise cancelling system to better allow conversations during the flight. Quickly taking a seat and buckling in, Sam motioned that they were ready. The pilot got clearance from the command center and proceeded with lift off, rising through the top of the building. Once the jet engines kicked in, the aircraft flew off and vanished into the clear blue sky.

CHAPTER 35

Once they reached their targeted cruising speed and altitude, Sam released his buckle to move toward the center of the group. "Our flight to New York will be much faster, thanks to Senator Steinberg and Mike's engineering skills. We are going to land on Long Island and head to our destinations from there, drawing as little attention to ourselves as possible. When you give the destination to your cab driver, get dropped off a block or two away from each target. Recent reports indicate that many criminal organizations are paying for information and early warning if they suspect any activity that might compromise their operations. I have no doubt The Tribe uses this same tactic to stay one step ahead. Be careful not to discuss too much information while in the taxi where the driver can overhear your plan. The more you act like a tourist, the less suspicious you will be. It'll be best to act like you're sightseeing and possibly visiting family."

The girls nodded while setting down their bags, obviously having heard these instructions before, but Alexavier soaked it all in.

"The building we will be landing on top of has a government contract that allows for limited landings and takeoffs. With our civilian clothes we will be perceived as employees being brought in from outside the city. I can't say that we will not draw suspicion since there could be Tribe sympathizers nearby. We'll make our way casually through the building and down to the street." Sam turned to Alexavier. "I will keep the conversation light, mostly to give the perception that you are part of an internship program. It will sound believable, since you look like a college student. I shouldn't be as recognizable after shaving my beard, but if someone happens to notice me, go on ahead to the front of the building, and I will meet you there as soon as I can."

"Got it," Alexavier responded.

Sam turned to Beth and Bobbie. "Fill me in on your mission."

Beth leaned closer, "The Major has us in the field for up to four days. First, we have a store in the Bronx that's possibly being used by Tribe activity as a cover for their getaways, until the heat dies down. This intel is promising. It comes from a reliable informant that has on more than one occasion seen Tribe members ducking in after crimes had been reported around New York City."

Bobbie handed Sam several papers. "Before we head there, the Major wants us to scout a large office building in Lower Manhattan that's on the way. There's been quite the activity among a few tenants every time The Terror Tribe pulls a job. One is a financial institution that may be laundering money for them."

"The other business to look into provides legal services for travel throughout the country and across the world. The Major suspects they're helping to hide any villains working with The Tribe."

Sam handed back their instructions. "Sounds like someone there might have a particular interest in The Terror Tribe. There is likely a handful of powerful corporations and financiers who wouldn't mind easy paydays for helping them. Some of the wealthy are actually outspoken Tribe sympathizers. The government's consistent over-regulation of nearly all aspects of business and foreign trade has alienated a huge portion of corporate America. It's going to be tough to infiltrate them. I would advise observation first. Try making connections with the worker bee employees throughout the companies. They will be less restricted to talk to outsiders, but be careful not to stir up too much which may raise suspicions."

“What have you guys got planned?” Beth inquired.

“We’re paying a visit to an old friend.” Sam refused to divulge more information. “This will also give me the opportunity to spend time with Alex on some field work.”

“I’m jealous!” Beth exclaimed. “You’re so lucky.”

Alexavier agreed, “I know. I can’t believe I’m actually doing this.”

Sam watched his protégée start to open up and show some much-needed emotion. “Okay. Let’s concentrate on what’s at hand. We will be landing on a predetermined helipad, one of many we use to avoid becoming too predictable with where we enter the city. We should be landing in a few.” Sam took his seat, performing one last check of his gear.

Once the helicopter had landed, everyone exited quickly to have the aircraft back in the air and lessen any attention that could come their way. After stepping off the aircraft, Sam pulled out a baseball cap from his backpack and placed it on his head, followed by sunglasses. The wind whipped around the top of the mid-level, business skyscraper. As lift off commenced, Sam led them through the building’s security and down the elevator to the street. The light pedestrian traffic allowed them to congregate on the sidewalk for further instructions.

Trying not to be too obvious was a bit difficult for Alexavier. He was actually in the city on a recon mission with his idol, the greatest superhero of all time. He cautiously looked up and out of the corner of his eyes, taking in the surrounding of New York, still in awe of where he was standing.

Sam faced them, shielding himself from onlookers. “You have your Com-Links?” Beth and Bobbie nodded. “Good. Keep communications to a minimum, unless absolutely necessary. Check in at each site with the complex, so we can have a trail to follow if something happens.”

“Yes, sir,” Bobbie said, adjusting her backpack.

"Stay safe. Watch each other's back. Let's get The Tribe." Sam's words brought goose bumps to Alexavier, making him pause. His fellow heroes had probably heard this speech many times, but him hearing it for the first time was exhilarating.

Focusing on their roles, they prepared to leave noting which direction to set off in. Bobbie melted in with the other pedestrians, almost vanishing as a part of the crowd. Before joining her tag-team partner, Beth quickly reached up and kissed Alexavier on the cheek. The surprise on his face gave her a smile and a giggle, as she trotted off to join Bobbie further down the sidewalk.

Once Alexavier was standing next to him, Sam began to look around. "One of most important things to remember when doing recon is to remain as inconspicuous as possible. Depending on where you are and what you're trying to accomplish could mean a great many things. Being that we're in New York City, I'll focus on what we need to do for a large metropolis."

"Okay."

"With all the commotion and everything going on, what you really want to do is to blend in. Saying you're a tourist has advantages, particularly if you need information, and you're not from the area. The bad part is you stand out by asking questions, sending the wrong signals, especially if you don't want people to know you're looking for them." Sam started walking, and his pupil followed. "You can do a little bit of both just by saying that you're from another borough of the city, and that you're not as familiar with this part of town. Even if you have some uncertainty, always make them think that this is where you're from. Walk from point to point with a certain kind of purpose or intent. If you marvel at the fact of all the hotdog vendors lining the streets, then you're giving away a side of you that you don't necessarily want to show. But it's all right to stop and pick up a hotdog if you're hungry, because that's what a New Yorker would do. Does that make sense?"

"Yeah."

"Doing recon in a smaller town has a lot of other things to consider. We'll go over some of those if we get the chance to head out to a rural area. For now, we're going to head over to the spot where a couple of crimes occurred, and the local authorities are a bit unsure where to go and what to do next."

"I'm guessing that since we're going to check it out, the crime was done by somebody with superpowers?"

"Precisely, but it wasn't just one crime, it was multiple crimes happening at the same time, all by the same individual."

Alexavier looked confused. "Same person? You mean like a teleporter?"

"Not a teleporter, a multiplier. His name is Scott Norfeld. He is known as Multiplicity."

"I've heard of him. New York City is so big, how do you think we'll find him?"

"I don't think finding him will be a problem." Sam appeared melancholy. "In fact, I'm pretty sure I know where he is."

"How did you find that out?"

"It's not hard to know, especially when he was somebody trained to be a hero. He graduated Project: Hero and left, but was never able to establish himself as a hero when the Major refused to have him join The United. That is probably the reason he turned to crime, needing to supplement his income. The likelihood is that he's been committing crimes that never fell on anyone's radar until he decided to pull off several jobs all at the same time. Having multiple versions of himself would create confusion and throw off police agencies. Only a Meta human could achieve this. They would also have a tough time dealing with a superpowered bank robber. The hope is that I can find him and talk some sense into him before a stray bullet does something worse."

"That's why you said we were visiting an old friend?"

"Yes," Sam sighed. "I worked so hard to get him to the level of being a great superhero. To see that he could be doing a one-eighty is disheartening." Sam looked around and was satisfied with where they were heading. "Follow me. And remember, real names, unless we encounter villains then mask up."

With a quick nod from Alexavier, they headed toward the end of the block, which put them on a busy road with lots of traffic, exactly the place to get transportation. Sam hailed a cab, finally getting one to see his request and slow down. Sam opened the door, allowing Alexavier to hop in first. With the door closed, Sam instructed the driver, "72nd and 3rd, please."

The driver nodded, and the cab pulled away, fighting with the heavy morning traffic. The casually dressed heroes removed their backpacks to sit back and get comfortable. Alexavier was still on edge, waiting for the talk about his performance as of late, but continued to focus on the mission ahead.

To not be overheard, Sam leaned in to talk at a softer register. "So, where we're heading is on the Upper Eastside. When Scott first got here, he needed to stay out of sight until he could get set up as a member of The United. I remember him mentioning this location as a safe place, but I never got a chance to see it. I'm wondering if he's still using it, thinking no one knows about it. He was turned down from joining The United, but did stay in town. At first, he was doing some small-time crime fighting on his own, but that doesn't pay the bills. With his good deeds going unnoticed and still not getting recognized by the Major to join The United, I believe he began committing small crimes, hoping that no one would notice. He got a little brazen the other day when he tried multiple crimes simultaneously. I think he wanted authorities to dismiss the crimes if several reports had the exact, same person committing them. He didn't wear his hero outfit to be recognized, so he was in civilian clothes. The description I obtained from the police fits him perfectly."

"From what I remember, he can duplicate himself a number of times, but doesn't have any other superpowers."

"Correct." Sam unzipped his jacket and took off the cap. "He has the advantage in numbers, but not in skills. As much as I tried to reinforce the need for proper combat training, he never fully reached his potential. He's more than capable of putting up a good fight with strength in numbers, but our skill levels are better than his. He can create up to 10 copies of himself, but no more than that. The hardest part will be fighting them all in a confined space where it's easy to get overwhelmed. We need to watch our backs and the areas around us."

"I take it we're going inside a building."

"I had a chance to view satellite images and intel over the last few days. His place is in a secured apartment building. His place isn't large, but has many rooms. If he is aligning himself with others, it's a perfect place to position your team and store valuables without suspicion. The building has good security, since it used be a factory. Lots of stone and brick make it a great bunker for those who don't want to be disturbed. The doors are industrial grade with impressive locks that aren't usual for an apartment building of any kind. There are windows to the outside of the perimeter residences, but have heavy metal frames and glass with steel reinforcing. Essentially, we're trying to get into a vault that happens to have an address."

Alexavier looked out the window, noticing some of the buildings passing by. "If the building is really secure, it would make sense that it could be a hideout. What if he started his own team, and there's more heroes or villains that we'll have to face?"

"Interesting thought. I don't know that we can answer that for sure, but it's something I'll keep in mind when we get there. We'll just need to be very careful."

"The Terror Tribe would definitely have the kind of funding to make that place a fortress."

Sam paused. "It would be unfortunate to find out that Scott made that kind of turn." He became quiet, and Alexavier let the silence linger, hoping Sam would be the one to break the silence. He didn't.

The cab finally reached Sam's requested destination. Alexavier was the first to hop out, while Sam paid the fare. Once the vehicle drove away, Sam joined his protégée on the sidewalk. Setting down his bag and putting on the baseball cap, Sam surveyed the area. "Keep your eyes open, but don't be obvious about looking. We're only about a block away from the location."

Alexavier casually turned to the restaurant behind him, glancing at the menu in the window. After a few seconds, he returned to Sam. "Not sure if the staring is on purpose, but there's a guy several businesses down at a table. He's eating, but also hasn't stopped looking at us. He's now on his phone while watching us."

"It might be nothing, but we need to make him think we're not a threat. Follow me, but wander about the next couple of restaurants as if we are looking for a place to eat."

Two stores down, Alexavier pointed to a deli. Sam nodded, "Keep motioning and walk by."

As they continue toward the end of the block, every new storefront gave them an opportunity to look out of the farthest point of their field of vision. The suspicious man kept eating and observing them. To ensure they looked like tourists, Sam continued to browse the business windows, as well as checking out those on the opposite side of the street.

"If Scott had established contact with any locals, that guy may be helping him in return for being a part of whatever operations he's pulling off. It might be no coincidence that he hasn't taken his eyes off us yet."

Sam stopped at one window, putting his hand up to the window to block the glare. He backs up and tilts his head to see the sign. A nod and a point inside sent Alexavier inside a local eatery. Sam followed, catching up and explaining, "If he's wondering what we're doing, hopefully he thinks we're hungry and decided to eat."

"Are we going to wait inside and scout his movements?"

"Actually, we're masking our movements by pretending to find a place to have an early lunch. I noticed a backdoor entrance to this establishment, so we can make our way out the back and go around to the possible hideout. He'll think we're still in here eating and wait for us to exit. It will probably be a few minutes before he questions our intentions for food, so we need to head out the back now."

They graciously moved through the patrons, getting to the back entrance. Once in the alley, Sam scoped the long tunnel of litter, dumpsters and trash cans, identifying the building a block down through the alley that they intended to enter. Keeping their heads on a swivel to notice anything out of the norm, they swiftly got to the closest corner and put their backs to the wall. A quick observation showed no signs of people, so they walked briskly to the building in question.

Sam pointed, "The window to the far side should be the living area. We won't get by it without being seen. We need to go around to the back."

Alexavier nodded, following Sam's lead. The wall they moved along didn't have many windows, which helped hide their presence. When they reached the back corner, Sam paused.

"We're going to hide our gear and go in as civilians, just in case someone in the building sees us. We'll put our bags in these dumpsters, but bring your belt."

With a quick grab of the loaded belt before stuffing the backpack into the huge metal trash container, they proceeded to the back door. Sam placed his hand on the knob. Just as he thought, it was locked, so he bent down to have a closer look.

"It's definitely a high-end lock system," Sam whispered. "Although I don't think it's anything too difficult to pick."

Alexavier pulled out his pick set and began fiddling with the picks and keyhole. With the skill level and precision that he had impressed everyone back at the complex, he was able to bypass the complex lock tumbler in just a few seconds. Alex opened the door, and Sam led the way, giving the young hero a nod and a smile as he quietly moved ahead. Alexavier allowed the door to close silently, before following close behind. The hallways were empty, cleared of objects and people. The conversion from a warehouse to apartments left the high ceilings and mechanical equipment from lighting, heating and cooling visible. The cement floors were a blessing, not creating any noise as they moved through the two hallways toward the front of the building. The atmosphere felt almost too eerie without any sounds.

None of the residences had windows to see into the hallway. The only way anyone could know they were there was through their peepholes, so getting close to the targeted door was simple enough. Checking the door to what was possibly Scott's apartment, Sam found it was locked and motioned to Alexavier, who moved around and quickly unlocked it. Sam motioned him to fall back, slowly turning the handle and open the door. They slid inside and quietly shut the door behind them. Sam methodically checked out every room, not finding a soul. Each of the back rooms didn't contain anything of interest, but Sam wanted to see the furthest one down the hallway.

Alexavier joined him, but had some questions. "Could we get in trouble for being in here? We're not the police with a warrant."

"True, but I know he's committing crimes. I'm hoping that my intervention can knock some sense into him before he gets arrested. We had a strong relationship, so I want to give him a chance before needing to do something drastic."

"What if we don't find anything?"

"I'd love to be proven wrong." Sam arrived at the closed door to the suspected room that may hold proof of guilt or innocence. This door wasn't locked, which surprised Sam. What was inside didn't surprise him either, but it did disappoint him. It was loaded with huge amounts of valuable items and property. What hurt Sam most were the hard briefcases piled in the corner. He knew what he would find upon opening them, and it was all cash. Alexavier could see the changing look on his idol's face, but didn't have any words. Sam did. "I think we should call this in."

As Sam turned to put in his Com-Link, Alexavier looked back towards the door, pointing to the front entrance. There was no noise, but Sam had faith in that unusual sensation that Alexavier possessed, so they moved behind the doorway to the room to stay out of sight. Within seconds, the front door swung open, but no one entered. Sam knew they were caught, so he shouted, "It's me, Scott! I've come to talk!"

The sound of rapid footsteps getting softer had Sam rush for the door. Two bodies were tossed aside, landing in the doorway. Both got up, seeing Alexavier heading their way. They were clones of Multiplicity and looked to block him from leaving. Having trained to take on multiple targets, Alexavier was quick to engage them. Using a combination of kicks and punches from one clone to another, he was able to keep them from getting too close and deliver significant damage.

Within moments, more clones piled into the apartment, reducing the space he could use to fight them off. Needing some separation, Alexavier reached into his belt and pulled out the small metal rod. A press of the small button activated the spring that shot out the ends, creating the large staff that he urgently needed. He began swinging quickly and precisely, aiming first for the closest clones and their legs to reduce their mobility. Once they had felt enough pain, he moved to the next wave of clones. Before he could make his way through them, Sam had been rushed by a couple of clones and forced back into the apartment. Not able fend them all off, he was shoved through a window and into the alley.

Alexavier continued to swing his staff and thrust it into a clone's stomach, but the fight was only progressing so far. Not knowing the status of his mentor outside the building, he decided to exit out into the battlefield. Using the staff to vault over the majority of attackers, Alexavier landed on his feet and shot himself through the window, rolling on the ground and positioning himself to face the hoard of advancing clones.

Sam's fight had him swinging with enough power to land massive punches, doing as much damage as possible. His super resilient skin allowed him to absorb incredible impacts without much pain. The accumulating shock never hurt him, but made him adjust his plan to create enough distance to prevent from being overwhelmed. Sam and Alexavier collected themselves, coming back-to-back and being surrounded by a horde of angry duplicate versions of Scott. They circled the heroes, strategically getting into place before slowly advancing forward for one last assault.

"Scott, listen to me. I'm here to help. Really, I am"

"We are Multiplicity." The clones slowly closed in on their prey. "We don't want your help."

Before engaging in one last encounter, Sam tilted his head to speak softly, "These clones don't feel pain like humans do and won't affect Multiplicity. Even if we take him out, the clones will continue to fight. Use extreme aggression and brutality to take them out. But don't kill or destroy them, or another will appear. We need them down, but not dead."

Alexavier nodded and suddenly, something flipped in his brain. Before Sam could coordinate an offensive, the young hero stepped forward with every swing loaded with the absolute, most power he could generate. One smash to an arm and a spin around to attack another's leg led to an accurate jab to the stomach. Alexavier spun his staff to slice through the air to make contact from one clone to another, setting up finishing strikes sprinkled in between.

The clones converged on Alexavier in greater numbers in hopes of taking advantage of who they believed to be an inexperienced trainee. Being caught off guard by the quickness of Alexavier's attack, Sam rushed a couple of clones, hoping to land shots and remove a couple away from the center of the battle. Sam's power was his strength, rather than his quickness. He focused his attacks to cause severe damage quickly and allow him to move to the next target. Each of the other clones started to swarm, but Sam's slightly wild punches and a random front kick continued to push each back, eventually taking its toll and allowing for Sam to power through their attacks.

As each twirl of the staff created huge momentum and landing crushing blows, the clones started to fall quickly, lowering the number of threats, allowing the young hero to drop the surrounding horde like flies.

Once the non-stop combat came to an end, as Sam dropped an unconscious clone, he looked around. "How many do we have?"

"I count ten."

Both knew what the number meant. Sam gave Alexavier a slight nod and started glancing around the area as a signal. Alexavier took a moment to let his mind clear and sense his surroundings. When the feeling finally came to him, he opened his eyes with a small motion to his left. Understanding the message, Sam gave him a slight nod, and Alexavier quietly snuck off to his right.

As Sam worked hard to catch his breath and make sure the antagonists they took down stayed that way, a dark shadow appeared in the alley, but remained hidden enough out of sight. A few moments passed without any acknowledgement and the figure slowly crept forward. Before he could get into any position to potentially cause further trouble, Alexavier snuck up from behind and wrapped his arms around the man, applying an effective, rear naked choke. As the struggle ensued, they moved into better lighting to show Multiplicity himself being entangled in Alexavier's web of control. Jumping on the villain's back, Alexavier wrapped his legs around and tightened them to secure a takedown. Multiplicity fell back and struggled to free himself, but it wasn't long before his desperation faded, just like his consciousness, and he went limp.

Alexavier let go of the passed-out guy and rolled to sit on his rear. A sense of accomplishment was mixed with that awkward sensation of a presence. Turning around quickly, Alexavier faced up at a figure standing before him. From the side of the building, he saw several outlines of others from the roof above, but their identities were blocked by the sun shining behind them. Any sense of fear vanished when he focused to see the hero Downtown standing before him with an outstretched hand. "This is a pleasant surprise."

Alexavier grabbed the hand, pulling himself up. "Thank you."

Sam came over. "Glad to see you and the team."

"Weirdly, we were scoping out a possible small time Tribe operation several blocks over when a passerby commented on a fight going on towards this direction." Downtown motioned for the others to join. "We thought to investigate and maybe help. As always with you, we're here and you've already done the heavy lifting."

"Not true," Sam grinned. "Last time we saw each other, I remember getting thrown through a few buildings before you intervened and took care of things."

"All I did was show up. Once Terrorcide got distracted in seeing me, you took him down. However, I'll take an assist any time I can get it."

"Done." Both smiled, then Sam added, "You remember Dread from the complex."

"Absolutely. Nice to see you again."

"Nice to see you too, especially your outfit."

"Oh, thanks." Downtown fiddled with his suit. "It's my first try for something new. The rest of the team didn't like the old one. Nobody likes those Project: Hero suits." Downtown looked back, checking on the group's progress. "We'll help secure these guys before they can get back on their feet."

Sam waved him away. "Don't worry about them. Once Multiplicity's clones have been out for a few minutes, they'll vanish. We will need to bind the real Multiplicity, so he can't create more clones when he regains consciousness. Use the zip ties to bind his wrists so they touch. That won't allow the separation of the clones from his body."

Downtown and Alexavier took turns watching the clones, while Sam cinched the zip tie on Multiplicity. With enough time passing of each clone's incapacitation, they began to deteriorate into dust. After a few minutes, the alley was filled with a hazy smoke of once animated individuals. This was short lived with the movement of Downtown's team members arriving from the rooftop, dissipating the thick dust cloud. Appearing before them stood the team in colorful and intricately designed outfits. Downtown proceeded to stand before them for an introduction. "So, Dread. I'd like to formally introduce you to my team, The United Outcasts!"

Alexavier responded with a smile, "Awesome."

"Let's wrap this up." Sam tapped his earpiece. "Come in, command center."

A few seconds passed before a response came back. "Go ahead."

"I have a capture for extraction. I'll send you location coordinates to meet us shortly. We've apprehended Multiplicity. Please inform Major Constantine."

"Roger. We'll prepare a flight and await the further details."

"Patriot Warrior, out." After a final push of the Com-Link button, Sam turned to view the same unusual sight as the others. The remaining dust from the deteriorated clones gradually blew away in the mild breeze flowing through the alley.

"Can never get used to it," Transcend mentioned. "I saw it happen hundreds of times in training, but it's still a bit weird."

DLX exclaimed, "But it sure is fun to see when your punches send their heads flying in a rocky dusty mess."

"Man, you're crazy," Anthem responded.

"Yo! You know it don't hurt them." DLX's smile did little to persuade them to his side.

Sam gave a look in Multiplicity's direction, but got an angered stare in return as he regained consciousness, before the disgruntled, former hero turned away. Alexavier could see the saddened expression and walked over. "What will happen now?"

"Knowing the Major," Sam paused. "First there will be incarceration and interrogation before being tried as a criminal. He will probably spend a long time locked away." Sam went over to join the group of heroes guarding the prisoner with Alexavier accompanying him.

Some members of The United Outcasts used their extensive powers of flight to transport the prisoner to the top of a building and away from the crowd that had slowly been gathering. The helicopter eventually arrived and had the prisoner loaded aboard. Sam's mood was still one of being down and evident to all gathered near him. Talking was kept to a minimum, as they all waited for the jet helicopter to depart. Watching the helicopter rise into the sky, Sam stared one last time, wishing things could have been different. As the aircraft began to vanish in a distance, Sam admitted, “I considered him a friend, not just a student.”

“I think all of us considered him a friend,” Downtown admitted. “It’s too bad that we couldn’t get the Outcasts up and running sooner. He would’ve been such a huge asset to the team.”

With a pat on the back, they turned to join the rest of the heroes waiting patiently. Epic wondered, “What’s on your agenda?”

“Actually, we finished our mission fairly quickly,” Sam stated. “We still have a couple of days that were blocked off to give us time if we needed it. We’ll need to get our backpacks.”

Downtown motioned over toward Alexavier. “Should we show you our secret hideout?”

Alexavier nearly jumped up and down. “Yes, please!”

CHAPTER 36

As with most superhero teams, having a headquarters was pretty much mandatory. If the place you call home doesn't include any caves nearby, then your secret lair must be a building. Where that is located then depends on the actual city you reside in. For The United Outcasts, that city is New York City, and their home is a very tall building. The difficulty in having a base in the sky is access, particularly when you have to leave or return. Anonymity is crucial. You can't just fly in and out, without anybody noticing. That's how you can get attacked and killed. When this team was being created, great planning and even more funds went into designing a quick entrance and exit, which is camouflaged from the public in a different building across the street.

Sam and Alexavier were escorted through a complex tunnel system and emerged at an apartment penthouse turned command center. Twenty-feet tall ceilings with floor to ceiling glass windows encompassing the whole floor allowed for complete three-hundred-and-sixty-degree views of the city. Several feet of space created a ring around the inner command area, which included essential computers, monitors and other communication equipment. Center to that was the area used for socializing. With the team settling into the lounge area and taking off their masks, Sam joined them and set his backpack on the center table, but Alexavier paused and gave a quick look around, with the scenery out the window being very mesmerizing.

"Nice, huh?"

"Sure is, Downtown."

"Call me Robert." The leader of The United Outcasts joined Alexavier to take in the amazing view. To stand with such an important hero and see the amazing city, made this already incredible experience so much more surreal to the young hero. After a moment of gawking, Robert brought the young hero back to the where others were relaxing.

"Team, this is Alexavier Vankendreh'd, also known as Dread. I had the privilege to meet him back at the complex. Welcome to The United Outcasts' headquarters."

Everyone gave out a warm welcome and wave, as the two made their way into the very comfortable social area of the command center. Robert commented while taking a seat, "That new helicopter sure is nice. It's such an improvement over the old one. How were you able to get it? It must have been hard, since Project: Hero isn't actually an officially recognized part of the government."

"That's part of the reason why we could get it," Sam explained. "The helicopter itself isn't actually an on the books operation either. Senator Steinberg worked some of his magic to get us an early prototype that Mike was able to tweak with his own special skills. Once the super-secret engineers saw what Mike could accomplished with the prototype, it was ours, but only if Mike would help modify the others. It is more than twice as fast as the old one and better for holding equipment. With the recent string of Terror Tribe activities, this new aircraft can help us intercept them faster. Unfortunately, the pattern of their recent string of robberies has us confused of their plan."

DLX wondered, "Do you think it's a diversionary tactic for something else? We were talking about this earlier. What if it's not about banks? I mean, if they're not breaking into the bigger banks for the bigger haul, then..."

"We've been wondering that too. The Tribe members involved weren't any from the main team, but they did have an affiliation. It wasn't until Alex stopped Landfill that they brought in Natural Disaster." Sam placed his coat on the table next to him. "That could be true."

Epic added, "If the true Tribe members are planning something different, the trail they're putting us on is pretty smart for throwing everyone off their next big heist. We know they've hit institutions ten times bigger in the past. Their next target could be military or government."

Robert noticed Alexavier still looking around the massive penthouse. "What do you think of our headquarters in the sky, Dread?"

"It's pretty incredible. I didn't think anyone outside The United would have a place like this."

"Thanks to Sam and some creative government funding, we're able to have a real place to run our operations. It makes keeping the city safe a much easier job."

Robert quickly realized that an introduction was in order. "Sorry, Alexavier. You got to briefly meet everyone back in that alley, but let me formally introduce the team. That was Roy Tanner, better known as Epic. His power of harnessing UV radiation from the sun nearly rivals that of Intergalactic. He was deemed too old, out of shape and not the right look for The United. He can fly, shoot energy blasts and harness enough energy to produce a protective shield. He's one of the best heroes in the world, even though he's never been in The United."

Next to him is one of our many heroes of African descent, the mighty DLX. He prefers to not use his real name, which is for personal reasons. His ability to pull energy from others and use it to power himself makes him dangerous for even the most powerful villains. He's actually the only hero to have ever come close to beating Natural Disaster."

Alexavier gave a wave.

"Next is our hero-slash-weirdo, Todd Carlin or Giggle Stick."

"I'm glad to resemble that remark."

Robert continued, "Todd is another one of our heroes of African descent and has been deemed by the Major to be too unstable to join The United. His use of weapons, staffs in particular, makes him a formidable force against any villain. His quickness in combat is second to none. With his retractable staff, he may be the best hand-to-hand fighter since Sam, not to mention he has an invulnerability to be able to bounce off things without really getting hurt."

"Our master planner and strategist is Transcend. Her real name is Melina Levante. This Latino powerhouse is small in stature, but mighty in mental abilities. Her abilities vary greatly and are quite unusual. One of the most amazing things she can do with the slightest touch is detect that person's previous connections to other people and even things."

"It's quite similar to what Tyber can do, but much more broadly," Sam added. "She has the ability to prevent any kind of mental attacks or powers that affect the mind, but with the amount of focus, she unable to use her powers."

Robert pointed to the far couch. "Sitting next to her is the first gay couple of the superhero world, Getaway and Rosé. These ladies have just graduated Project: Hero. I think just before you arrived. Getaway's name is Tisha Borland, and Rosé is Megan Keel. Another hero of African descent, Getaway uses fast speeds for flying in linear patterns to escape and evade capture, also using some weird form of luck!"

"It's never luck when you're this good," Tisha replied.

Robert grinned, "Rosé can use the power of persuasion to bend people to her will, making her great for infiltration. She doesn't really force people to do want she wants, but they somehow feel the need to do it.

Of course, that is the famous hat and smile of Ordinary Joe. Preferring to be called Joe, he is Joe Donnelly, an anomaly among super powerful people. Testing higher than anyone else as a Meta Human, he has shown no real powers, yet he's still one of the greatest heroes in the world. When things are at their worst, he's at his best.

His tag team partner is Hellhammer. This behemoth from Down Under is Neal Van Til, the only person able to lift a couple of rare space rocks, which he uses as a hammer and club to smash bad guys. Once he harnesses those weapons, he becomes nearly invulnerable. He is also one of the few heroes in North America never having been through Project: Hero.

Then we have our newest additions, Apex, Livevil, Anthem and Radical.

Apex is Anthony Laviolette, a Canadian who has amazing speed, whether it's flying, running or swimming. He can't reach supersonic speeds, but he's fast, no matter where he is. Best part of his powers is that he never seems to tire or lose energy.

Livevil doesn't want to use her real name either, but what she does use is amazing. We needed a nasty, must be able to do the deed kind of hero, and she is it. With the unusual ability to survive physical injury to an otherworldly level, she will not hesitate to end any villain and send them to their grave."

Todd gave her a golf clap, which she in return gave him a dirty look and point of her knife.

"Muhammad Abdul Kahfi is Anthem." Robert looked to his left for a fist bump. "Even though he is Muslim, he was inspired by Sam and wanted to become the next generation's Patriot Warrior. His powers are much like Sam's, but much more powerful in some areas. Unfortunately, having the skin color he has, being an example for this country wasn't in the cards for joining The United for some reason. He had a tryout, but the Major denied him joining. But that doesn't matter. We're thrilled to have him with us." Sam patted him on the back, sporting one of the biggest smiles.

"And last is Berlin Kensington, known as Radical. He is the first transgender hero to come from Project: Hero. He can increase in muscle mass or thin down. Which means, he becomes super strong or super-fast, plus adding a bit of invulnerability as well."

Alexavier remembered him and asked, "Aren't you Dynamic's brother? I can see how your powers are a bit similar."

"Yes, I am," he stated.

"That must be so cool."

A disappointed look washed over his face. "We haven't spoken in years."

"Oh, I'm sorry," Alexavier responded, feeling bad for bringing it up.

"It's okay. We haven't been close for a long time. I'm just happy that Downtown wanted to have me as a part of the team."

Robert gave an approving nod. "I'm thrilled you accepted my offer. I know you had taken some time off, so I didn't want to rush you back. But then of course, there's me. We had the pleasure of meeting back at the complex. I can stick to objects, which makes me perfect for fighting crime in New York City with all these big buildings."

"Most importantly," Sam added with pride in his voice. "The world's first openly gay superhero and of color as well."

"I feel like I needed to open that door for others who didn't feel they could truly be themselves. But in the end, that probably didn't help me when I was trying to get into The United."

"Have you heard from Gary Hughes?" Sam wondered.

"I saw him just the other day," Robert replied with uncertainty. "He hasn't given me an answer about joining, although he told me he's now called The Hatriot. We also wouldn't have been able to do this without Beta Star and his team, Vincent Dreadnought, Ginger Riot, Citadel and Ranier for help in legal matters and setting up our headquarters."

Alexavier had a confused look. "I don't understand. All of you are just amazing and some of the best heroes ever to come out of Project: Hero. I would be thrilled to have you on my team. Why wouldn't you guys become members of The United?"

"The Major doesn't want us on his team." DLX's statement appeared to resonate with the rest of the team, who all agreed.

"In his eyes, we're not good enough." Muhammad's comment brought another collective agreement.

"His loss is our gain," Robert stood up. "It doesn't matter if The United is well funded by the government, and they get thrown into the spotlight whenever possible. This team is going to change the way the world fights crime. It all starts here, in New York City."

A collective approval brought a more positive response, as Sam added, "Even if the world wants to look at The United as the measuring stick, that stick might not be long enough to measure this team. The ability of this team to quickly handle situations is unparalleled."

"There's so many of you who can go really fast," Alexavier marveled. "I don't think I've seen that many ever assembled together."

"Response time has always been a concern whenever The Terror Tribe makes a move. Everyone is always late to catch them, especially The United." Robert placed his hand on Anthony's shoulder. "This will be the team to react quickly and intercept them when they're in the act."

"Since a couple of us with speed can also fly, we can bring the others that don't. We don't need to wait on any aircraft to warm up," Roy added.

Anthony looked back at Robert. "And it's the speed we have that will bring them down, leaving The United to find petty criminals to arrest."

An agreeing chuckle came over the room as Sam looked to continue the conversation. "I feel this group that has been put together is the best team out there. I have faith in all of you. I believe in your leadership with Robert guiding you. I am going to back you and give you the support you need. And here." Sam motions for Alexavier to hand him his earpiece and then passes it to Robert. "I will also look to acquire some of these so everyone can be in constant and instantaneous communication. If The Tribe is here to cause problems, I can trust that you will be there to shut them down."

"We won't let you down," Muhammad responded, followed by a nod from the others.

"Since we're here." Sam stood up. "I know Alex hasn't been to the monument at the epicenter of the blast. I'd like to take him there before we leave."

Robert handed the earpiece back. "We can definitely accommodate the future of Project: Hero. Let's get out of our suits, and we'll walk on over."

Sam quickly added before everyone got too far, "Actually, keep your suits on under your clothes and just bring your masks. After we have a few moments to ourselves at memorial, I think it might be good for you guys to mingle with public in your hero suits and let them get to know you better. We'll just have you hold off putting on the masks until after we get there."

Robert and the team agreed, as they went down the stairs to the living portion of the penthouse. Having a few minutes before leaving, Alexavier walked over to one of the huge windows. Looking into the city, he could see the square that had the monument amongst the buildings that was ground zero. He began to feel anxious knowing that within minutes, he would be on his way there to experience something he had long wished he could.

CHAPTER 37

The walk through the streets of New York City was accompanied by much anticipation. Alexavier had been to New York City a few times previously for Project: Hero activities, but never the opportunity to visit such a historic site. He enjoyed the company and conversation, especially with so many heroes he had followed since their own time with Project: Hero. Hearing each person's story about the city and their adventures on every avenue, kept a smile on Alexavier's face. Voices were kept to a lower volume to not alert the citizens passing by with their colorful details of battle, but everything changed once they turned the final corner.

As the image of the statue came into view, his eyes widened, just like his mouth. Seeing pictures and images online while surfing the World Net is one thing, but being in the presence of such an impressive monument was beyond imagination. Having seen the tribute to the fallen heroes and those who lost their lives during the nuclear attack brought about a lot of emotions. The statue was an abstract piece, all in unpolished aluminum that has an organic flowing design. It rolled and swayed up from the ground, rising in the air as if reaching for the sun. The base was a very standard circle of granite with the contrast provided by the bronze plaque that encompassed half of the base's circumference.

Everyone noticed Alexavier's reaction and let him roam at his own pace. He looked everything over, in awe of every inch of the display. Making it halfway around, he found himself in the path of sunlight reflecting into his eyes.

Shielding them to see, the plaque's inscription finally caught his eye. The bronze, with its many raised letters, glistened and shined. Roy tagged along as they made it to the front of the inscription, standing next to him and read the words aloud.

"For the heroes, for the citizens, for those who lost their lives, let this memorial be a tribute to their sacrifices. Let this statue be a reminder, that no matter what brings us down, we will always rise back up. As this monument reaches for the sun, we reach for a brighter tomorrow"

Roy looked over. "Pretty powerful, isn't it?"

"Yeah."

Robert and the rest of the team joined Alexavier, with Todd placing his hand on Alexavier's shoulder, who admitted, "My first time too. I've only seen pictures, since I'm from Oregon and have only been here a short time. You get a certain feeling that's completely different when you're standing in front of it."

"To know you're here, where it all happened is a whole different feeling. To think about 30 years ago, everything within several hundred feet was obliterated." Roy looked around. "Where we're standing was leveled. If there was anything left, it was melted or charred."

Robert looked around. "Not many of the buildings you see around the memorial were able to be saved. Almost three dozen that weren't destroyed from the blast had to be demolished."

"It's said that there are bodies that were never recovered," Roy pointed out. "Some may have still been in the damaged buildings when they were leveled."

Alexavier looked around in utter disbelief. "Oh man."

Joe added, "Officials say that just over a thousand people died in the blast, along with the original Human Battery and Golden Wing."

Melina walked by. "It's also estimated that another tens of thousands may have suffered complications from the radiation."

Sam arrived, with several adoring fans in tow. "Not to mention, many more who will still develop issues down the road."

"We lived less than a mile away," Robert explained. "We could feel the heat from the blast. With the intensity of the explosion, we thought we were going to die."

"It was intense, to say the least. So, I'd like you all to help me with something." Sam pulled his backpack off and set it down. Upon opening it, Sam pulled out a small, decorated box. "When we realized that the bomb was going to detonate, Human Battery and Golden Wing sent me away to try and get the others out. Unfortunately, the elevators didn't work. As I raced down the stairs of the building, I noticed a woman with a disability unable to get to safety. Her name was Dorothy Sommers. I did what I could to help her, but I knew we weren't going to make it. I decided to look for a place to hunker down and hope we could shield ourselves from the blast, eventually finding a heavily fortified lab on one of the lower floors. We covered up, and I told Dorothy to close her eyes, but I knew the lab wouldn't protect us. She stayed strong when the blast happened. After the sound, heat and light subsided, we realized we had somehow survived. Once we had made our way to safety, both of us had gotten checked out and suffered only minor burns. As time went on, we became good friends, and I would visit Dorothy as often as I could. Unfortunately, she developed cancer a few years ago, including an inoperable brain tumor, which left her in a coma for the last year. She passed away a few days ago. I went to her funeral to pay my respects while in D.C., and so I could fulfill her last wish. When she was diagnosed with cancer, she asked me to promise that she was to be laid to rest at the memorial." Loosening the top, Sam walked to the flower beds encompassing the memorial. "She said that in her death, life would flourish." He tilted the urn, pouring the ashes to rest amongst the vegetation. "Go to God, Dorothy. I will miss you."

Upon finishing, Sam returned and placed the urn on the statue. After backing away, he remained silent, while a tear ran down his cheek. Alexavier stepped forward to stand by Sam. The rest of the Outcast team followed suit. Soon, it became much bigger than just for those heroes, as the citizens visiting the site realized what was happening and joined them to bow their heads in silence.

CHAPTER 38

The gathering of people around the monument grew, particularly with the presence of a hero. It took a few minutes, Sam was recognized by the more observant and garnered instant attention. Unlike Sam, the heroes of The United Outcasts wore masks at all times while in their hero personas. They were unrecognizable without them, and hadn't put them on yet. The time had finally come, and Sam went over to Robert to instruct him, "Tell your team to mask up. It's time for The United Outcasts to take center stage."

Robert motioned to the others with hand gestures to secretly put on their masks. It took a few moments for the people around to realize that members of The United Outcasts were in attendance as well, particularly since they were dressed in street clothes. As the whispers grew, an electric feeling spread through the crowds with the realization they were in the presence of the next great team of superheroes.

The spectacle of superheroes at the New York monument gave Alexavier a new look into what the real world would be, if and when he were to graduate. Being dressed in his basic, gray, hooded sweatshirt allowed him to blend in with the regular people. He could really appreciate being able to observe the heroes interacting with adoring fans. It's something that no training or textbook could show him or that he would experience otherwise.

As much as there were people who loved heroes, there were others who thought they were a part of the problem and were willing to make their voices heard. The longer the heroes stayed to mingle with the public, the more detractors showed up to speak their minds about how superheroes were the real threat. Eventually things got to the point where Sam realized they couldn't stay. Seeing how the situation could escalate in a wrong way, Sam weaved through a crowded area, eventually finding Robert.

The adoring fans made it difficult to hear, so Sam leaned in. "I think we should head back. I don't want to wear out our welcome. Plus, this should be the time for you and your team to shine in the spotlight."

"Thank you for everything, Sam."

"Stay safe." With one last handshake, Sam parted ways, leaving the heroes of New York to get acquainted with their people. Sam gathered Alexavier, who was near Anthem and Radical at the closest street corner. They arrived with several onlookers still in tow, as Sam hailed a cab. Within seconds, a yellow van pulled up to the curb. Sam opened the door, motioning for Alexavier to get in. Questions were being directed toward Sam, one in particular about Alexavier. "Who is that with you, another superhero?"

Sam quickly closed the door before turning to the crowd gathering around and explained, "This is a young man who is getting the opportunity to join me for a day. Soon, I will be providing a chance for more of you to see what it is like in the day of a superhero. We will let you know more coming up shortly. Thanks! See you soon!"

Sam climbed into the van, shutting the door behind him. "We need to get to the helipad to go home." Sam leaned forward to address the cab driver. "Can you take us to Long Island? I'll let you know where we need to go once we're in the borough."

The taxi driver turned to acknowledge Sam and realized who was in his cab, even without his signature beard. "Holy crap! You're him! You're The Patriot Warrior!"

"Yes, I am. Glad to meet you."

Realizing that he was gawking, the taxi driver waived to Sam in acknowledgment, and they were underway.

Sam sat back and settled into his seat. "I think that worked out pretty well as a cover story. Major Constantine is going to love having to figure out something like the hero for a day thing I had to come up with. Being that you're a part of this Secret Garden that we call it, we need to make sure that your anonymity is kept safe. Unfortunately, going on missions and recon has a downside as people can see you and begin to wonder. I've heard that the D.C. mission where you captured Landfill has stirred up public interest again not knowing who you guys are. When we're out in public, especially around me this time, try to keep yourself from being noticed or standing out if fans start coming over. "

Alexavier nodded, "Okay. I understand."

Taking a deep breath, Sam let out a sigh, "I really hated having to lie, especially to the people who trust me. If they find out, this will give the ones who don't trust us the justification for what they're already saying. We shouldn't be hiding you guys, yet the Major won't have any of it."

"Do you think he might reconsider or change his mind?"

"Not likely. He believes that keeping a low profile is safest. I understand that, especially if you're worried about groups like The Terror Tribe that might look to disrupt the training process of young heroes that might one day bring them down. Some of our former recruits have actually joined The Tribe, putting the various complexes in a risky situation, since they know these locations. We may need to move some complexes to new locations. Now that I'm going to be around more often, the way the Major thinks might change. I might be able to do it if I can get Senator Steinberg on board."

"I know a lot of us feel better whenever you're around."

“If need be, I can make a permanent move and stay at Project: Hero full time. Then I’ll be around in case there is anything to worry about. Our program has turned out some of the greatest heroes the world has ever known, like Dynamic, Riva, The, DLX, Downtown and Epic. Why can’t we showcase the next generation of heroes, like you?”

Alexavier had a warm feeling sweep over him when he heard those words. After a couple of lackluster workouts and a fight with Killus, he felt he still wasn’t in Sam’s good graces. “Like me?”

“Sure. You’re going to one day be bringing down every bad guy out there, and the world should see that. We just have to work on your motivation and execution, particularly when it comes to workouts. There cannot be any hesitation. You need to be on point at all times, just like you are when we’re out here chasing down members of The Tribe.”

“I don’t know. There’s a different feeling I get when I’m out here.”

“That needs to stay the same out here. Our worry should be if things change where instead of being hesitant during training, it happens out here where you could get injured or even killed. When you were in Philadelphia, we didn’t think there would be a worry, especially since you excelled at everything. Our hope was that you would transition to the new complex and be out hunting villains with The United in no time.”

Alexavier tried to look confident and reassuring. “I still hope to do that.”

“Then what you need to do when we return is to focus on your training, particularly when it comes to the workouts. No more holding back. No more standing on the sidelines. You need to be as dominant as you were before, just like in Philadelphia.”

“Yes, sir.”

"Keep working on your other skills, but work on combat and sparring. You shouldn't have to worry about who is in front of you, whether it's Dave, Harvey or myself. Just go out and perform as well as you should every time."

"I will."

"Glad to hear." Sam patted Alexavier on the back and turned to face forward. "We will need you to continue your training in tactical and battlefield analysis. You're coming along extremely well. Your sense or instincts for situations is beyond everyone else. I would love for you to further that skill into problem solving larger events. Trying to figure out how not to be one step behind The Tribe all the times is getting tiring. The only time we react is when there has already been a heist or robbery."

Alexavier hesitated, "Uh, speaking of robberies, I was thinking about the last couple of bank robberies. Were they on days when there would be lots of cash on hand?"

"I can't say for sure, although not any more cash than normal."

"I overheard people saying that they thought the banks were hit because they were smaller and had less security."

Sam rubbed his chin. "I'm not a believer in that theory, not when you have someone as powerful as Landfill. He could have taken out or disabled the guards of any bank, not matter the size. What are you thinking?"

"Not sure. With Tribe activity, there seems to be patterns, but we find out what they are afterward. I guess I was wondering if they had a preference on smaller banks that we could look into."

Sam tilted his head and pondered, "Maybe. Usually, you get good at one thing and perfect it. If The Terror Tribe has a liking to hitting certain kinds of institutions, we should probably profile them all to see where they might strike next."

"I'm just thinking about the two heists and why those banks."

"I will say, the Pittsburgh heist happened, but didn't seem odd. Then they have made their way from Washington, D.C. to Pittsburgh, while trying to flee, and just happened to stop along the way to rob another bank? If you're trying to get away and stay out of the lime-light, I could be wrong, but wouldn't you try to not bring attention to yourself, like steal from a bank in broad daylight? I asked about that, but no one had any clue or could make heads or tails of it."

"Could it have been a plan to do all along to hit them both?"

"There have been a couple of times that they would go on a robbery spree and head from one area to another, hitting up multiple businesses and institutions that were on their way. If they were heading toward Cleveland or Detroit, they would have been there by now. If they're heading to Chicago, that's too far into the Midwest. The Tribe usually don't spend that much time in the Midwest. They prefer going right to the West Coast, where there's serious money to be stolen."

"They did in Cleveland when Beth captured Mortymer."

"That's true. But if I remember correctly, that was only one heist and not connected to any others. They also relied on a lot of local muscle."

"Do you think there's a pattern? Have they ever robbed these banks before?"

Sam reached for his backpack. "That's a good question. I don't know offhand. They've robbed so many institutions over the years that it's hard to keep track, but I know someone who might know."

"I've always wondered if they've got somebody on the inside, so they can target certain banks over and over again. Maybe someone is getting paid by The Tribe to work for all the banks or a company that services them."

Sam put his Com-Link in his ear and quickly tapped the button. "Patch me into Major Constantine. Tell him I have a couple of questions."

"If we can find an inside man, maybe that will show us a pattern."

"Hello, Major. It's Sam. Can you tell us if any of recent Terror Tribe heists were locations which they had robbed before?"

A pause happened before Sam responded, "Really?" The surprised tone in Sam's voice had Alexavier look up. "Only the two most recent? Do you know if there is any connection between the two? I'm hoping to find someone who might be that connection, maybe working for… None?"

The disappointing answer had Alexavier searching for another possible idea. Suddenly, the sun found his eyes and brought back the dream he had of the bright light shining and the woman in white. The images reached out from the light like the church steeple just outside. The words she said in his dream now made sense. "What about the first time both were robbed. When was that?"

"Major, did you hear Alex… Yes… So, you're saying both banks were first robbed in 1988, only a couple days from each other… I want to say that's a coincidence, since it wasn't the same day, like what just happened. We need something better to connect them."

Alexavier waved his hand to interrupt. "Were there more that happened with the first time? Did they only stop at two? Were there three or four?"

There was a pause, then Sam spoke, "Yeah, probably got overlooked… Really… Where and when… We are heading to Long Island for an extraction now… Alright… I'll get back to you."

"What did he say?"

Sam looked over. "Back then, there was a third bank hit a couple days later on Long Island. But if that was actually their next target, that would have happened a couple of days ago."

"Has there been a third robbery."

"There hasn't been. That doesn't follow the pattern."

Alexavier stared out the window, puzzled by the inconsistency, but hoping there was a connection. He then wondered, “If a bank gets robbed, like they did long ago, don’t they change things up? I mean, not just security, but their other processes and procedures to throw criminals off if they were to try and rob them again.”

“Most institutions do change things, or at least to some point if there’s a possible breach of data or suspicion of activity of a criminal nature on top of increasing security.” Sam tapped the earpiece. “Any information about the bank on Long Island? Do we know what their monthly procedures are for security, deliveries and transfers?”

A few moments of silence let Alexavier continue looking out the window, until Sam exclaimed, “Really! All three? I’ll be in touch.”

“What did they find out?”

“When the banks were robbed in 1988, they were hit the day after large deposits were made from large area businesses. Similar deposits are still happening the same way, and that’s what occurred in D.C. and Pittsburgh. The bank on Long Island changed their schedule for large scale deposits.”

“When do deposits like that happen?”

“Major?” Alexavier grew anxious with Sam’s silence, until Sam looked over. “That was yesterday.”

Alexavier sat up. “They’re robbing it today!”

“Major, we’re on our way there and should arrive in just a few minutes… Yes… Sam, out.” Sam leaned forward. “Driver? Is it possible to get to The Cities National Bank of Long Island? And if you can get us there quicker, I’ll quadruple the fare.”

“Anything for The Patriot Warrior.” The cab driver nodded and put his foot to the floor. Alexavier noticed Sam changing into his hero outfit and proceeded to do the same. It wouldn’t be long before they were on the scene, hoping to prevent another Terror Tribe heist.

CHAPTER 39

On a semi-busy street in Long Island, a security guard held the door open for a bank customer. She thanked him for the courtesy and walked into the nice cool air, leaving the heat and sun outside. Once she had made it into the lobby, the guard let go of the door so it could swing closed.

That was not to happen. Sticking his hand between the door and its frame, Natural Disaster pulled it open wide and made a quick entry to the lobby. The guard turned and noticed the monstrous villain and attempted to pull his gun. Natural Disaster was too fast and unleashed a strong, energetic blast that threw the guard back, hitting the wall hard enough to have him rendered unconscious.

The Infamous One followed, entering the bank with several other Terror Tribe members falling in behind. "We're here for your vault, not your lives! It will be very easy to keep it that way!"

Terror swept through the lobby, as patrons yelled and quickly cowered on the floor or behind fixtures. Any tellers or bank employees that could started running for a back exit, while the others caught within eyesight of the frightening villains tried to hide the best they could. Screams and cries eventually settled into a subdued drone.

After scanning the lobby and deducing there was no threats anymore, The Infamous One ordered, "Game Over, if you please."

"I would have said this is a stick up. But then again, I'm one for the classics." Game Over passes everyone by and went straight for the stone column. A hefty tug brought it away from being seated between the floor and ceiling. With weapon in hand, he waved it at the employees and patrons. "Or how about hands up? You need to go retro, bro."

"I do what I do and say what I need to say. It's about content, not style."

Game Over question, "When was the last time you watched a movie?"

The Infamous One strolled by, heading for the counter. "I appreciate the written word and not commentary driven, over produced cinema."

Game Over shook his head and cleared the way toward the back with the column. Scurrying in from the outside, Empty and Bootlegger followed behind, a little anxious being with the big guns of the team. Empty placed several of his portals around the bank. The employees were boxed in, scared of what the odd spaces around them would do. Bootlegger flew around back, scoping out the vault. The Infamous One eventually joined her. Upon evaluating the enormous, steel door, the evil mastermind knew what was needed to get inside. A glance to the lobby notified Game Over that his presence was needed. Natural Disaster stood guard while his tag team partner dropped the column and went to the back. Looking the door over, Game Over chuckled, knowing how easy this would be. With one hand on the handle and the other securely on the bottom, he gave a hefty tug and ripped the vault door from the steel shell holding it together.

"Ha! Just like opening a can of tuna." Game Over tossed the metal door into an office area, crushing some desks and computers, sending debris into the air.

Bootlegger slipped inside inspecting what she could possibly carry. Empty joined them, but went towards the wall beside the door and placed a portal. The hole opened large enough for more Terror Tribe members to walk through. The very stocky Rumble and slender Terrorcide quickly began transferring money through the portal.

They were interrupted when Carnevil, the demented clown began pushing his way through to help. Struggling to make it through, he stepped on someone's foot and fell backwards, landing on the ground, causing his top hat to roll away. Carnevil pulled himself up and dusted off his pants. A short waddle had him picking up the hat and looking inside the vault. Satisfied, he grabbed some money and threw it into his hat. But as quickly as he could toss some in, the money flew back out. Feeling annoyed, he stuck his hand into the hat searching for something. Not finding it, he moved deeper where the hat was now up to his shoulder. Once he found the object, he pulled his arm out, holding a white bunny. A comical stare down ended with Carnevil showing the bunny the cash. "Funny little bunny, green means good. It's like lettuce, but with lots more germs. Don't forget to wash your hands and brush the teeth of your comb." Stuffing the bunny back inside, Carnevil began placing as much money as fast as he could into the top hat.

In between money exchanging hands, Cavalio stepped through the portal. She looked over the operation while placing herself next to The Infamous One. She put a hand on his shoulder and leaned in. "How long do we have?"

"Once the portals link together, we have less than five minutes. Thankfully they're close together. If they're more than a mile apart, we would have had approximately twenty seconds."

"We could always use these portals to leave for somewhere warmer."

The Infamous One put his hand to Cavalio's face. "Very shortly, you and I can retreat far from this chaos."

"I look forward to it."

The moment of sentiment was interrupted by Bootlegger. "I've got all I can carry."

"Take the bags and return to the drop point."

"Yes, sir." Bootlegger flew into the portal.

Game Over was disappointed again. “C’mon. I’m just waiting for those words of nostalgia. You mean to tell me that you don’t get that warm feeling when you hear a cliché?”

“Everything about you is only a cliché.” Cavalio’s words hurt.

The Infamous One continued directing the collection of money during the conversation. “I do appreciate your love of vintage verbiage. There’s been so many times that I’ve looked at you as less than civilized. Maybe I should give you the benefit of the doubt just once.”

“Just for me,” Game Over poked “C’mon. Tell me how we’re doing.”

“Everything is going according to plan.”

Game Over smiled and nodded, “You see. Classic.”

CHAPTER 40

Sam and Alexavier were within moments of arriving at the bank. Both were completely geared up and ready for action. Sam was receiving an update from the Major, as Alexavier scanned the skyline, looking for signs of bad guys. A hazy cloud could be seen hovering just above the buildings, possibly from the bank. Once they got to a cross street, their line of sight improved, and they could see their destination.

“Okay. Bye.” Sam tapped his earpiece. “Looks like your intuition was right. Moments ago, several individuals entered and began robbing that exact third bank that was robbed long ago. Reports are a bit sketchy, but eyewitnesses say they did have super powers. From what the Major can determine, there could be as many as five Tribe members involved. Washington, D.C. only saw three villains. Pittsburgh only had the two remaining after we got Landfill, but they got another. Now, if we are looking at five, maybe more, there could be some of the prominent members involved. I had the Major contact local law enforcement and tell them to stay back. The police will be easily outgunned.”

“Should we get back up?”

“That's not a bad idea. Driver, pull over here.”

The taxi pulled to a stop about a block before the bank. Sam and Alexavier grabbed their stuff and got out quickly. Sam handed the driver a stack of bills. “Get out of here so you don’t get hurt.”

The gracious man zoomed away, not wanting to be caught in the crossfire. Sam headed toward the sidewalk on the same side as the bank, backing up to the wall of a building. Alexavier followed close behind, taking a position right by his side.

“I don't think they could see us. Let me make a call before we're too close and give ourselves away from talking.” Sam tapped his Com-Link. He listened for a moment before a voice came back. “Major, it's me. We're out here on Long Island... Major?”

“What happened?”

“I don't know. I heard his voice and then the only thing I could hear was static.” Sam tapped the earpiece again. “Come in, Major.” After a brief listen, he tapped it again. “Nope. Just static. If I were to guess, they might be prepared for a confrontation, and they're waiting. Give me your feelings on things.”

Alexavier closed his eyes, focusing as much on what he could sense. “I don’t feel anything. It's too quiet. I want to believe they're still inside. We got here too fast for them to cleanly get away.”

“I agree. They could be trying to hide or maybe heading towards the back door.” Sam leaned forward, hoping to see a clear path. “Follow me. Stay close.”

They slowly, but steadily walked down the block. Once an alley came up, Sam ducked in, finding a dumpster. They both took out their masks, with Alexavier doing a quick switch to his black hooded sweatshirt. Sam opened the dumpster and placed his bag inside. Alexavier followed suit, and Sam closed the lid softly. Once back on the sidewalk, they quickly moved toward the building on the corner.

“Are you sensing anything?”

Alexavier paused before shaking his head. “Nothing.”

“When we get to the door, stand to the side, out of view. Once situated safely, look through the windows to see if there is anyone inside. If we both give the thumbs up that it’s all clear, we'll go inside. Masks on. You ready?”

"Yes, sir."

Sam looked around to scope out their next move, but saw civilians watching from across the street. He tried waving them away from the possible danger, but they recognized him and began pointing and talking loudly. Sam again attempted to hush them. This time they complied, but the damage might have been done. The commotion was substantial enough that if anyone was watching from the bank lobby would have seen it.

Realizing that the people wouldn't get to a safe area, Sam decided to move forward. Once he knew Alexavier was ready to follow, he sprinted to the closest vehicle, and then to the front door. He motioned to Alexavier to move to the opposite side of the truck. When they were in place, Sam gave the signal to go. With lightning speed, both of them were at the entryway, taking their place on opposite sides. Slowly, each one took a turn peeking into the lobby. Sam gave a thumbs up, followed by one from Alexavier. With the coast all clear, they snuck through the doors and hid behind the closest counter.

Sam put his hand up, holding back his protégée. "What do your feelings say?"

"I'm not sensing any danger."

"That's odd. We'll try to stay together. But in case we get separated, your first priority is to capture any Tribe members you might encounter. Watch your back and continue to try the Com-Link. Meet back here when you're able to. We're going to check out the vault first."

With a quick nod from Alexavier, Sam stayed low, leading the way. A quiet and steady pace led them through the back-office area and staring at a wide-open vault door. Sam held up his hand, keeping Alexavier back, but then waved him forward. Sam crept along until he could peek inside. As the mostly empty vault came into view, Alexavier suddenly got that feeling of dread. "Look out!"

The attempt to warn Sam was futile. A massive energy blast tore through the front wall of the vault, sending Sam back through the front of the building. Alexavier jumped away for cover, trying to shield himself from the shrapnel. After landing near a desk, he looked up to see that Sam was nowhere to be found, only debris from the wall he had been sent through. Scrambling to his feet, he was met by Natural Disaster. That feeling overcame him again and he leaped onto the closest bank teller counter and into the air as a blast of energy ripped through the office, sending desks, chairs, computers and paper flying through the back of the bank. Alexavier reached for a light fixture, swinging far into the lobby and landing near the front door. Once he righted himself, he stood face to face with the deadly villain, just staring him down.

“So, it's that little, black hooded, wannabe hero.”

“Yeah, and I'm here to stop you from stealing any money.”

“Well, that was the plan. Let's see how this turns out.” Natural Disaster began to build up a charge of energy, distorting his image as the energy flowed in and through him, coming out his arms. Feeling the need to move, Alexavier jumped away. With the release of such a violent blast, it impacted the wall behind, sending shards of concrete in all directions. Alexavier rolled with the wave of debris, standing up and charging toward the monstrous villain. Caught off guard, Natural Disaster attempted to throw up a shield of energy, but Alexavier took to higher ground for some offense. Natural Disaster needed more time to build up his energy for more powerful attacks. In general, he only has limited on-demand energy for use. Alexavier's quick use of the bank teller's counter didn't provide enough time for even the smallest recharge. Running along and jumping at the end with as much force as he could throw into a two-legged dropkick, Alexavier was met with a projection of energy that was released from the shield. The subsequent contact created a surge that shot

Alexavier back across the room, forcing him to twist and turn to land on his feet. Once stabilized, he readied for another attack.

But before either had the chance to engage the other again, Sam came charging in and tackled Natural Disaster through the back wall of the building. Alexavier eased up for a second, until that feeling told him to evade. He ducked and rolled, narrowly getting grabbed by Bootlegger, who flew in from behind. The aerial villain hovered while circling, hoping to throw off the young hero. “You're new. I don't remember you at Project: Hero.”

Not knowing enough about who he was facing, Alexavier decided to establish some dialogue. “I am. Name's Dread.”

She sported a devilish smile. “You're that kid they're all talking about. This works out perfect. I get to take care of their little problem and solidify my status with the team.”

“All you can do is fly. That's not that special.”

“That doesn't matter.” She stopped and floated high into the vaulted ceiling. “When their team really doesn't have anyone that is good at flying, I'm a hot commodity that can do this.” With that comment, she swooped down, aiming for the young hero.

Now knowing for sure that her only ability was being able to fly, Alexavier thought the best strategy was to join her where she's most comfortable. He started running toward the vault, making his opponent chase. He waited until she was right on top of him before bouncing off a pillar, landing on his feet and running the other way. Bootlegger twisted her body to turn and followed. Alexavier headed toward a chair, which he used as a springboard, bounced high and kicked off the wall. He timed his leap just right to grab ahold of her leg. The added weight twisted her body, sending her into a spin and flying through the hole in the crumbling wall towards the outside world.

Bootlegger's ability to fly is a delicate balance of speed and agility, coupled with maneuverability dependent upon the way she holds her body, arms and legs. The added baggage of Alexavier caused her to fly out of control, and Alexavier sensed that. He attempted to reach her other leg through the turmoil, eventually getting his grip on it and allowing her to gain partial control of her flight. She looked back with a scowl. “Get off!”

He knew she could try to shake him or she would risk flying out of control again, so he hung on tight. Frustrated, she swung her arms and spun around. Alexavier twisted with her body, continuing to hold on. With limited options to get rid of her unwanted passenger, Bootlegger dove down attempting to use the building tops to scrape him off. As she swung down, his momentum brought his feet close to touching several rooftops and the ventilation equipment scattered throughout. She kept trying, but Alexavier's maneuver to avoid contact with the high-rise architecture threw her off enough to never get too close. She eventually decided another tactic, altitude. Bending and adjusting her body, she zoomed straight into the clouds.

Alexavier knew this joyride wasn't going to end merrily unless he was the one driving. He began to throw his body about, trying to get a feel for what he could do to her flight patterns. Unfortunately, his limited thrashing around wasn't able to dictate where she would go, and he became concerned that he would soon get tired and lose his grip. He had to take full control, which meant adjusting his position to being on her back. He swung his legs, disrupting her trajectory and forcing her to move awkwardly. That allowed him to take one leg and wrap it around her body. He clamped on with the other, allowing him to transfer his torso up to hers. A quick squirm while being in not so controlled flight had him on her back, grabbing her arms and finally taking control.

"Let go!" Bootlegger wanted to contest the takeover, but understood it could mean plummeting to earth. She stayed compliant, waiting to see what Alexavier was going to do.

"We can end this calmly."

"This will only end if you get dropped on your head!"

Alexavier tightened his grip. "Nobody has to get hurt if we can just head back to the bank."

"How about I show you who's going to get hurt?" she gave up trying to talk and threw her body into an awkward position, causing them to spin uncontrollably in the air. Their decline in speed meant a quick descent through the clouds and toward the street below. Alexavier wasn't thrown off, yet used the free fall to whip his body around and latch onto her body with his legs, now pointing opposite the way she way flying. She began to panic and worked to regain stability. Throwing her arms out, she lifted her head and evened out at street level, skimming various vehicles, which didn't faze her passenger. Feeling the need to up the danger, Bootlegger aimed for any standing structure, including buildings. Swooping in and out of streets and back and forth near skyscrapers put Alexavier's grip to the test. He had to readjust his grip several times, but the G forces would eventually prove too much for his slowly failing grasp of her body. Sensing this, she increased her angle of flight toward objects, getting Alexavier to slip even more.

Being backward on her body, he had minimal control, but really need to do something drastic. Every time he tried to rearrange his position, he would almost lose his grip. Finally, he let go with his hands, tightening his legs wrapped around her body. The disruption of balance sent them spiraling along a main road, nearly taking out business signs and canopies. As Bootlegger desperately tried to regain her balance, her thrashing allowed Alexavier to swing around with one arm and grab the back of her suit. He quickly squirmed into position and ended up back on top.

Now that he was on her back, he reached up and put her in a full nelson, giving him full control. His limited piloting experience made for a few close calls slamming into buildings, especially when Bootlegger struggled. An attempt to head back to the bank came up short, as she ducked her head, sending them into several uncontrollable flips. The situation finally deteriorated to the point that Alexavier felt like getting off the ride. Being out of control meant a guessing game of when to jettison. He closed his eyes. When the moment felt right, he let go and let his body fall free. With the world spinning quickly, he wrenched his body around, going against the spin. Having a glimpse of the ground, Alexavier twisted to get more aligned to what was the inevitable landing. The attempt to tuck into a roll didn't provide enough of a brace, resulting in a harsh landing. He rolled several times, eventually coming to a stop next to a set of mailboxes. His disorientation subsided enough to watch Bootlegger slam into the building in front of him. Her body slid down, coming to rest face first on the ground.

Letting the dizziness fade, Alexavier pulled himself to his feet. A quick cinching of zip ties for restraints had him feeling confident that with Bootlegger's state of unconsciousness, she would no longer be able to interfere. Gauging where he was and the distance back to the bank, Alexavier began the rapid journey back to help Sam.

#

Crashing through the back wall wasn't his first idea, but it allowed Sam to get Natural Disaster away from the bank. They both hit the ground, but Sam rolled off to gain distance between them. Getting a running start, he leaped forward, hoping to land a hard attack. Natural Disaster quickly put up a shield to block and the force propelled Sam over his head. Sam landed hard on his back, rolling onto his side.

Getting to one knee, it became a staring contest as Natural Disaster amped up his energy field. Sam didn't want to be sitting duck, so he raced to a dumpster and shoved it hard. Natural Disaster blasted it, sending it back Sam's direction. Sam leaped over, palette in hand and threw it into the air. A blast incinerated the wooden projectile, but drained most of Natural Disaster's energy. Taking the chance that he could penetrate his defenses, Sam sprinted headfirst. Natural Disaster braced for impact, letting Sam get close before unleashing as much energy as possible. Sam was thrown back, landing hard on the concrete. He groaned, rolling to his stomach, but noticed the villain defenseless. With a long grunt, Sam pushed himself up, grabbing a trashcan. Throwing it first, the distraction had Natural Disaster pay attention to the silver projectile, as Sam rushed in and tackled the monstrous man. They wrestled each other before getting back to their feet. Sam grabbed an arm, twisted his body and threw Natural Disaster to the ground,

Sam rose to his feet for another attack, but had no time to try again, as Game Over hit him square in the chest with a telephone pole. Game Over's power was to lessen the gravity of any object he touches. He took this opportunity to take a several hundred-pound chunk of wood and swing it like a Louisville Slugger. Flying backwards toward the bank, Sam's body broke through more of the crumbling wall and slammed into the marble column, causing significant damage. Each impact did its own damage, taking a bigger toll on Sam as he struggled to get back on his feet. A quick glance saw Game Over swing again, but Sam was quick enough to dodge the next telephone pole attack. It pounded the column again, sending splinters and shards everywhere.

Finally, a brooding Natural Disaster made his way back into the bank. He kept a small field energy around him as he slowly approached Sam. Both villains moved in opposite directions, trying to corner Sam, like lions on the African plane. Sam scooted back on one knee until a chair stopped his retreat. Scanning the immediate vicinity, Alexavier was nowhere to be found and there was no way out. He realized that the situation just went from bad to really, really bad.

Hoping to slow things down, Sam tried a little dialogue. “I don't know how many times I've tried, and it never works, but maybe just one last time to talk you guys out of this.”

Game Over waved the pole around. “Talk is cheap, especially when you keep coming after us.”

“You've left me with no choice.”

“And you've left us none as well.” Natural Disaster stopped close to the front entrance to block any escape. “Now, we take you out, and then your little friend.”

“I think I want the kid's head on a pole,” Game Over joked, waving the pole vigorously.

Sam kept eyeing Natural Disaster, who had a clear shot to do some real damage, yet was reluctant to do so. “We'll get you, no matter what it takes.”

“Oh, poor Sam. You were like an uncle to me.” Game Over smirked. “Come to think of it, I hated my uncles.”

Game Over's erratic waving of the telephone pole continued to knock things around, as well as hitting the walls and center column. Every time it did, a little dust and debris would fall from the ceiling. It quickly became obvious to Sam that Game Over had no clue about the building, but Natural Disaster did. That's why the enormous villain was cautious in unloading a barrage of energy blasts to cause any more damage. This could work to Sam's advantage if he could create a bit of chaos.

Feeling the time was right to escalate things, Sam reached back for the chair behind him, whipping it as hard as he could, like a baseball. Game Over easily swatted it away aiming for Sam, who quickly ducked out of the way and rolled to his side. Ending up near a small table, he grabbed the lamp that was on it and tossed it toward Natural Disaster. He then took the table and aimed it at Game Over. Both villains deflected the projectiles away with ease.

Sam jumped over to the counter near the teller windows. He reached for any object laying around and hurled them with force. Game Over's swing easily went through the objects. He turned his attention to Sam, taking a swing like an axe to chop wood, smashing the counter as Sam rolled away. Natural Disaster moved from side to side, hoping to contain the hero.

"You stupid, son of a..." Game Over's frustration came out in every swing, which also meant being reckless. Each time he brought the pole back, the next attack was much stronger and much faster. That meant carelessness and Sam used it to his advantage. Moving away toward the door, where Natural Disaster stood, Sam quickly dove back underneath, rolling to his knees and narrowly missing the telephone pole heading in their direction. When Game Over attempted to slam the patriotic hero again, Sam leaped to the side, allowing the pole to smash into the column, shattering the pole and cracking the column further. The realization hit Natural Disaster that the rumbling sound was the building losing its structural integrity and was starting to crumble. Sam planned his maneuvering appropriately, leaving enough room to race toward the hole in the back wall of the bank. The ceiling came down around the legendary Tribe members, effectively trapping them inside the collapsing structure.

Sam came flying out of the bank, landing in a harsh, uncontrolled roll. Once he could move, he scrambled to distance himself from the random concrete and debris being thrown from the collapsing bank only several feet away. The mad dash to safety ended with his back against the adjacent building. With the cloud of dust quickly thickening around him, Sam scanned his surroundings and raced for safety further down the alley, toward a parking lot between a couple of nearby businesses. Once at a safe distance, he glanced back, wondering if his recruit was alright. "Dread, come in." The static was still present, leaving him to call out verbally, "Dread!" With no response, his thoughts went to the possibility that communications were being intentionally blocked or scrambled. Scanning the nearby adjacent buildings, a figure stood out, standing near the edge with his arms spread wide. It was the Tribe member, Xstatik and he needed to be taken down. It was critical for Sam to stop Xstatik from using his power to disrupt radio signals.

Sam sprinted forward, and his foot made contact with a dark area, which suddenly appeared transcending the narrow alley. A jolting, psychological wave of terror coursed through his mind, causing his legs to buckle beneath him. Sam started to fall helplessly, as his body rolled forward crumpling to the ground. Opening his eyes slightly, Sam pushed back the searing pain and gathered as much energy as he could to lift his body up and rest on his knees.

As Sam stared up at the sky, his worst reality was now a daytime nightmare. The buildings were in ruin. The darkened sky had shades of red with clouds painted with blood. Acid rain was falling all around him. The freedom of his world had deteriorated into a lifeless landscape that swallowed all hope. His very soul began to die. Looking at the building before him, he notices a woman standing at the top, watching his agonizing realizations. His breathing shortened, and his heart rate increased. Sam was under attack, and it took all of his energy to utter one name. "Helen..."

CHAPTER 41

Seeing Major Constantine rushing through the halls of the complex is a sight hardly seen. When communications with Sam were lost, the former military man wasted no time getting to the command center. Everyone was in a panic, frantically searching for some kind of answer for the Major, all to avoid the wrath of the man in charge.

"Somebody tell me something!"

No one had an answer. Thus, no one was safe from the Major's glare. He waited, but still no one indulged him. With the lack of response lingering, his blood pressure rose even higher. "Does anyone have anything for me or do I start throwing people around the room?"

A reluctant communications technician slowly moved closer. "We lost contact with Sam about a half hour ago."

The Major struggled to stay calm. "You told me that ten minutes ago. Somebody give me an update now!"

A frightened Sergeant spoke up, "We haven't heard from him, and we don't know why."

"Maybe that's what you should be trying to figure out!"

"It might help if we contacted someone in the area. You know, to see if it's just a communication problem in New York?"

"And who would you expect us to call, Sargent?"

"With The United half a country away, our only real choice is The United Outcasts."

"Not an option."

The puzzled Sargent asked, "I'm not sure we have any other-"

"We always have another option! Do we know any politicians?"

"Sorry, Major. We've burned most of those bridges bef-"

"Damn it! I need somebody over there! Do we know any reporters or news anchors?"

"I can try to get through, sir. But how should I say where we are from and identifying as?"

The Major's frustration level peaked, as he became speechless. Then one of the corporals spoke up, "Sir! I have Booby Trap on the line!"

The Major rushed over, yanking the headset from him. "I need you two to head to Long Island immediately where a bank is being robbed. You should be able to see it by the smoke in the distance. Hurry! We've lost communications with Sam and Alex."

"That might take us a bit, but we'll get there as fast we can. Out."

Letting out a big sigh, the Major closed his eyes. He was once again not in control of a situation and had no real answer to solve this riddle. One that had two of his people's lives in danger.

#

Sam's muscles constricted, the mental attack consuming his mind. The world he lived in had now been replaced by one that haunted him. The concrete buildings and dirt-filled roads were morphed into crumbling structures that burned, painting the skies in hues of red and orange. Hysterical people ran around, tearing down and destroying whatever they could grasp. Sam's eyes saw the silhouette of the woman, with a man hiding behind her. He mustered all the power to fight this mental horror. "Helen... please."

The woman approached the edge of the building, leaning forward. Finally, Hellabond revealed herself. Her flowing hair that was an inferno of raging fire matched her anger and hate. “Don't you dare call me that! You destroyed her! You didn't care about her!”

“This isn't… you. You… would never do-”

“Shut up!” Hellabond screamed. “Your mind games killed her years ago! Helen Bordeau died alone. Her heart rotted like the piece of useless flesh that it was. Did you ever come to see her or help her? No! Your selfishness and lack of feelings destroyed anything that could have been saved! Now I'm going to repay you for what you did. My Field of Screams is what you deserve!”

“I know it's not... you. Stop this.” Sam struggled to lift his head. “Is this… what you want, Beauperon?”

The mysterious man standing in the background walked over to his enraged comrade. His thick French accent exuded arrogance. “So, my friend. You do not like to see your old acquaintances, no?”

Sam tried to hold onto his consciousness. Her Field of Screams began swelling, and Sam had a hard time keeping his thoughts separate from the surreal mental images. “Beauperon…this is not… why… would you do this?”

Beauperon sneered, “Soon, my dear Hellabond will own you, just like I own her.”

“This is... not like you, The Tribe? Where.... is your cohort, Vliet?” Sam's body quivered with spasms.

“You never really understood us.” Beauperon leaned over to enjoy the view. “You never cared about us. You tried to kidnap me. Your actions hurt Vliet, and for that, you’ll pay.”

“You committed crimes… you’re wanted for killing-”

“No! No, Samuel! My country has deemed me to be a free man, a hero to the people even. I am bigger than you are to your own country. It is you who will be my greatest accomplishment." Beauperon smiled, "I will bring you back to stand trial for your crimes. I place you under arrest by the authority of the country of France, dear Samuel."

Sam's vision started to completely transform. His reality became one with the illusion that was infesting his brain. The decaying world of his worst nightmares dragged him down to hell, and he was helpless, except to scream.

#

After what seemed like a lengthy run from several blocks over, Alexavier finally made it back to the bank, seeing only the outermost structural portions of the building standing. As he gaped at the sight, he could feel the ground start to shake, getting stronger and more violent. After a few seconds, it beginning to subside, allowing him to hear the sound of somebody in trouble, off in the distance. Trying to sprint around the rubble to see who needed help, he was greeted by the new Tribe member, Empty, who was extremely nervous. Alexavier knew this villain wouldn't be a problem in a face-to-face confrontation, since his powers were for escaping. But catching him would be a whole other story with his ability to create portals. Rather than engage in a lengthy chase, Alexavier tried to at least reason with the skittish bad guy.

"I know you don't want to fight me. Just give up now, and this doesn't have to get physical."

Empty laughed through the nervousness, "You ain't taking this away from me. I've worked too hard. I'll bury you in a loop of portals for eternity if I have to."

Empty opened up his hand, creating a hole of nothingness. With his other hand, he stretched it until it was almost as big as he was and threw it to the ground. Running as fast as he could to put distance between himself and

Alexavier, he continued to create portals and place them around the streets and walls. Alexavier took off chasing him, but had to be careful where he took each step.

Studying villains as much as Alexavier did in the library, he was familiar with how these portals worked. Each pair is specifically linked to each other, making it hard to track which pairs were connected when there are multiple portals surrounding him. He had to be careful not to get caught falling into or stepping on one and ending up in an unusual place.

The chase around the street in front of the bank was a game of cat and mouse, but with mousetraps for the cat. Empty would throw a portal in an odd location and then drop another on the ground. Over and over again, Alexavier would continue to dodge portal after portal.

Even with Empty throwing out as many portals as he could to disrupt any chance for physical engagement, Alexavier was quick to bypass each and every one of them. The only downside with all the portals was Empty could easily keep his distance. With portals having been placed everywhere, it was getting confusing as to where each one led.

Although, Alexavier had thought of a plan, he had no idea whether or not it would even work. The only way to know would know was to jump right in. So that's what he did. Seeing the nearest portal, he jumped in feet first. But what goes in feet first, comes out upside down, Alexavier's orientation made for a messy landing on the pavement. Having no clue which portals were connected with each other, the only logical thing to do be to try them all.

Another rumble shook the ground strong enough that Alexavier stumbled forward into another portal. This exit proved beneficial as he ended up behind the confused villain. But Empty produced a couple more portals, causing enough disruption for Alexavier to attempt a direct attack. So again, he jumped into another hole in front of him. This time he came out of the wall across the street. With every entry into a portal, he began to figured out each destination, until Alexavier had a plan for using Empty's portals to his advantage.

Another tremor started, slowing the battle, but this one lasted longer. Keeping their balance was a bigger task than it was before, especially being out in the open. As the shaking died down, Alexavier took advantage of the confusion and dove headfirst into one of portals on the ground. He popped up from another in the middle of the road, landing on his feet. He quickly dove into another, coming up in a different location. The cycle happened three or four more times causing Empty to panic. Finally, after numerous transitions from one area to another, Alexavier found the right portals that were connected and jumped in feet first. The subsequent transitions from portal to portal had left Empty even more confused. Finally, Alexavier exited a portal stuck to the wall of the building next door, which happened to be right next to Empty. Alexavier landed on one knee and pulled out the steel rod, pressing the button on top. The compact staff extended to full length and locked into place. With one swift swing, he was able to sweep Empty off his feet. With another quick sweep, pouncing on the bad guy's neck, he shoved the end of the staff directly against his Adam's apple. Empty attempted to struggle, but couldn't move from the pressure of the metal staff pushing him to the ground.

Once again, Alexavier heard the sound of someone in distress. As much as he would like to bring down a Tribe member, who is already in his grasp, the need to help whoever was in trouble pulled him more. Letting go of Empty, Alexavier rushed through the alley, heading along massive chunks of debris from the bank. The remaining walls began to disappear, as he entered an alley that was adjacent to an open lot. A chance look to his left just for the briefest of moments revealed a person kneeling on the ground. Such an odd sight made him stop and redirect his course of action. Alexavier slowed down, until he could see who the distressed person was. A shock overwhelmed him as he realized that it was Sam Nelson, the Patriot Warrior. Alexavier began sprinting, but his plan was quickly derailed when a man in plain street clothes stepped out of a door from the nearest building.

Alexavier shouted, “What are you doing? Get back inside!”

Realizing that the young hero was unaware of who he is, The Infamous One looked to take advantage of the situation and inquired, “Are you one of them?”

The unknowing Alexavier rushed over to the man and moved him closer to the wall. “Stay down and don’t make any noise! If they hear you, they’ll come after you. This isn’t the place to be walking around right now.”

“But if I run real fast, I bet I could-”

Alexavier grabbed a hold of the man's shirt. “Look, these people are killers. They won’t hesitate to kill you if they catch you. If you value your life, go back in and hide.”

The eyes of The Infamous One looked out into the lot between the buildings. He broke free from Alexavier and darted toward the center of the open area yelling, “They won’t catch me!”

Fearing for the man's safety, Alexavier was quick to go after him. Once he caught up to the man, Alexavier attempted to restrain him. “You’re going to get yourself killed.”

“Let me go!”

“Stop, you don’t know what-” Alexavier tried desperately to hold onto him when The Infamous One whipped around, pulling out a chromed semi-auto pistol.

“Sorry, kid. It’s a waste that your life has not yet begun, and it is about to end,” The Infamous One taunted.

Alexavier took a step back, nearly stumbling over a baseball-sized rock. He regained his balance and placed his foot behind the rock. “I’m trying to help a friend over there. We can leave here, and both of us can walk away. Neither of us has to get hurt."

"Really?" The Infamous One produced a sly grin. "Currently, I do not think that you have anything useful to bargain with. I'm not staring down the barrel of a high-powered handgun. There is nothing that you can bring to the table to barter with."

Alexavier bluffed, "I can let you walk away."

Alexavier's lack of fear coupled with his own confidence made The Infamous One curious. "It is interesting. You are such a new hero to your team, yet inexperience has given way to the knowledge of years of battle. I almost regret that you will become an unremarkable ink blot on the map that history will draw."

"I'm no artist, but let me paint you a picture. You're going to be tied up and headed to a prison cell."

"My appreciation for the arts puts me in the prime spot to deal. You are no Van Gogh. You are no Monet. Alas, you have nothing of worth." The Infamous One pulled back the hammer to the massive pistol. "This plan was perfection, like a priceless Picasso. This was better than I imagined. Instead of your whole team, it's just the two of you. We got you to come right to us. You had no clue this was an invitation to your funeral, especially after you messed with our resources and operations. This plan has been all about you. You followed the trail of crumbs right to us and now, you will become a memory."

With care, Alexavier cradled the rock with the toes of his boot. With a swift motion, he swung his leg and hurled the rock, smacking The Infamous One's head. While his enemy was off balance, Alexavier pounced forward, knocking away the gun with one hand and delivered a well-timed, leaping punch. Stunned, The Infamous One tumbled to the ground.

Alexavier crouched down, getting on top and grabbing him by his throat. "Who are you? What do you have to do with this?"

"You are so naïve. You have no clue," The Infamous One stated.

"I don't need clues, just a name!"

A smile appeared on The Infamous One's face. "Samuel Nelson."

Two words, one hero's name. It was more than enough meaning to the young man that completely changed his focus. Alexavier looked up, hearing Sam yell. The Infamous One seized the small window of opportunity and kicked Alexavier, flipping him over The Infamous One's head.

The Infamous One stood up and slowly backed away, reaching down and pulling out a black mask. "Very shortly, Sam will be under the permanent control of Hellabond and her mental powers. Once she infests his mind long enough, he will become her slave forever. It is up to you to choose whether to save him or not."

As The Infamous One pulled the mask over his face, Alexavier finally realized who had tried to put a bullet in him. He had a tough choice to make, yet each possibility had its reward. Alexavier gave The Infamous One a reprieve and jumped up to help Sam. The Infamous One rushed off to a safer location amongst the shadows of the buildings, occasionally looking back to make sure that the young hero wasn't following him.

Seeing Sam kneeling on the ground was very distressing, so Alexavier raced over as fast as he could. Once he was within arm's reach, his eyes fixated on the most unusual of things. The ground resembled waves of water, but continuing to shift and morph in ripples of energy. Centered in the middle of the weird field, Sam was not aware that Alexavier was so close.

Sam's pleas continued in his mentally altered world. "Please! Just hear me, Helen."

"Call me Hellabond!" she screamed.

"Please. I need you to hear... me."

Brimming with confidence, Beauperon said, "You could do yourself a favor, Samuel, and let her mind take yours. The pain will go away. You will feel nothing."

"Let Sam go!" Alexavier yelled out, grabbing their attention.

Beauperon sighed in disgust, "Dear boy, do you have any idea what he has done? Have you ever heard about the unspeakable crimes he has committed?"

"He's a great man! He's a hero to many people!" Alexavier stated.

"He's a bastard! He's a liar and a thief!" Hellabond's hatred flowed through each word, just like her Field of Screams. "His pain and suffering will end when he joins my side. He will fulfill my every wish. He will love me again!" The words were uncomfortable to Beauperon, whose reaction was less than enthusiastic.

Alexavier tried to stall, hoping to figure out a solution to the situation. "Okay, so you care about him. Can you be happy if he doesn't care about you, because you're forcing him to? Deep down, he will resent that."

"No, you have no idea. Sam let her ruin my life! Julie Beckenstein caused it with her lies, and he let her do it. I will hurt her the best way I can, by stealing him from her!" Hellabond's eyes glowed with the red shade of anger, while her hair raged up like flames of fire.

Alexavier realized that Hellabond was angry at the original Beacon of Light, a hero from the old team before The United. Noticing Beauperon showing some uneasiness about her plans, he tried another approach. "Is what you want for him to be her servant?"

Beauperon fired back, "He will not become a part of us! He is going to pay for his crimes, and his life will be his payment."

Hellabond turned around, furious. “He will not be used and thrown away! It is only for me to decide what will happen to him! I will decide how he will serve by my side!”

Beauperon pleaded, “He has caused you pain, my dear. If he is allowed to stay with you, he could only cause more by leaving again.”

Alexavier's ploy to cause a rift was slowly working. “That's right. Do you want to get hurt again? If you let him go, then that will never happen.”

“Shut up! Shut your damn mouth!” Her field gradually lessened around Sam. “You want to let him hurt me and get away with it? You are just as much the liar as she is! You are just as bad as he is! You're trying to screw with me!”

Feeling uncomfortable, Alexavier looked down at the ground and saw Hellabond’s Field of Screams moving closer to him from behind. His only avenue of escape was a small brick wall that jutted out of the closest building. He used the corner to run and climbed up to the lowest fire escape platform. He catapulted himself up, grabbing the bottom bar. Upon pulling himself up, he looked down and saw her Field of Screams slowly climbing the wall. In one fluid motion, Alexavier jumped to the rail and leaped across the narrow alley to the fire escape on the other side. One hand caught the bottom of the lowest platform, leaving him hanging precariously vulnerable. He reached with his other hand and pulled himself up. A frantic dash up each set of stairs ended when the stairs stopped only three floors up, too low from the roof. Alexavier noticed a streetlight jutting out from the nearby telephone pole. Being his only safe haven, he jumped as far as possible. His left hand touched the bar and slipped off. Luckily, he was able to swing his right hand up, grabbing onto it. Swinging freely, he took a moment to get his wits about him. The Field of Screams had engulfed everything but the light pole. But that gradually changed, as the flux of energy began creeping up from the bottom.

With escape not possible, the thought to attack them might divert The Field enough to get away, but he couldn't get far enough to not get consumed in it. Taking one hand from the bar, Alexavier dug into his belt, pulling out a couple of throwing needles. Contorting his body, he gained the momentum to twist back and heave the needles at the two villains. The one aimed toward Hellabond slammed into her Field that radiated from her body and disintegrated. He got lucky with the second one that pierced Beauperon's shoulder, causing him to scream in pain and fall to one knee. His cries caused his cohort to turn and see the blood.

"You little worm! You helpless little worm! You think a mere physical object can hurt me? Your lack of originality in fighting me is typical of what Sam has taught you. He has now led you to a certain and painful end!"

Seeing the young hero wiggle around, without an advantageous place to go, Hellabond cackled while speaking. "Your escape is an invitation to hell. In moments, Sam will be mine, forever! Soon, you will scream for me, and you will become my slave to toy with as well. You will suffer at my fingers for the vile words that have come out of your mouth!"

Realizing this was a no-win situation, and he'll never be able to get through to her, Alexavier made a hard choice. One free man was better than none. He pulled himself up, chest high to the bar and started to swing. A couple of swings back and forth had given enough momentum, and he launched himself forward into the air. Extending his body as far as he could, Alexavier tucked in, preparing to land. With sufficient force, he leaped forward upon hitting the ground. His body slammed into Sam, knocking him away and clear of the Field of Screams. Sam was now too far for another one of her attacks, but Alexavier on the other hand was caught. He sat up on his knees. The horrific look in his eyes showed the effects of her torturous, mind-altering powers. Alexavier's plan to sacrifice himself was successful. He had temporarily saved his idol, but the price he might pay could be his soul.

Hellabond cried out in horror, “You worthless little… your attempt to save Sam left you to me! No matter. You'll soon be mine. Then I'll come back for Sam and have you both!”

The mental struggle for Alexavier was one of futility in the nonsensical and bogus world that Hellabond’s Field of Screams created. The sights brought terror to his eyes. The real world vanished, transformed into the nightmare that was hidden in the back of his mind. Cries slowly turned to screams.

The Infamous One watched with utter joy at the sight of the two heroes on the ground, but turned his attention to the remnants of the bank. The shaking began again, so he backed away. With one last intense rumble, slabs of concrete and debris were shot out from the base of the fallen bank, revealing a tired Natural Disaster and Game Over. After the final concrete projectiles had come to rest on the ground, The Infamous One hurried to his comrades, pulling them out of the crater. Once they could see that both heroes were down and out, gasping for air was replaced by sighs of relief and maniacal laughter.

“We got him!” Game Over exclaimed.

“Hellabond has him trapped. Killing him doesn’t have to be our only option,” Natural Disaster stated. “With her powers to corrupt and control, he can be ours!”

The Infamous One smiled, “Absolutely. In the meantime, we have The Patriot Warrior to deal with.”

The three most dangerous villains of The Terror Tribe gradually found their way through the rubble to a crawling and injured Sam. Even being who they were, caution was taken in case the hero was playing possum. Their methodical stalking cast a shadow, alerting Sam to their presence.

Sam finally turned over, slowly gaining back strength. "What a miss match. The three toughest men The Tribe has to offer. Surely you don't need three more to beat me down?"

"Oh, this will be fun," Natural Disaster said with a chuckle.

Game Over grabbed a large chunk of cement. "What was it your dad always said? This is going to hurt you more than it'll hurt me. Maybe that was just my dad. Either way, this is gonna sting a little."

Sam laughed, "You're just so outnumbered."

"How do you figure that?" The Infamous One halted, sensing that something might be off and turned quickly.

Sure enough, flying in his direction was several members of The United Outcasts. Epic led the charge with DLX and Radical holding on tight. Apex followed, carrying Downtown and Transcend. Epic let go of Radical, who bulked up for his landing, hitting the ground with a thud and heading directly for Natural Disaster. DLX needed a softer landing, but followed close behind. Downtown took a position slightly away from the battlefield and began to climb the nearest building, which put him just across from Hellabond and Beauperon. To keep from being discovered, Downtown used hand signals instead of vocal commands to guide his team and secure the fallen heroes. Epic used his ultraviolet, charged blasts to keep Hellabond off balance while performing aerial flybys. Apex dropped off Transcend and then followed suit, zooming in and out, too fast to be attacked from The Terror Tribe below and diverting their attention.

Game Over freaked out, desperately trying to find a weapon. Natural Disaster stood his ground, waiting for his energy level to rise to the point of being able to be unleashed. Radical slimmed down super thin, racing at incredible speeds around the Tribe members, keeping them off balance. The diversion allowed DLX to come up on Natural Disaster and pull the charged particles from him that he was building up. With enough power harnessed, DLX delivered a powerful blow that shattered Natural Disaster's remaining protective shield. In the meantime, Game Over had picked a couple of cinder blocks and hurled them at DLX. Putting up a slight energy shield of his own from what little stored energy was left in his body, the chunks of cement broke apart and fell onto the ground. Feeling the time was right to strike, Natural Disaster slowly pulled up a bit of energy for a swing, but was met with a massive punch from Radical that snapped his head back, sending him butt first to the ground. For the first time since becoming the vicious villain the world knows as Natural Disaster, he felt his own blood pouring out his nose and lower lip. Seeing his partner looking out of sorts, Game Over began reaching for larger slabs of cement from the bank and repeatedly threw them toward DLX. Radical bucked up from his slim stature and jumped in to lend a hand, using his increasing strength and invulnerability to deflect away each and every projectile.

While the other villains were preoccupied, Transcend walked briskly down the alley to the edge of Hellabond's Field of Screams. The swirling and bubbling field of energy had an ominous look to it, but not one that Transcend was afraid of. She picked up one foot and cautiously sat it down, causing the Field of Screams to back away from the ground she was occupying. She kept moving forward until the parting of The Field allowed for Alexander to be clear and unaffected. He slumped forward and fell to the ground. Transcend quickly leaned down to help the drained, young hero onto his feet. As they hurried away from the battlefield, The Field continued to dissipate away from wherever she stepped until they were cleared and safe. Feeling exhausted, Alexavier dropped to the ground, needing the rest to recuperate.

Under pressure from what felt like all sides, Hellabond's Field of Screams became erratic, extending into various directions and back again. She continued her guttural yelling with each pass of the heroes. Unable to have her Field entangle anyone touching the ground, she began to focus her hatred to extend The Field out through the air and in all directions. Beauperon freaked out, stumbling back, trying to stay out of the way while holding his shoulder.

On the rooftop of the adjacent building, Julie Beckenstein, the original Beacon of Light, stood poised and still. The sight threw Hellabond off, causing her to stumble over to the roof ledge and her Field to vanish. Upon regaining her balance, she looked over to see that Julie had disappeared. Angry and confused, the thoughts began to pound in Hellabond's head, seeing the woman she blames most. The only thing she could do was scream, “NO!”

Beauperon finally made it back to his feet, hearing his accomplice's distress. “What is wrong? Why are you screaming?” Not receiving a response, he carefully walked to where she was standing. Her Field of Screams was erratic, so he kept his distance for the moment.

“She's here. Damn it, she's here!” Hellabond looked around feverishly. “Where are you?”

“Who are you talking to?” Beauperon wondered.

Hellabond's ranting continued, “Stop hiding! Come out, you tramp!”

In a desperate attempt to shake her from her angered state, Beauperon placed his hand on her shoulder, trying to stop her persistent screeching. “Helen, please.”

“NO! Leave me be! Get away from me!”

“Ma chère, we should go!” Beauperon tugged at her arm.

“LET GO!” Hellabond unleashed her powers at Beauperon. Her Field took control of his consciousness, leaving him only with his voice to scream. It pierced Hellabond’s ears and jolted her back from her rage to realize what she had done. Her Field of Screams vanished instantly.

Beauperon fell to his hands and knees. "Helen, we need to leave. We are not safe."

Hellabond took a quick glance to the opposite rooftop. "But-"

"They will be coming for us. Helen!" Beauperon grabbed her arm again. She reluctantly allowed him to pull her away, but still looked back for the women she eternally despised.

#

Being out in the open and in bright sunlight, The Infamous One was at a huge disadvantage. He had no shadows to hide in. The most he could do was fend off the attacks with his firearms. Rather than engage in a pointless battle and waste ammo, he found a spot near the destroyed bank where he could no longer be seen. Game Over tried to find any object to pick up and throw, while Natural Disaster continued to recharge, hoping to shoot a wave of energy towards anyone he didn't like. Both thought better and joined their fearsome leader, taking cover.

Through the chaos, The Infamous One shouted, "Our fortunes have changed!"

"You really think so?" Game Over responded sarcastically.

"I'm not done yet," Natural Disaster muttered, still looking to fight on.

The Infamous One placed his hand on Natural Disaster's shoulder. "The time has arrived."

Natural Disaster would rather fight than run, but with constant pressure caused from DLX and Radical, the three most deadly villains alive started to fear for their freedom. Not wanting to get captured, they quickly retreated from the scene. Game Over grabbed dumpsters and pallets, just to wave around in defense. After providing enough head start for his brethren to get away, Game

Over lobbed the last dumpster toward the downed heroes in an effort to divert the chasing heroes. Epic used a focused energy beam to catch and hold the dumpster and everything inside. He set the metal container softly away from the battlefield before once again joining the fight.

As the villains backed away, reinforcements arrived with Anthem, Livevil and Giggle Stick rushing towards them. Knowing there was clearly no way to win this fight, the remaining members of The Terror Tribe retreated as quickly as possible. Hoping to hold off the heroes from advancing, The Infamous One turned back to fire a shot from his pistol, but it did little other than bounce off Epic's energy field. The added pressure of more heroes meant extreme measures needed to be taken. Natural Disaster stopped and turned to face the oncoming heroes. He raised his arms and built enough power to unleash a blast of energy that radiated outward, obliterating both buildings nearby. The rainstorm of flying debris provided a necessary distraction and forced Downtown to shift to an adjacent building or get buried underneath the rubble. Anthem weaved through the raining shards of concrete as Radical bulked up even more to punch away those pieces that came his way. Epic flew over and stopped between the stone projectiles from the destroyed building and reached out his arms. With all his might, he extended out his energy field to ensnare every piece of concrete that could pose a dangerous threat to the team's safety. Once all the flying debris was encapsulated with his energy field, Epic released his hold, allowing the stone fragments to safely drop to the ground.

As Epic descended to the ground to rest after the strenuous use of his powers, other members continued their pursuit of the villains. Never the ones to give up on a fight, even when it's over, Livevil and Giggle Stick continued to chase after the deflated bad guys. You could hear them hoot and holler, excited to chase down members of The Terror Tribe.

CHAPTER 42

On his hands and knees, Alexavier tried desperately to look back, not to the rooftop where Hellabond stood, but the one across from him. Once the Field of Screams subsided, he caught a glimpse of the woman from his dreams. Transcend continued to assist, helping him to sit up. He continued to breathe heavy and scan the buildings. He knew she wasn't an allusion. Although the Field of Screams can make you see things that aren't there, he knew that she was real.

With the area now secure, Downtown hurried down the side of the building to check on everyone, and in particular to assist Anthem in helping the legendary hero still resting on his knees. "How are you doing?"

Sam leaned back and worked to catch his breath. "A bit groggy, but that will clear up with time. How's Dread?"

"The kid's resting," Anthem stated. "He was getting his brain scrambled by Hellabond. Were you hurt? Did The Tribe-"

"Actually, it was Hellabond who did the most damage."

Downtown wondered, "I thought Dread was in the one in her field."

"The only reason he was there is because he saved me. She had me trapped for quite some time. If he hadn't come along when he did, I might have succumbed to the Field of Screams."

Anthem added, "We saw The Tribe standing over you."

"Yeah. Not sure what that was about. They've killed people much quicker than that."

"The Infamous One has such an ego," Epic stated. "I think he wanted to relish in the fact that it was you he had in front of him. The wars between you go way back, don't they? I'm sure he was thinking that this was finally going to be the end of things."

Downtown directed the others to continue to ensure the area was secure, and maintain the integrity of possible evidence. Epic and Apex hovered around the perimeter, making sure the growing crowd of curious citizens didn't get too close. The returning Livevil and Giggle Stick also helped to secure the site, as large chunks of cement continued to fall from the leftover skeleton of the bank. Transcend had moved Alexavier closer to a medical team for an evaluation. They had kept him on the ground, even though he felt he could stand. Sam motioned for him to stay down.

"I'm okay. Really, I am."

Transcend countered, "We just need to be cautious. Her effects can linger."

"You good?" Sam stared, observing the young hero.

"Yes, sir."

Feeling confident in the coherent response, Sam nodded and motioned to allow him to get up. "How's your head? Her Field can make your mind cloudy for long stretches after being in it."

"I feel fine. I wasn't in there that long."

Anthem informed Sam, "We noticed the smoke in the distance being much more than a normal fire, and Transcend detected a weird aura about this area."

Transcend added, "The mental signature of powers being used was so strong that there must have been something big going on. I couldn't identify who was creating the disturbance, which meant we needed to investigate."

"Downtown was concerned," Anthem stated. "So, he had us head over here as quickly as our guys could fly. You were down, but luckily not out."

"Both Natural Disaster and Game Over were waiting for us." Sam patted Alexavier on the back. "I'm glad to see you're alright after getting separated."

"I had to fend off Bootlegger and Empty. When I finally got back here, The Infamous One pretended to be a bystander. Then he pulled a gun on me and told me it was their plan to bring me here."

Downtown asked Sam, "Can I use your Com-Link to inform the Major. Hopefully he can send reinforcements."

"Last I knew, communications were down. Xstatik was blocking all signal, but give it a try." Sam handed over the earpiece.

"Wait," Downtown paused. "Why would they want a recruit?"

"It happened before," Sam responded. "Last time we had to deal with them, they had captured Beacon of Light."

Anthem wondered, "The Terror Tribe was never known for targeting trainees."

Sam explained, "We weren't sure if they really did target her, or if she was just in the wrong spot. If this was on purpose, we have a big problem. A lot of The Terror Tribe consists of former Project: Hero recruits. Some of them know where our complexes are located."

"What did The Infamous One say exactly?"

"He said it was their plan for me to come here."

Sam thought hard. "You did figure out the bank robberies. What if that's what they had in mind, that you would figure it out and thus be here?"

Anthem asked, "Why would they want him specifically?"

Sam took a deep breath. "Our last encounter with them had our team in New Jersey, trying to rescue Beacon. While most of the team was taking on part of The Terror Tribe, Dread found out where they held Beacon and disrupted their plans. We know they had focused on Beacon, because she could make it too bright for The Infamous One to use his powers to hide. After what

Dread did to their hideout and ruining their operations, I can see why he is now their target."

Various police and government authorities had arrived and began taking control of the crime scene. The rest of The United Outcasts returned, with Epic informing everyone, "Not sure who's going to do it, but the feds are going to want you to fill them in."

Sam said, looking over to the front of the bank, "I'll do it, but give me a minute. Right now, I have to talk to you guys. We are in need of help. Before The Outcasts are fully operational, I would like to have a few of you come to the complex and spend some time working with our current recruits. We need to fine tune some of their skills, especially with those who can fly."

"I'm open to going," Epic volunteered. "If that's okay?"

"Yeah. I wouldn't mind giving back. I would love to see some of this guy here in action." Downtown pointed to Alexavier. "We've heard so much about him."

Alexavier grinned, "I would be honored to have you with us. I'm sure there's so much I could learn from you."

"I would love to as well, but I think I need to track Hellabond," Transcend proclaimed, still looking around. "For her to be involved with The Tribe is odd. She's up to something."

"I agree. Beauperon was with her, but no Vliet," Sam stated. "The three of them have always been a group, but they've never really associated themselves with The Terror Tribe."

Livevil added, "The only time they wanted help, they came looking for a bunch of us renegades a few years ago. At that time, we heard they were planning something big."

Transcend said, slowly walking away, "Then I really need to locate them. I'll update you if I find anything."

Downtown nodded and turned to Sam. “You get the authorities squared away, and I’ll get with Major and finalize who will go back to the complex.”

“Great. I need to speak to the Major as well. He’s been yelling in my ear. I’ll take care of everything and be back shortly.” Sam headed toward the closest official.

Anthem proclaimed, “I’d love to have more time to work with Sam.”

Downtown pulled out his phone. “Let me ask the others to see if they’re also interested.”

“I think I’ll tag along with Transcend,” Giggle Stick slowly turned away. “Picking a fight with a Meta like Hellabond sounds like fun.”

Livevil followed, pulling out a couple of long knives and backed away. “I vote for hunting bad guys.”

Alexavier stood near Anthem, smiling. Anthem noticed him and said, “You did good. I’m sure Sam is proud.”

“Thank you. I hope so. I’ve been worried about my performance lately.”

Anthem placed his hand on the young hero’s shoulder. “If there’s anything I can do to help with your training, I’ll be joining you for a visit.”

“I really appreciate it.” Alexavier had a huge grin on his face, which only got bigger as Bobbie and Beth arrived. Alexavier couldn’t have felt any better, but the hug from Beth was the cherry on top of the sundae. He had been getting training from his idol. Now he had the hero touted to replace Sam, offering guidance and training. His path to becoming a hero was becoming a reality. Even with all the events, Alexavier gave one last glance at the rooftop across the way, where the woman in white had stood.

CHAPTER 43

The roof to the hanger was wide open with a cyclone of air wreaking havoc on everything not nailed down. The returning helicopter was coming in fast, and the whirling blades brought stronger than normal winds. There was an urgency about the complex, much more than normal. Mike and Jonathon were waiting with several members of The Elitesmen Guard to handle the prisoners. Various recruits, as well as Wally in his wheelchair, found places to welcome the heroes, as well as see who they captured. The touchdown was a bit rough, but somewhat expected. The cargo door opened slowly, allowing Bobbie, Beth and Alexavier to walk down the ramp. Once at the bottom, they cleared a path for Guard members to rush the cargo area to retrieve Bootlegger, their detained villain. After waiting for them to clear out the bad guy, Sam exited with several heroes in tow, including Downtown, Epic, Anthem and Radical in tow.

Mike was thrilled and greeted them first. “Nice to see you guys again. How's the knee holding up, Roy?”

“Haven't had an issue since the doctor gave it the magic touch,” Roy replied.

“Fantastic.” Mike turned and reached out his hand. “How is the Anthem suit holding up?”

Muhammad replied, “Awesome. Doesn’t even feel it’s there. Hey, speaking of the doctor, can Jean do something about my shoulder? Game Over took a good swing and hit it pretty hard.”

“I'm sure she'd love to say hi. How long has it been?”

Mike led Muhammad away, leaving Jonathon to finish the greetings. Robert was first up. “Long time, no see. I hear you're doing well.”

Robert shook hands. “Hectic is the word. When you're starting a new team from scratch, there are so many things to do, even when you're fighting the bad guys.”

“I see you added a few new members, including one that's a little....Radical? How are you?” Jonathon joked.

Berlin grinned, “I'm thrilled to be back doing what I love.”

“I'm sure Robert is happy to have you.” Jonathon turned to Sam. “So, what happened? Apparently, it went from a bank robbery to a full-scale war.”

“As much as I can piece together, this whole series of robberies they carried out lately has been to target Alex. First, they wanted to eliminate Beth because of her light powers negating The Infamous One's ability to hide in the shadows. After Alex saved Beth in Jersey, they must have thought it necessary to focus on him. Their hope was to get us to see the pattern of bank robberies, realize that they were similar to some that occurred years ago and figure it out. With no surprise, Alex did. We happened to be on Long Island where the last bank robbery was targeted and raced over there, arriving to encounter most of the group, not to mention Hellabond and Beauperon.”

“I didn't think they were associated,” Jonathon added.

“Me either,” Sam agreed. “I always thought their goals were always different and conflicted. Somehow, they were working together, and it was a perfect plan, especially with Alex and I, being the only ones trying to stop them. Luckily, The United Outcasts weren't that far away and noticed the commotion from their headquarters. I don't think The Tribe counted on them assisting us. Alex sacrificed himself for me as Hellabond had me in her Field of Screams. A few minutes longer, and I would been under her control. That's when The Outcasts came in and saved us. The Tribe tried for a brief moment to fight them off, but quickly knew they were no match for the heavy firepower from The United Outcasts. Radical even got her chance to extract a bit of revenge on Natural Disaster."

"I think that's the first time I've seen him bloodied." Berlin smiled, "It felt so good."

"Your brother would be proud." Sam put his hand on Berlin's shoulder, although his expression showed that Sam's words weren't very reassuring. "The best part is that all of the money has been accounted for. The Tribe got none of the cash."

"That's awesome!" Berlin exclaimed.

Robert added, "Bank robbery, foiled. Taking out Dread, failed. I'd say they're furious right now."

Roy noticed the old helicopter at the back of the hanger and marveled, "Now you've got two helicopters? Nice! Surprised you kept the old one."

"You can thank the Senator for the new one." Sam moved closer to the new helicopter. "It's a major improvement and worth having such an advanced tool."

"When you now have access to more than one helicopter, you might not get the shiny new one bringing you back home, if we start going on more missions." Jonathon had to bring the reunion to an end. "Regardless, Major Constantine is waiting for you in his office. He said it was urgent."

"Don't worry about us." Robert nodded. "We know our way around."

The rest of the team began welcoming everyone back, but Alexavier urgently needed to talk to someone. "Sam!" Alexavier halted his idol before he could leave. "I'd like to talk to you about the lady from my dreams."

Sam nodded. "Just give me a few minutes to take care of some business, and we'll sit down, okay?" Alexavier nodded, and Sam patted him on the back.

"Get your evaluation done with the doctor before you forget. I'll catch up with you a bit later."

With a friendly wave, Sam exited the hanger, throwing his outfit jacket over his shoulder. The operation wasn't a complete success, but showed enough good results that he could have a smile to end his day.

#

After getting a quick checkup with Dr. Dennis, Alexavier was joined by the other heroes that were headed into the complex. As their journey through the sparsely populated hallways continued, more of the heroes departed the group. Eventually, Alexavier and Beth branched off and turned the corner to Alexavier's room. Beth removed her gloves, while Alexavier went into the closet to get out of his hero gear and suit. Once he was completed with his wardrobe change, including putting on his favorite gray, sweatshirt jacket, he returned where Beth began discussing the day's events.

"I wish I could have been there. I mean, we did find a couple of local yahoos, but nothing too much. Our leads really didn't pan out."

"She was there, Beth. The lady from my dreams was there and I know who it is."

"Really? Who?"

"Liberty's Light or the original Beacon of Light. She was on the rooftop above me. She was distracting Hellabond, which allowed Transcend to come in and move me away from the Field of Screams."

Beth's eyes grew big. "You mean Julie Beckenstein? The one that was involved with Sam?"

"Yeah."

"No way!"

Alexavier sat down on the couch. “Yeah. She was there, just staring at Hellabond. It had to have affected Hellabond, because she had a hard time focusing on me.”

“Didn’t Hellabond have a thing for Sam, but he was dating Beacon at the time?”

“If I remember correctly she did.” Alexavier rubbed his face. “I tried to talk to him, but he needed to take care of stuff and said we would talk later.”

Beth wondered, “Maybe he doesn’t know she was there to help.”

“The only thing I know is that she saved me.”

“I thought she wasn't helping us anymore.” Beth sat next to Alexavier. “When the Major told us about what happened, it sounded like she abandoned Project: Hero and turned her back on Sam. The Major said she had a breakdown and went crazy. I found some news articles while going through the library saying that she killed a police officer, just by looking at him.”

“Yikes! That’s scary to have that kind of power to kill by looking at someone.” Then Alexavier realized, “She was there, but I don’t think Sam saw her. She had to be there to help.”

“Maybe she still has feelings for him and couldn't let him get hurt.”

“Actually, she showed up when I was trapped, not him.”

“That's weird. Why wouldn't she be there to save him? Maybe she just got there late?”

Alexavier paused with a look of confusion. “She was the one coming to me in visions while I was sleeping.”

“But wouldn't she show up in his dreams too? They used to be really close. Did he mention anything about her and visions?”

“No. It was just like any other training mission. Everything was very professional. I even got to go to The United Outcasts’ headquarters and meet all of them. If something was happening, he didn't say anything.”

“But why would she only appear to you?”

“Maybe she couldn't help and needed to warn me or let me know something. During the visions, she talked about needing to look up and see into the light. That happened twice while in New York. The first time was when Sam and I were driving back to get picked up by the helicopter, and we were talking about the robberies. I saw the sun behind a church steeple, and it reminded me of the vision of her when she said, ‘Enough is never enough, as there will always be another.’ That's when I asked if the first two robberies matched any previous ones. We found out there were, so we headed over to the third bank and caught them in the act. The second time was when I looked up in the Field of Screams. I felt helpless until I saw a shining light in the sky. When I focused on it, I could see that it was her. Somehow, her light was cutting through Hellabond's field.”

“Some doctors have said that Beacon's powers grew to where she could see the future.”

“If that's true, couldn't she do something about the robberies? I thought she was one of the most powerful people on the planet.”

“I don't know. What if she's losing her powers and needs your help?”

Alexavier pulled his favorite gray, hooded sweatshirt over his head. “Why couldn't she just ask Sam?”

“Maybe because of their history?”

“Should I really say something to him? I asked to speak to him, but he had to talk to the Major.”

“That's up to you. It depends on if you feel comfortable enough to approach him about her trying to contact you and not him.”

“Ugh. Maybe I should sleep on it.”

Beth stood up and grabbed his arm. “How about we celebrate a great win as a team and talk about it some more? I invited everyone for some ice cream.”

“I'm only going if I get two.”

With the biggest smile, Beth agreed, “Deal.”

For them both, life couldn’t appear much better than this very moment, as they ventured down the hallway. Watching from the shadows, Harvey could only stare at Alexavier and brood.

#

Sam entered Major Constantine's office feeling better than he had in a very long time. Having limited success against The Terror Tribe had brought a lot of anxiety. The hard work he had put in for so long into this program felt like it was finally paying off.

“Taking Alexavier with me to New York was the right idea. He performed just as any high-level recruit should and more. He listened. He executed. He’s everything we want. It was a pretty successful operation. Not only did The Terror Tribe not secure any of the money, but we also thwarted their plot to take out Alexavier. It was a pretty elaborate plan, even with its simplicity.”

The Major had quite the concerned look. “Wait! They’re targeting recruits? I needed to discuss the problem with Mike and his so-called trauma, but this is a bigger problem!”

“I agree.”

“First was Beth, which could be dismissed. Now they’re going after Alexavier. Our whole program could be in jeopardy. This requires a serious, heavyweight response. I’ll contact Dynamic and Riva to get The United on this.”

“Bring them back immediately. We don’t need our success turning into a nightmare.”

The Major hesitated before providing an update. "I should inform you that things have been busy while you were away. You did intercept The Tribe, but they were also on the other side of New York City."

"Really. That's pretty gutsy of them, especially since all of their big guns were at the bank with us." Sam threw his gear on a chair.

"They were. Killus said Nib and Everlorne were doing the dirty work. Cavalio and her girls were working behind the scenes."

"Hold up. What about Killus not going on mission did you not understand?"

"We are talking about various members of The Tribe, including Everlorne and Nib. Killus was the best option, and thankfully he was here for me to send. Unfortunately, we were undermanned and didn't stop them."

"Wait. Why weren't the others sent instead?"

"Dave and Harvey were on assignment, and Wally still hasn't fully recovered."

Confused, Sam asked, "What assignment?"

"Sources had several possible super-powered humans close to Washington, D.C. with a threat to the White House. Since Killus couldn't go, that left Dave and Harvey. I know you wouldn't want Killus to be all by himself, so I sent Hank with him."

"What about Michael, or even Manny? You know what? I don't even care. This just made my decision even easier. I had eased up my schedule to spend more time here. I really wanted to fulfill my duties in Washington and abroad, but not anymore. I feel I would do better take over the general operations and work through every recruit's development."

By this time, the Major was angry, just looking for any way to change the subject. "So, then you don't want to know what happened in New York with the other members of The Terror Tribe?"

Sam turned with a look of frustration. "What happened in New York?"

The Major handed Sam a folder. “They hit Dynamic Tech’s controls testing lab in Lower Manhattan, just as you were responding to the bank heist on Long Island. Luckily, having the second jet copter made it possible to intercept them, especially with its speed.”

“Intercept them? That's a long flight. How were you hoping to get there and still find someone around?”

“We got lucky, particularly having the new helicopter back here. Something held them up and Killus and Hank were able to get there in enough time to engage them.”

“Did they have any success?”

“Killus said they may have injured Nib, but he couldn't tell for sure. Before they really got a chance to fight them, they fled, retreating really fast. Hank and Killus weren't able to stop them from escaping.”

“Did we figure out why there were there?”

“We were able to determine that it was a robbery.”

“Was anything taken?”

The Major was reluctant to answer. “We did get there quick enough to drive them away before they could take too much. The information we have is very premature and-“

“What did they steal?”

CHAPTER 44

It was becoming a tradition. Finish a mission and relax at a café. Whether the results were good or bad, it led to refreshments. This time, several members of The Terror Tribe met up in the East Village, sitting outside and enjoying the sunshine. Saving a seat for the others was Everlorne, Cavalio and Nib, who kept a long duffel bag under their chairs. They sipped on lattes and relaxed, biding their time. Nib was nervous and focused on being inconspicuous, keeping his head down as pedestrians walked by the sidewalk. He was visibly agitated, but tried to sit still. Eventually, a welcomed face appeared, as their leader came strolling around the corner. The Infamous One blended well with unknowing civilians, since he was wearing more conventional clothing. With only a nod, he took a seat next to Nib. They kept quiet when the waiter came over. "Can I get you gentlemen anything?"

"Chamomile tea, please," The Infamous One ordered.

As the waiter walker away, Nib was itching to get the conversation started. "I hear you didn't get the kid."

"It was unfortunate," The Infamous One informed them. "But not as bad as it could have been. Plus, I've learned a bit about our new hero. He's creative, very intuitive and quick. I didn't think he would be as far along in his combat readiness for such a new recruit."

Hobbling along came Game Over, being escorted by Natural Disaster. As the café tables were small, only seating four people, Natural Disaster grabbed a couple of chairs from an adjacent table.

"Wait. Our fearless leader wasn't prepared?" Game Over said sarcastically.

"That's funny coming from the guy who forgot his boots the last time we were going to hit Wall Street," Natural Disaster quipped.

"Hey! I had to dry them off, and you didn't want to wait."

"Our operation for taking down Dread didn't go as planned, and we weren't able to make our way from Manhattan with any of the money." The Infamous One looked around the table.

Nib grimaced, but opened his hand, creating his crimson energy blade. "You needed me with you to take out Dread."

"I needed your services elsewhere." The Infamous One closed Nib's hand, dousing his glowing blade. "You were exactly where you needed to be. The success of our plan depended on it."

"Still don't care." Nib sat back. "The kid has payback coming."

"Next time, my friend. Next time," Cavalio assured him with a smile.

"I take it you guys were successful," Natural Disaster said.

"We nearly made it out without a problem," Everlorne explained, still keeping his head down. "Killing Machine made it more difficult than it should have been."

Cavalio leaned in to talk softer. "The fact that his brother doesn't like him really helps."

"This success is just the first. With all the years of planning, decades really, our hard work and sacrifice that has caused unnecessary turmoil amongst our ranks is finally coming to an end." The Infamous One smiled. "We knew it. We planned it. We executed it to perfection."

Game Over hushed them as the waiter came back with tea. Once the waiter left, Everlorne continued the conversation. "We're still a long way from completion. I wouldn't celebrate until we've won."

"A war can last a lifetime. Battles are frequent and can bring change, especially just one victory."

Cavalio agreed with their leader, "This was the victory we needed."

"Let's just use this momentum to push us forward. We've had to take so many steps back lately," Natural Disaster stated.

"But we did get it?" Game Over wondered.

"Yes," Nib responded, being more annoyed and in pain.

The Infamous One smiled, "Now, we are one step closer to our ultimate goal. A goal that shall be achieved, because I have foreseen it."

Like a little boy on Christmas, Game Over couldn't help himself. "Can I see it?"

"Why do you need to see it?" Everlorne questioned.

"Because I've never seen one."

Game Over was getting on Nib's nerves, who replied, "That doesn't mean you need to see it."

"But Dad, quit being such a grouchy pants." There had been multiple times in the past that many of The Terror Tribe had wanted to kill Game Over. Add this one to the long list.

Reluctantly, Everlorne obliged. "Okay, you can look, but don't touch."

Game Over looking down, but quickly became disappointed. "So that's it? Not what I imagined it would look like, boss."

The Infamous One leaned closer. "So, tell me, Game Over. What did you think the detonator for a nuclear weapon would look like?"

Glossary

<u>Heroes and those involved with Project: Hero</u>:

Alexavier Vankendreh'd (Dread): Has increased physical abilities, including strength, speed, agility and healing. Is skilled in all forms of combat, with or without weapons. Possesses a unique 'feeling' that warns him of dangerous people and situations that cause him to react unknowingly to stay safe.

Anthony Laviolette (Apex): Can achieve supersonic speeds when running, swimming or flying, but never tires.

April Dandridge (Appendage): Has extra limbs, including arms, legs, wings and even a tail that are hidden on her body. She can pull these out, attach them to her body, which come to life as her own.

Berlin Kensington (Radical): Can bulk up for strength or slim down for speed. The more he does, the more invulnerable he becomes.

Beth Breckenridge (Beacon of Light): Has light-based powers that can intensify to become used as heat or shoot beams of light. Can create a nearly indestructible defensive shield.

Bobbie Terpstra (Booby Trap): Touches objects that become traps to distract enemies. Highly skilled in various forms of combat, stealth and reconnaissance.

Dave Headley (Dead Head): Has the ability to return to life after he appears to die.

Dirk Henderson: Leader of The Elitesmen Guard. Wears an armored battle suit.

DLX (Real name unknown) Pulls energy from others to use for strength, power and an energy shield.

Dwayne Cygnus (Sickness): Inflicts various sicknesses and diseases when making contacting with someone's skin.

Frank Steinberg: U.S. Senator and financial backer of Project: Hero.

Gary Hughes (The Hatriot, *Pronounced: Hay-tree-ot*): Hero with powers similar to the Patriot Warrior, but is a vigilante. Has a high level of increased strength, speed and endurance, which includes limited invulnerability.

Glen Euw (Glu): Secretes sticky substances from his pores and mouth.

Hank Malberg (Hack 'N Maul): Has increased strength and invulnerability that reacts to the ferocity of the attack. Invulnerability becomes stronger against more powerful attacks, but the weaker the attacks, he becomes more vulnerable.

Harvey Stringer (Heart Strings): Has a limited magnetic control over very small iron particles, particularly in someone's bloodstream. Can cause anything from dizziness to complete stoppage of blood flow throughout the body.

James Killus (Killing Machine): Maniacal psychopath who has no regard for human life. Appears to have no powers, but also no fear. Is highly skilled in combat, particularly with weapons.

Jean Dennis: Doctor who possesses various healing abilities.

Jennifer Xiaohan (Syphon): Draws energy from her surroundings, which can be used for electric bolts. Can become transparent, fly and move through solid objects.

Joe Donnelly (Ordinary Joe): Is classified as a Meta human, but has yet to show any powers.

John Constantine: The Major, retired, who is the head of Project: Hero and coordinator for The United.

Jonathon Bender (Time Bender): Uses a field of energy that appears to change inanimate objects into a different form of its stages of existence or evolutionary state.

Julie Beckenstein (Beacon of Light, the original): Has various, light-based powers, as well as a vast array of abilities, particularly mental powers. The full level of her real powers is yet unknown.

Livevil (Real name unknown, *Pronounced: Liv-evil*): Demented hero who has the ability to survive incredible amounts of physical damage to the body.

Manny Batista (Human Battery): Can absorb or draw energy from various sources, which can be transformed into various forms of energy weapons or shields.

Megan Keel (Rosé): Uses the power of persuasion to make people do her bidding.

Melina Levante (Transcend): Has nearly unlimited mental abilities. Can become impervious to mental attacks, which then limits her use of her other mental powers.

Michael McKnight (Mecha): Has skin that can turn into flexible, yet tough metal plates, which can open and transform, revealing many mechanical items, including guns, rocket launchers, wings, booster and tools.

Mike Mackinaw (Mr. Machine): Has a high level of understanding and expertise in all things mechanical, electrical and computers.

Muhammad Abdul Kahfi (Anthem): Has powers similar to the Patriot Warrior but with more increased strength, speed, endurance and high level of invulnerability.

Neal Van Til (Hellhammer): Can lift a couple of heavy space rocks that he uses as weapons. Has a high level of invulnerability while holding them.

Percy Shottenheimer (Precision Shot): Has uncanny level of accuracy for anything he throws, shoots or aims. Highly skilled in use of weapons.

Robert Baun (Downtown): Has the ability to adhere to solid objects. Once he's using his ability, he can lift objects many times his weight.

Roy Tanner (Epic): Absorbs ultraviolet waves from the sun to fly, shoot energy blasts and create a force field.

Sam Nelson (The Patriot Warrior): Technical advisor and consultant for Project: Hero. Has a high level of increased strength, speed and endurance, which includes limited invulnerability.

Tisha Borland (Getaway): Can fly in straight lines, making sharp turns and has a lucky streak that helps her escape.

Todd Carlin (Giggle Stick): Has a high level of invulnerability and uses a staff as a weapon or for protection.

Wally Ryder (Wave Rider): Uses various sources of energy to obtain flight.

Villains:

Air Raid: Has the ability to fly and can carry nearly unlimited amounts of items and weight.

Beauperon: Can influence those who are susceptible to mental persuasion to do his bidding with a hold that can last long after he's stopped using his powers.

Bootlegger: Has the ability to fly, but not hover and has a protective shield used while flying that can encapsulate those she carries.

Carnevil: *Pronounced: Karn-evil*, Demented clown who has a hat that can hold a nearly unlimited number of objects, including weapons and his pets, carnivorous bunnies.

Cavalio: Girlfriend of The Infamous One. Establishes a mental link with persons who obey her every wish. Is highly skilled in various forms of combat.

Dodgeball: Has great accuracy when throwing objects that have different effects, like electrocute, smoke and explode.

Empty: Creates portals that link together to aid in escaping.

Everlorne: Has various and extensive magical powers that only work on inanimate objects.

Faducia: Can manipulate inanimate objects, like a sword-shaped rock and changing them into a real sword.

Game Over: Negates the gravity of whatever he touches to become feather-lite, allowing him to pick up massive objects with ease.

Hellabond (Helen Bordeau): Creates her Field of Screams that reaches out along objects like the ground and walls to create fear and panic. Long enough exposure can lead to being under her mental control permanently.

Landfill: Can manipulate the dirt and soil within several hundred feet around him to make various things from mounds to projectiles.

Multiplicity (Scott Norfeld): Can create up to ten copies of himself that function separately, but still under his control.

Natural Disaster (Nate Disantine, son of Major Disaster): Can produce massive amounts of raw energy to use as blasts, shields or to propel himself short distances.

Nib: Creates an energy blade from his hand that drains an enemy's stamina and disorients them. Putting both hands together creates a death blade, which can kill.

Rumble: Creates an energy field from hands that can be projected outward for attacks or as a shield.

Terrorcide: Has demonic looking mouths around his body that open up and unhinge to bite through almost any object. Also has the ability to take incredible amounts of damage and not die, including having amputated limbs that can be reconnected.

Tether: Can use mental energy that becomes a physical tether to grab or hold onto objects.

The Infamous One: Formerly Known as Midnight Thief and current leader of The Terror Tribe. Can blend into shadows or areas that are shaded to become nearly invisible. Has been considered one of the most intelligent people on the planet. Is highly skilled in all forms of combat, including weapons.

Topher: Can shape inanimate objects into the shapes of other objects.

Made in the USA
Middletown, DE
05 October 2023